No Love Lost . . .

"Was there a gun in the house, ma'am?" asked Leo.

"Boris had one. Stole it from a German corpse during the war."

"Might be a Luger," Elena murmured to her partner. "Could you show us where the gun is, Dimitra?"

"You want me to get up? My poor hip is aching and you want me to go looking for a gun."

"Maybe you could just tell us where it is, ma'am," suggested Leo.

"In the desk. Second drawer down."

No gun was found in the desk, no shell casings near the body. "You have any idea what he might have done with it, ma'am? Could he have given it away?"

"Boris was tight as shrunk pants," Dimitra snapped. "He wouldn't give it away."

"Do you notice anything else missing?"

"What would be missing? God's not a thief."

MORE MYSTERIES FROM THE
BERKLEY PUBLISHING GROUP . . .

JENNY McKAY MYSTERIES: This TV reporter finds out where, when, why . . . *and* whodunit. "A more streetwise version of television's Murphy Brown." —*Booklist*

by Dick Belsky

BROADCAST CLUES

THE MOURNING SHOW

LIVE FROM NEW YORK

SUMMERTIME NEWS

CAT CALIBAN MYSTERIES: She was married for thirty-eight years. Raised three kids. Compared to that, tracking down killers is easy . . .

by D. B. Borton

ONE FOR THE MONEY

THREE IS A CROWD

TWO POINTS FOR MURDER

FOUR ELEMENTS OF MURDER

KATE JASPER MYSTERIES: Even in sunny California, there are cold-blooded killers . . . "This series is a treasure!" —Carolyn G. Hart

by Jaqueline Girdner

ADJUSTED TO DEATH

THE LAST RESORT

TEA-TOTALLY DEAD

MURDER MOST MELLOW

FAT-FREE AND FATAL

A STIFF CRITIQUE

FREDDIE O'NEAL, P.I., MYSTERIES: You can bet that this appealing Reno private investigator will get her man . . . "A winner." —Linda Grant

by Catherine Dain

LAY IT ON THE LINE

WALK A CROOKED MILE

BET AGAINST THE HOUSE

SING A SONG OF DEATH

LAMENT FOR A DEAD COWBOY

CALEY BURKE, P.I., MYSTERIES: This California private investigator has a brand-new license, a gun in her purse, and a knack for solving even the trickiest cases!

by Bridget McKenna

MURDER BEACH

CAUGHT DEAD

DEAD AHEAD

CHINA BAYLES MYSTERIES: She left the big city to run an herb shop in Pecan Springs, Texas. But murder can happen anywhere . . . "A wonderful character!"

by Susan Wittig Albert —*Mostly Murder*

THYME OF DEATH

HANGMAN'S ROOT

WITCHES' BANE

LIZ WAREHAM MYSTERIES: In the world of public relations, crime can be a real career-killer . . . "Readers will enjoy feisty Liz!" —*Publishers Weekly*

by Carol Brennan

HEADHUNT

FULL COMMISSION

ELENA JARVIS MYSTERIES: There are some pretty bizarre crimes deep in the heart of Texas—and a pretty gutsy police detective who rounds up the unusual suspects . . .

by Nancy Herndon

ACID BATH

WIDOWS' WATCH

WIDOWS' WATCH

Nancy Herndon

BERKLEY PRIME CRIME, NEW YORK

WIDOWS' WATCH

A Berkley Prime Crime Book / published by arrangement with the author

PRINTING HISTORY
Berkley Prime Crime edition / August 1995

ISBN: 0-425-14900-5

Berkley Prime Crime Books are published by
The Berkley Publishing Group,
200 Madison Avenue, New York, NY 10016.
The name BERKLEY PRIME CRIME and the BERKLEY PRIME CRIME design are trademarks belonging to Berkley Publishing Corporation.

PRINTED IN THE UNITED STATES OF AMERICA

10 9 8 7 6 5 4 3 2 1

For my brother and sister-in-law
Robert and Susan Fairbanks

Acknowledgments

Special thanks to my editor, Laura Anne Gilman; to fellow writers Joan Coleman, Elizabeth Fackler, Terry Irvin, and Jean Miculka, all of whom were so generous with their time and suggestions; to Mari Herman of the El Paso Public Library, who told me intriguing stories about the Berkeley Free Speech Movement; to Marion Coleman for information about military twenty-one-gun salutes; to Nadine Prestwood and her daughter, whose condo provided one of the novel's settings; to Chris Burton of Ride-on-Sports and James Smith of Schwinn of El Paso for information about bicycles; and again to all those friendly, knowledgeable members of the El Paso Police Department, Sheriff's Department, and District Attorney's Office.

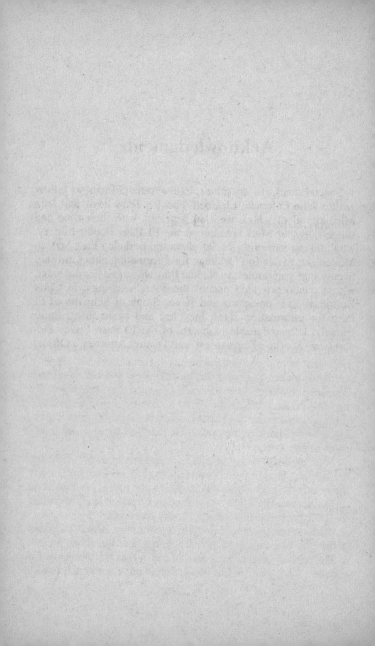

1
:.

Monday, September 27, 2:23 P.M.

Boris Potemkin was a short, paunchy man with powerful shoulders, ropy arms, and large, heavily veined hands. Gray hair bristled off his head in untidy clumps. Although the temperature in his house felt like the hot blast of air from an open oven, he wore a raveling gray sleeveless cardigan sweater over a long-sleeved denim shirt, as well as tan cotton work pants and carpet slippers. And he was scowling.

Medicare and Boris' A.A.R.P. policy weren't covering the expenses of his wife's broken hip—damn her! He sat in a creaking rocker, studying the brochure for a health insurance supplement, which he had saved from the Sunday paper. He had just reached the clause on exclusion of preexisting conditions and muttered, "Bastards," when he heard discreet knocking from the back of the house. He shuffled through the living room to the kitchen.

"What are *you* doing here?" he asked sourly as he unlatched the screen. Then he shuffled back toward his rocker, leaving the visitor to follow. Once in the living room, he turned to repeat his question. He had only one surprised second to feel the cool pressure of steel against his forehead.

"This is for Dimitra," said the visitor, and Boris fell, dead before his body hit the floor. He didn't hear the shot.

The visitor scanned the hands and wrists of the body for jewelry, then went to the desk, removed a small Christmas

1

cookie tin brightly decorated with green holly leaves and red berries, checked the contents, and left, the screen door swinging softly closed on the silent house. Less than three minutes had passed from knock to departure.

2

Monday, September 27, 5:02 P.M.

The day Boris Potemkin died, Los Santos Crimes Against Persons Detective Elena Jarvis was feeling particularly cheerful as she drove home in five o'clock traffic. The sky was bright blue, the temperature a comfortable eighty-eight degrees—comfortable when she considered how many hundred-degree days they'd had that summer. The mountains that rose in stark brown peaks dividing the east and west sides of the city held a fading remembrance of green from the August rains, but the air was desert-dry again. Just the way Elena liked it.

Smiling, she brushed a strand of black hair away from one high cheekbone, tucking it back into the heavy French braid lying against her neck. It had been a good day, two cases closed, lots of laughs. Leo, her partner, had rushed home from their eight-to-four shift to impregnate his wife. He'd had a call over the police radio that morning with a message from Concepcion. "I'm ovulating," was what it said—to every Los Santos cop on the road. "What am I supposed to do?" he'd complained to Elena. "Drive home for a quick one while you wait outside in the car?"

"I could hang out in your kitchen. Have a cup of coffee."

"Yeah, right. I gotta talk to that woman. She didn't have to tell the dispatcher."

"You want to be a daddy, you have to make some sacrifices," Elena had replied. Leo had a low sperm count. He and

3

Concepcion were trying the rhythm method in reverse. Probably right about now.

In a burst of exuberance, Elena had blown the insurance money she received from the Mafia vandalism of her living room on a state-of-the-art drip irrigation system, which now rattled pleasantly in the bed of her pickup. Elena liked greenery in her yard, but the summer water bills were killing her, not to mention getting up before sunrise and out after sunset because of water rationing. With this new apparatus, designed in Israel to provide the most growing stuff for the least moisture, she could stop financing Los Santos Water Utilities. Maybe she'd dig the first trench tonight.

She turned onto her street and spotted a new Chevrolet pickup in her driveway. Frank! She'd finally caught him. She wheeled in, cutting off his escape route and sprinted around the side of the house to the back door. Open! And she'd had the doors locked, the security system armed. How did he do it? She had house and car alarms, barred windows—the whole enchilada. Well, her ex-husband was through sneaking into her house and shifting the furniture, through reparking her truck so she couldn't find it. She'd cuff him and haul his ass down to jail.

She drew her revolver from the shoulder holster under her loose linen jacket, easing the kitchen door open, whirling inside with the gun in a two-handed grip, leveled at—her mother. "Mom?"

"That's not exactly the welcome I expected," said Harmony Waite Portillo, who was sitting on a yellow and green Mexican ladderback chair, sipping tea and talking to Dimitra Potemkin, one of Elena's elderly neighbors. Dimitra occupied the fold-down seat of her walker. She was recovering from a broken hip, poor woman.

Elena smiled at her neighbor, then said to her mother, "I thought Frank was in here. He's not, is he?" She looked around. Given her ex-husband's sneaky nature, he might be lurking in the pantry among the staples and cleaning supplies.

"He left after he let me into the house and moved the loom in for me," Harmony replied.

"He has a *key*?" Elena scowled and holstered her revolver. "That does it. I'm getting a restraining order."

"Have a cup of tea, dear. It's very calming."

After leaning down to kiss her mother, Elena sank into a chair while Harmony poured a cup of the herbal tea she compounded herself. "It's wonderful to see you, Mom, but how come you're here?"

"I'm here to do something about your living room, Elena," said Harmony, voice crisp with disapproval.

Elena's conscience blipped. The living room had been vandalized in late May, and not only had she failed to refurnish, she'd just spent the money on pipes, hoses, and timers. She should have known that disaster area would be preying on her mother's mind. Disasters reminded Elena of her ex, which reminded her of the unidentified pickup in her driveway. "Whose truck is that out front?"

"Mine," said Harmony. "I won it at the Penitentes raffle."

"Come on! When did they start giving away trucks?"

"Last Easter."

"Well, I guess a raffle is more socially acceptable than a crucifixion," said Elena, grinning. Dimitra's mouth dropped open.

"Now, Elena, you know the Penitente Brotherhood doesn't do that anymore. Your father wouldn't allow it. In fact, he claims they never did."

Still grinning, Elena settled back in her chair. Having her mother in the kitchen was almost as good as being home in Chimayo, a small New Mexico town in the Sangre de Cristo Mountains. "How are you, Dimitra?" Elena asked. "Hip giving you any trouble?"

"I'm better," said the old lady, "but Boris is dead. That's what I came to tell you."

"Oh, Dimitra, I'm so sorry." Elena put down her cup and leaned forward to clasp her neighbor's hand in sympathy. "I hadn't heard."

"No reason you should. He was fine when I left at noon— mean as ever."

"He died *today*?"

"I came right over when I found him."

"You mean he's—" What had seemed sad, but not unexpected, given Boris' age, was taking on a bizarre twist.

Dimitra's head bobbed, every corkscrew curl bouncing like a little aluminum Slinky. "Dead on the floor," she affirmed. "I guess God finally decided to kill him. High time too. That *zloy stareek*."

"You mean he's been dead while we were sitting here talking?" asked Harmony, blue eyes wide.

"Dead as an icon," Dimitra affirmed. "Not likely he's gone anywhere. I thought you'd know what to do, Elena, you being a policeman."

"How come you didn't call 911?" asked Elena.

"Oh, Boris hid my glasses again, and I can't seem to remember telephone numbers anymore."

"I'll go right over." What if old Boris were alive and in need of a doctor?

"The door's open," said Dimitra. "Was when I got home, still is. I don't know what that *zloy stareek* did with the key. He never lets *me* have one."

"I'll follow with Dimitra," Harmony offered.

Elena nodded and sprinted out the screen door, then paused and turned back. "What does that mean, Dimitra? Zoy streak?"

Dimitra thought a minute. "Mean old bastard."

"I see." Elena tried not to stare at her newly widowed neighbor. "Lock up, Mom," she called over her shoulder. How long since Dimitra Potemkin got home and found Boris? And why hadn't she mentioned his death to Harmony? Well, Dimitra had been a little odd and a lot absent-minded since she broke her hip. Poor woman, this would be a great blow to her. Or maybe not. She'd called him "the mean old bastard" twice. Elena had never realized Dimitra didn't like her husband.

Across the street and three doors down, Elena dashed up the Potemkins' cracked sidewalk, through the wooden gate and across the small, weedy courtyard. As Dimitra had said, the door was unlocked. Elena turned the knob and burst in, then stopped short. Boris was indeed on the floor. She bent for a closer look. And he was indeed dead. There was a bullet hole in his forehead.

3
..

So as not to contaminate the crime scene with her own fingerprints, Elena got a pair of latex gloves from her purse and put them on before she called headquarters. The detective from her squad on the twelve-to-eight shift was away from his desk, so she contacted Leo Weizell at home, then Identification and Records, explaining in each case that she was first officer on the scene because the murder had been committed on her block. Finally she notified the office of the medical examiner.

By that time Dimitra was trundling her walker through the courtyard, Harmony beside her. Elena hurried to the front door. "Listen, Mom," she said, "I have to secure the scene."

"I'm sure, dear, with you here, we'll be perfectly secure. I can see the gun under your jacket."

"Secure the *scene*, Mom, not us."

"Oh. Well, I won't touch anything. Here, Dimitra, let me help you get that walker over the sill."

"Mom." Harmony backed into Elena in the effort to help Dimitra, who was muttering, "I don't need any help." Elena sighed. Since the widow had already been here, there was no reason to keep her out, and Elena despaired of talking her mother into leaving.

Dimitra looked down at Boris. "If he fell over and hit his forehead, he'd die face down instead of on his back, which proves—"

7

"Dimitra, he was—"

"—struck down by God," finished the old lady. "You think it was a bolt of lightning?"

"It was a bullet," said Elena, "and as far as I know, God doesn't use guns to mete out divine retribution."

"Grandmother Portillo is always saying that God works in mysterious ways," said Harmony.

"Yeah, well, if God's at work here, it'll sure hurt my chances of making an arrest." Before they could debate the matter, Leo arrived and met Harmony, to whom he said, "Wow, Mrs. Portillo, you're even more of a babe than Elena."

To which Harmony responded, "Well, aren't you sweet?"

Dimitra said, "You need to put on some weight, young man." Leo was over six feet and probably didn't weigh more than one hundred and sixty. Elena figured a lot of that weight was muscle he'd developed pursuing his hobbies, tap dancing and, more recently, trying to get Concepcion pregnant. Elena had always considered sex great exercise, not that she'd had any lately.

"Who's she?" asked Charlie Solis as the I.D. & R. team crowded in.

"My mother," said Elena.

"It's all right, Officer," said Harmony. "I'm not sitting down. I'm not touching anything. I do understand about securing the crime scene. My husband's the sheriff in Rio Arriba County, New Mexico."

Charlie's mouth quirked. "Well, we appreciate your cooperation, ma'am, but unless you're a witness, maybe you could leave."

"No, I couldn't," said Harmony. "I'm here to console the widow."

Dimitra was sitting in the seat of her walker, staring balefully at the body of her husband. "I don't care what you say. God killed him."

"What was that?" asked Charlie.

"Mom, Dimitra, why don't you sit out in the courtyard?" Elena suggested.

"It might be cooler," Harmony admitted. "It's at least ninety-five in here."

"That's because Boris won't turn on the air conditioner Lance bought me," said Dimitra. "Boris *deserved* to be struck down by God!"

Leo was scribbling notes. Elena figured that if Dimitra wanted to get herself arrested for murder, she was going about it just right. "What time was it when you found him, Dimitra?" asked Elena.

"I don't know. Margaret Forrest dropped me off after the bridge game, and there he was, so I started out for your house. Then, let's see, I stopped to chat with Gloria Ledesma. About how hard the weather is on the flowers. All the rain in August, and now it's bone-dry again. Flood or drought. That's Los Santos."

Elena wouldn't have equated Los Santos' eight-inch average annual rainfall with flood, but they had suffered a wet August, comparatively speaking. "Then you're not sure when you got home? Did you say you stopped to talk between here and my house *after* you found Boris?"

"Yes. With Mrs. Ledesma."

"Did you tell her about Boris?"

"I don't think so."

Elena and Leo exchanged glances. Then Leo said, "When did you last see your husband alive, Mrs. Potemkin?"

"Before the bridge game. I had to make him lunch. You'd think the man could make his own. He didn't break *his* hip. But, oh no, I have to cook breakfast, lunch, and dinner just the way I always did."

"I guess we can ask this Margaret when she dropped Mrs. Potemkin off," Leo murmured to Elena.

Dimitra Potemkin's head bobbed. "Margaret will know. She's good with numbers. Remembers every card that's been played. Now, me—I don't play bridge that often."

"Oh? How did you happen to be playing this afternoon, ma'am?" asked Leo.

"Lydia Beeman had something else to do. That group plays every day."

"Where?" asked Elena.

"The Socorro Heights Senior Citizens Center. Your mother's going to give us weaving demonstrations."

Elena glanced at Harmony, who nodded enthusiastically. That meant Dimitra had been arranging for a weaving demonstration while her husband was lying dead on the living-room carpet, unreported. "Who made up the foursome, Dimitra?"

"Margaret, Emily Marks, and Portia Lemay."

Before they could ask another question, Onofre Calderon, the medical examiner, bounced in. "Got another croaker for me?" he said to Elena.

She frowned at him and nodded her head toward Dimitra. "This is the widow, Mrs. Potemkin."

"Afternoon, ma'am. Sorry for your loss."

"If you had known him, you wouldn't say that," muttered Dimitra.

Nodding solemnly, as if widows always took spousal death that way, Onofre went over to examine the corpse. "Right between the eyes at pretty close range," he said. "Maybe a 9 mm." Calderon lifted the head, looking for an exit wound. "Slug's still in there. He must have had some tough skull."

"He has a metal plate in his head," said Dimitra. "Once we went to visit my family, and Boris set off every metal detector between here and New York City. Used that as an excuse to keep me from going back. Boris was a real *zloy stareek*," she muttered, then added, "That means bad-tempered old man. In Russian."

Flash bulbs were popping, fingerprint powder being spread over the house. "Look at the mess you're making," Dimitra protested. "Are you going to clean up afterward?"

"Ma'am, would you have telephone numbers and addresses for those ladies you played bridge with?" Leo asked.

"No," said Dimitra.

"For heaven's sake," said Harmony. "Why don't you stop pestering this poor woman. She's just lost her husband."

"Mom!" warned Elena.

"You can be sure that your father wouldn't handle things so unfeelingly," Harmony said to Elena. "Dimitra, you must come down to the house and have dinner with us. In fact, maybe you'd like to stay the night."

Dimitra shook her head energetically. "I'm not leaving my house a target for thieves."

"No sign of a break-in here," said one of the I.D. & R. men. "He must have let the shooter in."

"There'll have to be an autopsy, ma'am," said Onofre Calderon. "I know the family sometimes objects, but—"

"Do whatever you want," said Dimitra. "But you'll find it was God that killed him."

"Was there a gun in the house, ma'am?" asked Leo.

"Boris had one. Stole it from a German corpse during the war."

"Do you know what kind it was?"

"How would I know that?" retorted Dimitra, surprised.

"Might be a Luger," Elena murmured to Leo, who nodded. "Could you show us where the gun is, Dimitra?"

"You want me to get up? My poor hip is aching and you want me to go looking for a gun."

"Maybe you could just tell us where it is, ma'am," suggested Leo.

"In the desk. Second drawer down."

No gun was found in the desk, no shell casings near the body. "You have any idea what he might have done with it, ma'am? Could he have given it away?"

"Boris was tight as shrunk pants," Dimitra snapped. "He wouldn't give it away."

"Do you notice anything else missing?"

"What would be missing? God's not a thief."

The crime-scene team finally finished with their photographs, their fingerprint-dusting, their evidence-gathering. The medical examiner arranged for removal of the body, and Dimitra refused to leave her house, for which Elena was very grateful. She didn't want her lieutenant complaining that she was personally involved again with suspects, and Dimitra *was* a suspect. Just as Elena's friend Sarah Tolland had been the first suspect in the acid bath case last spring, although the murderer turned out to be Karl Bonnard, whom Elena had met and *dated* during the investigation. When Lieutenant Beltran wasn't glaring at her, her fellow detectives were making jokes. She wished everybody would just forget that damn case.

"Do you have any family we can call?" asked Harmony.

"I certainly do," said Dimitra, perking up. "My son, Lance. He'll be delighted to hear that God has finally taken Boris."

Startled, Elena realized that she knew a Lance Potemkin, but why had she never seen him around the neighborhood if he was Dimitra's son? Bad blood between him and his father? She and Leo would have to question Lance. Family members were always prime suspects.

"We'd better interview the neighbors tonight," said Leo as they left, "then catch the bridge players tomorrow at that center."

Elena nodded. She still couldn't believe Dimitra Potemkin had not only sat around talking with Harmony while Boris lay dead on the floor but had stopped to chat with another neighbor.

"Mom, do you remember when Dimitra showed up at the house and how long she was there?"

"I've no idea," said Harmony. "I was unpacking when she arrived, but I'm not even sure when *I* arrived. You know I don't believe in watches. And then we were chatting about the senior citizens center. Dimitra told me she usually goes to play chess but that she's taken classes in shuffleboard, Ping-Pong, and country dancing. I gather her husband didn't approve of the dancing. Isn't that sweet? Jealousy at their age. Of course, since she broke her hip, she's pretty much limited to chess. Russians are mad for chess."

Elena turned to Leo. "Even if we can pinpoint when she was gone, the high temperature in there may screw up the coroner's estimation of how long Boris was dead."

"Well, dear," Harmony said, "no matter what your evidence indicates, Dimitra is not your murderer. Her aura was a nice, composed blue. A killer's aura would be red, or gold with red flashes."

"A killer's *what*?" asked Leo.

Elena rolled her eyes. What were you going to do with a mother who thought she could look at someone and see colors that told her what kind of emotions the person was experiencing?

4
##

Harmony went back to Elena's house to start dinner. Leo and Elena began their canvass of the neighborhood with Mrs. Ledesma, who confirmed her conversation with Dimitra that afternoon.

"We talked about roses," said Gloria Ledesma. They had found the lady sitting on a swing in the back yard, scowling at her rose bed. "All that rain in August," she grumbled. "I've got black spots, aphids. It's the greenhouse effect, you know. People using deodorant. Who cares what armpits smell like?"

"What time was it when she stopped to talk?" asked Leo.

"Speak up, young man."

Leo shouted his question.

"What do you care? Two old women talking about roses. I suppose it's against the law to grow roses, just like it's against the law to water them. You ought to be out catching criminals instead of bothering old ladies."

"Boris Potemkin was killed today," shouted Elena. She'd never been overly fond of Gloria Ledesma, who was a grouch.

"I know that. Police cars all over the street. Like I said, why aren't you trying to find out who killed him?"

"We are," said Elena. "Did Dimitra mention his death to you?"

"No. And if you're thinking Dimitra killed him, she didn't.

13

Although she had reason," Mrs. Ledesma added, her small brown face screwing up angrily.

"What would that reason be, ma'am?" asked Leo loudly.

The old lady squinted at him, then turned away. "How would I know?" she muttered. "And I don't know what time Dimitra was here. You think I'm running to look at the clock every ten minutes so I'll know what time my neighbor stopped to chat?"

"Was it early afternoon or late?" Elena asked patiently.

Mrs. Ledesma scowled. "I stopped having gas from lunch, so I suppose it was late. Every meal I eat—gas and heartburn. I'm lucky to have an hour when I'm not in pain, and then it's time to eat again. Got gas right now."

"What time do you eat dinner?" asked Elena mildly.

"I eat at five on the dot every day. A healthy TV dinner."

"Do you know of any problems in the Potemkin family?" asked Leo. "Did you ever hear any arguments or see any evidence of physical abuse?"

Gloria Ledesma got up and plucked a mildewed leaf. "They were great ones to squabble," she admitted. "Always shouting at each other."

"What did they fight about?"

Mrs. Ledesma glanced at Leo scornfully. "How would I know?" she said. "In case you haven't noticed, I'm hard of hearing. I get the noise, not the words. And abuse?" The old lady shrugged. "People of my generation don't talk about that sort of thing. But Dimitra—she had a lot of accidents."

"What about Lance?" asked Elena, wondering if Boris had abused his son as well as his wife.

"Lance wasn't allowed home. Boy's a sodomite. Did you know that? His father kicked him out. Well, I can understand that, except that maybe Lance wouldn't have been what he is if it weren't for Boris."

"You mean you think his father abused him sexually?" asked Elena, astonished.

"No, of course not. Boris didn't like men. *Or* women. But Lance—he was a good boy, always real nice to me and Mr. Ledesma. Never heard a word against him until Boris kicked him out. That's when Lance got a job at one a those men-only bars. You know what I mean? Where the men dance with each

other. Maybe that job got Lance started on unnatural behavior."
Mrs. Ledesma shrugged. "I never did like Boris."

"Did you see any strangers in the neighborhood this afternoon?" Leo asked.

"There's a new mailman," said Mrs. Ledesma. "And a young fellow in a big brown truck. Delivering parcels."

"No one loitering around?" Leo asked.

"Just Dimitra and me." Mrs. Ledesma snickered.

"Don't you find it odd that she didn't mention Boris' death?" Elena doubted that a dead husband would have slipped Dimitra's mind.

Mrs. Ledesma shrugged. "I think when Dimitra broke her hip, she must have broke her head too. She's been sorta batty since then."

Elena didn't argue. She'd noticed the same thing.

"I'll tell you who probably killed him. That little weasel, Ashkenazi."

"Omar?" asked Elena, surprised. "Why do you say that?"

"Oh, he's had his eye on Dimitra," said Gloria Ledesma. "The two of them used to sneak off to that senior citizens center and play chess. Dimitra got around. She had her gentlemen friends."

"You're surely not saying she was unfaithful to Boris?"

"At her age? Don't be dumb. But he knew she was attractive to men. That's one of the things that made him so mean, I wouldn't be surprised."

Elena had certainly never thought of Dimitra Potemkin as a *femme fatale*. How many *femme fatales* did you find pushing walkers? But then Dimitra had been pretty spry before she broke her hip.

"Ashkenazi probably figures he can marry her now. Get his hands on Boris' pension. How much can a retired rug salesman make?"

"I thought he owned that store," said Elena. "I remember him saying his father founded it."

"His father did, and the old man held the reins until he dropped dead doing his income taxes, but it wasn't ten years after Ashkenazi inherited that he went bankrupt. He's a dumb little weasel. Always talking about those stupid rugs. As if they were better than a painting of the Blessed Jesus. As if they were holier than a statue of the Virgin of Guadalupe. After he went bankrupt, someone bought the place and hired him on as a salesman. That's what he was most of his life. A salesman. And then he claimed he slipped a disk lifting carpets. Filed for workmen's compensation. Now he sits around his house pretending something's wrong with his back.

"Well, Dimitra's a fool if she marries Ashkenazi. Now she's got rid of Boris, she might as well enjoy herself."

"Neat lady," said Leo as they walked to the house on the other side of the Potemkins'. "Mr. Ledesma probably died to get away from her." Elena laughed. "Still, she's given us a lead. Love and greed are popular motives for murder. Maybe the rug salesman offed Boris."

"I doubt it," said Elena dryly. "He's a tiny atheist pacifist. But how about her theory that working in a gay bar turns you gay?"

"Maybe she's right," said Leo.

"Bull," said Elena. "There's evidence that it's genetic. Differences in the brain, that sort of thing."

"Yeah, well." Leo shrugged. "Looks like the son might have reason to kill the old man. And Mrs. Potemkin had a motive."

Elena nodded. All this had been going on in her neighborhood, and she'd never noticed. Some detective she was. *Dimitra had a lot of accidents.* Gloria Ledesma's words echoed in Elena's head.

"So did we learn anything there besides the fact that she thinks the carpet guy did it?" asked Leo.

"The possibility that Boris abused his wife and the fact that he turned against his son." Elena thought back over the conversation. "If Gloria Ledesma eats at five on the dot and has gas until an hour before meals, Dimitra came by between four and five."

"I can just see the D.A. cross-examining Mrs. Ledesma about flatulence," said Leo, grinning.

"Hey, you don't know it's flatulence. Maybe she belches. And if the coroner says Boris died before four o'clock, Dimitra's in the clear. Probably."

"Maybe Mrs. Ledesma killed him."

The two of them went laughing up the walk to the residence of Amy and Ben Fogel, a couple who had lived together so long that they looked like twins. They were perched on a nubby brown sofa watching the taped recording of a game show, Amy crocheting an antimacassar like the ones that protected every chair-back in their crowded living room.

"What a terrible thing," said Amy. "Shot in his own house."

"Makes you wonder whether he was shot with his own gun," said Ben.

"Do you know what kind of gun it was?" asked Leo.

"Handgun," said Ben Fogel. "Look at that, Amy. She's just won that dining room set, and I knew the answer to that question." The winner on the television screen was jumping up and down, screaming, hugging the game show host.

"Yes, dear, but *we* wouldn't want that dining room set. It's tacky. We saw him just this morning," said Amy. "Boris. He was shouting at the dogs for doing something—well—indiscreet in his front yard."

Elena wondered what. Dog sex? Dog urination?

"Would you know what time that was, ma'am?" asked Leo.

"Twelve-thirty."

"Would that be exact or approximate?"

"Exact," said Ben. "Today was our day for flexible sigmoidoscopy. Once a year, you know. Have to watch out for colon cancer. We always go together."

"We do everything together," said Amy.

His and hers colon exams? Elena suppressed a grin.

"And we allow ourselves plenty of time to get there," said Amy.

"Haven't had a speeding ticket in fifty-five years of driving," said Ben. "Don't intend to get one in my golden years." He chuckled and stroked the tip of a knobby index finger over the white hair that grew from the rim of his ear. "So we know it was twelve-thirty because that's when we planned to leave, and we always leave on time."

"We believe in timeliness," said Amy.

"Ambulance and police cars everywhere when we got back," said Ben. "Had a hard time getting into my driveway. We always go out to eat after flexible sigmoidoscopy. Can't eat before, you know. Otherwise, we might have heard the shot."

"Did you ever hear any arguments between the Potemkins?" Elena asked.

"All the time," said Amy Fogel. "The worst was the day Dimitra broke her hip."

"You think Boris was responsible?"

"We wouldn't know that," said Amy guardedly.

"But they were quarreling because he found out she'd been in touch with Lance," said Ben Fogel. "Boris was an unpleasant person. I'm sorry to say it, and I realize that Lance has his peculiarities, but he was a kind boy and always good to his mother."

"Did you ever hear any arguments between Lance and Mr. Potemkin?"

"Oh, yes. After Dimitra broke her hip, Lance and Boris had a terrible fight. Lance came to the house to visit. Bringing flowers. Dimitra loves flowers," said Amy.

"It was the day Boris usually went to the V.F.W.," said Ben. "He came home early and caught Lance in the house, chased the boy out to the back yard by the bomb shelter."

"I think Lance was the one who insisted that they go outside. He wouldn't want to upset his mother by yelling at Boris in the house," Amy objected.

"That was where Dimitra broke her hip. During one of Boris' air raid drills," Ben explained.

"Air raid drills?" echoed Leo.

"Boris held them every month. He was sure the Communists were going to destroy Los Santos with nuclear missiles."

"The end of the Cold War must have been a big relief to him," Leo muttered.

"Not at all," said Ben Fogel. "Boris thought *glasnost* was a Communist plot to catch us off guard. He upped the drills to once a week."

"Until Dimitra broke her hip," Amy added. "She can't manage steps anymore."

Elena shook her head. She'd never realized how really squirrelly Boris Potemkin was.

"Boris told me once that he had to keep a gun in the house to protect himself from the K.G.B.," said Ben.

Elena wondered if she was supposed to add the K.G.B. to their list of suspects. "You were saying about the argument between Lance and Boris out by the bomb shelter."

"Oh, yes. Well, Lance said his father ought to be shot for what he did to Dimitra, and Boris shouted back that if Lance ever showed up at their house again, he'd do worse."

Leo whistled softly. "Does Lance strike you as the type who would—"

"Of course not," said Amy Fogel. "He was a lovely child. Prettiest blond curls I ever saw, and he used to help me carry my groceries in. Wouldn't take a penny. Such a nice boy. I don't care what they say about him. Oh look, Ben. Look at that grandfather clock they're going to give away."

"Did you see Mr. Ashkenazi today?" Elena asked.

Amy Fogel dragged her attention away from the clock on the television screen. "Why, yes. He was out on his porch meditating in the lotus position. Omar says he owes the rehabilitation of his back to surgery and yoga."

Elena nodded. She too had seen Omar Ashkenazi on his front porch with his legs crossed, but she didn't really think he was meditating. More likely he was watching the goings-on in the neighborhood.

"He waved goodbye to Dimitra when some woman came and picked her up," said Amy.

"That's right," Ben agreed. "We were getting the booklet the Avon lady left. Omar told Dimitra to have a good time at the center and that he wished he could be there playing chess with her. And she said, 'That's not possible anymore, Omar,' and climbed into the car."

"They used to be good friends," said Amy, "but I'm afraid Boris was the jealous type. Not that there was anything to be jealous of," she added hastily. "Boris was just bad-tempered. Omar was still meditating when Boris yelled at the dogs. One of the things Boris said was, 'Go over to the rug dealer's yard, you mutts. Give him something to watch.'"

"That's right. He did say that," said Ben. "And Omar never looked up, even when Boris shouted something about not coveting thy neighbor's wife. I don't suppose Omar even heard, since he was meditating. Boris gave up and went in. Slammed his door."

Omar Ashkenazi could come out of meditation to speak to Dimitra, thought Elena, but he played possum when he was insulted by Boris. Could that have been the last straw for Omar? Maybe he'd gone over and shot Boris because he *had* heard that Bible quote about coveting a neighbor's wife.

"Mr. Ashkenazi has the most beautiful rugs," said Amy wistfully.

Elena and Leo moved on to the Ituribes', on the far side of the Fogels' house. "So we know he was alive after his wife left for the center," said Leo, skirting a fall of orange pyracantha berries on the sidewalk to the front door.

"Right. Now the question is whether he was dead when she got home, maybe killed by her admirer. Or her son. Or by her, and then she waited around to report it."

The Ituribes were in their late seventies, a widow and her brother-in-law. Mrs. Ituribe was short and built like a truck. She had a rosy, smiling face and arthritic knees. Mr. Ituribe, her brother-in-law, was like a bantam rooster on the edge of starvation, a stocky man gone thin, with a full face that had collapsed as a result of weight loss. Elena knew that he had metastasized prostate cancer.

The Ituribes, when questioned about Lance, clammed up disapprovingly. *Homophobes*, thought Elena. Neither admitted hearing the family fights, although they'd heard the gossip, about which they were very discreet when questioned. Had they seen Boris any time today? They hadn't.

"We sleep a lot," said Mrs. Ituribe. "Because of the painkillers."

Had they seen any unusual people or happenings in the neighborhood?

"The chair," said Juanita.

"The bicycle," agreed Jose. "We were taking this old chair out to the alley. You leave it there, the scavengers will pick it up."

"It's nice to know some poor person will get use out of your discards," said Juanita.

Elena could see Leo eyeing the rest of their furniture,

wondering what kind of condition the chair had been in if these two considered it discardable.

"I was an upholsterer," said Jose Ituribe. "In my younger days, I could have fixed that chair good as new."

"When was it we took the chair out, Jose?"

"I dunno. Two-thirty, three."

"Too late anyway," said Juanita. "It was hot for two old folks like us trying to get that chair out to the alley. And what do we see when we get there? A beautiful bicycle. Now, why would anyone leave a beautiful bicycle out for the scavengers?" Both shook their heads. "If I could ride a bicycle, I'd have taken it myself. But I've got the arthritis. In the knees, you know. Everywhere. And Jose's got the cancer. We're too old for riding bicycles. But I was tempted. Weren't you, Jose?"

"Why not?" He shrugged. "If someone's leaving it out, that means you can take it. You know about that, Elena?"

She nodded. "Whose house was it in back of?"

"Fogels'?" suggested Juanita.

"Dimitra's," said Jose.

"It might have been Gloria Ledesma's."

"Gloria doesn't have a bicycle," said Jose. "Anyway, it was behind Dimitra's."

"I'm short-sighted," Juanita apologized. "I'm not sure where it was, but Jose, he sees pretty good. Maybe Lance was visiting Dimitra."

"But it wasn't Boris' day to be out of the house, so it wouldn't have been Lance," Jose objected.

"What did it look like?" asked Elena, thinking they'd forgotten Lance was grown and wouldn't be riding a bike.

"Looked good to me," said Juanita.

"Color?" prompted Leo.

"I've got the—what is it I've got, Jose?"

"She don't see colors too good."

Leo looked inquiringly at Jose.

"Green?" Jose guessed. "The sun was pretty bright. Hard to tell in bright sunlight. But it looked good."

"What about the handlebars?"

Jose nodded, eager to be of assistance. "It had handlebars. And tires. Had a seat too."

"A black seat," Juanita agreed. "But it could have been something else, since I don't see colors too good. I've got the diabetes. And cataracts."

"Did you see Mr. Ashkenazi today?" asked Leo.

"I didn't," said Juanita. "Did you, Jose?"

"I didn't. He was probably sleeping. Like us."

"Not like us," said Juanita, turning to Elena. "Did you know that Mr. Ashkenazi sleeps whenever he gets tired? One night he might be up all night; next he's sleeping at night. Sometimes he takes catnaps. Omar claims that's the best way, that working an eight-hour day isn't what humans were meant to do. He says his health has improved two hundred percent since he started sleeping whenever he feels tired."

"Dumb," said Jose. "Now a siesta I can understand, but even that's old-fashioned. No siestas at the upholstery shop."

Leo and Elena asked a few more questions and moved on, wondering whether the strange bicycle in the alley behind the crime scene was significant. Leo didn't think a murderer would use a bicycle for transportation. Elena reserved judgment. Maybe they'd find someone else who had seen it and could describe it more accurately.

"Jeez, gettin' old's hell, isn't it?" said Leo as they left the Ituribes' yard. "Isn't there anyone young on your street?"

"Me," said Elena. "And there are a lot of old people in better health than the ones you've seen. Actually, Mrs. Ledesma's in good health. So was Dimitra before she broke her hip." They continued to canvass the neighborhood, reinforcing their suspicion that the Potemkins had been a troubled family. Lots of quarrels. Possible abuse. Nobody would admit that Boris had pushed Dimitra down the steps of the bomb shelter, but some hinted. No one else had seen the bicycle. Several had seen Ashkenazi meditating on his porch while Boris shouted insults.

"How come you missed all the problems with the Potemkins?" Leo asked Elena as they left the last house and went over to Omar Ashkenazi's place.

"Cause I'm three doors away, and Hispanics don't talk about family abuse. Older Anglos either. It happens, but it's covered up. Even taken for granted. You ought to know that."

Leo shrugged. "I'm gonna catch some Hispanic abuse if I

don't get home to my wife sometime tonight." He rang the doorbell. No answer. Pounded on the wood. No answer. "His car's in the driveway," Leo muttered. "Police! Open up!" he shouted.

"Come on, Leo," said Elena. "The man's probably asleep."

"He's not deaf, is he?"

"No, but when he decides he's tired, he sticks in earplugs and wears a sleep mask." She turned away from his door. "I'll come back later tonight. He's bound to be awake within the next few hours. And tomorrow we'll talk to Dimitra again. See if she's found anything missing. Talk to the son, Lance. Then drop by the senior citizens center at noon to catch the bridge players."

"Suits me," Leo agreed.

"You wanna stay for dinner? Mom will have fixed something."

"So will Concepcion, and I'd better turn up to eat it—even if it's grown mold while we were talking to your neighbors."

"It takes more than two hours to grow mold, Leo, unless your refrigerator's already full of it."

5

..

Monday, September 27, 9:15 P.M.

When Elena let herself into the house, she heard the familiar thump, thump of her mother's loom coming from the living room. Harmony was, as usual, setting out to make order and beauty out of chaos.

"Your dinner's in the microwave," she called. "Set the timer for four minutes." Elena did as she was told, peeking under the plastic wrap her mother had laid on the plate. Beans and brisket. It looked great. Harmony must have brought the brisket with her.

"Guacamole in the refrigerator," Harmony called.

Elena closed the microwave door, set the timer, and snatched a can of Tecate from the refrigerator. Once she had sprinkled the top with salt, squeezed a cut lime over the salt and taken a deep swallow, she removed her jacket and shoulder holster, placing the gun in a locked drawer. The microwave buzzer went off, and she carried her dinner into the living room.

In the early days after the vandalism, she'd reshelved the books that had been tossed everywhere, thrown away those that were badly torn, along with broken lamps and end tables, swept up the glass underfoot, and ordered miniblinds to replace the ravaged draperies. Then she'd put off the rest. Consequently, a jagged hole gaped at her from the television screen, and the slashed upholstery had not been replaced. Somehow she hadn't found the time for any major shopping expeditions. Now the insurance money was gone. She sighed and put her dinner and beer on the tiled hearth of the round corner fireplace while she unfolded a TV table and set it up. Then she sat down on the hearth to eat.

"Who's looking after Pop?" she asked.

Harmony continued to weave. "Josie and Armstrong are back in Chimayo, so your father's staying with them."

Elena nodded. Her middle sister Josie had married the artist Armstrong Carr when she was eighteen. During the tourist and opera season, they lived in Santa Fe, where he had a studio and gallery. In the fall they moved back to his house in Chimayo with their nine-year-old daughter, Cleo. "Armstrong's going to go crazy with Pop's calls coming in day and night."

"Armstrong's taken to painting with earphones on. Then he names the canvas after whatever music inspired it, usually something from the chamber music programs. He'll never hear the telephone." Harmony settled onto a high stool she had carried into the room, and studied the first six inches of her pattern. Then she turned to Elena, who was dipping tostados into guacamole. "I brought you a cordless telephone and an answering machine."

"How come?" Elena wrapped a slice of the brisket in a flour tortilla, garnished it with beans, and bit into her improvised burrito.

"Because I haven't been able to get hold of you for three weeks." Harmony had resumed her weaving. "They're in the bag by what's left of your television."

"When I'm home, I'm usually out back," said Elena, feeling guilty that she hadn't written or called in so long. "I've been working on the rock wall."

"I thought it was something like that," Harmony murmured. "I do worry about you, Elena. Now you can answer from outside or return my calls."

"Sorry, Mom. I promise to do better." Elena finished the last bite of her dinner and rose to examine the two gifts. Very high-tech. "Listen, Mom, these are way too expensive. You better take them back and—"

"Nonsense. I bought them at a discount store in Albuquerque. Besides that, I have more money than I know what to do with."

"Since when?"

"Since I started using my fabrics to make coats and dresses for the Santa Fe tourists. Armstrong's gallery on Canyon Road is handling my *creations*." Harmony laughed. "He can't very well charge his mother-in-law a commission, and the last coat sold for twelve hundred dollars."

"You're kidding!" said Elena, astonished. That was more than she and Frank had put down on the house when they took out their V.A. loan. "How does Pop feel about it? You must be making more than he does."

"Not yet, but I'm thinking of hiring other weavers. And your father hasn't complained." Harmony finished her row and started a new one. "How's Dimitra?"

"Celebrating, would be my guess." Elena carried her plate to the sink and tossed her beer can into a large wooden waste basket, handsomely antiqued in green and lined with a plastic garbage bag. "How *come* Pop doesn't mind?" she called, rinsing plate and silverware and putting them into the dishwasher. Her father was the quintessential Hispanic male. She couldn't imagine that he'd be cool about his wife making tons of money.

"Ruben's busy trying to find out who's been taking more than their share from the *acequias*," said Harmony, "and it's not as if our lifestyle has changed. I'm using my profits to send Maria spending money while she's in med school, and I've put some into Johnny and Betts's business."

Elena had returned to the living room. "Right. Portillo Southwestern kitsch."

"Now, Elena," chided Harmony, "not all of the tourists can afford Pueblo pottery or Armstrong Carr paintings. Johnny and Betts provide a welcome product—tasteless, but popular." Laughter sparkled in her blue eyes. "Next I plan to make a down payment on a new pickup for Two and Rafaela." Two was Ruben, Junior, third oldest Portillo and a deputy sheriff under his father.

"You want a beer, Mom?"

"Not so close to bedtime, Elena. Now, why don't you tell me

what happened between you and Frank. You've been pretty vague about that divorce, and your grandmother Portillo was horrified, needless to say."

Should she tell her mother that Frank had turned out to be a man who'd knock his wife down during a quarrel over his infidelity? Elena had picked herself up, got her gun from the locked drawer, driven him out of the house, and filed for divorce. Goodbye, Frank. If she told Harmony, Harmony would find someone to put a curse on him. If Harmony told the sheriff, he might come down and shoot Frank.

Elena sighed. Pop had been dead-set against the marriage. He hadn't liked Frank, whom Elena had met backpacking in the Gila Wilderness. Pop didn't even like the Sierra Club, which sponsored the trip. And he had a fit when Elena announced that she was marrying Frank after one month's acquaintance—two weeks camping and two weekend visits to Albuquerque, where Elena was a student at New Mexico University. But Elena hadn't paid any attention to her father. She'd been in love.

"Part of it was professional jealousy, Mom," she hedged. "Frank couldn't hack it when I did better on the exams and promotion lists, and did it faster. He got to be a real pain. Still is," she added, remembering that Frank had let Harmony into the house with a key. She'd have to pay that locksmith a visit, ask a few pointed questions, demand a free lock change. And get a restraining order against Frank. She should have done it that one time he hit her, not waited through the divorce and his stupid, post-marital bids for attention.

Determined to make up for lost time, she went to the kitchen to call a lawyer who owed her a favor. From now on if Frank came within a hundred yards of her, her house, or her car, she'd have him thrown in jail. That ought to go over great with his lieutenant. Once Frank bailed out, they'd can him, or at least shift him from Narcotics to Traffic.

Elena grinned at the idea of her ex-husband, who thought being an undercover narc was more fun than sex, getting assigned to Traffic. Or Community Relations. He could run around giving lectures to grade-schoolers. He'd have to shave off that dirty blond stubble and put on decent clothes. She was still grinning after her conversation with the lawyer.

"Elena, what are you up to?" asked her mother when Elena came back into the room. "I haven't seen that look since you and your brother Johnny tried to sell the tourists bottled lemonade with lizards in the bottom."

"Hey, we thought if the Anglos would buy mescal with worms, they'd love the lizards. A lizard's cute; a worm's disgusting." Elena excused herself again and went to the front yard to check Omar Ashkenazi's house. The lights were on. "Back in a half hour, Mom," she called through the door.

Omar had a nifty live oak in his front yard that Elena coveted. It looked as if it had spent two hundred years in a strong wind and survived with a very gnarly character. She knocked on Omar's door, then rang his bell, hoping he'd remembered to take his earplugs out. When she got no answer, she peeked in the window and saw him puttering around in his front room, so she knocked on the window. When he turned to pick up a newspaper, she waved her arms. His sleep mask was pushed up above his eyes, and he squinted, came over, and peered out the window. Then a big smile blossomed across his unwrinkled, shining brown face, and he rushed to open the door.

"Elena, what a nice surprise."

"Hi, Omar."

"What?"

Elena pointed to her ears, and Omar Ashkenzai laughed merrily, removing his sleep mask, then his earplugs. He was a short man, dressed in a peculiar gray-green jumpsuit with black epaulettes and black and gold buttons down the front. His head was perfectly bald and dome-shaped, the skin a satiny light brown, his nose a thin hook with pinched nostrils. His eyes had a peculiar slant, not quite Oriental. From the back, the shells of his ears flared out like tropical flowers from two-inch stalks. From the front, the protruding earplugs had made his ears look like double mushrooms.

"Sit down, Elena. Sit down. Can I offer you something to drink? A kiwi and mango cocktail? I created the recipe myself."

"Sure. Why not?" While Omar bustled off to prepare the

fruit juice, Elena stared at his living room. It contained a small inlaid parquet table with a green and white onyx chess set from Mexico. Elena had seen a hundred sets like it in the shop windows along Avenida de Juarez, where eager shopkeepers stood out on cracked sidewalks trying to lure the *gringo touristas* in to buy. Two wooden chairs, intricately scrolled, sat at the table. Other than these pieces and a chair at the window, the room held no other furniture, but it did have a spectacular rug, so splendid in color and design that Elena skirted it to take the window chair. She couldn't imagine actually stepping on such a beautiful thing.

"Here you are," said Omar, handing her a glass of green liquid swirled with yellow. He sat down cross-legged on his beautiful carpet, facing her with his hands resting, palms up, on his knees.

Elena took a sip of her kiwi and mango juice and gasped. "Is this alcoholic?" she asked.

Omar nodded enthusiastically. "I ferment it myself. Kiwi-mango hard cider. I'm applying for a patent."

"Well—" Elena cleared her throat. "It certainly has a kick. Are you aware of what happened in the neighborhood this afternoon?"

"Can't say that I am," said Omar, "but I always enjoy a good gossip." Then his face fell. "I hope you're not going to tell me that both Fogels have colon cancer. I know they were scheduled for their yearly—"

"They're fine," Elena interrupted, not wanting to hear any more about flexible sigmoidoscopy. "It's about Boris Potemkin."

"That old fart! Someone ought to lock him up in his bomb shelter and throw away the key. Here, he's married to a beautiful, intelligent, charming woman like Dimitra—"

Beautiful? wondered Elena.

"—with hair, as the young people say, to die for."

Elena pictured the aluminum slinky curls on her neighbor's head. They were unusual. But beautiful?

"Dimitra's a charmer," said Mr. Ashkenazi. "A chess player par excellence." He lifted one small brown hand and circled the thumb and forefinger, smiling delightedly. "So what happened to Boris? Did she finally turn him in to the police? High time."

"He was murdered," said Elena, watching Omar closely.

"Murdered? What luck!" cried Mr. Ashkenazi and scrambled off the rug. "I must go right down to console Dimitra."

"She's gone to bed," said Elena.

"Oh, of course. Dimitra keeps conventional hours. Have I told you my theory of natural sleep?"

"Yes, you have," said Elena. "I'm afraid I have to ask you where you were this afternoon, Omar."

"Well, I was right here. Snoozing. I just got up a few minutes ago." He looked at his watch. "Nine hours sleep. I may not need any more for a few days."

"Did anyone—ah—know you were asleep here?"

"Probably not. I was sleeping on this very rug. If you nap on a beautiful carpet, it's not only good for your back, but it gives you splendid Oriental dreams. 'In Xanadu did Kubla Khan a stately pleasure-dome decree'"—Omar was waving his hands excitedly—"'where Alph, the sacred river, ran through caverns measureless to man down to a sunless sea.' Coleridge had his opium; I have my rugs. Would you like to hear one of the dreams I dreamed this afternoon?"

"Ah—some other time," said Elena. If, when she and Leo came thumping on his door earlier in the evening, they'd looked through the window, would they have seen him sleeping on his Oriental rug? "No telephone calls or anything?"

"While I was asleep? I wouldn't know, my dear. My earplugs are exceedingly effective."

"Any ideas about who might have killed Boris?"

"Goodness, I'd have done it myself if I weren't a pacifist. That was one of the troubles between Boris and myself, you know. Aside from the fact that he treated the enchanting Dimitra so badly. We disagreed about war and violence. I do not believe in violence. Happily I am of an age to have missed the various wars this country fought. But I would have been a conscientious objector had I been called. Perhaps served in an ambulance unit. Unarmed. Saving the lives of young men maimed by nationalistic jingoism."

"Omar—"

"Boris, however, believed in violence. He was hoping our

Government would make a preemptive nuclear strike against Russia during the years when we were at each other's throats, figuratively speaking. I have myself overcome a violent heritage."

"Oh?"

"Yes, my ancestors were Mongol warriors. I could well be descended from Attila the Hun or Genghis Khan. Which says something for the evolution of the human soul. Unfortunately, Boris never evolved. He could have *been* Attila the Hun. I think he always regretted having been assigned to an engineering rather than a fighting unit. The man's most cherished war memory was blowing up a bridge with a German army contingent on it, although he also expressed admiration for the Nazis. Good lord! The man was at war with harmless ground squirrels. I can't understand why you didn't arrest him for shooting them."

"I never realized he was," said Elena. "I never *heard* any gunshots in the neighborhood."

"Well, he had a Machiavellian soul. He probably did his shooting while you were on duty. The rest of us certainly knew about it. And he frightened poor Dimitra into covering up for his cruelties against her."

"You could have called the police yourself, you know," said Elena.

"The fair Dimitra begged me not to. She said he'd kill both her and me if I reported him."

Elena squinted at Omar. "Were you and Dimitra having an affair?" she asked.

"Only an affair of the soul, my dear. Of the mind. Not that I don't desire the adorable Mrs. Potemkin. I burn for her. Have you read the poetry of Omar Khayyam, whose namesake I am? 'A jug of wine, a loaf of bread—and thou beside me singing in the wilderness.' Dimitra has a voice. You probably didn't know this. We could have made beautiful music together. Perhaps we still can. If she weren't addicted to regular sleeping hours, I'd rush over there right now and invite her to a movie. If it were forty or fifty years ago, we could have gone to a musical film. Has she ever told you about the Eugene Onegin movie made in—"

"Omar, I have to get home," said Elena hastily. "It's certainly been nice to talk to you. And thank you for your— ah—frankness."

"And thank you, my dear, for bringing the good news. I shall watch Dimitra's house from now until the time when, to paraphrase Byron, 'she rises in beauty like the sun'—unless, of course, another sleep period comes upon me."

Elena nodded. "You do that." She bade him goodnight, handed back the empty glass, and walked home giggling as a result of the alcoholic kiwi-mango cider and Mr. Ashkenazi's poetic and forthrightly stated crush on Dimitra Potemkin. Of course, that made him a suspect, and he didn't have an alibi. Elena sighed. They'd need to work the neighborhood again to see if anyone had spotted him sneaking around the Potemkin house.

"Hi, Mom," she said when she got home. "Found another suspect. Seems that Dimitra had a soul mate right here in the neighborhood."

"Did she really?" said Harmony.

"Yep. He's ready to snap her up now that Boris is out of the way."

"How romantic! And how fortunate for Dimitra. Now she won't be lonely."

"You want her to marry someone who might have killed her husband?"

"Well, maybe she could settle for an affair until the case is solved," said Harmony cheerfully. "And then there are social security considerations. Dimitra could lose hers if she . . ."

Trust Harmony to take delight in a weird idea. Dimitra Potemkin and Omar Ashkenazi having an affair. Over the chess set, no doubt.

6
..

"Elena was absolutely right when she said you're as handsome as her father," said Harmony, smiling at Lieutenant Beltran, the head of Crimes Against Persons.

Elena suppressed a look of astonishment. She might have said Lieutenant Beltran looked *like* her father, Sheriff Ruben Portillo. Both were stocky, graying, middle-aged men. But handsome? Well, Elena supposed her mother had thought the sheriff handsome when she was a twenty-year-old hippie dropout from Berkeley, living on a commune outside Chimayo, and Ruben Portillo a twenty-three-year-old deputy sheriff raiding that commune's pot patch. The way her mother and father told the story, it was love at first sight between the unlikely pair, an Anglo flower child and a young Hispanic lawman whose family had lived in the Sangre de Cristos since Spanish colonial times.

Lieutenant Beltran seemed to be completely bowled over by Harmony. And why not? thought Elena. Her mother was a beautiful woman: still slender, white-skinned, blue-eyed, with long black silvered hair that hung to her waist, still wearing beads and bright, flowing clothes that she wove and designed herself. Harmony bowled over every man she met, including some young enough to be her sons. Lieutenant Beltran, smitten, was telling Harmony what a fine policewoman her daughter was. As if, ever since the acid bath case, he hadn't

33

been treating Elena like an unwanted spider in a pfitzer juniper. It seemed as though every detective not out on the streets crowded around to meet Harmony, who had driven Elena to work after leaving the Penitentes' pickup for servicing at a Chevrolet dealership on Montana. She was telling them about the problems of loading and off-loading her loom.

"Men are so chivalrous," she said. "I'm afraid some macho old fellow at Socorro Heights will want to help me and end up with a hernia."

"I can take care of that problem," said the lieutenant, who evidently didn't want to be outdone in *machismo* by some "old fellow." "I'll put wheels on the loom for you and a winch on your truck."

"Aren't you thoughtful," said Harmony, beaming.

Elena decided that if her mother stayed in town a month, she'd probably talk Beltran into giving Elena sergeant's stripes without a civil service exam.

7
..

Before Leo and Elena could revisit Dimitra Potemkin, their sergeant, Manny Escobedo, sent them off on a car-jacking with injuries. Rosa Munoz, a single mother and college student with a job at Burger King and a full class-load, had been driving to the University of Texas at Los Santos around seven-thirty when a guy jumped in her car at the Delta light, smashed her head into the driver's side window, pushed her out onto the median strip, and drove away in her '85 VW. When they interviewed Rosa around nine at Thomason General, she said that the *hijo de puta* who'd knocked her out and stolen her car had a tattoo of the Virgin of Guadalupe on his right fist.

"Mano Alvarez," said Elena. They picked him up playing street handball in the Lower Valley, had his picture taken and developed in the basement photo lab at headquarters so it wouldn't have the usual mug shot name and number, and took the photo along with five others to Rosa Munoz, who said, "Number three. They ought to cut off his hand. It's an insult to the Holy Mother." They charged Mano with assault and grand theft auto. Case closed unless Auto Theft could find the car.

They didn't get to Dimitra until eleven o'clock, although she had called headquarters earlier to report the theft of a "czar's medal." Elena and Leo interviewed Dimitra in her kitchen, where she was making cabbage rolls.

"For after the funeral?" Elena asked.

35

"For me," said Dimitra. "I like cabbage rolls, and Boris would never let me freeze them. Now I'm going to make a whole year's worth and freeze every one." She rolled cabbage leaves around another lump of ground meat mixed with mysterious ingredients. "Would you like a few?" she asked Elena.

Accepting would probably be considered a breach of ethics by Lieutenant Beltran, but he wouldn't complain if Harmony got the rolls. "Thanks," Elena replied. "My mother adores ethnic food."

"Peculiar woman," said Dimitra. "My baba told me about women like that in the old country. Did you know your mother thinks she sees colors around people's heads? A gold circle, I could believe, if you're a saint or a member of the Holy Family, but colors? And she doesn't understand why I'm not putting on black and crying over Boris. But then she probably likes your father."

"Speaking of families, Dimitra. Have you heard from Lance?" Elena asked. Detective Beto Sanchez had tried to reach the son, Lance, by telephone to set up an appointment. No luck.

Dimitra shook her head. "He wasn't answering his phone last night. And the English Department said this morning that he'd called in sick. I was real disappointed not to be able to tell him the good news."

"You reported that something was missing besides the gun?" Leo reminded her.

Dimitra wiped her hands on a striped dish towel, thinking. "The czar's medal." Obviously pleased that she'd remembered, she folded the towel, now spotted with bits of meat and herbs, and laid it neatly over the back of a tan plastic kitchen chair. Then she scooped up a huge glob of meat stuffing from a blue Pyrex bowl.

"Boris' family were czarists. He came to this country in '39, when he was seventeen. Chased out of Russia by the Communists—that's what he said. But maybe he ran so he wouldn't have to fight in Stalin's army. Didn't do him any good. He got drafted here in '41 and had to build roads and bridges. You want a glass of tea? Bet you never had tea made in a samovar. Boris never let me offer refreshments. That *zloy stareek*!"

Elena and Leo declined with thanks. Dimitra looked disappointed. "Anyway, Boris spent most of the war in Europe; that's until he got the back of his head blown off and they put the plate in. When he got out of the hospital, he became a guard in a prison camp near here. Boris loved that—pushing Nazi officers around. Then he came home to Coney Island after the war, so handsome in his uniform." She sounded wistful. "That's when he met me."

Leo was showing signs of impatience, but Elena kept him from interrupting. With Dimitra so uncharacteristically talkative, they'd find out more about the family, hopefully something bearing on the murder.

"He always hated my people," muttered Dimitra. "Called Papa a Communist. Of course, they weren't—Mama and Papa. Even in the thirties they didn't belong to the party. They were socialists, trade unionists," she said proudly. "Papa was a presser in the garment district. Now Boris—his favorite American was Senator Joseph McCarthy, but then what can you expect of a man as mean as Boris?"

"You're always saying how mean he was, Mrs. Potemkin. Could you give us an example?" Leo asked.

She squinted at him. "Well, there was Lance. You'd think when I finally had a baby—I was forty-two when Lance was born—you'd think Boris would have been happy. But he got meaner than ever. Lance must have been three, maybe four, and I wanted to start saving money for his college. I could tell even then he was going to be special, a Chekhov, or an Einstein, maybe a Robert Redford."

Elena nodded politely. She remembered Lance as being cute but no Robert Redford, and his secretarial job in the H.H.U. English Department didn't mark him as any Einstein. Now, Chekhov—maybe Lance wrote plays.

"You know what Boris did?" demanded Dimitra, highly incensed. "He took out a loan and built a bomb shelter in the back yard. To protect us from Communist H-bombs, he said. You'd think to hear Boris talk, my father was going to come down here in a Russian MIG and explode a bomb on top of us.

What with paying off the house and the stupid bomb shelter, I never could put away any money for Lance."

"How have relations been between your husband and your son in recent years, Dimitra?" asked Elena.

"What relations?" Dimitra wrapped her tray of cabbage rolls in foil, yanked open the top compartment of her refrigerator, and shoved the tray in. "Boris was the papa from hell, the Rasputin of fatherhood, the—"

"Yes, but specifically what—"

"He wanted Lance to be an engineer—not on trains, on buildings. Boris was a carpenter. Worked construction all his life, but he had to compete with the illegals from Mexico for jobs, so he never made good money. He wanted Lance to be one of the bosses. But Lance, he signed up to be an English major, so Boris stopped speaking to him. Two years later, he made my boy leave the house."

"What was that quarrel over?" Elena asked.

"Oh, they just didn't get along," said Dimitra evasively, her thin, veined hands patting and rolling, flying between the work surface and the tray. "Who could get along with Boris?" she muttered.

"Tell us about the czar's medal," said Elena.

"Sure. Boris bragged about that medal to everyone who'd listen. The czar, the one the Communists killed, gave it to Boris' grandfather—for leading a bunch of Cossacks into the Pale and killing seventy-five Jews—grandfathers, women, children. Boris didn't like Jews either, but then he didn't like anyone.

"And the medal! You should have seen it. Seventy-five lives for a bit of green ribbon and a round coin-like thing. Wasn't even gold. Of course, Boris, he said it would be worth a fortune some day—when the Communists were gone. So after Gorbachev and Yeltsin, I said, 'Boris, why don't you sell it?' 'What, sell my grandfather's medal?' he says. 'At least, put it in a safe deposit box,' I tell him. But not Boris. He says he's got a gun. Anyone tries to take the medal from him, he'll shoot them. But why would anyone want the ugly old thing? It's probably bad luck. Blood on it." She paused, a smile of surprise and delight dawning. "You know, it's nice to say what

I think for a change. You want to know about our family? I could talk for hours. Never got to before."

Poor Dimitra, Elena thought, remembering how silent the woman had always been while Boris was alive. Now she couldn't stop talking. "Did Boris ever say how much the medal was worth?" Elena asked.

"It wasn't worth anything—except in his head."

Could Boris have been shot for a worthless medal? Elena wondered. Someone heard him bragging about it, maybe thought it was gold, covered with jewels, got into the house, Boris pulled a gun, the thief took it away from him, shot him in the struggle or after forcing him to tell where the medal was. Or maybe when he saw that it was nothing special, the thief shot Boris for spite. Muggers did that. Beat up the victim because he didn't have any money. "How did you happen to notice it was missing, Dimitra?"

"I was looking in the desk for his life insurance policy and noticed the box was gone. Boris kept it in a fruitcake tin Amy Fogel gave us one Christmas."

They could check the pawn shops and fences, Elena decided. She doubted anyone in Los Santos would pay the thief anything for it. As a result, some fence might be willing to get on her good side by giving her a name.

"How did you and Mr. Potemkin get along?" asked Leo.

"We did things his way. How do you think?" said Dimitra. "Never did anything *I* wanted to do. Wouldn't put my boy through college. He didn't even want me to see Lance. Soon as that first batch freezes, I'll take out six or eight for you and your mother, Elena."

"Thank you," said Elena. "You were saying about Boris."

"He never wanted to go to the movies," said Dimitra. "If it weren't for my hip and the fact that I never learned to drive, I think I'd go to a movie this afternoon. I loved the movies back home in New York. We had a Russian-language movie house. You probably didn't know that."

"No, I didn't." Maybe Dimitra had a pleasant surprise coming. If Omar hadn't fallen asleep again, he'd be along pretty soon to invite her to the movies.

"I saw *Eugene Onegin* there when I was fifteen. I was born

in this country, but Russia looked just the way my baba described it. Long fields of snow. You should have seen the duel scene between Onegin and Lenski. Lenski's aria, it's the most beautiful music! You know it?" She glanced up from the cabbage rolls.

Neither Leo nor Elena did.

"Well, you come by some evening. I'll play it for you." Then she sighed, her nostalgic smile fading. "I forgot. Boris broke my records. If I have any money on his insurance, maybe I'll go back to Coney Island and visit my family. See if there's anyone left."

Elena felt a pang of sadness for the woman, who didn't even know whether she had family still living.

"'Fraid you can't leave town till your husband's murder's solved, ma'am," Leo warned.

Dimitra glanced at him with no evidence of alarm. "Well, I don't suppose there'll be enough money for me to go, anyway. Just wishful thinking. I'm too old—too crippled up."

"How did that happen, Dimitra—the broken hip?"

Dimitra hesitated. "I fell down the stairs to the bomb shelter." Silence followed. Then she added, "During air raid practice."

Air raid drills. Czar's medals. Communist plots. Boris must have been paranoid. And the rumors of abuse. Elena had to wonder whether Dimitra had been pushed. People hinted, but Dimitra wasn't admitting it. As open as she'd been about her dislike of her husband, wouldn't she have mentioned physical abuse if there had been any?

As Elena and Leo walked to the car, Elena said, "Someone could have killed him for the czar's medal."

"It doesn't sound like a big prize to me," said Leo.

"Still, we better check it out." Elena told him about her interview with Omar Ashkenazi. "He could have done it. He was as happy to hear about Boris' death as Dimitra."

"Maybe she asked him to kill her husband," Leo suggested.

"I suppose that's possible," said Elena.

"The Potemkins don't come off as a loving threesome," said Leo. "And another thing. She was careful not to mention that her son's gay. Lance is the one we need to get hold of. If the old lady didn't kill the husband, probably the son did."

"Still," said Elena, "I think I'll run Omar's name through the computer. He claims to be pacifist, but who knows? We might find fifteen agg assaults."

8
..

The Socorro Heights Senior Citizens Center was housed in an old building, thirties vintage, of native red rock with a new cement-block addition in back and cactus, oleanders, and nonbearing mulberry trees in front. The parking lot, with numerous spaces reserved for the handicapped, had dozens of cars slanting drunkenly over the lines. "How you doing with the baby-making?" Elena asked as she and Leo walked toward the entrance.

Leo groaned. "I'm too old," he muttered.

"Yeah, right. Thirty," said Elena.

Leo shrugged. "She takes her temperature, the right time hits, and we screw like rabbits for a couple a days. We're so tired when the time's up, we go to bed about eight o'clock and can't hardly wake up for the alarm."

"Gee, Leo. Really tough. Have you considered giving up sex and adopting a kid?"

"*I've* considered it," said Leo, "but Concepcion wants her own. All of her brothers and sisters have kids. When the family gets together, they act like if she hadn't married an Anglo, she'd have six babies by now."

"Aren't you glad you don't?" said Elena, stopping to ask where they'd find the bridge group. A member of the administrative staff pointed them toward the aroma of the noonday

42

meal. Meat loaf and pickled beets. Elena wondered how the Hispanic seniors felt about that menu.

The bridge game was underway in a large room where Ping-Pong and a sing-along to music from an old record player were also in progress. Hundreds of notices were posted on bulletin boards: classes to be held in the side rooms, second-hand goods for sale, rooms for rent, health fairs with free tests and shots. Seniors ate stale popcorn from a machine where they scooped their own into a bag and left a dime. Piles of used paper coffee cups in plastic holders littered a table that held a big coffeepot. Classroom doors, some open, some closed, lined the right side of the large room.

Leo and Elena introduced themselves to the four female bridge players. Emily somebody said, "Four no trump," and the rest, including her partner, tut-tutted.

"I'm Lydia Beeman," said a lean, vigorous-looking woman in tailored beige slacks and blouse. She rose to shake hands. "You're here about Boris Potemkin, I imagine. That's Margaret Forrest." She gestured toward another tall woman with beautifully coiffed white hair. "Margaret gave Dimitra a ride yesterday. And that's Portia Lemay, my bidding partner for today." Lydia nodded toward a third woman. "Portia's single. Sold more houses than anyone in Los Santos before she retired."

"I still know where the good buys are," said Portia, blue eyes twinkling in an unlined, rosy face.

"And this is Emily Marks, who just made the world's most ill-conceived bid," Lydia concluded and sat down. "Double," she said to Emily.

"Redouble," said Emily gaily.

Elena judged that Emily Marks was a bit younger than the others, who appeared to be in their middle seventies. Emily's hair was dyed brown-blond and teased into an elaborate halo around her head. She had the look of a woman who'd had a face lift that was just beginning to sag.

"Emily's the only one with a living husband," said Lydia, "and a good thing too, since she needs a lot of looking after."

Elena figured that if she were doing a statistical study with this group as its basis, she'd come to the conclusion that marriage caused wrinkles. A brief, polite argument ensued over who would be questioned first. Portia Lemay, the dummy, volunteered. Leo and Elena insisted on Mrs. Forrest.

"I don't have anything to tell you that the others can't hear," said Margaret Forrest.

"What's goin' on he-ah?" The words were slow, the accent drawling, the tone suspicious.

Elena looked across the bridge table to a man who stood behind and slightly to the side of Lydia Beeman. He was tall and thin, with skin as seamed, brown, and rough as an overripe kiwi. Straight and sparse, his white hair hung a good inch below his ears, and his eyes were blue and faded amid the squinting wrinkles of a man who had looked too long into the sun. Hanging loosely from bony hips, his jeans were held up by a wide leather belt with an ancient rodeo buckle. A worn sports jacket cut Western style with pointed yokes partially covered a clean but poorly ironed white shirt highlighted by a string tie. His boots were high-heeled, scuffed and tooled, a soiled yellow color with brown curlicue insets around the tops. Elena took him in at a glance and thought, *Portrait of an old cowboy*.

"These are detectives investigating Boris Potemkin's murder," said Lydia.

"Well, whyfore they botherin' you ladies?"

"Because Dimitra played bridge with us yesterday," said Margaret.

"Don't like to see ladies bothered."

"This is T. Bob Tyler," said Lydia to Leo and Elena. "He's a retired rancher who doesn't know what to do with himself, so he hangs around here being chivalrous in a minor way." T. Bob Tyler patted Lydia Beeman's lean shoulder as if he understood that her sharp words were a sign of affection. "T. Bob, meet Detectives Weizell and Jarvis. Jarvis is the woman. How do you like that? Bet they didn't have any lady sheriffs out in Otero County, New Mexico, when you were ranching. They never did in East Texas when I was a girl."

"No ma'am," said T. Bob and placed a showy Stetson over his heart as he smiled shyly at Elena. She was sure he'd have swept the hat off had it been on his head.

"Mrs. Forrest," said Leo, nodding his head toward an empty classroom.

"Whar's Miss Margaret goin'?" asked T. Bob in an alarmed tone.

"They're about to give her the third degree," said Lydia dryly. "Don't you want to go along to protect her?"

Elena heard the tap of his boot heels coming after them. She turned and said, "Don't worry, Mr. Tyler. We won't do her an ounce of harm."

T. Bob stopped, looking confused, probably because he didn't know how to gainsay a woman. They escaped into the classroom with Margaret, leaving him behind, mumbling. Leo, Elena, and Margaret took seats in the uncomfortable desk-chair combinations that looked like discards from the school district.

"We're primarily interested in time, Mrs. Forrest," said Elena.

"And state of mind," added Leo.

"Well, I certainly feel guilty. I should have gone into the house with her, especially considering that she has to use a walker. Poor thing. I was anxious to get home to work on my mums. I decided just yesterday that they needed to be pinched back one—"

"Mrs. Forrest," Leo interrupted.

"You're not familiar with chrysanthemum strategies?" asked Margaret Forrest, misunderstanding his interruption. "You pinch some buds to make the rest of the blossoms larger."

"What time was it when you dropped her off, ma'am?" Leo asked, cutting off the mum lecture.

"Three-thirty," said Margaret. "And I suppose you'd like to know when I picked her up. That was quarter-to-twelve. We always have lunch together before we start playing. The food isn't very good here, but it's better than cooking."

Elena reflected that they had yet to find a witness in this case who didn't want to tell them more than they needed to know.

"I still enjoy my garden," Margaret was saying, "but—"

"About *Dimitra's* state of mind that afternoon," Elena cut in, feeling like some ill-brought-up youngster.

Mrs. Forrest looked surprised but obligingly replied. "She

seemed cheerful. Now, of course, she's probably thinking that if she'd stayed home, Boris might still be alive."

"You have the impression that Dimitra was fond of her husband?"

"Well, used to him. Heavens, they've been married for years. You get used to living with a person."

"But how did she *feel* about him? Did she say anything about him yesterday?"

"Oh, the usual. Everyone knows Boris was difficult."

"Do you think Dimitra was a battered woman?" asked Elena.

"A what?" Margaret looked uneasy.

"Did her husband abuse her physically or emotionally?"

"Goodness, I couldn't say." Then she added hesitantly, "Dimitra did mention several unkind remarks he made. Is that what you mean?"

"Yes. Like what?"

"She'd forgotten to bring in the paper that morning."

"He made her go out for the paper?" Elena liked Boris less with each new story she heard about him.

"He did," said Margaret. "And Boris was quite able to go out and get his own paper. But he expected her to do everything she'd ever done before she broke her hip."

"Do you have any idea how that happened?" asked Leo.

Margaret Forrest's face closed. "It's hard to say. Her hip might have given way on its own. Because of osteoporosis, which strikes so many older woman. I hope you're getting lots of calcium while you can, Detective Jarvis."

"You saying her hip just crumbled?" asked Leo incredulously.

"I really have no idea," said Margaret. "It could have crumbled before the fall or broken after."

Wow, thought Elena. *Maybe I better drink more milk.* "She was with you from quarter-of-twelve to three-thirty?"

"That's right," said Margaret. "I just wish that I'd seen her into that house."

"Did she seem to *want* you to?"

"No, she said, 'Get back in your car, Margaret. I know you're anxious to start on those mums.' And I was. So I did."

"Did someone invite Dimitra Potemkin to play yesterday," asked Leo, "or did she offer?"

Margaret Forrest frowned, shook her head. "I'm not sure, but Lydia could tell you. She's the one who needed a substitute."

When Mrs. Forrest had left, Elena murmured, "You think Dimitra was setting herself up with an alibi?"

"Could be. If she and the son were both in on it. Maybe the son was in the house with the body. Or she could have been afraid he'd be." Leo got up. "We're going to be here all afternoon if we can't get these people to stick to the point," he muttered. "They're as bad as your neighbors were last night."

"Older people have plenty of time. They like to talk."

"So we'll interrupt them," said Leo. They went out to the bridge table. Emily Marks had been set, doubled and redoubled, on her four-no-trump bid, and a new round of bidding was in progress.

T. Bob Tyler sat at the corner of the table between Lydia and Emily Marks, his eyes fixed on the classroom door.

"Maybe Mr. Tyler could take a hand," said Elena, anxious to get on with the interviews.

"Don't play nuthin' but poker," said T. Bob. "Bridge and suchlike are women's games."

"Fiddlesticks," said Lydia Beeman. "I probably play a better hand of poker than you do, T. Bob." She turned to her fellow players. "Since Portia's got the bid at four hearts, you go in next, Emily."

"I've never been questioned by the police," said Emily. "Should I have a lawyer?"

"Don't be a ninny," snapped Lydia. "You haven't done anything."

"You want me to go along, Miz Emily?" asked T. Bob. "Don't want you frightened by no lawmen, even if one is a woman."

Emily giggled. "You're such a dear, T. Bob," she said. "Almost as chivalrous as my George."

"Don't reckon your George ever handled a six-gun," rumbled T. Bob.

"I hope you're not packing one, Mr. Tyler," said Elena. "If you are, it's concealed, and that's against the law."

"Too many folks got sissy ideas about guns these days," said T. Bob glumly. "Ah sure am willin' an' able to go in an' look after you, Miz Emily."

"Well, I—"

"Get on in there, Emily," said Lydia.

"You mustn't let Lydia's gruff ways mislead you," said Emily once they'd arranged themselves in the desk chairs. "She's a wonderful woman. My big sister."

"You're related?" asked Elena, surprised.

"She was the best friend of my real big sister who"—Emily looked as if she might cry—"who died several years back. Lydia's been so good to me. She took me into the bridge group when she knew I wasn't a very good player. Although I've improved. You wouldn't believe it."

Elena didn't believe it.

"Between Lydia and my dear husband, George, I never have a worry in the world."

"That's real nice," said Leo. "What we wanted to ask you about was Dimitra Potemkin."

"Oh, yes. I plan to take her a bowl of my cream of squash soup. That should—"

"Do you think she liked her husband, Boris?" asked Leo. Having had to listen to the mum dissertation from Margaret Forrest, he was evidently determined to miss whatever Emily Marks had to say about squash soup. Elena cleared her throat to keep from giggling.

Emily looked shocked and said, "I'm sure she did."

"She never said anything unfavorable about him?"

"Well, of course, but she didn't mean it."

"What did she say about him yesterday?" asked Elena.

"Goodness, I don't remember. I have enough trouble remembering what's been bid, and as for remembering what's been played—"

"Time, Mrs. Marks," said Leo. "We need to know when Dimitra Potemkin was here at the center." But Emily didn't remember—that or much else of significance.

"Senile?" Leo murmured to Elena when the lady had left.

"Just a twit," Elena replied and followed him out.

"Portia's free," said Lydia. "I'm playing two hearts."

"Miz Lemay, she don't know nuthin' 'bout murders," said T. Bob Tyler. "She's a maiden lady. In my 'sperience maiden ladies is mighty squeamish 'bout blood."

"We don't think she killed anyone," said Elena, who was getting tired of the old rancher's interference.

Portia Lemay patted T. Bob Tyler on the shoulder as she passed. "Don't get yourself in a fuss, T. Bob," she said.

"Don't know why the police would be hangin' round a bunch of old folks anyway," said T. Bob to Lydia.

"You may consider yourself an old folk. I'm not," retorted Lydia.

Portia Lemay wanted to give Leo advice on refinancing his house since interest rates were at an all-time low, but Leo circumvented that by refusing to divulge his current rate. Forced to talk about the Potemkins, Miss Lemay agreed that Lance and his father had had a sour relationship for years. She wasn't sure who had arranged for Dimitra to take Lydia's place at the bridge table.

By the time they had finished with Portia Lemay, Leo wanted to ask questions at random among the center's population.

"Lydia Beeman knows who suggested that Dimitra take her place," Elena pointed out. Mrs. Beeman rose and pushed back her chair without being asked.

T. Bob piped up, "How come you're goin' in, Miz Lydia? You wasn't even here yesterday."

"Neither were you from what I hear," said Lydia crisply. "Maybe they want to know where I was. Maybe they'd like to know where you were when Boris Potemkin was getting himself shot, you being such an admirer of Dimitra's."

As Lydia marched into the classroom, T. Bob was saying, "Ah was too here. Waz she mean by that?"

"You were?" asked Emily.

"Ah was. Where else would Ah be? This is where Ah always come of an afternoon."

Leo cleared his throat at the classroom door. "Why don't you

talk to Mrs. Beeman, Elena, and I'll see what else I can dig up."
Elena nodded and followed Lydia in.

"The other ladies think your partner is very rude, Detective
Jarvis," said Lydia. "He kept interrupting them."

Elena flushed. Questioning senior citizens was the pits, and
she wished Leo had stayed for this. He hadn't seemed to mind
being rude, while Elena remembered all those years of Grandmother Portillo rapping her knuckles with a weaver's shuttle if
she interrupted. If Mrs. Beeman was a blabbermouth, Elena
was going to be stuck because she'd grown up in Chimayo,
where everyone was scrupulously polite to their elders.

She cleared her throat self-consciously. "I realize you
weren't here yesterday, Mrs. Beeman, but I did want to ask
whose idea it was that Dimitra take your place in the bridge
game."

"I said I needed a substitute. Dimitra offered."

"So it was her idea?"

"Yes, but that doesn't mean she was providing herself with
an alibi."

Not much got by this lady, Elena thought.

"Dimitra couldn't have known until day before yesterday
that she'd be sitting in for me," said Lydia. "If she wanted to
have her husband killed, I imagine it would take more than
overnight planning."

On the other hand, thought Elena, Dimitra could have seen
her chance, called her son or Omar, and set the whole thing up
on the spur of the moment. Or maybe Boris did something that
night that triggered her to plan his death while she had the
opportunity.

"How long have you been a policewoman?" asked Lydia.

"Three and a half years," Elena replied, wondering if the
question was an evasive tactic indicating that Mrs. Beeman had
information she didn't want to divulge.

"It's a great and proud responsibility," Lydia declared. "I
hope you find your work satisfying."

Elena shrugged. "We arrest them, but the courts don't always
send them to jail. Now about—"

"There are certainly flaws in the system," Lydia agreed. "As
it happens, I take a great interest. Many of the men in my

family were judges, Texas Rangers, sheriffs, or contributed in other ways to law and order in the state. In fact, Farwell Brant, my great-great-great-grandfather, fought at the Alamo, which was certainly a struggle for justice. The Mexican legal system was an abomination. If you've read your Texas history, Detective Jarvis, you know that there *was* no law in Texas at that time. The Revolution was *not* just a land grab."

"Actually, I grew up in New Mexico," said Elena.

"And the Mexicans still follow the Napoleonic Code."

Elena tried to think of a question before Lydia started explaining the drawbacks of the Napoleonic Code.

"You're very lucky that women can make a contribution these days," the lady went on. "Such opportunities hardly existed when I was young—at least, not *professional* opportunities, opportunities for which one received a *salary*. I would never say that women weren't heard or active in matters of legal importance, just that we exerted *indirect* influence."

"I'm sure you did. Do you—"

"I suppose I might have joined one of the women's units of the armed forces during the Second World War. Instead I married a soldier, a career army man."

"An honorable calling," murmured Elena. She found Lydia Beeman's attitude interesting. Many older women didn't approve of Elena's profession. Grandmother Portillo certainly didn't.

"I shall watch with interest your progress on this case," Lydia was saying. "The police deserve all the support they can get in these violent times."

"Thank you." Elena wished her mother could hear this. Even married to a sheriff, Harmony still slipped and used the word *pigs* occasionally. Usually when referring to the good old days at Berkeley.

"Do you have other questions for me?" asked Lydia.

"Ah—yes." Elena had to collect her thoughts. "Does Dimitra often play bridge?"

"Occasionally. She *prefers* chess and plays that very well."

Dimitra might be having a chess game this very minute at Omar's house, Elena thought.

"The general perception is that women do not have the sense

of spatial relationships required for chess," said Lydia, making it clear that people who held that opinion were fools. "You even hear *women* saying that they have no sense of direction. In my opinion, this is a societal rather than a hereditary or gender-related trait. I, for instance, have an infallible sense of direction. Dimitra was an excellent chess player. Unfortunately," Lydia added, "her broken hip has affected her mental capacities."

"I noticed that myself," said Elena.

"You know Dimitra?"

"She's my neighbor."

"Good. I'm glad to hear there'll be someone looking out for her."

"Won't her son do that?" murmured Elena.

"If you mean in the sense that he'll move back in, I rather imagine Lance would prefer to follow his own lifestyle. It has been some years since he lived in the family home. You've met Lance?"

"In the course of investigating another case last spring."

"I'm surprised that you haven't talked to him in reference to this one."

"We haven't got hold of him yet," Elena admitted.

"I hope his mother has been able to reach him," said Lydia, frowning. "She'll need his help with the funeral arrangements and other problems. A husband's death generates reams of paperwork."

Reams of paperwork? That was a peculiar way to look at it. "Lance isn't answering his telephone."

"Nonetheless, I would not count on discovering that Lance is the murderer. A thief caught in the act would be a more likely suspect."

"Why do you say that?" Elena asked.

"Because the older population is a target for crime."

"Is there anything you could tell me about the family that would shed some light?"

"Such as what?"

"Do you think that Dimitra was a battered woman?"

"That is a question that you should ask Dimitra," Lydia

replied evenly. "It is not information that I would be likely to have, is it?"

"Well, if you were friends with her—"

"Acquaintances," corrected Lydia. And then she surprised Elena with a warm smile. "I wish you the best of luck, my dear. Both with this case and your career. If I can ever be of assistance, do not hesitate to call on me. It is my feeling that every citizen should contribute in whatever way they can to the cause of justice."

When Elena left the classroom, Leo was waiting for her. They walked out together, and she asked if he had come up with anything.

"Well, there's that old cowboy. He left as soon as he saw I was talking to people, and although he claims he was here yesterday afternoon, nobody remembers seeing him."

"That doesn't necessarily mean he wasn't here," Elena pointed out. "Some of these people are bound to be forgetful."

"Sure, but the thing is Mrs. Beeman said he's an admirer of Dimitra Potemkin, so I asked around. It turns out he was her country-music dancing partner here at the center, and her husband didn't like it. Dimitra and old T. Bob were a real two-stepping, Cotton-Eyed-Joe couple until she broke her hip, and we've got a pretty fair idea of who caused that. Think about it. Maybe this T. Bob Tyler, who everybody agrees just loves the ladies, felt it was his old-timey Western duty to rub out Boris for Mrs. Boris' safety. Maybe he feels responsible for that broken hip. Maybe he figures, with Boris gone, he and Dimitra can get together."

"Good grief!" said Elena. "Two boyfriends?"

"Two?"

"Omar Ashkenazi." Elena shook her head and opened the door to the car they had checked out of the police garage. "Weird case," she muttered, starting the motor. "We got one dead old man; one crippled-up, happy widow; an absentee son and two possible boyfriends as suspects. Not your usual murder case."

"Our usual murder case is a drive-by shooting. Be thankful for the change of pace."

9
..

Finding her mother at the stove cooking, Elena went to the refrigerator for salad ingredients. "How come I didn't see you at Socorro Heights?" she asked. "I thought you were going to spend the day there."

"Only the morning. Setting up weaving demonstrations and discussing the possibility of lessons. Have you heard rumors that Dimitra Potemkin was a battered woman?"

"Everyone dances around it, but the implication is there." After chopping green onions and tomatoes, Elena added lettuce to the salad bowl.

"Not that I think she killed Boris—even in self-defense." Harmony was dicing potatoes at the counter.

Elena agreed. "Her alibi probably covers the time of death."

"And she didn't have the aura of someone who just committed murder."

"Right, Mom." Elena grinned, tossing the salad while Harmony put the finishing touches on a skillet full of *chile verde,* which smelled ambrosial. "The son, Lance, might have done it."

"Why would you think that?" Harmony spiced and tasted the chile, then added the diced potatoes.

"Well, I've heard that he threatened Boris because of Dimitra. And nobody thinks they got along well. They didn't even speak in recent years—except for a few fights."

Harmony nodded. "Greek tragedy on the border."

"Right. Sophocles for seniors. Maybe Dimitra asked Lance to kill Boris."

"Nonsense."

"Anyway, it looks bad that we can't get hold of him. What'd you think of the bridge group? Did you meet them?"

Harmony put a lid on the skillet and leaned against the counter. "The bridge group," she mused. "Well, I find it very touching that those women have been together for so many years. They all went to the same private school here in town. Some as boarders, some as day students."

"I didn't know that." Elena got out beer and tilted a chilled stein sideways so that she could pour without getting too much foam.

"Of course, some moved away, but they all ended up back here."

"Lydia Beeman would be one of the ones who moved away. Her husband was in the army." Elena handed a stein to Harmony and filled one for herself. "She's an interesting woman, don't you think?"

"Lydia?" Harmony raised the lid to give her *chile verde* a stir, then took her first sip of beer. "I really didn't care for her."

"Why not?" asked Elena, surprised.

"The woman has an angry aura."

"Oh, come on, Mom. Lots of citizens are angry. It's a tough world. Especially if you're her age."

"That's true," Harmony agreed and changed the subject. "I can't understand why you haven't done anything about your living room, Elena."

"I did. I swept up the glass, put the books back on the shelves—"

"—and left your sofa and chairs in hopeless condition. Fortunately, your neighbor, Mr. Ituribe, has offered to work on the springs and help me with the upholstering. You'll have a designer living room before I leave." Harmony ladled the *chile verde* into large bowls as Elena scooped the salad into small ones.

Then they sat down to dinner, Elena savoring the first mouthful of her mother's delicious beef and green chile stew.

As she ate, she thought about the case. Lance Potemkin loved his mother and hated his father. Boris abused Dimitra, had even threatened to kill her if Lance didn't stay away. So if Dimitra hadn't killed the old man, Lance was the most likely suspect. That scenario made more sense than a robber killing Boris to get his hands on a medal that wouldn't be worth anything with a local fence.

"Have you seen Dimitra today?" asked Elena as she helped herself to more *chili verde*.

"Just briefly. She brought me cabbage rolls, but she couldn't stay to chat because one of the neighbors had invited her to go to the movies. A Mr. Ashkenazi."

Elena shook her head. Omar was another suspect. And if T. Bob Tyler was the murderer instead of Lance or Omar, Omar Ashkenazi might be the next victim. Maybe she ought to run all three men through the computer for priors.

10
..

They caught Lance Potemkin arriving at the English Department the next morning. He stowed a backpack behind his desk and said, "Aren't you the detectives who investigated the non-murder of Angus McGlenlevie last spring?"

"Right. Where have you been?" asked Leo. "We've been trying to get hold of you for two days."

"I've—" Lance looked surprised, then uneasy. "I've had the flu."

"It's too early for the flu," said Elena, thinking he really was cute. Blond curls, a clean-cut face, and nice build. He also looked guilty as hell.

"It's striking early," said Lance defensively.

"So where were you while you had the flu?" asked Elena. "We called your house."

"I—turned the phone off."

"Don't you ever read the Los Santos papers or talk to your mother?" asked Leo.

"I haven't seen a paper."

"You didn't listen to the radio or watch TV? You have to do something while you're sick," Leo prodded.

"I go to bed and sleep." Alarm suddenly flashed in Lance's eyes. "Is something wrong with my mother?"

Was he worried that his mother had been arrested, when he himself was the murderer? Elena wondered. Maybe both

57

Potemkins were guilty. Or innocent. If innocent, she and Leo
would be the first to break the news of his father's death. Not
that she expected Lance to take it hard.

"What's happened to her?" He sounded almost frantic.

"Your father died day before yesterday," said Leo.

"What about my *mother*?"

Not *What happened to Dad?* Elena noticed. "Dimitra's
O.K." Pity Lance didn't like women. At a guess, she didn't
think he was that much younger than she.

"But your father was shot in the head," said Leo. "Your
mother said he had a gun, but it's missing."

"Well, he couldn't have killed himself with his own gun,"
said Lance. "I have it."

"Oh?" Leo, who had been leaning against the desk, straightened. "We'll need to take a look at it," said Elena.

"Sure, but it's at home, and I don't get off till five, so—"

"We're going to have to ask you to come over to headquarters anyway," Elena interrupted.

"Now? I have to proof the galleys of the literary magazine
today."

"You're the editor?"

"Angus McGlenlevie is. He just doesn't do the work."

"Uh-huh. Well, maybe he'll have to this time."

Lance looked surprised, then laughed, then went back to
looking anxious. "I don't know anything," he assured them.

"We still need to question family members."

Reluctantly he agreed and excused himself to tell the
chairman.

They could hear through the open door Dr. Mendez's
condolences on the death of Lance's father, his groan when he
realized that he'd need to track down Angus McGlenlevie for
the proofing of the galleys, his heartfelt plea that Lance get
back as soon as possible because the department was falling
apart in his absence.

Elena found this all very interesting. Dr. Raul Mendez was
a noted scholar of Hispanic-American literature, according to
Elena's friend Professor Sarah Tolland. Now Elena was getting
the impression that Mendez might be the department chair and

Gus McGlenlevie the editor of the department's literary magazine, but Lance Potemkin, the secretary, was doing the work.

They escorted him to their tan Taurus, confiscated in a drug bust with three million dollars worth of cocaine stashed in the trunk in leaking baggies. Detectives joked about getting high inhaling if they had to change a tire, or vacuuming the trunk and retiring. "Am I a suspect?" Lance asked as he fastened his seat belt.

"At this point it's sort of everyone and no one," Leo replied.

Looking uneasy, Lance said, "We might as well stop by my place if you want his gun."

"How did you come to have it?" asked Elena.

"He threatened my mother. I took the gun so he couldn't shoot her."

"Did your father threaten her often?"

"Not just threats," said Lance darkly. "But she refused to tell the police."

"She was pretty up front about not liking him."

"In her place, would you like him?"

Elena was driving, talking to Lance, while Leo took notes as they pulled up to a prairie-style house, probably designed earlier in the century by Henry Trost, a Frank Lloyd Wright follower. Elena would have loved to own a Trost house, but they were too big and undoubtedly too expensive.

"I have the second floor," said Lance. They mounted outside wooden steps that must have been added later when the attic was converted to accommodate a renter. Lance had one large room and a bath. There was a Pullman kitchen behind slatted doors and a large couch upholstered in a nubby black fabric. It evidently opened out into a bed. A beautiful reproduction eighteenth-century writing desk and chair stood by the large dormer window, and a glass and wrought-iron dining set occupied one corner. Several large abstract paintings, whose predominant colors were black and white with touches of red, hung on matte white walls.

Elena found herself liking the paintings, although her taste usually ran to Indian and Southwestern art. The Hopi painters who had modernized traditional Hopi designs were among her favorites. If she were rich, she'd buy one of those corn-maiden pictures. They featured a muted shade of green that sent shivers up her spine. "Nice place," she said to Lance.

He thanked her with a pleased smile and added deprecatingly, "It's affordable."

The most interesting thing in the apartment, case-wise, was the streamlined bicycle hanging from the wall on pegs. Elena went over to inspect it and jotted down in her notebook "green Cannondale R600." The Ituribes had thought the bike in the alley was green.

"Do a lot of bicycle riding?" asked Leo casually.

Lance turned to follow the direction of Leo's gaze. "I'm a racer." His face lit with enthusiasm. "It's the greatest high in the world, riding a bike so fast the roadside blurs at the corners of your vision and the horizon hurtles into your face."

Very poetic, thought Elena and asked prosaically, "You own a car?"

Lance shook his head. "I bike to work."

"That's ten miles!" exclaimed Elena. Ten miles on a bike would probably lay her up for a week.

"Not quite, but it keeps me in shape for the next race. The gun's in the drawer of my writing desk."

Leo went to the desk, opened it, fished a gun out with a pencil, and dropped it, barrel up, into an evidence bag he pulled from his pocket. "Looks like a Luger."

Lance nodded. "My father found it on the body of a German officer during the Second World War."

Before he sealed the bag, Leo leaned over to sniff. "Smells like it's been cleaned."

"Probably. He'd rather disassemble and clean that Luger than read a book or watch TV."

"Ammunition in here," said Leo. He used a handkerchief to remove the box and open it. "Some gone."

"He liked to shoot ground squirrels out back."

"Surprised he didn't notice the gun was missing if he was so fond of it," said Leo.

"Maybe he did. I haven't talked to him or my mother since I took it."

"Nine millimeter hollow point," Leo murmured to Elena. The autopsy report had come in that morning. Boris had been killed by a 9 mm hollow-point bullet through the brain. It had smashed against the plate at the back of his skull, making it impossible for Ballistics to give them rifling information that would tie the bullet to a specific gun. The markings at the end of the cartridge, however, had been identified as probably coming from an old Luger. The gun, the bullets, and the bicycle made Lance a very good suspect, especially since he'd been overheard threatening to kill his father.

They left the apartment and went to headquarters at Five Points, where they put Lance in the large interrogation room with the one-way window. He sat down on the blue polka-dot sofa as Elena and Leo excused themselves for a private conversation in the hall.

"He was lying about the flu," said Leo.

"I agree. You'd think he'd at least come up with a better story. And he only rides a bicycle, which explains the green bike in the alley."

"You wanna question him while I listen?" Leo offered. "You know more about the mother."

"Sure. And let's get a warrant for his apartment. If we find the czar's medal, it would make our case."

"I'll fill out the form while you're talking to him."

Elena walked into the interrogation room and sat down on a brown vinyl chair facing Lance while Leo holed up next door, where he could listen and watch without being seen.

"You're about to ask if I want a lawyer," said Lance. "Don't bother. I didn't kill my father."

"Good. You said you were home with the flu. Did you go to a doctor?"

"Of course not. You have the flu, you go to bed, drink lots of liquids, take aspirin."

He seemed more comfortable with the story now. Elena figured he'd been thinking up elaborations on the way over. "Did you see or talk to anyone while you were sick?"

"No, I stayed in bed, only got up to use the bathroom and drink tea."

"Sounds like my mother's prescription."

"It's my mother's too."

"How come you didn't call her if you were sick?"

Lance gave her a hard look, belying the shy poet façade. "When I got in touch with my mother, it set my father off."

"Your mother never *said* your father abused her."

"That's right. Even when he pushed her downstairs and broke her hip, she didn't admit it. You've never met women like that?"

Elena nodded. There was anger there, enough to fuel a murder, she thought. "What was the problem between you and your father?"

"Just about everything. The way he treated her. It infuriated him if I tried to defend her. He'd probably rather they never had a child. Especially one like me."

"Could you be more specific?"

"He thinks writing poetry is unmanly—I'm a poet. Then he found out I'm gay; he *hated* that." Lance eyed Elena bitterly. "I suppose my being gay gives me favored status as the suspect."

"Neither Leo nor I have anything against homosexuals," said Elena, which was an evasion of sorts. There *had* been problems between the department and the homosexual community. "Are you—ah—out of the closet?"

"If you mean do I run around joining organizations, stumping for gay rights, marching in weird parades, no. It's neither a secret nor widely known. Do you run around talking about *your* sex life?"

Elena laughed. "Right now I don't have any. I suppose someone lives downstairs at your place."

"Sure. The owners of the house."

"Would they be aware that you were home sick?"

"I don't know."

"They might have heard you moving around."

"I didn't move around that much."

"Going up and down the stairs?"

"I didn't leave the apartment."

"You're telling me that you have no alibi."

"I don't need an alibi. I didn't kill him." He was sounding nervous and defensive again, as if it were beginning to dawn on him that he might be in big trouble. "And you can keep the gun. I don't want it back now that my mother's safe." He paused, then said, "My God, has she been trying to get hold of me?"

"She has."

"I need to get over there."

Leo came in from the listening room and said, "We're gonna have to ask you not to leave Los Santos until our investigation is complete, Mr. Potemkin."

"But I'm entered in a bicycle race on the High Road to Taos the end of the week."

"Sorry. Unless we've found the killer, you can't go."

"I'm under arrest?" He looked terrified. "Do you realize how gays are treated in jail? I can't—"

"You're not under arrest," said Leo. "But you are a suspect."

"Another thing. We're going to have to impound your bicycles," added Elena. "I assume there's a second at H.H.U.?"

"What am I supposed to use for transportation?"

"Rent a car. Take a bus," suggested Leo.

"What do my bicycles have to do with this?"

"One of the neighbors"—Elena almost said who but thought better of it—"saw a bike out in the alley the afternoon of your father's death."

Lance paled. "It couldn't have been one of mine."

"Still, sir, we'll need to impound them," said Leo. "If you refuse, we can get a warrant."

"What are you going to do? Have a bicycle lineup for one of my mother's doddering old friends?" he snapped.

Elena hadn't thought of it, but it was an idea.

Lance looked dejected and muttered, "Did it occur to you that someone might have broken into the house and killed him?"

"Sure, we thought of that, except the house wasn't broken into. We also thought of your mother," said Leo.

"Mother wouldn't." Lance looked horrified. "Good lord, she wasn't there when it happened, was she?"

Nice touch, thought Elena. "She says she was playing bridge at the senior citizens center."

He looked relieved. "I hope you're giving me a ride back to the English Department."

"Well, we'll have to pick up the bicycle there, and we'll want to search your apartment," said Elena.

"What for?"

"Evidence."

"But there isn't any," Lance protested. "I didn't *do* anything."

"The question is, do we have to get a warrant for your apartment?"

"If I give permission, what happens? You discover I have some homosexual novels and charge me with—"

"Lance, we're not interested in your library. You have my word that we won't take anything that doesn't pertain to your father." He looked scared and confused. If Lance was innocent, confusion was understandable. Either way, she could understand *scared*.

"Cooperation makes a good impression," said Leo, "but we can get the warrant. Take about two hours. We can hold you until—"

"But I have the magazine proofs to do." Lance now looked like a man on the edge of panic. "All right," he decided.

They left the Crimes Against Persons Division and started to turn right toward the side door.

"Sneaking me out?" muttered Lance.

"Not if you'd prefer to leave through the front," said Leo sharply and, taking Lance by the arm, headed him toward the hall that went to the public reception area. At the desk they ran into Harmony, chatting with a volunteer.

"Mom, you're kind of early to pick me up, aren't you?" said Elena.

"I finished at the center, so I thought I'd come down and get better acquainted. Your colleagues are so—" She stared at Lance, then exclaimed, "You're the poet who publishes in the *Desert Wind Anthology!*"

Lance flushed, much to Elena's astonishment.

"Your poem on saguaro against the sky was so moving," said Harmony. "If it doesn't take the prize this year, I'll be very disappointed. I'm Harmony Portillo." She shook Lance's hand enthusiastically. "Elena's mother."

"It's nice to meet you, ma'am," he replied. "I don't know too many people who've read my poetry."

"I'm definitely a fan," said Harmony. "And I've met your mother. Lovely woman. She gave me a dozen frozen cabbage rolls just yesterday. I suppose you're here about your father's death. I'm so sorry, dear."

"Thanks," said Lance.

"In fact, I drove Dimitra over to your apartment this morning to see if we couldn't get hold of you."

"I feel terrible that I wasn't there for her," said Lance. "How's she taking it?"

"Very well, dear. She's bearing up."

"Bearing up" was an understatement, thought Elena. Dimitra was just short of gleeful.

"Well, it's been a pleasure to meet you. If you're ever in Santa Fe, I'll come in for the reading." Harmony gave him a card.

"I've got a reading at the university tomorrow night," he said diffidently.

"Really. Which university?"

"Herbert Hobart. It's at seven. The first-floor auditorium in the Humanities building."

"I'll be there," Harmony promised.

"Now that I think of it, I wonder if I'll be there," he mumbled. "I've got to find a ride."

"Oh, I'd be glad to pick you up," said Harmony.

"*Mom!*"

"Give me your address."

Lance wrote the information on a slip of paper he borrowed from the desk sergeant. Elena gritted her teeth. Her mother was making friends with their prime suspect. Declaring herself his biggest fan. Offering him a ride.

"Time to go, Mr. Potemkin," said Leo. "Officer Blake here will take you to the university to pick up the other bicycle. You can either give us the key to your apartment or we'll meet you there."

Lance opted to be present during the search. Once the poet had gone, Leo turned to Elena. "We've got him on tape saying, 'My mother's safe now.'"

Elena sighed. "I noticed that, but he *was* cooperative. Didn't make us get warrants or anything."

"When I said we'd hold him, he thought I meant jail."

"Can't blame him for not wanting to spend any time there."

"I figure he thinks he's washed the bicycles down so good there won't be any evidence left that one of them was in that alley. As for the apartment, lots of perps think they've hidden things where no cop would ever think to look. But he's wrong. If the medal's there, we'll find it."

"Whatever are you two talking about?" asked Harmony. "That boy didn't kill his father."

Elena grinned. "Let me guess. He radiates the wrong color? Unfortunately, testimony about auras isn't admissible in court, Mom."

"Auras?" said Leo and stared at Harmony as if she'd just sprouted fairy wings.

Harmony went to the Chevrolet dealership to pick up her truck. Leo and Elena returned to Lance's apartment, where they found a lot of handwritten poetry stuffed in his desk. No czar's medal. No gun-cleaning equipment, no rubber gloves to eliminate fingerprints, no ski mask to hide his identity. No letters or diaries expressing a desire to kill his father. He did have an extensive library of gay literature and some videos, but Elena kept her promise and ignored them. And he had some sexy silk bikini underpants in bright prints, but she didn't think those were germane to the case, just interesting. Frank had never worn anything like that, nor had her brothers. Elena wondered how many men had sexy underwear. Maybe just gay men did.

"We still can't assume he's innocent," said Leo, interrupting her underwear speculations.

"I know," Elena agreed and got out of Leo's car. Since Harmony had left Elena's truck at the dealer's lot, Leo had offered Elena a ride to pick it up.

11
..

Having dug the first trench for her irrigation system, Elena came in from the back yard to find her mother weaving.

"Do you like the colors?" Harmony asked.

Elena studied the growing piece of fabric. "Yes," she said. "Especially the green."

Harmony nodded. "You always had a taste for that Hopi green, but what about the coral?"

"Depends on how much there is."

"Just touches," said Harmony. "Actually, I don't know why I'm asking you. You never give any thought to home decor."

"I trust your taste, Mom, but look at this stuff." She waved despondently at the sofa and love seat. Stuffing burst out of the pillows, springs from the frames.

"Not a problem. Mr. Ituribe will take care of it."

"How did you happen to meet him?"

"Why, I've introduced myself to all your neighbors. Jose perked right up at the thought of getting his hand in again."

"I'll have to pay him something."

"He'd be insulted if you offered."

"The poor man's dying of prostate cancer, Mom."

"I know, Elena. It will make him happy to know he's left something beautiful behind when he goes. Why haven't you replaced your TV?"

"I've still got the black and white in the kitchen. It's good enough for the news."

"Well, certainly the news is something one doesn't want to see in full color."

"Mom, about Lance Potemkin. I don't want you hanging out with a guy who probably killed his father."

"Elena, Lance is *not* guilty."

"O.K. Maybe he isn't, but he's a suspect. It looks bad to have my own mother connected to my suspect."

Harmony chuckled. "Listening to him read poetry hardly constitutes a close connection."

"You offered him a ride."

"Well, he doesn't have one. You took his bicycles." Harmony stretched her back, then returned to her weaving.

Elena gave up. "Have you seen Dimitra today? I wondered how she was doing."

"Just for a minute this afternoon," said Harmony. "She was getting dressed for a date with Mr. Ashkenazi. Since she couldn't locate her son, Mr. Ashkenazi offered to drive her to the mortuary to make funeral arrangements. Then they planned to take in a movie and go out to dinner."

Elena didn't know why she was surprised. Dimitra hadn't made any bones about being pleased over Boris' death, but for God's sake, the woman had accepted a date before she'd even buried her husband. And taking her boyfriend to the funeral parlor? Elena shook her head. Tomorrow she'd ask Lieutenant Beltran to assign two uniforms to recanvass the neighborhood, see if anyone had spotted Omar lurking around the murder scene. Claiming to have been asleep on your carpet wasn't Elena's idea of a great alibi, and dating the widow of the victim—that certainly looked suspicious—stupid maybe, but suspicious.

"You know, Elena, you're wasting time looking for evidence against Lance when it was obviously a robbery."

"You mean because of the czar's medal?"

"Well, that and the fact that it's not the first time this has happened. Several women from the center have lost their husbands in daylight robberies."

"They have? Are you saying there's a connection?"

"I have no idea, Elena, but it does show that older people are being targeted."

"Well, robberies are hard to solve, but we clear a good percentage of the murders. Much better than most cities."

"I'm sure you do, dear. I know you're a great asset to Crimes Against Persons—speaking of which, Lieutenant Beltran should be here any minute. With one of his sons. They're going to fix my truck and my loom so that I can get the loom to the senior citizens center handily."

Elena groaned. Just what she needed. Lieutenant Beltran and one of his sons getting chummy with her mother. Before she knew it, she'd have Mrs. Beltran over here complaining and Harmony inextricably entangled with both her case and her colleagues.

"I wonder what sign he is," mused Harmony.

"Boss. That's his sign."

"I meant zodiac sign, dear. I rather imagine he's a Taurus like your father."

12
..

Because Leo was working another case with Beto Sanchez, Elena and Officer Pete Amador from Central Division arranged a bicycle lineup. Besides Lance's two bicycles, a Merlin Titanium and a green Cannondale R600, Officer Amador borrowed one from the police bicycle patrol, a repainted blue and white mountain bike confiscated in a drug case. It had belonged to the dealer's teenaged son. To Elena the cocaine bike looked almost as expensive as Lance's, but what did she know? She just wrote down the names and descriptions as Amador produced them. He had called on his daughter for the fourth, a pink "ladies' cruiser" with a basket on the front.

Elena had some reservations about including girls' bicycles, since she doubted that Boris had been killed by a female, unless it was his wife, Dimitra. However, the coroner, even given the high temperature in the house, put the time of death between two and three, which was when Dimitra had been at the center.

The fifth bicycle, a black Rockhopper, had been taken from a newsboy delivering evening papers after sniffing spray paint. He'd run down an elderly lady and her dachshund. The lineup was still short a bicycle when Manny Escobedo, Elena's sergeant, said his daughter had one.

"Is it big enough to have been a murderer's?"

"Girls' ten-speed Schwinn," said Manny.

70

Elena called and got his ex-wife, Marcella, who was home with the flu but agreed to lend the green Schwinn.

"Slick—you not telling her it was my idea to ask," said Manny, who had been listening to Elena's end of the conversation. "How come she's home from work?"

"Got the flu. Isn't that something? End of September, and we're already into the yearly epidemic. Maybe Lance really did have it."

"Don't write Potemkin off," Manny advised. "He's got a good motive."

Elena sent Amador to pick up the green Schwinn and the Ituribes, whom she entertained with a tour of Crimes Against Persons while Amador wrested the Escobedo bike from the trunk of his patrol car.

The Ituribes were especially fascinated with the departmental computer. They watched with so much awe as a detective from Sex Crimes turned out a Wanted poster that Sergeant Escobedo offered to let them make one. He gave Jose instructions, the result of which was a "want" on Juanita. The crime: serving Jose cold *frijoles* for dinner on the night of September twenty-ninth.

"Who's gonna cook for you if I get arrested?" asked Juanita. She was folding up the souvenir poster and slipping it into an ancient brown handbag when Amador popped his head around the corner and motioned that he had the lineup in order. The Ituribes then trooped after Elena to the main interrogation room to look at the six bikes.

"What do you think about this one, Jose?" asked Juanita, pointing to Lance's green Cannondale.

"It's too funny-looking," said Jose. "I'd remember a bicycle that funny-looking."

Elena sighed.

"How about this one?" Jose pointed to the green Schwinn that belonged to Manny Escobedo's twelve-year-old daughter.

"Maybe," said Juanita. "It's green. Up close I can see that much. What do you think, Jose?"

"I don't know," said her brother-in-law. "The more I look, the more confused I get."

"Hey, look at this one, Jose. Cute, huh?"

"Pink with a basket? Yeah. The basket rings a bell," said Jose. "And the wheels look right to me. Fatter."

"Isn't it too small?" asked Juanita.

"How would we know? Neither one of us can see too good. Maybe it just looks small now because it's not so far away."

Elena winced. If the Ituribes thought things looked smaller close up, they were going to make rotten witnesses.

"But didn't you say green yesterday?" asked Juanita.

"Not yesterday, Monday." Jose scratched his chin. "I think I did. The green one's got a basket too."

Neither Ituribe had paid the slightest attention to Lance's Merlin Titanium. "You didn't say anything about a basket before, Jose," Elena pointed out.

"Didn't I?" He was studying the girl's green Schwinn. "I think it's this one, don't you, Juanita?"

"That or the pink one," Juanita agreed.

Elena thanked them and sent them home with Patrolman Amador. They'd just identified his daughter's bicycle as the suspect vehicle. That or the Escobedos' daughter's green ten-speed. Great! When Amador returned, Elena, who had been making phone calls, said, "Where was your daughter on the afternoon of September twenty-seventh?"

Amador grinned. "In school. Where the hell else would she be?"

"You're saying she's got an alibi?"

"Yep. 'Cause if she wasn't in school, her mother'd have told me about it."

"So much for that," said Elena. "Thanks for the help."

"Sure," said Amador. "Makes a nice break from chasing convenience-store robbers, and it's less dangerous than breaking up domestic brawls."

Elena drifted back to her desk, thinking about Omar and T. Bob Tyler, Dimitra's admirers. Time to run a computer check on them, she decided, and discovered that there was nothing on Omar except a few traffic tickets. On T. Bob Tyler, if he was the Thelonius Robert Tyler she found in the LSPD files, there was an assault charge. Three years ago Tyler had attacked some young guy in a bar. The responding officer reported that the victim had been making unpleasant remarks about old folks. Tyler had taken offense and knocked the young man down with an ashtray to the forehead. However, the victim turned out to have a want on him for aggravated robbery. He was hauled off to jail and evidently never filed charges against his assailant. Nothing else on Tyler in the LSPD files, but if he was easily offended, maybe there'd be something in Otero County, New Mexico, where he lived before he moved to Los Santos.

Elena telephoned the Sheriff's Department and asked if they had anything on T. Bob Tyler, maybe Thelonius Robert, giving his age and saying that he'd been a rancher there. The deputy transferred her to Sheriff Blankenship, who said, "Who wants to know about T. Bob Tyler?"

"I'm a detective with the Los Santos Police Department, Sheriff," said Elena and explained her case.

"Don't recall T. Bob ever shootin' anyone."

"Mr. Tyler was friendly with the victim's wife," said Elena, "and the victim didn't like it. We're exploring every avenue, and I wondered whether Tyler had a record in Otero County."

"Well, T. Bob was a feisty cuss," said the sheriff. "I got me his folder right in hand, covered with dust. Thelonius Robert Tyler. He musta took a poke at half the males in Otero County one time or another. Liked bar fights. Nothin' come of it, though. Ever'body'd sober up, an' nobody'd bring charges. But I gotta say, since you mention some fella's wife, T. Bob was a ladies' man. His own wife died—oh, musta been in the sixties, an' after that ole T. Bob was chasin' ever' skirt who showed up at an Otero County bar."

"Married women? Did he ever fight with any husbands?"

"Oh yeah. Nothin' serious like murder. A husband'd come along and take a poke at T. Bob, or T. Bob wouldn't like the way the fella was treatin' the wife, so he'd knock him down. Jus' yer usual stuff. T. Bob, he might be cussed with men, but he knew how to treat a woman. Reckon that ole boy got more ass in his day than anyone 'round here. Still, I can't figger him *shootin'* nobody over a woman."

"Even if the husband had done the wife serious injury, and Mr. Tyler felt somewhat responsible?"

"We-ell. Serious injury, huh? T. Bob sure as hell wouldn't

take to nobody doin' a woman serious injury. I recollect now he put Pete Dominguez in the hospital for three, four weeks one time. Le's see, that'd be back in—ah—'65, '66. Pete, he done broke his wife's jaw. Wife had it comin', but T. Bob, like I said, didn't hold with that stuff. Yeah, I s'pose he might kill someone if it was real serious an' he couldn't do nothin' else fer the lady in question."

"Thank you, Sheriff." Elena hung up and mused on what she'd heard. Now they had two good suspects and one not so good. Compared to Lance and T. Bob Tyler, Omar Ashkenazi, the self-proclaimed pacifist-vegetarian-yoga freak, didn't look particularly dangerous or motivated.

13
..

When Leo returned to headquarters, Elena told him that the bicycle lineup hadn't worked out.

"Couldn't they pick one?"

"Oh yeah—a pink ladies' cruiser and a green Schwinn—both with baskets. The suspect vehicles belonged to Pete Amador's daughter and Manny Escobedo's girl," said Elena dryly.

"Well, both of them admitted they couldn't see well. Even if they'd identified one of Potemkin's bicycles, they wouldn't have made good witnesses. So let's check into the son's background. Where do you want to start?"

"How about with the people who live downstairs? See if his alibi checks out." Leo agreed and they headed for the first floor of the prairie bungalow, where a bleary-eyed woman came to the door. They identified themselves, and Elena's first question was, "Are you ill, ma'am?"

"Don't I look it?" said Carlene Whittier. "If I didn't have the mother of all flus, I'd be at work. And if I were you, I'd stay down the end of the walk."

Elena and Leo cast startled glances at one another. "Do you think you could have caught it from Lance Potemkin?" asked Leo.

"Are you asking me if I'm having an affair with Lance?" said Mrs. Whittier, amazed. "I gotta sit down." Waving them in, she staggered back to her living room and sank into a large, pillowy orange recliner. "He's gay, and I'm happily married." She began to cough.

"Yes, ma'am, but he's your tenant," said Leo.

"Right. Best tenant we ever had. Pays on time. Isn't noisy. Doesn't have pets."

"We're interested in the period from September twenty-sixth to September twenty-ninth, particularly the twenty-seventh. Did you see him then?" asked Elena.

Mrs. Whittier fell into a coughing fit, then gasped, "Would you hand me that brown bottle on the coffee table?"

Elena gingerly picked the cough medicine up, glanced at it, and passed it to the woman. The label, sticky with spilled liquid, said "Phenergan with codeine."

"Haven't seen him in a couple of weeks," said Mrs. Whittier after drinking straight from the bottle.

"Did you hear him moving around upstairs?" Elena pressed.

"That's—ah—Sunday through Wednesday, right? Hand me that appointment calendar."

Leo passed Mrs. Whittier the notebook, and she thumbed through. "I was in Houston on business Monday. Probably where I caught the damn flu. Can you believe this? Flu in September? Anyway, I didn't get home till—I don't know—eleven-thirty Monday night. Didn't hear anything. I was at work Tuesday and Wednesday. Didn't hear anything those nights—or Sunday, and I was home all day getting ready for the trip."

"You didn't see or hear him on the steps?"

"Nope."

"Do you usually?"

"Nope," said Mrs. Whittier. She plucked two Kleenex from the box beside her chair, blew her nose, and tossed the used tissues on the floor.

Elena winced, picturing little flu viruses crawling across the carpet in her direction. "What about your husband? Did he mention seeing or hearing Lance?"

"Call him." Mrs. Whittier gestured toward the telephone. "The number is 555-7955."

Elena didn't want to pick up that telephone. She turned her

back to Mrs. Whittier, surreptitiously wiped off the receiver with her jacket sleeve, wishing she could spray with Lysol, and called Mr. Whittier, who hadn't seen or heard Lance either, not Monday night when his wife was away, or any other time.

"You didn't see him leaving for work in the morning?"

"No," said Mr. Whittier, "but then he leaves before sunrise. Rides a Merlin Titanium. That's a bicycle," he added.

"Right. Seems to me you might have heard him taking it downstairs since he keeps it hanging on his wall."

Mr. Whittier's answers were somewhat difficult to make out because Elena, virus conscious, was holding the receiver as far away from her ear as she could.

"He's a very quiet tenant. Is that my wife coughing?"

"Yes, she's pretty sick."

"Boy, I hope I don't get it," said Mr. Whittier.

Silently Elena echoed that thought.

"Why are you asking about Lance? Is he kin to the Potemkin who was killed earlier this week?"

"His father," Elena replied.

"And you think Lance did it? Well, everyone knows about the police department. If they can pin it on a gay, they will."

"Mr. Whittier, I assure you—"

"If you take him to trial, I'll testify as a character witness. He's the best tenant we ever had." Mr. Whittier hung up.

Mrs. Whittier, having finished her coughing spell, took another swig from the brown bottle.

"You can get pretty zonked out on codeine," Elena cautioned.

"That's the idea," said Carlene Whittier. "I'd rather sleep this off than stay awake coughing and sniffling."

"Do you know anything about Lance's relations with his family?" Leo asked.

Mrs. Whittier drank some orange juice and replied, "His father's a troll."

"A troll?" Leo looked surprised.

"A gnarled little guy with arms down to his knees and hair sticking up in every direction."

Elena nodded. That wasn't a bad description of the late Boris Potemkin. "How did you happen to meet him?"

"I didn't," said Mrs. Whittier. "He showed up here one evening, stood outside, and yelled at Lance for about fifteen minutes. Lance never even opened the door. I'm not sure he was there, but I gathered that the old man was furious because Lance had visited his mother in the hospital. Is that weird or what?" She plucked another tissue, blew her nose, then leaned her head wearily on one hand. "What's this about anyway?" she asked in a hoarse voice.

"Lance's father was murdered," said Elena.

"You're kidding."

"On Monday. Do you remember what Mr. Potemkin said— exactly? When he was in your front yard."

"He said he'd shoot Lance if Lance ever got near the mother and no flowers. He said don't send her flowers."

"And Lance didn't say anything?"

"Nope. So he's in the clear. Right?"

Neither Elena nor Leo commented on that dubious conclusion. As they were walking to the car, Leo said, "Now we know the old man threatened the son at least twice. Maybe Lance killed his father in self-defense. Went over to visit his mother, found Boris there instead; they got into an argument—"

"Boris didn't have a gun at that point," said Elena. "Lance had the gun. Did he tell us exactly when he took it?" Elena got her case notebook out to jot down the information from the Whittiers and to check Lance's statement.

"Well, he didn't say it was the day of the murder," Leo replied. "And Mrs. Potemkin didn't mention any other guns at the house. On the other hand, Lance may have really had the flu. Mrs. Whittier does."

"And Marcella Escobedo."

"Let's hope *we* don't get it," said Leo. "So maybe Lance is telling the truth."

"If he'd been coughing like his landlady, they'd have heard him," said Elena.

"If they were home. Anyway, we need to find out more about Lance—and his family. I couldn't pull up anything on them from the computer files."

"There's the university," Elena suggested. "He went to U.T. Los Santos. And we could hit that gay bar he worked at. He told me it was the Gemini Lounge. Maybe he still goes there."

"Yeah, we're gonna be real welcome at the Gemini. We might try for people who were taking English at the university when he was a student."

"Gay bar first. Bartenders know a lot, and it's easier to get them to talk when there aren't a lot of customers hanging around. Besides that, in the middle of the afternoon we're not likely to get mobbed by gays who have quarrels with the department."

They climbed into a blue Ford Escort, whose paint had long ago disappeared from the hood and roof, and headed for the Gemini Lounge, where they talked to Barney Allsop, bartender-owner.

"Sure I know Lance," said Barney. "So what's up? You cops gonna start harassing gays again?"

One cop steps out of line, and all the rest of us pay for it, thought Elena. "We understand Lance worked here."

"Yeah. Four or five years ago, when he was in college."

"How did he happen to choose this particular job?"

"It paid good, and he was trying to get through school without any support from his family."

"Family too poor to help?" asked Leo.

"The old man discovered Lance was gay and kicked him out."

So much for Gloria Ledesma's theory that Lance had caught homosexuality at the bar, thought Elena.

"Not that they were paying his tuition," the bartender continued. "His father was a first class s.o.b. Whoever offed him did Lance a favor, but if you're trying to pin it on Lance, forget it. He's not the violent type."

"You know who Lance's friends are these days?" asked Leo.

"If I knew, I wouldn't tell you." Barney Allsop turned away and began to rearrange his liquor shelves.

"Was Lance in here on Monday, Tuesday, or Wednesday?" Elena asked.

"Sure, he's in here all the time."

"Which night?"

"Every night."

"Was he in here Monday afternoon?"

"Sure was."

Elena looked around the bar, which was practically empty.

"He says he was home sick with the flu," said Leo.

"So maybe it was some other afternoon."

Elena and Leo made a few more stabs at pinning down smart-mouth Barney Allsop, failed, and went to the state university where they checked yearbooks for graduating English majors, then the alumni files. They found one creative-writing graduate from Lance's year who was listed as a shoe salesman in the Westside Mall.

When they arrived at Shoe-gri-la, the one salesman was trying to sell a pair of gold evening sandals to a woman with thick ankles. "They're wonderful for formal occasions," he assured her.

"I don't know," she said. "Ninety dollars is pretty expensive."

"Are you F. Scott Manning?" Leo asked the salesman, flashing his identification.

"Yeah, what's up?"

Leo drew him aside. "We understand you were a friend of Lance Potemkin at the university."

"I knew him," said Manning. "We were both creative-writing majors."

"We're looking into Mr. Potemkin's background," said Elena, edging F. Scott toward the counter in back.

"You think he killed his father? That *was* his father who got shot the other day, wasn't it? Or maybe you're looking for homosexuals. He's gay, you know."

"We know. Can you tell us anything about his relations with his family?"

"He wrote some very Freudian poetry in a class we took together. Father-figure as the Great Satan. You know." He glanced over at his customer, who was still preoccupied with the price of the sandals.

Elena wrote down "Great Satan," doubtful that you could convict a man on his poetry. "Could you tell us who any of his friends were at that time?"

"Well, I'll tell you who his *best* friend was. Professor Donald Mallory. That's how Lance got his A in Renaissance Poetry. A lot of us were really ticked off about that. We graduate and can't get decent jobs, and Mallory moves to Herbert Hobart to teach Shakespeare to a bunch of rich kids and takes Lance with him. Now Lance is getting published, and I'm selling shoes."

"Have you got a bow to clip on these?" the customer called, glaring at Leo and Elena. "I was here first, you know."

"A bow?" The salesman suppressed a look of horror and, grabbing a display card, circled the row of chairs separating him from the woman. "I have just the thing you want, ma'am." Selecting a pair of wide gold bows with gaudy rhinestone accents, he clipped them to the instep straps of the sandals. Elena, who could see the result from her place by the cash register, wondered how anyone could consider spending ninety dollars on a pair of shoes after making them look that bad.

Leo beckoned F. Scott back. "Would you know whether Professor Mallory and Mr. Potemkin are still—"

"—making it?" asked the shoe salesman snidely. "How would I know? Lance doesn't belong to any of the local writers' groups. Why should he? *He* gets published." F. Scott scooted away again. "They're stunning on you, ma'am," he said to his customer. "I'd never have thought of the bows."

The woman looked pleased.

"And those are wonderful shoes for dancing," added F. Scott.

"Well, I guess I'll take them, but I don't know what my husband will say about the price."

Elena and Leo thanked the shoe salesman for his cooperation and drove off in their Escort. "I hope we don't have to do any big movie-type car chases in this baby," said Leo.

"Yeah. Feels like it's going airborne on the curves," Elena agreed as they snaked their way up the mountain toward Herbert Hobart University, where they discovered that Professor Donald Mallory was out of town at a Modern Language Association meeting, his plane not due in Los Santos until six o'clock. They were informed of this by Lance, who flushed when they asked to see Mallory.

"Are you still investigating me?" he demanded. "I gave you my father's gun. I let you search my apartment without a warrant and take my bicycles. What more do you want? Do you have to—to harass my colleagues?"

Elena wished there'd been some way to get at members of the English Department other than going through Lance.

"You seem to be over your cough," said Leo.

"What cough?"

"You said you had the flu. Your landlady has it, and she's coughing."

"She didn't get it from me," Lance muttered.

"She didn't hear you coughing either," said Leo.

Looking anxious, Lance hit a button on his computer. The printer burst into noisy life, and paper began to inch over the roller to the accompaniment of ratcheting sounds. Elena wondered whether he was hoping to drown out further questions.

"Where do *you* figure you got it?" Leo asked.

Lance shrugged. "One of the students, I guess."

"Maybe we should check the clinic," Leo said to Elena. "See if any students have flu."

"You want to see anyone beside Dr. Mallory?" Lance asked, mouth tight.

"Who's in?" said Elena.

"I'm in," said Angus McGlenlevie, breezing into the departmental office. "Did you finish those proofs, Lance?"

"Someone had to," said Lance.

"And a fine job you do," said Gus. "I'm sure the printer won't mind waiting the extra day." He squinted at Elena and Leo. "I remember you," he said. "You're the cops who didn't offer me any protection last spring when Karl Bonnard was trying to kill me."

"We caught him before he got to you, didn't we?" said Elena.

"Well, he killed poor Howard. I'm having a hard time hiring post docs now. They think they're going to get murdered. I had two turn me down this fall."

Lance muttered something under his breath, which Elena took to be uncomplimentary. "Perhaps we could speak to you for a minute, Professor McGlenlevie," she said, and they trailed him down the hall to his office.

"*Rapture on the Rapids*," he said, gesturing to page proofs on his desk. "Should be out by Christmas."

"We'd like to ask you a few questions about Lance Potemkin," said Leo.

"He's not my lover."

"Whose lover is he?" asked Elena bluntly.

"Couldn't say. He and Donald Mallory were an item for a couple of years, but that broke up about six months ago."

"Do you know anything about Lance's family?" asked Elena.

"Didn't even know he had one," said Gus. "Are you still seeing Sarah?"

"We have dinner occasionally," said Elena. She didn't like the way he put it. Sarah was a friend, not a lover.

"Don't believe everything my ex-wife tells you about me," said Gus.

Elena grinned. "I don't have to. Everyone I interviewed on the acid bath case told me about you."

"All ladies, I presume. All good, I hope." Gus beamed at Elena. "I *am* popular with females—young and old."

"Except for Sarah," Elena murmured.

"Ah well, Sarah." Gus shrugged dramatically. "Sarah is a fine woman. Just a bit uptight about matters sexual."

Like flagrant infidelity in a husband, thought Elena.

14
••

Thursday, September 30, 7:30 P.M.

Harmony discovered, among those she met before Lance
Potemkin's standing-room-only poetry reading, members of
the English Department and students at Herbert Hobart University, poetry lovers who were familiar with Lance's sexual
orientation, and bicycle racers who were expecting Lance to do
them proud on the High Road to Taos. Lance had no sooner
read his last line of verse, received enthusiastic applause, and
been congratulated by English Department Chairman Raul
Mendez and Professor Donald Mallory, who was chairing the
session, than hands began to wave in the audience.

"I see we're going to have a lively discussion," said
Professor Mallory.

Without waiting to be called upon, a young man in a pleated
shirt rose to his feet and said, "Is it true, Lance, that the police
are harassing you about your father's death?"

"Gay activist," murmured Ferdie Baca to Harmony. He was
a graduate student in creative writing at the state university.
After being introduced to Harmony, Ferdie had stuck to her as
if he'd found his one true love. "His name is Orion Massine.
He's the lead male dancer in the Border Ballet."

Lance flushed. "They're questioning me," he admitted.

"What's this?" Professor Mallory looked alarmed. "I didn't
know anything had happened to your father."

"You've been at the M.L.A. meeting. He was murdered Monday," said Lance. "Probably a robbery."

"Of course, it was," said Orion, "but are they looking for a robber? No, they're after a gay."

Harmony was glad to see that she wasn't the only person convinced of Lance's innocence.

"Look, Orion—" Lance protested.

"Your civil rights are being violated," said the dancer, "and it's because you're homosexual." A murmur of assent rose from the gay activist contingent.

"There are three charges of discrimination against the police department by gay and lesbian officers," said a young man with the muscles of a body builder.

Harmony peered at him with interest.

"And there's Mac and Lennie," said a thirty-fivish woman with a Dutch-boy haircut and plaid knee socks. "They were asleep when some narcotics team kicked down the wrong door. Then when the cops didn't find any drugs, they arrested Mac and Lennie for being in bed together."

"That's one lawsuit we're going to win," said Orion.

"They've been raiding the Sappho Club ever since you filed that suit," complained the woman.

"Lesbian social club," murmured Ferdie. Harmony nodded. She'd never been to a lesbian social club. How interesting! Would Elena agree to visit?

"They've even been nosing around my store."

"Feminist bookstore," Ferdie murmured.

"As if a book about matriarchal society is going to corrupt the morals of American youth."

"Those of us who know you, Lance, know that you wouldn't have killed anyone, even your father, who probably deserved it. We've all agreed that we'll kick in for your defense fund," said Orion.

"I don't need a defense fund." Lance had turned pale.

"Have they brought you in for questioning?" asked Professor Mallory.

"Twice," Lance admitted. "Yesterday and today."

"Typical," said Orion. "They don't have enough to arrest

you, so they make a spectacle of you in front of your colleagues."

"That's not the worst of it," said a man who was painfully lean with a weathered face and a receding hairline. "They won't let him race at Chimayo." Rumbles of indignation circulated among the bicycle contingent.

Lance looked miserable. "One of my mother's neighbors saw a bicycle in the alley the day my father was killed, so the police confiscated both of mine as evidence."

"Lance is Los Santos' only hope to bring the cup home from that race," said the president of the Los Santos Cycle Racers' Association, who sported an aerodynamic crew cut and a double-breasted navy sport coat. "A local athletic hero, and he's being kept from bringing glory to the city. As all of you know, I don't hold with unnatural sex but, by God, when the police start interfering with serious bicycle racing, it's time to stand up and be counted."

"Thanks, Hoke," said Lance dryly.

Harmony thought the remark about unnatural sex rather tactless.

Then Gus McGlenlevie with his frizzy red beard and combat fatigues stood up and said, "You've got it all wrong if you think he's being harassed because he's gay."

"Sit down," yelled the gay activists.

"It's because he's a poet," shouted McGlenlevie. "Those police are vigilantes when it comes to people in the arts. For instance, last spring someone was trying to kill me, but the police wouldn't even give me protection.

"And before that, my ex-wife exploded a snail on my plate at dinner, and do you think they arrested her? They did not. And I didn't meet a single policeman or woman during that investigation who had read a word of *Erotica in Reeboks*, my best-selling poetry collection. I doubt any of them will read my book of poems on non-homosexual male bonding, *Rapture on the Rapids*, which should be in the bookstores in December just in time for Christmas. Nineteen ninety-five. Published by the Mile-High Press of Denver, Colorado."

"For God's sake," said Professor Donald Mallory, "we have a serious problem here, and you're using it to promote your book. And besides that, you misused the word *vigilantes*. Vigilantes are people who take the law into their own hands. By definition they can't be police officers."

"I was using it metaphorically, you twerp," snapped McGlenlevie and started pushing his way toward the lectern.

"Twerp!" shouted Mallory. "That from a man who writes pornographic doggerel."

"Is that your critical opinion? You, who've never written a line of original poetry in your life."

"I'm a renowned Elizabethan and Jacobean critic," snarled Mallory.

"With a following of four or five moldering old scholars who've read your pitiful efforts—"

"I'll have you know—"

"You wouldn't know a good poem if you—"

"If you'd stop screwing female students, maybe you'd find time to write some decent—"

"Would you be happier if I was screwing male students like you do?"

The dignified Professor Mallory raised his fist. Lance grabbed him and tried to pull him away while the chairman of the English Department rose from the front row and said, "Angus, this is beneath a poet's dignity."

"A poet's dignity is couched in the beauty of his verse," howled McGlenlevie.

"Let go of me, Lance," Mallory ordered.

Lance was still hanging onto his former lover, saying, "Come on, Don. This isn't helping anything."

"Gentlemen," said the chairman, "I'd appreciate it if you'd stop this embarrassing argument."

"He misused *vigilantes*," grumbled Mallory.

True, thought Harmony, and she didn't like McGlenlevie's aura—or his personality.

"I used it as a poet would—metaphorically," said McGlenlevie.

"Shut up," said the chairman.

"If I could have the floor," said the president of the bicycle racers.

"We're adjourning the meeting," said the chairman.

"It's obvious that, for whatever reason, Lance Potemkin is being unfairly treated by the police," shouted Hoke Mitchell.

"Right," Orion agreed. "I think we should mount a demonstration. Let them know that the public won't put up with the harassment of innocent citizens. While they're picking on Lance, the real murderer's getting away because the police are fixated on gays."

Once the bicycle racers had conferred, their president said, "We'll support a demonstration. When and where?"

"Police Headquarters tomorrow morning," said Orion with noisy agreement from the gay activists.

Harmony perked up. She did love a protest.

"I'll be happy to support a fellow poet," said Angus.

Lance didn't look happy to receive that particular offer, and Harmony wondered whether he disliked McGlenlevie, who seemed quite dislikable, as well as aura-impaired.

"Are you coming, Mallory? How about you, Dr. Mendez? Is the English Department behind us?" asked Angus.

Lance, looking alarmed and embarrassed, stammered, "Look, I really don't—"

"Oh, stop being so nice, Lance," said Orion. "We're supporting you whether you want it or not."

Harmony stood up. "If I might make a few suggestions—"

"Who are you, madam?" asked Dr. Mendez.

"I'm Harmony Waite Portillo, a weaver from Chimayo, New Mexico, and an admirer of Lance's poetry."

"If you plan to suggest that we stay home," said the bookstore owner in the Dutch-boy haircut, "let me point out that it's about time women took their places in the front lines protesting police harassment."

"My dear young lady," said Harmony, with some heat, "I was in the front lines of the Berkeley Free Speech Movement before you were born. I collected my share of bruises opposing the war in Vietnam. As an experienced protester, my suggestions are of a practical nature. First, if you want to get radio and TV coverage, you should hold your protest in the afternoon so you can co-opt the lead story on the six o'clock news. Second, I can promise more protesters if I have the morning to round them up."

"Who?" demanded Orion Massine suspiciously.

"Socorro Heights senior citizens." There was muttering about that idea. "Lance's mother is a member. None of them think Lance killed his father, but people at the center are extremely worried because the police are investigating Lance instead of looking for these daytime robbers who have killed several elderly men. I think the senior citizens would be delighted to join you at Police Headquarters.

"My third suggestion," continued Harmony, raising her voice over the hubbub, "is that you need training in safe protest tactics, which I am willing to provide right now to this group and tomorrow morning to the seniors."

"What kind of training?" asked Hoke.

"How to go limp so the police have to drag you away. That makes good TV footage. If they're using nightsticks, how to fall safely, protect your head and vital organs."

"Madam," said Donald Mallory, "surely you don't anticipate—"

"One never knows what the police will do, Professor. I was attacked by them in my younger days. I'd hate to think that any of us might be seriously hurt."

"Injuries might help Lance's case," said Orion.

"I don't want anyone hurt on my behalf," said Lance.

"Well, I think she's got it right about the time. How about two, tomorrow afternoon? Anyone object?" asked Orion.

No one did. "Good," said Harmony. "Now if those who are planning to join the protest will just move away from their chairs, I'll demonstrate some of the tricks."

Bicycle racers and gay activists joined Harmony's class enthusiastically and were soon dropping to the floor under her directions, rolling up in balls to protect their heads and vital organs, going limp in one another's arms. The English faculty stayed aloof until their chairman, Raul Mendez, had introduced himself to Harmony and suggested that people might be injured during the lessons.

"Why, you're the renowned critic of Latino literature!" said Harmony. "What a pleasure to meet you."

After that, every English professor or student who hung back got a sharp look from the chairman. For lack of room,

Harmony soon moved her class out into the halls of the Humanities building, although one professor pointed out that the university's insurance might not cover those who were injured while learning how to keep themselves from injury.

As they were driving home, Lance said hesitantly, "What's your daughter going to think of this protest?"

"Elena's known me all her life," said Harmony cheerfully. "This is just what she'd expect."

Lance sighed. "I've always liked to keep a low profile. It seems to me that after this, everyone in town will know the police think I killed my father."

"The media will get hold of it anyway, and in the meantime, maybe we can force the police to let you attend your bicycle race."

"Really?"

"Absolutely. There's nothing like a good protest to get the blood running and shake up the power structure. Enough so that they'll make concessions to shut us up."

"I hope they don't put me in jail to shut *me* up," said Lance. "People of my sexual orientation have a hard time in jail."

"Well, dear, if they arrest you, we'll insist on solitary. Then you'll have all that time to write poetry. Think of what going to jail did for Oscar Wilde."

"Yes," said Lance. "He had to exile himself after he got out, and he died in a French apartment with dreadful wallpaper."

"You went to that poetry reading, didn't you?" asked Elena when her mother got home. Harmony had been gone when Elena returned from work, late as usual.

"Of course, I did," said Harmony. "And his poetry was delightful. It was a *very* interesting meeting."

"I don't want to hear about it," muttered Elena. "Did Dimitra go?"

"No, she had a date."

"She went out with Omar *again*?"

"No, she went to a country-dancing club with a Mr. Tyler from the senior citizens center."

"She can't dance," said Elena. "She's in a walker."

"I realize that, dear, but she'll enjoy the music."

"For Pete's sake, Boris died Monday, and she's already had two dates. They're not even burying him until tomorrow. Isn't she supposed to be at the funeral parlor greeting the mourners?"

"She decided to cancel the visitation. The graveside ceremony's in the morning at Fort Bliss. Ten o'clock. I think you should try to be there, Elena."

"I'll do that," said Elena. She thought about Dimitra and T. Bob Tyler, the man described by Sheriff Blankenship as prone to assault. "Tyler might have killed Boris," she murmured.

"I thought Lance was your prime suspect," said Harmony.

"Well, he is," Elena replied defensively, "but I heard some stuff about Tyler that makes me nervous. I wonder if Dimitra knows that he's a barroom brawler?"

Her mother went to bed, but Elena sat up fretting, watching the Potemkin house, which was dark. Finally an old truck pulled up in front at ten-thirty. T. Bob Tyler, be-Stetsoned, ambled to the back of the pickup and removed Dimitra's walker, then pushed it to the passenger side. Elena watched him lift Dimitra down as if she were Snow White and he the handsome prince. What a sight those two must have made at the country-music club. Elena wondered whether T. Bob had decked anyone for making remarks about senior citizens.

Once he'd returned to the truck, Elena hurried down the street to knock on Dimitra's door.

"Who is it?" Dimitra yelled. "I've got a gun."

"It's me. Elena."

Dimitra opened the door immediately. "You want more of my cabbage rolls, right? Well, I decided to take your advice and serve them after the funeral. Maybe I'll make some more tomorrow after we've put Boris in the ground." She consulted an appointment calendar on a lamp table. "No, I can't do that. I'm going to the movies tomorrow afternoon with Omar."

At least it wasn't T. Bob Tyler. "Look, Dimitra, there's something I've got to tell you. I hate being a gossip, but I ran a check on T. Bob Tyler. That's who you were just out with, right?"

"I certainly was. We had the best time watching the young

people two-step. I've decided that if there's enough money, I'm going to have the physical therapy Boris wouldn't pay for after my hip replacement. I don't want to spend the rest of my life on the sidelines."

"Yeah, well, I'm glad you had a good time, Dimitra. Was there any trouble?"

"Why would there be trouble? T. Bob Tyler would never let anyone lay a hand on me."

"That's what I'm afraid of," muttered Elena.

"What's that supposed to mean?"

"T. Bob's got a long history of assaults."

Dimitra paled. "Who'd he hit?"

"A lot of guys in Otero County and one in Los Santos."

"Did he hit any women?"

"No women," Elena admitted.

"Then why are you telling me? It's men who hit women you have to watch out for."

"Still, Dimitra—"

"I'm having a lovely time, young lady. Don't spoil it. And I'll thank you not to be spying on me. I had enough of that with Boris."

15
∴

Elena stood at the graveside with Harmony and Leo. Never having been to the Fort Bliss National Cemetery, she found it surprisingly beautiful—green grass, trees, the battalions of white crosses in the older section. You could almost forget you were living on a desert mountain.

As the Russian Orthodox priest prayed over Boris Potemkin's casket, Elena tried to look attentive, although she was, in fact, studying the mourners. A large contingent from Boris' V.F.W. Post clustered across from the family, one old soldier in a wheelchair, two hunched over canes, some middle-aged, who might be veterans of Korea or Vietnam. Neighbors had come, the Fogels, the Ituribes, and Gloria Ledesma, scowling at Leo as if she thought he planned to make an arrest during the ceremony. Lance evidently expected to be the arrestee. He was visibly nervous and looked more often at Leo and Elena than he did at the priest.

The bridge group and other people from the senior citizens center were also in attendance. Emily Marks wore a chic black suit and a hat with a black veil. Several of the veterans had taken her for the widow and come up to express sympathy. Causing great astonishment, she replied that she hadn't known the deceased well, but wasn't it terrible how many violent crimes were committed these days?

The mistake didn't surprise Elena, since Dimitra had on a

yellow flowered dress and a bright blue straw hat with yellow daisies bobbing on the brim. She looked quite festive, flanked by her admirers, Omar Ashkenazi in a green polyester leisure suit—Elena hadn't known those were made anymore—his smooth brown scalp glowing in the morning sunshine, and T. Bob Tyler, who was glaring at the casket and then at Omar with such enmity that Elena decided he was a better suspect than she had figured.

Lance, standing to the right of Omar, reached over and patted his mother on the arm. The gesture earned him a beaming smile, and Elena heard Dimitra whisper, "Be sure to come for the wake. Cabbage rolls and vodka."

"Might as well," Lance muttered. "I can't go to Santa Fe."

"Now, don't pout," said Dimitra, as if he were ten years old. "There'll be other races."

The bearded priest glared at them and continued his interminable prayer. Even the seven-man honor guard was starting to fidget. After the final amen, a ramrod-straight old man stepped forward, his uniform hanging loosely from a gaunt frame. In a loud voice that echoed across the cemetery, he said, "Before we have the military salute to our fallen brother-in-arms, Boris Potemkin, I would like to say a few words on behalf of the members of V.F.W. Post 8550." He scowled at the civilian mourners. "Boris Potemkin was a soldier. He served his country honorably in The Great War, one of the few wars in recent memory for which the public feels any affection."

A Vietnam veteran muttered angrily under his breath.

"Boris built the bridges and the roads that allowed the army to march through France, through Germany to slay the Hydra-headed Fascist monster, the evil followers of dictatorship. Let us all remember Boris and his service to his adopted country, for Boris came from Russia, that hotbed of Communism."

"It's not a hotbed anymore," said Lydia Beeman. "You ought to keep up with the times, Conrad."

"Boris never believed the Communists were gone," said Dimitra from across the open grave.

"This is a man's tribute," rumbled the old soldier. "If women want to say something, they can do it when I'm through." He cleared his throat forcefully. "So we, his fellow soldiers, bid farewell to a departed patriot, Boris Potemkin."

The officer with the honor guard barked, "Fire!" Seven soldiers discharged their rifles, the first of three volleys in the traditional twenty-one-gun salute. The Vietnam veteran jerked as if he'd been shot and, shouting, "Gooks! Hit the dirt!" dove toward the grave, taking a little old lady with him.

"Fire!" The soldiers, trying not to stare, fired.

"For heaven's sake," cried Harmony, "the man's having a flashback. Stop that shooting."

"Fire!" Their rifles no longer at the proper angle, the honor guard fired one last time. Seeing the smoke drifting from rifle barrels aimed every which way, the widow, her beaus, and the nonmilitary mourners scattered like protesters under a tear-gas attack.

"It's O.K., man," said Lance, leaning down to pat the shoulder of the trembling ex-warrior, who was sprawled on the casket. "They're using blanks, not bullets."

"Gooks," whispered the veteran, pointing to Omar Ashkenazi.

"Sh-sh," said Lance. "He's my mother's boyfriend, not the Vietcong." Lance managed to help the old lady to her feet and onto the artificial grass beside the grave. Harmony kept up a soothing murmur to the trembling veteran while she disentangled him from the red, white, and blue carnations sent by the V.F.W.

"This has got to take the cake for graveside disasters," Elena muttered, stepping forward to help her mother with the veteran.

"This is what happens when the country sends young men off to kill women and children for no good reason and then sneers at them when they come home," said Harmony to the old veteran, as if the war in Vietnam had been his fault.

"Mom!" Elena hissed. That's all she needed—for her mother to get into a political squabble. She and Harmony had turned the victim of the flashback over to Leo.

"Madam," said the old soldier, "I fought my way from the beaches of Normandy to—"

"And got kissed by pretty French girls all the way, I

imagine," retorted Harmony. "How many children and old women threw grenades at *you*."

"Lance always was a sweet boy," said Dimitra. "Did you see him go to the rescue of that poor woman?"

"He's a fine-lookin' young fella," said T. Bob Tyler. "It's an honor to meet him."

"Nice to know somebody likes my son," said Dimitra. "Boris didn't."

"I always liked Lance," said Omar, not to be left out of the liking-Lance competition. "The boy has taste in rugs. I remember you bringing him down to my store when he was ten, Dimitra."

Had Dimitra and Omar been friends for that long? Elena wondered. Fifteen years or so?

"His favorite was the most expensive carpet in stock," said Omar admiringly. "Amazing taste in a child."

Lance had turned red because the conversation was being carried on rather loudly. "Is the ceremony over?" he asked the bearded priest.

"No," said Dimitra. "You and me, we gotta each put a flower on Boris' casket."

"The hell with that," Lance muttered. Then he glanced nervously at Leo and Elena, changed his mind, and rejoined his mother on the family side of the grave. Lance accepted a rose, studied it, and said, "This came from the bush he wanted to dig up and throw away."

Dimitra gave her son a twinkling smile and dropped her offering on the casket, which looked to Elena as if it was the cheapest one Dimitra could find. No doubt, Omar knew where all the casket bargains were. "Goodbye, Boris," said Dimitra as Lance flipped his rose onto his father's coffin, whose only other decoration was the trampled V.F.W. wreath. "We won't be seeing you anymore, Boris," said the widow.

"There's always the afterlife," the priest pointed out reprovingly.

Dimitra shrugged. "If anybody's going to hell, it's Boris Potemkin, and I don't plan to join him there. Now, everyone's invited to my house tonight for the wake."

"We don't have wakes," said the priest angrily. "That's an

Irish custom. If you wanted a wake, Mrs. Potemkin, you should have held it before the burial and contacted a Roman Catholic priest for the service."

"Vodka and cabbage rolls," said Dimitra with blithe indifference. She looked around at the staring crowd. "So if that's it," she announced, "T. Bob and I have to get over to the senior citizens center."

"So do I," Harmony murmured to Elena. "I'm late."

Elena wondered what the big rush was. Maybe T. Bob and Dimitra had signed up for Harmony's weaving class.

Dimitra went on tiptoe to kiss her son on the cheek. "Eight tonight," she said. "I've saved you twenty frozen cabbage rolls to take home."

"Aren't we going to a movie this afternoon, Dimitra?" asked Omar, and got a possessive glower from T. Bob Tyler.

"Oh, I'm sorry, Omar. I can't. We've got big plans at the center," Dimitra replied.

What big plans? Elena wondered. A shuffleboard tournament?

"Maybe this evening. No, that's the wake. How about tomorrow afternoon?"

"Tomorrow it is," said Omar. "If I feel myself drifting into sleep, I'll give you a call to reschedule."

"You do that, dear." Dimitra kissed him on the cheek and T. Bob Tyler muttered, "Come on, Miz Dimitra. We've got us important things to do." With that, the mourners dispersed.

"I've never seen a funeral like that," said Leo as they climbed into their unmarked police car. "Anyway, I'm free to get back on the case. Maybe we should split up."

"I was thinking of hitting the pawnshops," said Elena. "We ought to make an effort to find the czar's medal. If we don't try, some defense attorney will claim it was a robbery-murder and we ignored the possibility in order to make an easier collar."

"Like it wasn't the son or a jealous boyfriend with a quick temper," Leo agreed. On the way over, Elena had told him about her conversation with the Otero County sheriff the day before.

16
..

Elena dropped into her chair at headquarters. Brief consideration convinced her that the department didn't need a report on the bizarre funeral of Boris Potemkin, since she hadn't learned anything there. Picking up her ringing telephone, she said, "Detective Elena Jarvis."

Pete Amador at Central told her that he and his partner had canvassed her neighborhood looking for anyone who had seen Omar Ashkenazi the afternoon of the murder. They hadn't found a murder witness, but they had found a little boy peeking in Ashkenazi's window. "He was watchin' the suspect, who was lyin' on a rug, snorin'," said Amador. They had caught up with the child, whom Elena identified as Beanie Montoya, in his back yard across the alley, but Beanie had been too frightened to say anything. "My partner thought it might be better if you talk to the kid yourself in case he was lookin' in your guy's window on Monday afternoon."

"I'm surprised he was out of the house," said Elena. "His grandmother treats him like an egg she has to sit on or he won't hatch." Elena hung up. There was a slim possibility Beanie might be able to eliminate Omar from her list of suspects, although what were the odds of a five-year-old kid spending two afternoons watching Omar Ashkenazi asleep on his Oriental carpet? On the other hand, what if the kid liked to follow Omar around? Maybe Beanie was playing detective. Maybe he'd seen Omar go over to the Potemkins' Monday and—well, she'd just have to find out. She'd hit a few pawnshops, have lunch, and show up at the Montoyas' around one, when Beanie was home from play school.

Amarinta Montoya, Beanie's grandmother, filled the door when she answered Elena's finger on the bell. Three hundred pounds if she weighed an ounce was Elena's guess. Amarinta was as tall as her son Belen but double his weight, and she had a better mustache. "Mrs. Montoya, remember me? Elena Jarvis?"

"Sure, sure," said Amarinta.

"I'd like to talk to Beanie."

"What about?" asked Amarinta suspiciously. "If we got graffiti artists in the neighborhood, it ain't Beanie."

"Beanie didn't do anything." Elena could see the little boy, a loose Western Playland T-shirt drooping off his shoulders, twig legs sticking out beneath baggy shorts, socks sagging onto his sneakers. He looked scared to death. "Hey, Beanie," called Elena, giving him her best kids' smile. "*Que paso*? You're about to become a cop's best friend."

"Come here, Rudolfo," said his grandmother. "You ain't in any trouble. This is Mrs. Jarvis. She lives one street over. Don't you remember her?"

Beanie nodded, took two steps forward, and stopped by a lavender and pink couch, the latest in Southwestern chic, although the pillows had already lost their shape, so Elena figured the Montoyas must have bought it at some double discount store or off the back of a truck.

"So why are you here if he didn't do nothing?" asked Amarinta.

"I just need to ask him a few questions." Beanie was sneaking a terrified look at his grandmother. So that was it, thought Elena. Somehow or other he'd been getting out of the house without Amarinta knowing it. Now he was afraid Elena would reveal his secret.

"Come on in," said Amarinta.

"Actually, I thought I'd take Beanie out to the car," said Elena, figuring his grandmother would listen if they stayed inside. "Kids love police cars. You know? We'll just sit and chat, and then I'll send him right back in."

"You're taking Rudolfo out of the house? You got a warrant or something?"

"I don't need a warrant," said Elena.

"Well, let me see your badge. I don't want Belen coming home and getting after me because—wait a minute. How come you're looking so relieved, Beanie?"

"I'm not, Abuelita," he said in a scared voice.

Abuelita? thought Elena. Little grandmother? Now there was a misnomer! "Here's my badge, Amarinta. Come on, Beanie." She held out her hand to the child, and he edged across the room to take it. They walked out to the car together.

"It's not a police car," he said, disappointed.

"No, it's a detective car, but I got a flashing light I can stick on top."

"Yeah?" Beanie looked interested.

Elena fished the light from under the seat and stuck it on the roof. "There," she said. "It's official. Hop in."

Beanie stared a minute at the light. Then he scrambled across the seat to the passenger side. "Do I need to fasten my seat belt?" he asked.

"Nah," said Elena. "We're just gonna sit here and talk." She turned on the air conditioning.

"Is Mr. Ashkenazi mad at me?"

"Mr. Ashkenazi doesn't even know you were looking in his window. Do you do that often?"

"Are you gonna tell Abuelita?"

"Everything we say is confidential."

"What's that?"

"Secret. It means I won't tell."

"I go every day when Abuelita's asleep."

"Ah-huh. How long is that?"

"I don't know," said Beanie. "After lunch she goes to sleep. She don't wake up till Barney the Dinosaur comes on TV."

"What time is that?"

"When the little hand gets to the four."

Elena thought a minute. That meant Amarinta slept about

three hours each afternoon. "And you watch Mr. Ashkenazi every day from one till four?"

Beanie shook his head, thumb in his mouth.

"How often, then?" asked Elena.

"Only if he's in the living room."

"How come you watch Mr. Ashkenazi?" It didn't sound like a very exciting pastime to Elena. Surely the kid would rather watch TV or play with his toys, even if his *abuela* wouldn't let him play with other kids. Not that there were any along his street. Elena and the Montoyas were the first droplets in the wave of the future, the first younger people to move into a neighborhood of aging residents. She could see that Beanie didn't want to explain why he watched Mr. Ashkenazi. God, what was the old man doing in there? "You can tell me, Beanie," she said gently.

After an obviously painful moment of inner debate, Beanie whispered, "He's a space alien."

"He is?" Elena suppressed a grin. "How do you know that?"

"He looks like the alien in my comic book."

Mr. Ashkenazi *was* kind of different-looking. "Anything else besides the way he looks?"

"I seen him put his legs behind his head. An' sometimes he stands on his head or waves his arms an' legs around funny."

"Ah-huh." Yoga exercises, Elena guessed.

"An' when he sleeps, he makes loud, space-language sounds."

"I see."

"I'm waiting for more aliens to come. When it happens, I'm gonna be there an' see it all. Maybe a flying saucer an' green people an'—wow!" Beanie's eyes got as big as tortillas. "It's really exciting!"

Poor kid, thought Elena. The highlight of his afternoon was watching a retired Oriental-rug salesman snore and do yoga exercises.

"Mr. Ashkenazi doesn't eat meat," said Beanie, shyness overcome by his desire to confide these wonders to an interested party who had promised secrecy. "He can speak Earth language too. An' he told me meat was bad for me. 'Course, I know that's just an alien thing, 'cause Abuelita is always telling me to eat my meat 'cause it'll make me big an' strong an' smart."

Abuelita evidently hadn't heard about fat and cholesterol, thought Elena. "So tell me, Beanie, do you remember whether you were watching Mr. Ashkenazi on Monday? That would be the day you went back to school. After Sunday and Mass. The day all the police cars were on my street."

"I remember," said Beanie. "Me an' Mama went to see them."

"Did you watch Mr. Ashkenazi that day?"

His head bobbed. "First I had to eat all my *frijoles* an' my *arroz con pollo*. Then Abuelita gave me a popsicle 'cause I ate everything on my plate. I can make a popsicle last a long time," said Beanie proudly. "Then Abuelita sat down an' went to sleep, an' I went over to Mr. Ashkenazi's."

"That's a neat watch you got there." She admired his dinosaur watch. "Where were the hands when you left?"

"They were both on the one. An' I went home when the little hand was on the four so I could see Barney. No space aliens came."

So Omar had been under surveillance by Beanie Montoya from one to four, and the coroner said Boris died between two and three. Elena rolled down the car window when Amarinta knocked and shouted, "Ain't you through yet?"

"Your grandson is one smart kid," said Elena. She leaned over and whispered in his ear. "I'll never tell about the aliens."

Beanie gave her a conspiratorial smile and whispered back, "Abuelita might be scared if she knew." Then he scrambled out of the car.

17

Friday, October 1, 2:05 P.M.

"Who are those people out there?" demanded Captain Stollinger, head of the Criminal Investigations Division.

"I think half of them are from the media," replied Sergeant Mosson of Community Relations. "The protesters, according to their signs, are poets, gays, people from H.H.U., and bicycle racers."

"You're kidding." Captain Stollinger peered out the front door. He was six three with short gray hair and a hawk nose upon which were perched large rectangular bifocals framed in dull silver.

"They're all supporting Lance Potemkin, the guy C.A.P. thinks murdered his father," added Mosson.

Stollinger glowered through the door. "Get Beltran out here."

With so many factions milling around, Harmony despaired of a well-organized demonstration. She decided to deal with the senior citizens first, since she had got them together after the funeral, drilled them in safe-protest practices, and set them to work making signs that said things like "Protect Golden-Agers," "Senior Citizens Aren't Safe," and "Criminals are Killing Us." Unfortunately, many of the sign carriers were resting on the front steps. Granted, their presence impeded foot traffic into Police Headquarters, but Harmony had been hoping for a more active participation. The only senior citizen actually walking up and down was Lydia Beeman. Although Harmony didn't care much for the woman, Lydia was physically active, so Harmony approached her.

"Could you organize the Socorro Heights group into a picket line?" she asked.

"Do they look as if they're up to walking around?" retorted Lydia. "I had them bring lawn chairs for just that reason. As soon as they get their second wind, they'll be putting up the chairs."

"Wonderful!" said Harmony, willing to compromise. "Form a lawn-chair barricade so the police cars can't get in and out."

Lydia looked as if she were about to refuse, then nodded briskly and marshaled her forces. Harmony could hear various elderly ladies wondering if they might not be run down. "Of course not!" snapped Lydia. "Do you really think the police are going to kill someone's grandmother? They may ignore our problems, but they know better than to injure us."

The lawn-chair blockade formed up nicely, those without arthritis marching behind with the signs. Dimitra sat in her walker, while T. Bob Tyler stood behind her protectively. Harmony thought they made a charming couple. Satisfied with the senior citizens, she turned her attention to Hoke Mitchell, president of the bicycle racers. They were carrying signs that said "Let Lance Ride," "Los Santos Athletes Support Lance," and "We Want A Win In New Mexico." They'd come on their bicycles.

"Could you ride in some sort of close-order pattern and stop traffic on Raynor and Montana?" she asked.

Hoke agreed and strode off through the bicycle racers, calling out orders like a drill sergeant.

"What about us?" asked Orion, who had watched Harmony's organizing tactics. His group carried signs that said, "LSPD Harasses Gays," "Los Santos Lesbians for Lance," "Cease and Desist, LSPD Homophobes," and "Stop Gay Bashing."

"Form a human chain in the public parking lot," Harmony suggested. The gays fanned out, joined hands, and effectively kept anyone from leaving. Once the bicycle brigade began looping in figure eights, nothing came in. Police had to park farther out and walk to headquarters, as did civilians. Police cars already in their slots were blocked by the lawn-chair contingent.

"Looking good," said Harmony to Donald Mallory, who carried a sign that said in Renaissance lettering "H.H.U. Supports Its Staff." He was trying to ignore Gus McGlenlevie, who had arrived late carrying a sign that said "Vigilante Police Menace the Poetic Muse." "The senior citizens have left the front steps," said Harmony. "Why don't you Herbert Hobart people parade in front of the entrance so the police inside can see that the city's richest institution is mad at them?"

Gus, Mallory, Chairman Raul Mendez, Professor Anne-Marie LaPortierre, and a gaggle of fashionably dressed English majors trooped over to the steps. In fact, Gus bounced up like a red-bearded Christmas elf and pushed his sign against the glass where Captain Stollinger looked out. Ten minutes of Gus McGlenlevie, and the police ought to agree to anything, thought Harmony smugly.

"What the hell does that mean?" demanded Stollinger. "Police can't be vigilantes."

"That's Angus McGlenlevie," said Lieutenant Beltran. "That dumbass poet from H.H.U." Beltran had come from his office in Crimes Against Persons at the summons from the Community Relations sergeant.

"So what have we got to do with the poetic muse?"

Beltran stared out at the human chain of gay activists in the public parking lot, beyond them to the looping bicycle racers where the traffic was building up in all directions, approaching gridlock. If the department didn't act, there'd be cars backed up to the freeway, to downtown, to Bassett Center and beyond. And they couldn't get units in or out because the police lot was jammed with old folks in lawn chairs, chatting with one another and waving their signs if any cop came near.

"I don't know why McGlenlevie's here," Beltran admitted. "It's Jarvis and Weizell's case, and they're out gathering evidence against Lance Potemkin, who's a gay bicycle rider. We've got a pretty good case against him."

"Well, that explains why the gays and the bicyclers are protesting, but not the H.H.U. people," said Stollinger.

"Or the senior citizens," added Beltran.

"What senior citizens?"

"They're sitting in lawn chairs blocking traffic in our lot," said Sergeant Mosson, "carrying signs that say we're letting them get killed. Very bad public relations, sir, especially with all the media people out there."

"I think we've got a bunch of nut cases on our hands," said Captain Stollinger in disgust. "Get Captain de la Rosa to clear the parking lots and streets. It's a traffic situation."

"Captain de la Rosa's at a meeting in Austin," said Sergeant Mosson.

"So find the ranking officer in Traffic!" Stollinger tramped off, leaving Lieutenant Beltran to watch while a gay activist, approached by a police officer, fell limp into the cop's arms. The cop dropped the young man and leapt away as if burned.

Sweating profusely in the afternoon sun, Lieutenant Kurtz surveyed the line of elderly men and women sitting in lawn chairs, chatting with one another and passing around thermoses of lemonade. "O.K.," he said to Sergeant Lopez. "Start with that tall, thin old lady in the slacks and sun hat. She seems to be the ringleader."

"What am I supposed to do with her?" asked Lopez.

"Ask her to leave. Tell her she's guilty of demonstrating without a permit, interfering with officers in the performance of their duty. If she won't move, have two guys pick her up in the lawn chair and carry her across the street."

"What about the bicycle riders?"

"That ought to interfere with their operation. They're not gonna run down some old lady in a lawn chair. Assign your men in pairs. Take her and five others. Then we'll have a lane open and can move the rest out."

"Yes, sir." Lopez felt unhappy about his assignment, but he grabbed Patrolman Allen Mobley, who was big enough to lift three old ladies, and the two of them headed for Lydia Beeman.

"Ma'am, we'll have to ask you to move out of the way. You're blocking traffic."

"That's the idea," said Lydia.

"If you don't move, ma'am," said Lopez politely, "we're going to pick you up, lawn chair and all, and transport you across the street."

"Just try it, young man," said Lydia belligerently. "That's about what I'd expect of the police. Indifference to the safety of women."

"We're not indifferent, ma'am." He nodded to Mobley, and the two of them braced themselves to lift Lydia Beeman. Each put a hand on a chair arm and one under the seat. Lydia, who was wearing sensible, heavy-soled walking shoes, stood up— right on one of Mobley's big feet.

"Ye-ow-w!" cried Mobley.

Madre de Dios, thought Lopez. *I'm going to have to arrest somebody's grandmother for assaulting an officer.*

"My apologies," said Lydia. "I didn't see your foot."

As Lopez gave thanks that it had been an accident, Lydia folded her lawn chair and walked away.

Two chairs down, Emily Marks, who thought the whole operation a lark, slipped out of her chair and rolled into a ball on the pavement when two patrolmen tried to pick her up.

"Sergeant," shouted the officer on her left, "she's had a heart attack."

"Don't be silly," said Emily, peeking up at him. "I'm protecting myself against police brutality." The TV cameras were rolling.

"What did you do to that there lady?" roared T. Bob Tyler. He leapt from his station beside Dimitra and grappled with the patrolman who was taking Emily's pulse.

"Aren't you gallant, T. Bob!" said Emily.

T. Bob blushed happily.

"Sir, I'll have to arrest you for interfering with an officer in the performance of his duty," said the pulse-taker's partner.

"Who, me?" T. Bob looked surprised. "Ah thought you was hurtin' Miz Emily."

"Emily, get up!" Lydia had returned when she heard the commotion. "T. Bob, you come along too. He's just a foolish old man, Officer. You'd be embarrassed if you arrested him."

The officer looked embarrassed.

"I can't leave without Miz Dimitra," said T. Bob, looking around. "My lord, she's done disappeared."

Lieutenant Kurtz, who hadn't been there to see Emily's spectacular collapse or T. Bob's gallant rescue, was in front of headquarters. "You folks are blocking access to a public building," he shouted through a bullhorn. "Move along." No one moved. Kurtz then chose Gus McGlenlevie as the worst flake in the bunch. If his men had to haul this guy off, it would look a lot better on television than taking the man in the suit and tie. He approached Gus.

"I am a renowned poet, Officer," said McGlenlevie loudly. "Angus McGlenlevie, author of *Erotica in Reeboks*, author of *Rapture on the Rapids*, which will be in your local bookstores in time for Christmas gift-giving, Mile-High Press, nineteen ninety-five. Did you get that?" he asked a newspaper reporter scribbling beside him. Then he smiled and bowed with a flourish to the cameras from Channel 9.

Glancing uneasily at the TV cameras out of the corner of his eye, Lieutenant Kurtz turned to Donald Mallory, who looked as if he might be more amenable to a warning from a representative of law, order, and traffic control. "Sir, we would appreciate your vacating the premises. On pain of arrest, I ask you—"

Mallory stared down his nose loftily. "I am a professor of Renaissance and Jacobean poetry, sir, and your detectives are unfairly harassing a member of our staff and a talented poet." Mallory had raised his voice to auditorium volume. The TV people had to adjust their sound levels.

"And a gay," cried Orion Massine, rushing in from the public parking lot.

"And a Los Santos bicycle racer," said Hoke Mitchell, who had broken ranks on the street and bicycled up to the steps of Police Headquarters, skidding to a dramatic stop, displaying his Los Santos Cycle Racers T-shirt for the cameras.

"Lance Potemkin wouldn't kill a soul, much less his abominable father," said Orion to the reporter.

How the hell did Captain de la Rosa always manage to leave town when there was a problem? Kurtz wondered.

"And Los Santos will miss the acclaim when Lance wins the bicycle race on the High Road to Taos," warned Hoke Mitchell. He had collared a Channel 7 reporter. "The police have stolen his bicycle and refused to let him leave town."

Lieutenant Kurtz had no idea what they were talking about. Where the hell was Community Relations when he needed them? "Mosson!" he yelled through the door.

"I'm Lance's mother," cried Dimitra. "He didn't kill Boris." One of the traffic patrolmen had made the mistake of escorting Dimitra in her walker around to the front of the building. "Boris was struck down by God for his sins and his nasty disposition," said Dimitra to a *Herald Post* reporter, "and T. Bob Tyler was just trying to rescue Emily Marks. No matter what you people say, he's not a brawler."

Because of all the media people grouped around Dimitra, Sergeant Manny Escobedo, who had been sent out to represent the C.A.P. case against Lance Potemkin, couldn't get through the crowd. Sergeant Mosson of Community Relations tried to call Chief Gaitan, but the chief, according to his secretary, was giving a speech to the Rotarians on the department's plans to move operations out to area divisions in order to increase contact with the citizens of Los Santos. "Community-based law enforcement," Chief Gaitan called it, but Mosson didn't think this kind of interaction with the citizens was what the chief had in mind.

18
••

Friday, October 1, 4:30 P.M.

Elena spent two hours canvassing the pawnbrokers with a description of the czar's medal. At her last stop on Alameda, Jesus Bonilla said, "Don't sound like much. What would I want with it?"

"Historical stuff sells for thousands if you have the right buyer," she replied.

"So if I had it, I wouldn't be tellin' you, would I?" Jesus had a pawnshop *cum* fencing operation and a smart mouth.

"Gee, that's too bad, Jesus," said Elena, leaning her elbow on a glass case displaying handguns with nicked grips and unoiled barrels. "We're watching this one real close. If we find that the medal's passed through your hands—"

"Yeah, yeah. You're gonna drag me straight down to headquarters for questioning."

"No, we're gonna arrest you as an accessory to murder."

Jesus bit down so hard on his cigarillo that it broke and dropped sparks on his leather vest. Ten years earlier, he had been a member of the Scorpions and had barely beaten a murder rap after spending a year in the Los Santos County Jail.

"Hey," he said, grinding the cigarillo into the grimy floor with a booted heel. "You got no call to hassle me. I ain't seen the thing."

"That's not exactly what you said, Jesus. I took your answer to mean, 'I wouldn't tell you if I had.' "

"Well, I ain't seen it. Swear on my mother's soul."

"Your mother's dead."

"So she's a soul in heaven. All the better. Listen, I got a kid now. See 'im? Jesus, Jr."

Elena glanced down the aisle and didn't see any kid. "Jesus, Jr., seems to have skipped town."

"*Madre de Dios!*" exclaimed Jesus, Sr., and clacked off in his high-heeled cowboy boots. She could hear him in the back room yelling, "Hey, *malcríado*, fingers outa that cartridge box."

He returned carrying on his bony hip a pretty child with smooth brown cheeks, which by the time he reached maturity, *if* he reached maturity, would probably be pocked with acne scars like his father's.

"If that medal comes into your hands," said Elena, "if you even hear about it, you call me. Got it?"

"Got it," said Jesus, scowling at her in such a way that she could see in the man the boy who had once been the terror of the barrios and then moved on to prey on the young *cholos* who used him as a fence.

"You got no solidarity with *la raza*," said Jesus.

"*My* people," said Elena, "are on my side of the law. You ought to try it."

"I ought to starve too," said Jesus, but too softly to be quoted.

It was 4:45, and Jesus was her last stop. More overtime coming on her paycheck, and nothing to show for her day's work except the elimination of Omar Ashkenazi as a suspect. Her police radio stuttered to life with a warning that headquarters at Five Points was inaccessible due to traffic gridlock. Astonished, Elena headed home and parked the unmarked Taurus in her driveway. She jogged around the house to the kitchen and the black and white TV. As she locked up her gun, the news was coming on, shots of Los Santos, the mountain, cactus flowers, downtown bank buildings. She pulled a Tecate from the refrigerator and popped the tab as the newscaster said, "There's a giant protest going on at Police Headquarters this afternoon. It's tied up traffic for at least a mile in every direction for the last two hours. . . ."

"Protest?" Elena picked up the can and sat down, the first long sip sliding down her throat like wet silk.

". . . on Monday when seventy-one-year-old Boris Potemkin was shot to death in his home on Sierra Negra. A varied group gathered at Five Points this afternoon to protest police harassment of his son, Lance Potemkin, who is a suspect in the murder."

"Oh shit," muttered Elena and took another long gulp of cold beer.

"Among the groups represented in the protest are the Los Santos Gay Rights Association, professors and students from Herbert Hobart University—"

She spotted Gus McGlenlevie waving a sign about the cops interfering with the poetic muse. Donald Mallory, Lance's former lover, glared at McGlenlevie from the edge of the screen. The English Department was evidently supporting its secretary.

"—the Los Santos Cycle Racing Club . . ."

TV cameras showed a long shot of people wearing tights, pancake helmets and fanny packs, riding bicycles in figure eights on Raynor and Montana.

". . . headed by Lance Potemkin's mother, Mrs. Dimitra Potemkin, and Mrs. Harmony Waite Portillo of Chimayo, New Mexico—"

"Mom?" Elena stared at the black and white image of her mother.

"Among those arrested were Dr. Donald Mallory, Mrs. Portillo . . ." The list went on. "At this time the suspects are being held at Five Points because there is no way to get them to the county jail."

Elena rose, draining her beer can, then made a perfect hook shot into the wastebasket. She snapped off the television set, unlocked the drawer to get her 9mm in its shoulder holster, shrugged into her jacket, and headed for the departmental Taurus. If she had to walk in, she'd do it. Her own mother! They'd probably planned the demonstration at the poetry reading last night, and Harmony had conveniently failed to mention it.

19

Friday, October 1, 5:35 P.M.

Chaos prevailed at Police Headquarters: traffic gridlock on the streets, protesters milling outside, the leaders under arrest and held in the public reception area because the police had no way, short of teleportation, to get them downtown for booking. Harmony loved it. She was jammed against the desk sergeant's counter, guarded by a harassed patrolman and gleefully giving Lieutenant Beltran, whom she had demanded to see, melting looks that turned the poor man to putty.

Harmony knew she was looking her best, long black hair windblown so that the silver streaks showed, cheeks flushed from her afternoon outdoors. She had on her black hat with the silver and turquoise band, her favorite woven peacock-blue tent dress nipped at the waist with a concho belt, and her black sandals studded with turquoise.

"It's so sweet of you to come to my rescue." She gave Beltran a smile that turned him pink, while she ignored the imperious Captain Stollinger. Harmony considered herself only a partial feminist. She wasn't above using female wiles to achieve her ends. While Beltran was blushing and stammering, Harmony spotted Elena pushing through the mob of prisoners, police, and media people.

"Mom!" exclaimed Elena when she reached the desk. "How could you—"

113

"Where the hell have you been?" demanded Lieutenant Beltran, shaken out of his befuddlement.

"I've been working on the Potemkin case," Elena replied.

"This woman is your mother, Jarvis?" demanded Captain Stollinger as Lieutenant Beltran was muttering, "Maybe in the future, you could convince members of your family not to demonstrate against the department."

"I'd appreciate it if you wouldn't speak to my daughter in that tone of voice, Lieutenant," said Harmony indignantly.

"He's her superior," said Stollinger. "He can talk to her any way he wants . . . as long as it doesn't constitute sexual harassment," the captain added hastily.

"And here I thought you were being so gallant, Lieutenant," said Harmony reproachfully.

"I was. I mean it was certainly my pleasure to—"

"What's going on?" boomed the rich, baritone voice of Armando Gaitan, Chief of the Los Santos Police Department. "Can't I leave headquarters for three hours without my department being bombarded by unfavorable media attention?"

Elena put her hand over her mouth to hide a grin. If there was one thing the chief hated, it was unfavorable media attention. He liked to think of himself as the darling of the press. By and large he was, being a tall, trim, handsome man in the best Hispanic tradition, a bachelor who put a tremor in the hearts of ladies all over town, including media ladies.

"Chief," called a reporter from Channel 4, "do you have any comment on the accusations that have been leveled against the department by this group?"

"I don't even know what the accusations are," boomed the chief, "but I shall certainly look into them."

The reporter glanced down at her list as she trailed him toward Stollinger. "That police harass gays, that you're preventing a local hero from attending a bicycle race on the High Road to Taos, which everyone thinks he'll win, that—ah—the police are acting like vigilantes against poets."

"Vigilantes?" The chief looked astounded. "What poets? I don't know any poets."

"I, sir, am a poet," said Angus McGlenlevie, eluding his personal police attendant and grabbing the chief's arm. "The young man who is receiving your unwarranted attention is a poet. I assure you, poets all over the country, including myself, whose book *Rapture on the Rapids* will be in the—"

"By God, McGlenlevie," broke in Professor Donald Mallory, "if you plug that book one more time—"

"And for failing to protect senior citizens," concluded the reporter. "Could you please comment, sir."

"Senior citizens?" muttered Armando Gaitan. He shook off McGlenlevie and glared at the lieutenant. "What senior citizens haven't we been protecting?"

"I think they mean in general, sir," said Sergeant Mosson, who, from a place near the hall, had shouldered his way toward his leader, cutting off an interview with a reporter from Mexico to do so. "However, we had a lot of old folks in lawn chairs obstructing traffic in the parking lot."

"One older lady was dragged from her chair," said Harmony reproachfully. "That's no way to treat one's elders." It was then that Chief Gaitan first noticed Harmony Waite Portillo, and his eyes lit with the gleam of a bachelor on the prowl. Female politicians and city administrators, members of museum and symphony boards, even female members of the media were fair game for Chief Gaitan. Elena hoped he didn't favor married women. She'd never heard that he did.

"Chief, this is my *mother*, Harmony Waite Portillo," she said quickly. "Of Chimayo."

Chief Gaitan clasped Harmony's hand and gave her a charming smile. "Dear lady, what a pleasure, and may I say that your visit graces our fair city?"

TV cameras were rolling.

"The pleasure is mine," said Harmony with an equally charming smile. The two positively radiated good will and sex appeal.

"Mother's been arrested," said Elena loudly, "for picketing the police department. Probably in her younger days she even called us pigs."

"Elena!" exclaimed Harmony. "That was years ago! Before you were born." She smiled at Armando Gaitan. "In the late, bad sixties." Long, black eyelashes dropped flirtatiously onto flushed cheeks.

"We're contemporaries," said the chief.

"Are we? Did you ever call a policeman a pig?" Harmony asked gaily.

"No," said Gaitan. He was taking the conversation amazingly well.

"Do you plan to put Ms. Portillo in jail?" asked the pretty Channel 4 reporter sharply.

Elena decided there were at least two people in the crowd jealous over the flirtation between the chief and Harmony, Lieutenant Beltran being the other one.

"Everyone knows the LSPD is a bunch of gay bashers," said Orion Massine combatively, then turned to his guard and snapped, "Watch the pleats," when the patrolman grabbed the back of his shirt to keep him from escaping into the mob.

"Nonsense," said Chief Gaitan.

"Chief, there are a lot of senior citizens who are nervous about driving after dark and would like to get home as soon as possible," said Harmony.

"We haven't arrested any senior citizens," said Lieutenant Kurtz. He had come out of Sergeant Mosson's office to the left of the reception counter. "They can pack up their lawn chairs and leave, even the old guy who grabbed an officer. He evidently *thought* he was protecting some lady. *She* thought she was being subjected to police brutality. In other words, it was just a mix-up, so they can go home. The old folks." He looked hopeful.

"Well, I believe, sir," said Harmony, "that they're staying to see that nothing untoward happens to *me*, since I came with them from the Socorro Heights Center."

"Nothing unpleasant will happen to you, my dear Ms.—may I call you Harmony? My feeling is that we should all retire to the conference room—"

"What about Lance?" shouted Hoke Mitchell. "He's our best chance to win that race."

"—and discuss the complaints of those who have been protesting here today. I'm sure we can reach a compromise that will make everyone happy," said the chief soothingly.

"You're knuckling under, Chief?" asked the jealous Channel 4 reporter.

"I'm being responsive to public concerns," snapped the chief. Then he turned courteously to Harmony. "If you would represent the senior citizens, Ms. Portillo—"

Elena said, "Mrs.," but no one heard her.

At the chief's orders, police officers shepherded those who had been arrested into a utilitarian conference room with a lectern for the chief and an array of uncomfortable chairs for everyone else. The media was relegated to the hall. Protesters sat down, Gaitan took the lectern, and the complaints began.

"Where is this Lance Potemkin?" asked the chief after he had heard from gays, poets, and racers.

"He's much too retiring to take part in noisy protests," said Donald Mallory, "but I have a complaint."

"What is that, sir?" asked the chief.

"In the first place," said Mallory with dignified restraint, "the work of the English Department at Herbert Hobart has been seriously disrupted because of your unwarranted harassment of Lance Potemkin, our secretary. In the second place, McGlenlevie is misusing the word *vigilantes*. By its very definition, *vigilante* cannot be used about police in the pursuit of their assigned duties."

"Harassing gays is an assigned duty? I knew it!" shouted Orion.

"We do not have a policy of harassing gays," said the chief, "but we do have to investigate murder cases."

"Well, as I told my daughter," said Harmony, "your investigation is misguided. Lance is not the murderer."

"My dear lady, do you have evidence to support that?" asked the chief.

"Certainly. No one with Lance's customary aura—"

"His customary *what*?"

"Mom," moaned Elena.

"Aura," said Harmony clearly.

The chief looked taken aback. "Thank you for your input," he mumbled.

"And besides that, this is a case of robbery-murder, and not the first in your city. A number of old people have been killed in their homes by robbers. One of our purposes was to demand that the police department provide better protection for older citizens."

Armando Gaitan sighed and leaned his elbow on the lectern, brushing his neatly clipped mustache with a thoughtful finger. "Ms. Portillo, no one is more cognizant than I of the problems of the older population. We do the best we can to offer protection. Unfortunately, we cannot assign an officer to each elderly citizen."

"You've assigned an officer to each of *us* because we were exercising our right to free speech," said Gus.

"And it is certainly not my policy to target any group for harassment—not gays, not minorities, not—"

"Lance is a minority," said Gus. "He's Anglo. People are always saying Hispanics are the minority, but they're not in Los Santos. Look at the police in this room. Three-fourths are Hispanic, whereas we protesters are all Anglos."

"I'm Hispanic by marriage," said Harmony.

"Right, and the chief of police has been a lot more sympathetic to you than to any of the rest of us," said Gus.

"If you're accusing me of racial or ethnic discrimination, sir, you're out of line," said Chief Gaitan, reminding everyone that he could be as hard-nosed as the next cop, as well as a lot more charming. "Now, it appears to me that the one thing we can do something about is this business of the bicycle race. We are not keeping the young man from doing his job, are we, Detective Jarvis?" he added, to placate Professor Mallory, who had opened his mouth to protest.

"No, sir. He's been in for questioning, but he's not under arrest."

"Lance will win that race if you let him go," said Hoke.

"I'm delighted to hear that," said the chief. "You and your partner can escort Mr. Potemkin to New Mexico, Detective Jarvis, and see that he returns afterwards."

"Yes, sir, but how are we supposed to keep track of him during the race? I doubt that either one of us has been on a bicycle in years."

"I'm a bicycle racer," said Lieutenant Maggie Daguerre, who was observing from the back of the room.

The chief looked at her and beamed. Maggie Daguerre, the

department's computer expert, was a sight to gladden the eye of any man whose testosterone was still flowing. She was five foot eleven and built like a Vegas chorus girl, with lustrous black hair and slanted green eyes.

Lieutenant Beltran, still looking grumpy, said, "If Potemkin's a sure winner, no *woman's* going to keep up with him."

"I've placed in bicycle races," said Maggie, "not to mention canoe races, foot races—"

"Good. You'll go with the other two officers," said the chief.

"And to show solidarity between the Sheriff's Department in Rio Arriba County and the Los Santos Police Department," said Harmony, "I'll put Lance up as well as the police officers. Also I can arrange to have deputies placed along the High Road so you'll feel easy in your mind about this generous offer you've made, Chief."

"Armando," he corrected. "That's extremely gracious of you."

"What does Chimayo have to do with the race?" asked Elena, puzzled. Her hometown was populated by reclusive descendants of early Spanish settlers. They hadn't even allowed the movie *Milagro Beanfield War* to be filmed there, because they didn't want a horde of outsiders disturbing their way of life.

"We need a new roof on the Sanctuario," murmured Harmony. "It was the only way."

"I hope that we have addressed as many of the protesters' concerns as we are able to at this time," said the chief.

"We're all still under arrest," said Professor Donald Mallory.

"But not yet booked. Lieutenant Beltran, you can take care of freeing these people," ordered the chief. "Now, is everyone happy?"

"Absolutely," said Hoke Mitchell.

"I'm not," said Gus McGlenlevie.

"Oh, be quiet," said Donald Mallory. "You may want to go to jail. I don't."

"I could have written a brilliant cycle of verses from the county jail," said Gus.

"The detention facility is full," said the chief.

"What about the senior citizens?" asked Harmony.

"My dear lady, why don't we dismiss the meeting and discuss that." Protesters and officers began to leave.

"Harmony, about the best I can do," said Armando Gaitan, "is look into this matter of senior citizen safety. I shall appoint a board to investigate. Now, to more pleasant matters. The department is having a talent show in several weeks. I hope that you'll attend as my guest."

"I'd love to," said Harmony, her eyes lighting up with a gleam that made Elena extremely uneasy. Surely her mother wasn't falling for the chief. Harmony was a married woman. She had five children, four grandchildren. Elena imagined her mother leaving Sheriff Ruben Portillo, marrying Elena's chief, causing a scandal.

"I have my own transportation, Elena," said Harmony, breaking into those disquieting images. "Don't forget that the party for Boris is tonight."

20

Elena glanced at the clock. Seven-twenty and her mother hadn't returned. Maybe Harmony wanted to avoid the wake. Elena had tried those cabbage rolls and found two problems with them: one, the filling wasn't spicy; two, she didn't like cabbage. For that matter, she didn't care much for vodka— especially if Dimitra expected her to drink straight shots. She'd read about that Russian custom.

"Mom, where have you *been*?" she demanded when Harmony let herself into the kitchen ten minutes later.

"I had to take four senior citizens home, not to mention their lawn chairs."

At least her mother hadn't been meeting the chief in some dark bar. "I've got a bone to pick with you, Mom."

"We don't have time. We have to dress for the wake."

"You look great, and I can dress in three minutes. Why did you join that protest against the department? Can't you see that it was embarrassing for me?"

"Well, Elena," said Harmony, dropping into a chair, "one has to have the courage of one's convictions, even if one's daughter is going to be a pill about it."

"I'm not being a pill. I'm just—"

"We were addressing serious problems."

"Sure. Like whether or not Lance Potemkin gets to go to New Mexico."

121

"That, and the fact that there are three, four, maybe five women at the center whose husbands were killed in daylight robberies while the wives were at Socorro Heights. People really do feel that they aren't safe in their homes."

"Over how long a period was this?" asked Elena, frowning.

"I don't know, dear. Within recent years."

"With them, recent years could be the last fifty."

"I mean recent recent years," said her mother sternly. "It's a serious problem, very important to older people, and your chief has agreed to address it."

"Yeah, Mom, that's another thing. Why were you flirting with Chief Gaitan? What would Pop think?"

"I wasn't flirting. I was being friendly. And very successfully, I might add. Lance is going to the race, Armando has agreed to look into senior citizen problems, and—"

"—and you were flirting," said Elena. "You accepted a date with him."

"What are you *talking* about?"

"The police talent show."

"That's not a date! He invited me to be his guest, which I presume means a complimentary ticket. I'll be going with *you*."

"Oh. Are you sure? What if Gaitan thinks he's got a date?"

"Married women don't date."

"I'm sure Pop'll be pleased to hear that."

"Before he hears from Armando," Harmony mused, "I guess I'd better call your father to tell him I offered protection along the race route. We'll drive up tomorrow since the event is Sunday."

"*We?*"

"Of course. It's a nice opportunity for us to see your father and the family. Anyway, I've offered to put people up at the house."

Elena sighed. "That's Lance, Leo, me, Maggie, and you. Concepcion won't be going. She's nauseated."

"Is she? I must congratulate Leo."

"Maybe she's got the flu," said Elena dryly.

"Don't be such a pessimist."

"Who, me? Anyway, we've got five people plus the bicycles and luggage."

"The Holymobile will seat five," said Harmony.

Elena giggled. "Grandmother Portillo would consider that sacrilegious—calling it the Holymobile."

"Very well. The Penitentes' pickup. So it's all worked out. I'll drive."

"Something's bound to go wrong," Elena fretted. "Maggie'll fall behind. Then Lance'll disappear into the forest and get me demoted."

"Nonsense. Whatever happens, we'll work it out, dear."

"That's what you always say, Mom. That's what you said when the *curandera* put a curse on Tia Josefina over the Eye-of-God business."

"I worked it out. She lifted the curse."

"But we had to drink Joaquina's miserable herbal tea for a year, while the control group got to drink Kool Aid."

"Joaquina likes to think she's very scientific," said Harmony. "She still wants to write a book about science, herbs, and magic." Harmony was nibbling tortilla chips that Elena kept in a lidded basket on the table. "Do you know what the most irritating thing about that protest was?"

"I know what irritated me most," said Elena as she pulled bean dip from the refrigerator. "Your participation."

"Lydia Beeman," said Harmony, leaning forward to sample the dip. "Every single person from the center waited until I was released. But not Lydia. As soon as the police started carting off people in their lawn chairs, she got up, folded hers, and said to me, 'We're making fools of ourselves and not doing a bit of good.' Can you imagine that? Lance is riding in the bicycle race, isn't he? Well, anyway, that's what she said to me. But then what can you expect of a woman who honors the memory of her late husband by polishing his gun collection every month? If she doesn't care about Lance, she should at least care about the safety of senior citizens. One also hears rumors about battered wives at the center. Perhaps I ought to organize a demonstration pointing out that the system fails to protect women."

"Terrific," said Elena, scooping up some bean dip to fortify herself against the cabbage rolls and vodka. "But in Santa Fe, not Los Santos, and target the women who refuse to press charges against their abusers, and the judges and juries who won't give the bastards long sentences or, in some cases, even convict them."

"Would you like some raw carrots with our snack?"

"I'm not crazy about raw carrots, Mom," Elena replied.

"They keep you from getting something—breast cancer, I think. I read that if you eat a raw carrot a day, you'll never lose a breast."

"Right," said Elena. "You turn orange instead."

Because the hostess and many of the celebrants were worn out from the afternoon protest, the wake lasted only forty-five minutes. Elena went to bed early and thought about the things her mother had said. It was sort of amusing, how antagonistic Harmony felt toward Lydia Beeman, but then they were two different kinds of women: Harmony extremely feminine, given to political and social causes; Lydia rather masculine and given to causes of a more abstract nature, like justice. Anyway, Elena thought that Lydia was an interesting person, even if she wasn't Harmony's cup of tea.

Then there were her mother's remarks about husbands of Socorro Heights women having been killed in daylight home robberies. Could there have been five? If so, that was a curious statistic. Was there some crime-ring operating out of the center, finding out when people wouldn't be home? But the husbands *had* been home. If she and Leo didn't manage to close the case on Lance, she'd have to look into her mother's information after the bicycle race.

21
..

As Elena was finishing her *huevos rancheros*, Maggie Daguerre telephoned and said, "Do you really need three cops in the truck? I know I'm an extra gun, not that I ever use one—"

"I think the bicycle riders and the gay activists would be pretty ticked off if all three of us shot Lance on the way to Chimayo," Elena replied dryly.

"Right," Maggie agreed. "In that case, Manny Escobedo wants to drive me up. He's got his kids this weekend and thought it would be fun for them to come along, see that race, camp out. I'll have my own cheering section."

As she hung up, Elena tried to picture Maggie Daguerre, Manny Escobedo, and his two kids, spending the weekend together in a tent. The kids wouldn't like their dad taking up with a gorgeous computer expert/police officer/bicycle racer. And camping out? Daguerre was the outdoorsy type. But Manny?

A half hour later Harmony, Elena, and Leo were in front of Lance Potemkin's apartment arguing about who should sit where. "I want Lance up front with me," said Harmony. "It's not often I get the Yeats of his generation all to myself." Lance looked pleased.

"You can't drive, Mom. He's a murder suspect, so I drive; he sits in back with Leo."

"My insurance doesn't cover you, Elena," said Harmony smugly, "and we have to use my truck. You've no place for a bicycle on a police car and no back seat in your own truck."

"You should have mentioned the insurance business yesterday, Harmony," said Leo, looking worried.

"It seems to me," said Lance sarcastically, "that it would be easier for you two to shoot me if you're both sitting in back."

Elena glared at him. He was Mr. Sweetie with her mother and Mr. Snide with her. "You're sitting in back with Leo, and not behind my mother," she snapped, having pictured him grabbing Harmony around the neck from behind. She sure hoped Beltran never heard that Harmony had done the driving.

"Maybe you'd feel better if you realized that I don't have that many fans, especially fans who can actually quote lines of my poetry. It's not likely that I'm going to try to take Mrs. Portillo hostage. In fact, if I weren't gay, I'd probably be in love," said Lance, smiling sweetly at Harmony.

Harmony's infectious laughter floated out into the warm morning air as she leaned forward and kissed him on the cheek. "What a lovely compliment, dear."

If he thinks he can escape by buttering up my mother, he can think again, Elena decided grimly and waved him into the back seat. Leo then handcuffed himself to Lance, who didn't like that at all.

Harmony climbed into the driver's seat, muttering that Lance had *not* killed anyone; they were just being silly. Giving Elena a pointed look, she said, "Now, Lance, you're very welcome to stay at our house. You can sleep in Elena's old room. It has an excellent bed, so you'll get a good night's rest."

"Actually, I have friends in Santa Fe," said Lance.

"Can they put us up too?" asked Elena, resentful that her mother had offered the suspect Elena's comfortable bed.

"I forgot about that," said Lance, looking sulky. "Thanks, Mrs. Portillo. I guess I'll have to impose on you."

"No imposition at all," Harmony assured him. "Leo, you can have the room Two and Johnny slept in, and Elena, you can have Josie's."

"Great," said Elena. "I remember what the beds are like in

there." She sat sideways, watching Lance. If he made a move toward her mother, he was dead meat.

"You're not competing in a race tomorrow, Elena," said Harmony. "Lance needs the firmest bed."

"Well, he can't have the room to himself," muttered Elena. "He's under surveillance."

"In that case, you'd probably feel more comfortable sharing a room with me, Detective Jarvis, more comfortable than your partner would," Lance suggested. He seemed to be enjoying the squabble.

"I don't mind," said Leo. "Gays never get the hots for me."

"You just want the good bed," muttered Elena.

"Well, settle it among yourselves, children," said Harmony. She revved the engine and peeled rubber down the quiet suburban street. "I *have* missed Ruben."

"Mom, you've been gone less than a week. And take it easy, will you? My mother thinks she's good enough to race in a Grand Prix," Elena added. By running two yellow lights, Harmony had made it to the interstate access road in about thirty seconds. "When we were kids, she used to say, 'Buckle up,' and then scare us all silly tearing over dirt roads to get to Mass on time. We all prayed on Saturday night that Pop wouldn't be out on a call when it came time to head for the Sanctuario on Sunday morning."

Harmony laughed merrily and, zooming onto Interstate 10, cut off another pickup. The irate driver leaned on his horn. Elena noted that their suspect was terrified. Served him right. "Slow down, Mom. The speed limit's fifty-five in the city."

Harmony took her foot off the gas, but by the time they passed the Executive Center exit, they were back up to sixty-seven, and Lance, who rarely rode anything but a bicycle, was clutching the leather strap that hung from the ceiling on his side. He could hardly reply to Harmony's critique of his water metaphors in a poem about resurrection. Elena was pretty nervous herself, since her mother kept taking her eyes off the road in order to turn and talk to the prisoner.

22

Lance glared at them while Leo patted him down. "Couldn't you have done this at the house where I wouldn't be embarrassed?"

"Hey, we didn't even have to let you come to this race. It's costing the department a bundle to guard you," snapped Elena. She was sick and tired of Lance, who was still doing the Dr. Jekyll and Mr. Hyde bit. He'd been charming to everyone at dinner, especially Harmony and Maggie Daguerre; then he'd demanded to have a bedroom to himself, once Harmony had gone to bed and Maggie had left for her tent, the plan being to sandwich the two kids in between her and Manny. Leo had been so pissed, he not only shared a room with Lance, he'd cuffed the prisoner to the hand-carved wooden bedpost. Elena had warned Lance that if he yanked on the cuff and damaged the post, Harmony would kill him, no matter how great his water metaphors were.

"What's this?" demanded Leo, dragging a sharp implement from Lance's fanny pack.

"It's part of the repair kit," snapped Lance.

"Then you better hope the bike doesn't break down," said Elena, confiscating the item, "because you're not taking it with you." She could just imagine him stabbing Maggie and riding

128

off onto some unpaved track where he'd meet a gay activist in a Bronco and escape into the mountains.

"Heavenly Father," intoned Dr. Sunnydale, president of Herbert Hobart University. His white hair was handsomely styled, his suit a beautifully tailored light gray, and his tan as California as it had been when he was a famous TV evangelist. In Chimayo, among the bicycle-racers, fans, and townsfolk, the university president looked as out of place as a poodle in a coyote litter.

"Who the hell is he?" demanded Sheriff Ruben Portillo. "Father Reynaldo is supposed to bless the racers."

"We ask thy blessings on our fellow, Lance—ah—"

"Potemkin," whispered Harley Stanley, Vice-President for Academic Affairs, who had offered to ride his motorcycle ahead of the racers, carrying first-aid equipment and refreshments. The sheriff had refused.

"He's the president of Herbert Hobart University," Elena murmured.

". . . who has been unfairly harassed by the vigilante police," continued the university president.

Harley Stanley hissed into his ear, causing Dr. Sunnydale to frown at Gus McGlenlevie, who had evidently urged on him the phrase *vigilante police*. "—who has been given his own escort to the race by the Los Santos Police Department," the president amended.

Lance grumbled. Elena stifled a giggle. Father Reynaldo looked as if he'd like to excommunicate President Sunnydale. Citizens of Chimayo, who would never have allowed the race to start in their town if it weren't for the leaking roof, were muttering angrily about the insult to their priest and the Sanctuario. This pushy Protestant had no right to give the blessing, they said, mostly in Spanish, but not always.

"We ask, Heavenly Father, that you smile upon this fine young man, whose troubles are legion but whose heart is pure," said the president.

Bicycle racers now muttered resentfully because one of their number was being given special clerical attention. Lance looked embarrassed and sulky while Harmony whispered to him consolingly and Maggie Daguerre gave him a comradely

slap on the back. Much good she'd be as a guard, thought
Elena. Maggie and Lance had met the night before at Harmony's table and talked white-water rafting over savory bowls
of *caldillo* and hot flour tortillas in the Portillo kitchen during
a noisy dinner served to family and guests.

". . . safety, Christian sportsmanship, and the American
competitive spirit," concluded President Sunnydale. "Amen."

Muttering under his breath, Father Reynaldo stepped forward and asked a proper blessing on the racers. At a blast from
a ram's horn, preserved from Spanish colonial days, the herd of
bicycle racers pedaled vigorously away on the High Road to
Taos.

"They just left Chimayo," said Sheriff Portillo into his car
microphone. He had deputies stationed along the route in case
Lance tried to make a break for it. "Don't know what your
superiors are thinking of," her father muttered to Elena.
"Letting a murder suspect roam around the countryside like
this."

"It's all right, love," said Harmony, whisking up to her
husband and giving him a fleeting kiss. "Lance is innocent.
Would I invite a murderer to dinner and to spend the night?"

"You not only would, *querida*. You *have* on at least one
occasion." Ruben caught his wife by the flowing sash that
circled her slender waist and pulled her back for a hug.

Elena sighed, wishing she had a marriage like her parents'.
Her father had returned from Josie and Armstrong's house last
night and had undoubtedly made love to her mother after
dinner, for they had retired suspiciously early. Elena and the
guests and relatives had to do the dishes, which was only fair.
Harmony had driven all the way to Chimayo, after all, then
cooked dinner for twenty-five people.

Elena rubbed the small of her back. That bed in Josie's old
room was a killer. Not that she had cause for serious complaint.
Maggie Daguerre, who was at this moment racing madly along
on a bicycle, had occupied a sleeping bag in the Portillos'
orchard, sharing a tent with Manny Escobedo and being kicked
by his unfriendly children, Tito and Virgie.

"I will say," said Ruben Portillo, "that Potemkin has good
taste in women."

Elena grinned. "He's in his twenties, Pop, and—"

Ruben tugged Elena's French braid affectionately. "I can tell when a man's in love with your mother. Quit that, you kids!" he roared.

Cleo, Josie and Armstrong Carr's daughter, was supervising a mass scaling of the adobe wall around the old plaza. Virgie Escobedo, when shouted at by the sheriff, fell off and glared at him. Tito scrambled over the top and dropped out of sight. Two and Rafaela's twins, Tres and Carlito, obeyed their grandfather by climbing into the gnarled branches of a tree that overhung the wall.

"Look at me, *Abuelo*," shrieked Connie, the three-year-old daughter of Johnny and Betts Portillo. They had left her in Harmony's care so they could drift through the crowd peddling tiny clay bicycle racers in sombreros and ponchos. The figurines had come out of Betts' kiln just the day before.

Ruben strode to the wall and snatched his capering grand-daughter from the top. Cleo sat astride the adobe playing the shepherd's flute on which she composed her own tunes. With Connie under his arm, Ruben stopped to listen. "That's a good one, Cleo," he said. "Now get your bottom off that wall."

"Daddy, I'm bored," complained Virgie Escobedo.

"You're getting to be a real pain, kid," said the sergeant. "I know who put that lizard in Maggie's sleeping bag."

"Not me. I'm too old for silly stuff like that."

"You're saying Tito did it?"

"So what if he did? She didn't care."

"That's 'cause she's a gutsy lady," snapped Manny.

"I don't want a stepmother," muttered Virgie. "And she's too tall for you, anyway."

"Who says I'm marryin' her?" growled Manny.

"Mama."

Six-year-old Tito dropped off the wall, yelled, "Snitch," at his sister, and ran for his life when she made a grab for him.

"Bringing those two was a big mistake," Manny muttered to Elena. "You wouldn't believe how they treated Maggie last night."

"Maggie didn't seem to mind."

"Yeah," said the sergeant gloomily. "I guess that means she

doesn't care one way or the other about me. Otherwise, she'd want my kids to like her."

"Elena!"

Elena turned to see her friend Sarah Tolland, the chairman of Electrical Engineering at Herbert Hobart, working her way through the crowd. Sarah was trim, gray-blond, fortyish, and pretty in a very conservative way.

"I can't believe it," said Elena. "I didn't know you'd be here, Sarah."

"I didn't know Gus would be here," said Sarah, scowling. Her ex-husband was at the edge of the crowd flirting with one of the village girls, whose father was watching them closely.

Elena grinned. "If Gus tries to make a move on that young woman, her father might just drown the author of *Rapture on the Rapids* in an *acequia*."

Sarah grinned. "Gus has posters all over campus announcing that book. They can write in *posthumous* under his name and double the sales."

"So what are you doing here? Supporting Colin?" Sarah's boyfriend, Colin Stuart, a professor in her department, was one of the racers.

Sarah nodded, but she didn't look particularly happy. "I've been wanting to call you about Colin. I wondered if you'd be amenable to a date with him."

"He's *your* boyfriend, Sarah," said Elena, astonished.

"It's not working out. He's a wonderful person, but it's causing trouble in the department, my dating one of my own faculty."

"I'm sorry," said Elena. "Good men are hard to find."

"Tell me about it." Sarah glanced darkly at her ex-husband. "Not that I mind about Colin. Nice as he is, there's really no—well—spark between us."

Elena grinned. "So you want to fix me up with someone you find boring?"

"I don't find Colin boring at all!" said Sarah indignantly. "Believe me, you'll like him. He's charming, intelligent, good-looking, and—"

"Snap him up," advised Elena's sister Josie, who had come in on the end of the conversation.

"I think I'll pass," said Elena. "The last time I dated a member of Sarah's department, he turned out to be a murderer."

"Which one is he? I mean Colin, not the murderer," Josie asked.

"Forty-five, gray hair, good-looking, green cycler's tights," said Sarah.

"Elena would love to go out with him," said Josie.

"I would not. He's too old for me," Elena protested.

"Older men are better," said Josie. "Look at me and Armstrong. We're perfect for each other, and he's almost twenty years older than I am."

"Your mother's invited us to a barbecue tonight. I'll introduce you then, Elena," said Sarah. "There's Paul Zifkovitz from the Art Department. I need to have a word with him." She edged away before Elena could refuse the introduction.

"Traitor," Elena said to her sister. "Why are Johnny and Betts talking to Dr. Sunnydale?"

"They're offering to sell him a collection of Southwestern folk art—wholesale."

Elena groaned. Surely Herbert Hobart University wouldn't— Her fears that her brother Johnny and his wife might end up charged with art fraud were forgotten when a voice behind her said tentatively, "Detective Jarvis?"

What a voice! *Mariachi* baritone with an Anglo accent. She hated to turn around and find out who went with it. However, the voice's owner couldn't be considered a disappointment. Out of professional habit, she committed his physical characteristics to memory: lightly tanned face; square chin, slight flattening at the bridge of the nose, probably from a break; thick, wind-blown brown hair; hazel eyes that picked up the green of his sport shirt; and a killer smile that said, I'm prepared to be your best friend if you're interested. She put him at five-nine or ten, one-fifty, late twenties, wearing tan slacks and a tan windbreaker over the green shirt, sneakers, hands in pockets, easy stance.

His smile widened to a grin. "I promise you won't find me on any Wanted posters." He held out his hand. "We haven't met, but I'm Michael Futrell. I've kind of been following your career. The acid bath case, that rape-murder last year."

A police groupie, she thought, disappointed.

"I'm an assistant professor of criminology at H.H.U."

No matter how cute he was, Elena didn't want to date any more professors. It was bad enough that Sarah wanted to fix her up. This one was the right age, but he probably just wanted to talk shop.

"I've been kinda of lying in wait, hoping to introduce myself," he said.

"You mean you followed me up here?" asked Elena. He looked O.K. She'd hate to think he was some kind of creep-stalker.

"No, I'm here because my twin brother is riding in the race. He's a professor too. I heard all the kids calling you Aunt Elena and then Sarah Tolland talking to you, and I thought, 'Gee, that's her.'"

"Does your brother teach criminology too?" she asked, trying to imagine a university department with twin professors. No one would know who was teaching what.

"Kinesiology," Michael Futrell replied.

What the hell was that? Elena wondered.

He laughed as if he could read her mind. "That's Phys Ed to those of us not into heavy athletic endeavors."

"Like me?" she asked suspiciously. Did she look out of shape or something?

"Actually, I meant like me. I don't mind hiking, but I prefer gardening."

Elena looked at him with new interest. Gardening and criminology? Had God thrown Michael Futrell into her path after playing so many romantic jokes on her? Like Frank the Narc, her ex-husband. Like her last date, the homicidal engineering professor.

"Unfortunately, my gardening has to be done in pots on my apartment balcony," said Michael Futrell ruefully. "Anyway, you don't want to hear about my world-class patio tomatoes."

Elena wouldn't have minded. She grew tomatoes herself.

Looking even friendlier, Futrell said, "I was hoping we could—"

"*Niña*, get yourself over here." She turned toward her father, who was standing beside his sheriff's car, squawks coming from the police radio. Elena excused herself and hurried away. If Lance had taken off across the mountains, she and Leo would be in deep shit with Beltran.

"Your Lieutenant Daguerre just went down," said Ruben Portillo. "Then someone rode over her leg."

Elena groaned. "Now we don't have anyone guarding Lance. Is she badly hurt?"

"Broken leg." The sheriff added wryly, "That's some murderer you got there. He came back to help her—only racer who did."

Eavesdropping Los Santos race fans groaned.

"'Tis better to be a good Samaritan than a bicycle-race winner," said President Sunnydale. "Herbert Hobart University is proud of Lance—ah—"

"Potemkin," snapped Vice-President Harley Stanley, who had been telling everyone who would listen that Lance's trophy would be on display at the Herbert Hobart administration building. Now there would be no trophy.

"Dr. Sunnydale," said Josie, giving the ex-evangelist a charming smile, "has Herbert Hobart University ever considered establishing a museum for that famous Southwestern artist, Armstrong Carr?"

"Your brother is driving Lieutenant Daguerre back," said Ruben Portillo to Elena. "She evidently advised the suspect to return to the race, so he's on the road again."

That was dumb of Maggie. "How many deputies has the Taos sheriff provided at his end?" asked Elena anxiously. Maybe Lance had arranged the accident, planning to fall behind. In front of the pack, everyone would see him if he tried to disappear, but if he were trailing, he could escape unnoticed. "Leo, we got a problem."

"Tell me about it." Her partner had just limped up. "There's a thorn in my Nike. I'll probably get gangrene of the foot."

"Yeah, and never tap dance again," Elena replied unsympathetically. "I told you to wear hiking boots." She turned to Manny Escobedo. "Did you hear, Sergeant? Maggie's out of the race. Broken leg."

Suddenly Manny was all cop. "Then no one's guarding the prisoner." He thought a minute. "Either of you ride a motorcycle?"

"Not me," said Elena.

"I'm wounded," said Leo. "Anyway, we don't have a motorcycle."

"There's a guy named Stanley who does," said Manny, who had started his police career in the motorcycle patrol. Announcing his intention to catch up and guard the prisoner himself, he went off to requisition the vice-president's Harley.

"I don't know how you can think that Lance is a danger to anyone," said Harmony, who had been listening. "Would he come back to assist a policewoman if he were planning an escape? Of course he wouldn't. Elena, could you help Aunt Josefina with the preparations for the barbecue?"

"Mom, I'm on duty," Elena protested.

"Behave yourselves," said Manny to his kids and roared off.

23
..

Sunday, October 3, 7:30 P.M.

A cool breeze whispered through the Chimayo Valley, rustling the leaves on cottonwood trees, stirring wild grasses and flowering fall bushes. Elena sighed with enjoyment, looking off toward clouds with underbellies blushing in the setting sun, mountains darkening. Crowds of racers and spectators mingled, drank beer, margaritas, and lemonade sold by townsfolk; watched the *cabrito*, wrapped in foil, being dug out of the cooking pits; sat at wooden tables eating the local cuisine.

Lance Potemkin, after rescuing Maggie, had come in fifteenth, which didn't seem to bother him. Los Santoans had to take what comfort they could in Mark Futrell's third-place medal. Riding right beside Lance at the finish was Sarah Tolland's friend, Colin Stuart. Hoke Mitchell complained that the two men had actually been chatting on the last lap into Taos. They were still chatting at a table under a huge cottonwood tree, Lance guarded by Leo.

Maggie Daguerre's leg had been set at a hospital in Santa Fe after Deputy Sheriff Two Portillo dropped her off at Emergency. Manny picked her up once he had returned the vice-president's motorcycle. As a result she and Manny were gorging themselves while Manny's children and the Portillo grandchildren, led by nine-year-old Cleo Armstrong, decorated Maggie's cast with elaborate, brightly colored pictures and

Indian symbols—flute players on her ankle, road runners circling her shin. Elena wondered how Maggie's captain was going to react to that garish display of folk art in the conservative precincts of I.D. & R.

In the serving line Sarah and Elena finally reached the tables where food was being dispensed. Their plates were heaped with local delicacies, the last of which was a large scoop of meat provided by Harmony.

Sarah, who had already had two margaritas, which were being sold at four dollars apiece, daintily plucked a shred of the meat off the plate and popped it into her mouth. "What is this?" she asked Harmony.

"*Cabrito*," said Harmony. "Young goat."

Sarah was so taken aback that she neglected to protest when Harmony ladled a thick red chili sauce on top of the *cabrito*. "Is that spicy? I don't think I—"

"You'll love it," said Harmony, "and it's extremely nutritious. High in Vitamin C, which, as you probably know, is an antioxidant."

"Well, I—"

"Protection against cancer."

Looking dubious, Sarah paid thirty dollars for her meal and Colin's. Her plate already contained a number of items Elena knew Sarah didn't care for—tamales, beans, a big helping of corn relish. "Blue corn?" Sarah had whispered doubtfully.

"The area is famous for it," Elena assured her.

Tia Josefina came up to relieve Harmony, who fixed herself a plate, then helped Elena carry back food for Leo and Lance. As she took a seat beside Lance, Harmony said, "When I was at Berkeley—"

"I didn't know you went to Berkeley, Mrs. Portillo," Sarah interrupted, sitting down by Colin. "I got my doctorate there."

"Poor dear," said Harmony. "By the time you arrived, things must have been quite boring, whereas '64 was the beginning of the free speech movement—a very exciting time."

"I understood that it was a *violent* time," said Sarah.

"Not until the next year. In '64 everyone was so idealistic and dedicated. I met all sorts of wonderful people, and hilarious things happened."

"Hilarious?" Sarah tried the *cabrito* with hot sauce. "It *is* good," she admitted.

"Of course it is. And think of what it's doing for you. Keeping all those free radicals from attacking your cells. Elena, show her how to use the tortilla."

Lance smiled at Harmony. "You're right about that, Mrs. Portillo. I take twenty-five hundred milligrams of Vitamin C a day. I figure you can't start combating cancer too early."

Big deal, thought Elena, who had squeezed in beside him as part of her professional duty. She was sort of irritated that he *hadn't* tried to run for it.

"I can't imagine anything funny happening during the sixties at Berkeley," said Sarah.

"You do it like this," said Elena. She lined a flour tortilla with blue corn relish, beans, *cabrito* and hot sauce, rolled it up, and handed it to Sarah. "A burrito. You'll love it."

Sarah bit in gingerly and looked horrified when meat and beans shot out the other end.

"Well, one of the really wonderful incidents," said Harmony, "was when a street person started walking around campus with a sign that said *fuck*."

Sarah turned to stare at Harmony, who was laughing gaily.

"It caused a delicious controversy. Faculty members and visiting parents were offended. Some students complained that his sign didn't say anything worthwhile, and a good many said that, no matter what the sign said, it was his right to display it, and that the movement would be defeating its own purpose if they turned against him. At the time, many students were interested in solidarity with the street people and felt making him leave would be discriminatory."

"Well, I really think," said Sarah, "that such words have no place in public forums. Didn't the administration do anything?"

"They didn't have to," Harmony replied. "One of the professors wrote a letter to the student newspaper and pointed out that *fuck* is a transitive verb, requiring an object, which the sign didn't have, which meant the university was condoning a grammatical error. The students pretty much agreed when it was pointed out to them, so the street person was asked to leave."

Everyone at the table laughed heartily, including Elena, who had heard the story before, but excluding Sarah, who looked astounded.

"So you see," said Harmony, "we radicals really did have an interest in higher education. We weren't just protesting because we didn't feel like going to class, or because we enjoyed irritating the establishment."

Sarah shook her head and took a gulp of her margarita. "That reminds me, Elena," said Sarah. "I want to introduce you to Colin Stuart. A member of our department."

What reminded her? "You've already introduced us." Elena had never seen her friend even mildly inebriated and found the spectacle amusing.

Colin said, "I don't know whether Sarah's told you or not, Detective, but she's dumping me."

"It's just campus politics," Sarah protested.

"And she's determined to fix the two of us up."

"So I've heard," said Elena dryly. "But really, Dr. Stuart—"

"For a policewoman," said Lance, "Detective Jarvis is O.K., and she's got a great mom. How did you happen to drop out at Berkeley, Mrs. Portillo?"

Harmony was studying Colin Stuart as she murmured, "Oh, things got so violent the next year, Lance, and we were really peaceful young people—my friends and I. I didn't like being bludgeoned and hauled off to jail. Here I was demonstrating for peace and love, and strangers were clubbing me. So I left for New Mexico to form a commune with friends, live off the land, and become part of an ancient, peaceful society. Did you know that the Spanish settlers never had guns?"

"That's why so many of them got killed off by the Indians, Mom," said Johnny. "Anyone want to buy a race souvenir? How about you, Lance? Betts can paint 'fifteenth' on it for you."

"Coming in fifteenth isn't that memorable," said Lance. "Maybe Colin would like one. We tied for that dubious honor."

"Not me," said Colin. "I'll remember the food and the company. Wonderful *cabrito*, Mrs. Portillo."

"Ruben and the other Penitentes did the meat," said Harmony.

"Penitentes?" Sarah looked alarmed. "I've read about them."

"No sweat," said Johnny. "They haven't crucified anyone in years."

"Johnny!" Harmony laughed. "Your father says they never did."

"Did what?" asked Ruben Portillo. He slid in beside his wife.

"Crucified people."

The sheriff frowned. "We're a Catholic lay organization, started in the old days when we had corrupt priests or none at all. A few people may have volunteered to be *tied* to the cross, but that was a long time ago. No one was *nailed* to a cross."

"I was just about to tell them how we met, Ruben," said Harmony.

He nodded and pushed back his Stetson. "Real romantic. She was growing pot. We raided the commune—"

"—and Ruben and I fell in love," Harmony finished. "But I *wasn't* growing pot! I was learning to weave."

"Looked like pot to me," said Ruben.

"Herbs," said Harmony. "You know I've always been interested in herbal and holistic medicine."

"I don't know of anything you *haven't* been interested in one time or another. This aura business is driving me nuts." He turned to Elena. "Your mother keeps telling me Efraim Ontiveros doesn't mean any harm; he's got a great aura. Everyone in town knows he's a thief. Water, apples, chiles. He'd steal the *frijoles* out of your pot."

"He's a kleptomaniac," said Harmony. "He needs therapy."

"In Chimayo we don't have therapy; we have jail," said Ruben.

"Dr. Stuart has a good aura," said Harmony. "If he asks you out, Elena, you should accept."

"Just what I told her," said Sarah.

"Me too," said Josie. "Here's your painting, Dr. Tolland. I padded and wrapped it." She handed a large parcel to Sarah. "Elena thinks he's too old," said Josie.

"How old are you, Dr. Stuart?" Harmony asked.

"Mom!" Elena protested.

"Forty-four," said Colin Stuart. He smiled at Elena. "Is that too old?"

"Of course not," she mumbled reluctantly.

"Fine. Lance has given me the name of an after-hours club. Maybe we could go next weekend." He shot Sarah a challenging look, as if she might change her mind about not seeing him when she realized he was going to accept her offer to fix him up with a friend. Sarah didn't seem to notice. She was eating her burrito.

"I'm a cop," Elena said to Colin Stuart. "At an after-hours club, I'd have to arrest the management."

Stuart looked disappointed.

Lance said, "If they ever decide I didn't kill anyone, I'll take you and introduce you around, Colin. The jazz there is fantastic. Quite a few university people go."

"We all know you didn't kill anyone, Lance," said Harmony.

Elena rolled her eyes and said to Lance, "She doesn't speak for the department."

"Maggie doesn't think I killed my father," said Lance.

Elena could understand that, given the fact that Lance was a white-water rafter who had lost his chance to win the race in order to rescue Maggie. Since he hadn't run, Lance's chivalrous actions made Elena wonder too. Maybe he hadn't killed Boris. But then who? Some medal thief? One of Dimitra's suitors?

"I remember you," said Sarah, staring, somewhat owl-eyed at Leo. "You arrested me."

"So did Elena," said Leo defensively.

"You're the tap dancer," Sarah added. "Did you go to Tap Day in New York City?" Sarah took a big bite of her second burrito, failing to notice that this time half the contents fell out the other end. "Thousands, possibly millions of tap dancers gathered to dance in the streets of New York. Together. I imagine it was very noisy." She stuck her fork into a fallen bean and popped it into her mouth, then took a swig from her plastic margarita glass. She had salt on her upper lip. "But nice for tap dancers," she added.

"I've never heard of it," said Leo, looking at her suspiciously.

"I saw it in the *New York Times*," said Sarah and finished off the last of her *cabrito*. "I bought one of your son-in-law's pictures, Mrs. Portillo," she said to Harmony. "On the advice of Professor Zifkovitz of our Art Department."

"Looks to me like you're dumping me for Zifkovitz," said Colin Stuart.

"Don't be silly," said Sarah. "I wouldn't dream of getting mixed up with another arty type. Mrs. Portillo, would you have a remedy for an upset stomach? I don't feel at all well."

"Too many margaritas," said Elena.

"You're quite wrong," said Sarah. "I am known for being able to drink with dignity. The problem is too much exotic food."

"I'd like to hear more about this Tap Day," said Leo, eyes gleaming with enthusiasm.

Oh God, thought Elena. *He's going to start one in Los Santos.*

"Look it up in the *New York Times Index*," said Sarah. "At present, I'm going to be sick."

"Johnny, go get the *curandera* for Dr. Tolland," said Harmony.

"What's that?" asked Sarah. "I thought maybe you or Aunt Josefina could—*curandera*? I don't think I—"

"She's a witch," said Elena, grinning. "Herbs, teas, curses, love potions—"

"Now, Elena," said Harmony. "Joaquina has a wonderful tea for an upset stomach. That business of the curse was years ago."

Sarah dropped her head into her hands. "I *know* better than to attend sporting events and eat Mexican food."

Harmony patted her on the shoulder and said, "You need to expand your horizons, my dear."

"I had hoped marrying Gus would be my last horizon-expanding experience," mumbled Sarah. "Because of him, I was charged with murder. By your daughter. And her partner, the tap dancer."

"Would that be Gus McGlenevie?" asked Harmony, looking astonished. "You married *him*?"

Sarah nodded.

"You poor dear. That man has a *terrible* aura."

"Wait till you read his poetry," muttered Lance. "His aura couldn't possibly be worse than his poetry."

"I wouldn't dream of reading anything he wrote," said Harmony. "He has absolutely no scruples. When we were picketing the police station, he was interested only in publicizing his book."

"You were picketing a police station?" exclaimed Ruben Portillo.

Elena found herself warming up to Lance. He didn't like Gus. He didn't like Gus's poetry. And he was really cute. Much more her age than Colin Stuart. But then Lance, unfortunately, was gay. Too bad. Elena had been wishing some eligible man would turn up in her life. Preferably someone under forty.

She glanced out at the crowd and saw Michael Futrell talking to his brother. Both were attractive. Of course, Dr. Futrell hadn't said anything about a date. He probably wanted to interview her for some crime book he was writing. Elena sighed. If you'd told her ten years ago that before she was thirty she'd be unmarried and without a date for three consecutive months, she'd never have believed it.

24
..

Elena sat in her gray tweed chair in her gray tweed partitioned cubicle on the last row in the Crimes Against Persons section. She was typing into the computer her report on the weekend spent guarding Lance Potemkin, excluding certain features of the adventure, such as her mother's quarrel with Joaquina. After receiving a report from Sarah Tolland's Santa Fe hotel room, Harmony had stomped off to confront the local *curandera*, who had evidently given Sarah something that had cleaned her system out completely.

"I cured her, didn't I?" said Joaquina indignantly.

There among the pots of herbs, the braided garlic and onion strings, and the chile *ristras* hanging from the *vigas* in Joaquina's kitchen, Elena's peace-loving mother had offered to punch the *curandera* in the nose.

"What do you care?" demanded Joaquina. "That woman was not one of ours."

Narrowing her blue eyes, Harmony said, "Watch yourself, Joaquina. There is a *curandera* of great power in Los Santos where my daughter lives. Maybe I will go to her and have her put a curse on you."

To which Joaquina replied, "Curses go both ways. I can put a curse on you or any of your family."

"Not if this woman of power blocks you. She speaks with the old gods who still linger in Mexico." Joaquina blanched.

145

"She is a *bruja* known all over Texas and Chihuahua. She is a—"

"All *right*," said Joaquina. "So I won't give purges to any more of your fancy Anglo friends."

Elena finished the report, blanked the computer screen, and concentrated on the Potemkin case. At this point, she wasn't that sure of Lance's guilt. So she thought about T. Bob Tyler, with his long history of assault and womanizing. Then she considered the gossip her mother had relayed about some indeterminate number of old men who had died in recent years during unsolved daylight robberies, men whose wives were connected with the center.

How would she go about retrieving the information she needed from the I.D. & R. central filing system? She didn't want to look at every murder case in the last five years. She wasn't even sure how much she'd find previous to 1991, which was when they'd started putting everything into the computer. Then she snapped her fingers. Maggie Daguerre, if she was in today, could get the information.

"Where you going?" called Leo from across the aisle as Elena slung the strap of her bag onto her shoulder.

"To see Daguerre," she replied and left Crimes Against Persons, heading for I.D. & R., and Maggie's small, glassed-in office. Lieutenants and sergeants got their own offices. Detectives had cubicles like Elena's. Officers on patrol used desks in some big room when they happened to be in the station houses. She skipped the elevator, took the stairs and, in two minutes, was knocking on the glass of Maggie's door, although she could see that Maggie's captain was there, embarked on a tirade. Maggie waved Elena in.

"Well, hell, Daguerre, can't you wash it off?" the captain was saying, pointing to her wildly painted leg cast.

"Sure, but the cast would disintegrate."

"Then go to the hospital and have them tape over it."

"It's a work of art," said Maggie reproachfully. "Most of it was done by the daughter of a famous artist."

"Shit! I don't care if it was done by Pablo Picasso."

"He's dead," said Elena helpfully.

The captain glared at her.

"Come on, Captain," said Maggie. "When they cut it off in six weeks, I'm going to have it sprayed with plastic and hang it on my wall. Thirty years from now I'll sell it and become a world traveler with the money I get. I even bought this great rubber thing to protect it when I take a shower."

"Well, wear the rubber thing when you come to work. Wait a minute." He squinted at her. "It's not some kind of goddamn giant condom, is it?"

"Yeah, I guess you could call it that," said Maggie, on the verge of laughter.

"Well, stay in your office," the captain ordered. "What if we have visitors? How professional will they think we are if one of my officers looks like a goddamn Mexican souvenir shop?" He stamped out, treading on Elena's foot, and slammed the door so hard the glass rattled.

"I think he broke my toe," said Elena as she sat down.

"In that case you want to file a worker's compensation claim." Maggie smiled hospitably. "What can I do for you?"

"I need to run a computer search, and I'm not even sure some of the things I want to do can be done."

Maggie clicked her tongue disapprovingly. "It's the age of electronics, kid. Get with it. You want me to give you some books?"

"I want you to give me some advice, or better, I want you to do it for me."

"Forget that," said Maggie. "Tell me what you need, and I'll type out directions on how to get it." She swung her chair to face the computer keyboard and screen, leaving her cast propped on an open desk drawer.

Elena sighed. "I want to read detectives' reports and everything else connected with robbery-homicides—well, maybe just homicides—of men over sixty-five. Well, no, make that sixty-two."

She watched Maggie think a minute, then attack the keyboard.

"Cases from the last five years," Elena added.

"That's a problem. The older stuff—you can call up the cases, but you're not going to get a lot of information from the computer. You'll have to pull the written files."

Elena nodded. "If it's possible, I'd like to narrow it down to men who were killed in their own homes, men who might have abused their wives and or even their children."

"So you want to cross-reference domestic violence cases?"

"Yeah, I guess so. And I want to know where the wives were when the men were killed. Particularly, I want cases where the wives were at the Socorro Heights Senior Citizens Center."

Maggie groaned. "I can give you some tips, but I'm not sure you can pull up cases that meet all those parameters without reading the files yourself."

Elena nodded glumly. Still, how many old men could have been murdered in the last five years? Surely not that many. She hoped not, anyway. She had thirty-nine cases presently active. She'd be lucky to find time. "I bet you could do this in an hour," she hinted.

"In an hour, I'm going home," said Maggie. "My leg hurts like hell." Even as she was talking, she continued to type. Her telephone rang; she picked it up, tucked it under her chin, and went on typing as she listened. "Leo wants you," she said, passing the phone to Elena.

Leo said, "Lance Potemkin's here. Says he's got an alibi for the day of the murder, wants to talk to us both."

Elena sighed. An alibi. If he really had one, she would *have* to run the computer search, check back with the pawnshops. They'd be scrambling for suspects. "I'll come right up." If Lance had an alibi, why the hell hadn't he told them in the first place instead of insisting he'd been home by himself with the flu?

25
..

"He wouldn't say anything until you got here," said Leo when Elena found them sitting silently in one of the small interrogation rooms.

"That way I won't have to keep repeating myself," said Lance, "and you can tell your mother about the whole thing. I really hated her thinking I might be a murderer."

"She didn't think that," said Elena.

"Well, she must have wondered."

"You're saying you're more worried about what Harmony thinks than us?" asked Leo. "She can't put you in jail."

"No one should. I didn't kill him."

"You going to tell us you were with someone on the day of the murder?" Leo looked as if he didn't believe it.

"Yes," said Lance. "Not only that day, but Friday, Saturday, and Sunday before and Tuesday after. I took some sick leave." He looked defensive. "Well, I've never taken any before, and everyone else does it."

"So you weren't in your apartment at all?" Elena asked. Surely he hadn't lied because he was afraid the English Department would find out he'd taken a bogus sick leave?

"I wasn't even in Texas," said Lance. "My friend has a place across the border in New Mexico. He grows grapes and vegetables, makes his own wine. Beautiful house."

"Yeah, yeah," said Leo. "What's your friend's name?"

149

Lance hesitated.

"Look, it's not going to do you any good unless we can check this out," said Elena.

Lance sighed. "His name is Bayard Sims. He's the chairman of Gourmet Cookery at the university."

"He's your lover?"

Lance nodded.

"So why didn't you tell us in the first place? It's not as if we didn't know you're gay."

"Bayard's getting a divorce. His wife's a lawyer here in town, and he wants partial custody of the children. He was afraid, if it came out that he's bisexual, he couldn't even get decent visitation rights."

"So he asked you not to—"

"No! It was my idea. I'd have felt terrible if he lost his children because of me."

"You'd have felt worse if you were convicted of your father's murder because of him," said Elena, frowning. Who was to say that this Bayard Sims wouldn't lie for Lance?

"There was a case where a lesbian mother lost her kids because of her sexual orientation," said Lance. "And the divorce was Bayard's idea. His wife is really mad about it. She wanted them to move back into town and stay together. Neither one of us doubted that she'd use the children against him if she had any idea about—well, about me."

"So how come you've decided to tell us now?" Leo asked.

Lance sighed again. "There's nothing to keep from her anymore. She left town on business and took the kids with her, so we thought—well, we thought we could have a long weekend together while she was gone, but she—she'd hired a private detective. When she got back Saturday she told Bayard that he either stayed married to her and dumped me, or he'd never see the children again."

"So Bayard dumped you." Elena shook her head. Adultery had sure changed. She wondered if Mrs. Sims had been surprised to find that her husband's lover was male.

"He did," said Lance sadly.

"And you were with him all day Monday? Never out of his sight?" asked Leo.

Lance nodded. "We were trying out recipes. Bayard is writing a cookbook. He's a brilliant chef."

"What's his phone number?"

"Do you have to call him?"

"Of course we do."

"Maybe you could call him at school. So his wife doesn't have to hear any more about me."

"O.K. What's his number at school?" asked Elena.

Lance produced it. "Maybe you could avoid mentioning to his secretary that it's the police calling."

"Does he know he's going to be hearing from us?"

Lance looked even more unhappy. "I'd have told him—after I decided I might as well admit where I was—but he doesn't want me to call him."

"Does he know you're a suspect in the case?"

"Surely I'm not anymore."

"You are until we talk to him," said Leo.

"I told him about being questioned when he told me about his wife's ultimatum."

"And he didn't offer to come forward for you?" asked Elena, thinking that was pretty tacky of the great chef.

"I'm sure he would have once he'd had time to think about it, but my mother—she's pretty upset about me being a suspect. I don't want her joining any more demonstrations. Maybe you could remind Mrs. Portillo that my mother isn't really up to—"

"Neither am I," interrupted Elena dryly. "Is that *Dr.* Sims?"

Lance nodded. "Bayard has a doctorate in French literature, although his cooking these days is usually Southwestern with unusual ingredients. For instance—"

"That's O.K.," said Leo. "You don't have to tell us about his menus."

"Christ!" he said when Lance had left. "I've never been on a case where you can't shut up either the suspects or the witnesses."

"What suspects?" grumbled Elena. "We're pretty much back to square one. Left with a thief or T. Bob Tyler, who swears he was at the center, or"—and she didn't believe this one herself—"or a serial killer."

• • •

"I have no idea what you're talking about," said Dr. Bayard Sims. "I was by myself on those dates. At my home in New Mexico."

"You don't know Lance Potemkin?" Elena asked, amazed.

"We may have met," said Sims cautiously.

"But he wasn't at your house Friday through Tuesday a week ago?"

"No."

"Great!" said Elena after she'd hung up. "Now what?"

"Kind of dumb for Potemkin to feed us this story if his alibi was going to deny it," said Leo.

"Telephone calls," Elena mused. "Let's see if they called each other. That'll be easy since Sims lives in New Mexico and Lance lives here in Los Santos."

"Worth a try."

"You do it."

"Why me?"

"Because I want to start a computer search."

"You and who else?"

"Me and Maggie Daguerre's instructions." Elena fished them out of her bag. "Unless you want to check for dead old men killed in their own homes while—"

"Not me. That's the dumbest theory I ever heard."

"My mother doesn't think so."

"Your mother isn't a cop. In fact, your mother, much as I like her, is kinda flaky. Auras, for God's sake?" Leo shook his head. "I'll take the telephone company."

26
..

Staring dismally at the computer screen, Elena picked up Maggie's instructions, accessed the central files, and entered her parameters. Crime: robbery/homicide. Victim: male, 62 plus. Scene of crime: victim's residence. Scope of search: five years. Maggie's suggestions for trying to find out where the wife had been were difficult. Maybe if there weren't too many cases, Elena could just scan each file.

The first case came up on the screen. Good lord! It was just three months ago. She read the patrolman's report and shook her head. The homicide had been committed in the projects on the far Westside, an elderly male Hispanic killed by a teenager who was in the act of stealing the victim's car, a 1978 Mercury with, as it happened, a dead battery. She rejected that case and punched *next*.

A year ago, Jose "Joe" Castro, a retired high-school principal, had been shot in his kitchen with a Japanese Nambu at approximately 2:30 P.M. while fixing himself a bourbon and ginger ale. Daytime drinker, thought Elena. Wife beaters were often heavy drinkers. The Castro murder was still an open file, no arrest. She scanned further. Robbery-homicide. She called up the next screen. A family ring and a watch given to the decedent on his retirement by the school system were missing, both presumed to have been taken off the body. The widow's name was Mercedes Castro.

153

Elena cross-referenced to Domestic Violence. No reports, which didn't mean there hadn't been any. Still, it would have been nice to have something clear-cut. She skipped back to the detective reports on the Jose Castro murder. Reading . . . reading . . . bingo! Mercedes Castro had been at the Socorro Heights Senior Citizens Center when her husband was killed. Excitement flowed through Elena's veins, something that rarely happened to her in front of a computer. Maybe there *was* something to the rumors. Two murders in one year. Both wives at Socorro Heights.

"Sanchez. Jarvis." Elena looked up at the sound of Manny's voice. "Shooting on the perimeters at Bowie." Elena poked her head out into the aisle. "You got anybody else, Sergeant? The Potemkin case just blew up in our faces, but I'm onto something else."

"What?"

"My mother's been telling me about other women at the center whose husbands have been killed in daylight robberies. Rumors about spousal abuse." Elena grinned. "Mom thinks it's divine retribution." This was a theory that Harmony had advanced on the drive home.

"Oh, right!" said Manny. "Do *you* think it's divine retribution? What do you expect to find? God in the computer?"

Elena shrugged. She didn't believe in divine retribution, but on the other hand, she didn't believe in big fat coincidences either. If any more of these murders showed up, she'd figure it was more than a coincidence.

"So what are we looking at?" asked Manny. "A serial killer based out of a senior citizens center?"

"I know it sounds crazy, Sergeant, but it's the only lead we've got beside the boyfriend—unless we get Lance back." But would Lance use Sims as an alibi if he hadn't been with Sims? The professor was probably lying to cover his ass with his wife.

Coming down the aisle, Leo heard the last sentence. "What's up?"

"Your partner's pursuing a case of divine retribution."

"The Potemkin case? The wife says God killed him."

"You want to take a shooting over at Bowie with Sanchez?"

"Sure. I'd rather go out with Sanchez than be in on accusing God. Concepcion would never forgive me. She'd figure she can't get pregnant cause I'm on God's shit list." He headed back toward Sanchez, who was talking to another detective where the two aisles intersected.

"Thanks, Sergeant," said Elena. "I've already found one killing that fits the pattern."

Manny rolled his eyes and left. Elena went back to the computer and took notes on the Jose Castro case. Hoping to interview Mercedes Castro, she wrote down addresses and telephone numbers for the family home, plus the son's place, then called up the next entry.

A year and a half ago an old man was shot in his home. The case was investigated as homicide but closed out as suicide. He had advanced cancer. Items reported missing by relatives turned out to be pawned to pay his medical bills, the last of which had been for an office-visit appeal to his doctor to give him a hundred sleeping pills. The doctor had refused. Elena shook her head. Poor old guy. He'd shot himself through the ear, blown his brains out all over the bathroom, and been discovered three days later by a neighbor lady soliciting for the American Cancer Society.

Elena called up the next file. Victim: Harold "Hank" Brolie. Shot in his home three years ago around one in the afternoon with a Smith and Wesson, case open. Stolen: a watch awarded him as Salesman of the Year for an independent insurance agency. The watch had probably been taken off the body. Elena nodded. Same as Jose Castro. But this one had a new wrinkle. Well, not new when you considered Boris. Hank Brolie's National Rifle Association shooting medals, usually displayed in a case in the living room, were missing. Medal theft number two.

Wife of the deceased: Chantal Brolie. Elena called up the detectives' reports. And smiled. Chantal Brolie had been— guess where?—at the Socorro Heights Senior Citizens Center. The whole afternoon. Dear God! There really might be a serial killer at work here. Chantal had been a French teacher in a local high school, retired at the time of the killing. Two high-school connections, thought Elena, Castro and Brolie. But not with the Potemkins.

She cross-referenced for domestic abuse. Three disturbing-the-peace calls phoned in by neighbors over a period of two years, but nothing a year prior to the murder. Elena bit her lip. The patrolman who answered one of the calls said the husband and wife claimed it was just an ordinary quarrel, maybe a little loud. Another noted that the wife had a bruised cheekbone and twist marks on her left wrist. She claimed a fall for the bruised cheekbone, burst out crying and wouldn't answer when asked about the wrist. Husband sullen and uncooperative, noted Officer Amalo Baile. The third officer smelled alcohol on the husband. Elena wrote down the names, addresses, telephone numbers, and parallels between the Brolie murder and the others.

"This is really creepy," she muttered and pulled up two more cases, the first an old man living alone in Sunset Heights. They'd cleaned out everything in his house. Neighbors had seen a truck and moving men but hadn't thought anything of it. It was a mind-your-own-business street. The body wasn't found for two weeks, until the mailman noticed an odor emanating from the mail slot and called the police. Newspapers piling up in the front yard might have been a clue, but nobody had investigated. One neighbor said he figured the old man had gone to visit his daughter in Carrizozo, maybe taken his furniture with him, although the neighbor couldn't explain why the furniture had been moved after dark.

The second was a murder-suicide over by the water-treatment plant. Husband killed the wife, then himself, although it had been investigated for a time as a double murder. Neighbors said the smell from the plant was enough to make anyone crazy.

Elena went out to lunch with a detective from Sex Crimes and had a salad, trying to ameliorate the effects of overeating during the bicycle-race weekend. At two o'clock she pulled up the death four years ago of Porfirio Cox. Since it occurred before the department began entering everything into the computers, there wasn't as much information, but it was listed as a daylight robbery-murder, unsolved, so Elena took the case number. She'd follow up by pulling the written files. The last one she could find that fit the pattern at all was Herbert Stoltz, another daylight robbery-murder. Porfirio Cox had a wife listed, Marcia Cox. Stoltz didn't. Still, Elena took down his case number and name.

She shut down the computer and headed for I.D. & R., only to be stopped by Manny, who said, "If you've got the time, Jarvis, we've got an agg assault at a pawnshop on Alameda, one Jesus Bonilla. Isn't he a buddy of yours?"

"No. Who did Jesus assault?"

"Someone assaulted him and cleaned out his gun inventory."

"Who'm I covering it with?"

"Me. We're out of detectives except for you, our computer wizard."

Elena made a wry face. "I'm just following Maggie's instructions, but I'll tell you, Sergeant, it's really getting weird. I've now got three old guys killed in the last three years, their wives all at the Socorro Heights Center when the deed was done."

"That is weird," Manny agreed. "I'll drive." The two went to the lot and hopped into an '88 Ford Escort, which had been turned over by the Mexican police, another of the hundreds of stolen cars that crossed the border weekly, but one of the few that ever came back. With all the identification numbers filed off, LSPD couldn't find the owner. The car was heartily disliked in the department because potholes and bumps, even the traffic humps at banks and schools, would turn off the fuel pump and leave you stranded until you delved under the carpet in the trunk to turn the pump back on. The Ford Company called it a safety feature that kept the car from catching fire after accidents; the detectives called it a pain in the ass and turned it in regularly to departmental mechanics for adjustment.

"I got two more possibles," said Elena, "but they're before everything went into the computer, so I'll have to look up the paperwork. You think I should chase it for more than five years?"

Manny wheeled out onto Raynor and headed for the inter-state. "Go with what you got now," he advised. "See how good it looks. If there really seems to be a connection, and that's hard to believe—I mean, what have we got here? Some nut who hates his grandfather, so he runs around killing old men every year or so. Anyway, if it looks good, we'll have I.D. & R. check it further back."

"Thank God," said Elena. "You wouldn't believe how many error messages I got just coming up with these cases."

"Sure I would," said Manny. "Everyone knows about you and computers."

They took the Paisano overpass to Alameda, where they found Jesus Bonilla insisting that he was not leaving his shop to go to the hospital no matter how big a lump he had on the back of his head. The *hijo de puta* pulled a gun on him, made him turn around, and whacked him with the butt. "Where are the police when you need 'em?" asked Jesus indignantly.

"You turned up anything on that czar's medal?" asked Elena.

"I been attacked and robbed, and you're worrying about some damned czar's medal. No wonder everybody hates the police."

Not everyone, thought Elena smugly, remembering Lydia Beeman. Just scumbags like Jesus Bonilla. By the time she and Manny got through taking Bonilla's statement, it was 3:45, too late to pull those I.D. & R. files and see if she could find two more Socorro Heights murders. Well, the last guy, Stoltz, had been a widower, so unless he had visited the center himself, he wasn't part of the pattern. If there was a pattern. Manny's joke about grandfather-haters wasn't going to fly. Someone in the center fingering houses for burglary? Nothing of great worth had been stolen. And the husbands had been at home. But the thief might have had some reason to think they wouldn't be. Maybe she should check for *successful* burglaries while the householders were at the center. The only other possibility was the spousal abuse factor and T. Bob Tyler or some other avenger of women. It worked for the Potemkins, for the Brolies. Nothing on the Castros. And one of the two remaining victims didn't even have a wife—well, not a living wife. His next of kin had been a son.

"That Maggie Daguerre is something else," said Manny.

"Right out of hospital emergency, with her leg in a fifty-pound cast, and she still wants to go to a barbecue and sleep in a tent."

"She's going home early today."

Manny looked alarmed. "Something wrong?"

"Mostly her captain," said Elena, grinning. "He doesn't like the cast. Thinks it's unprofessional."

"Yeah? Jesus," said Manny, "I thought it was a work of art. I never realized my kids had any talent that way."

They arrived back at headquarters, where Elena clocked out and headed for home, but the Potemkin murder was so curious that she wished it were tomorrow morning so that she could keep delving.

27
:.

Tuesday, October 5, 8:30 P.M.

Elena dragged a rocking chair from her bedroom into the living room so she could keep her mother company while Harmony was walking the loom. "That's really a great pattern, Mom," she said, examining the growing length of fabric.

"My patterns usually are," Harmony replied. "I don't know why that Lydia Beeman—well, we won't talk about her."

Elena stifled a grin. "What about Lydia?"

"It's just that I was beginning my weaving class—I have twelve ladies and two gentlemen—and I told them that weaving is a very practical skill. You can make fabrics for home decoration and for your own wardrobe. I mentioned this outfit as an example." Harmony gestured to her loose-weave overblouse and full skirt. The blouse had a high mandarin collar and wide, three-quarter-length sleeves. The deep purple fabric was banded at the sleeves and hem with rose and turquoise Indian designs. A silver concho belt inset with pinkish-red stones cinched the blouse at the waist. Elena hated to think what an outfit like that would cost in one of the Santa Fe boutiques. No wonder her mother was starting to make money. "So what did Lydia say?"

"She said my clothes are quite impractical because they aren't machine-washable, probably not even hand-washable."

"Well, I suppose it's true," said Elena.

"What does that have to do with anything?" Harmony

160

demanded. "There are people who don't even *have* washing machines. And most of my clothes *are* hand-washable. Comfort, color, beauty—those are the important qualities in clothes. The self-image they give you—"

"Mom, you'll have to admit that Lydia Beeman is the wash-and-wear type. She probably doesn't even wear skirts."

"She made remarks about my sandals too. Said I'd ruin my feet unless I switched to sensible walking shoes. There's nothing wrong with my feet!"

"I know, Mom. They're very pretty."

"*She* probably has ingrown toenails or bunions. That's why she wears those ugly lace-up shoes."

Elena sensed a real feud developing between her mother and Lydia Beeman, which was kind of unusual for Harmony.

"How's your investigation coming on the Potemkin case?" asked Harmony.

"Lance came in and told us that he'd been with some professor from the university the whole time."

"I knew it!"

"But the professor denies it."

Harmony looked astonished. "He must be lying."

"Quite possible," Elena agreed. "The man's married."

"What? To another man? I didn't know that was possible in Texas."

"It's not. He's divorcing a *wife* and wants partial custody of the children, so Lance didn't want to mention their—ah—weekend together."

"Well, of course he didn't. Very thoughtful and caring of him."

"We still have to question Professor Sims in person."

28
..

Wednesday, October 6, 9:00 A.M.

"Interviews this afternoon,," said Leo. "Two o'clock. Bayard Sims and Lance Potemkin."

Elena was getting ready to go downstairs for the backfiles on the Cox and Stoltz cases.

"Manny says you're making progress on the serial-killer angle."

Elena shrugged. "I'm keeping after it, anyway." She gathered up her notes and headed for I.D. & R., where she asked a clerk to pull the two files. Porfirio Cox first. The man had been shot by an intruder with a Russian Tokarev handgun in September, four years ago at around three in the afternoon. The intruder got in by knocking out a pane in the back door and unlocking it from the inside. The gun was never found. No fingerprints but the family's. A gold papal medal had been stolen, which Cox, a builder, had received for his donations of labor and materials to the Catholic Diocese of Los Santos.

Another medal. Was the killer a medal collector? Or just someone who liked to take a souvenir with him? Could you get anything from a fence for a papal medal? Los Santos was heavily Roman Catholic. She read on. There! The wife, Marcia Cox, had been at the Socorro Heights Senior Citizens Center when he was killed. Elena asked the clerk for a cross reference on family violence. Nothing turned up.

Her last victim within the five-year period—barely—was

Herbert Stoltz, a retired colonel. A widower. Killed around two in the afternoon. Murder weapon—an Italian Beretta Modello. Nice gun. Elena thought about the weapons. All World War II. Maybe. They didn't actually have the weapons to confirm the ballistics reports. No sign of breaking and entering, but there were a number of items missing, according to the victim's son: a Rolex watch—now that would bring some money, unlike the stuff she'd turned up on the other victims; a West Point ring—that too might be worth something; three military medals for valor. More medals. But no wife this time.

She began to read the detectives' reports. Lousy typing. They didn't have computers, so there were misspellings, X-ing-outs. "Oh boy," Elena breathed. No wonder this one didn't have a wife. He'd killed her.

Elena asked the clerk for the file on Frances Stoltz, and read slowly. Herbert Stoltz had shot his wife during a quarrel over her threat to file for divorce. He hadn't told detectives *why* she was filing, just that a man who had been married for almost fifty years had a right to expect that his wife would stick by him in his old age. So why hadn't he been in jail instead of at home where someone could ring his bell, walk in, and kill him? Suspended sentence. Elena called the D.A.'s office, got lucky. The First Assistant D.A. had tried the case himself and remembered it.

"He had a high-priced lawyer and a lot of character witnesses," said the A.D.A. "Everyone said this was a good man, driven temporarily nuts because his wife wanted to leave him for no good reason. Was that fair? his lawyer said. He's old and sick, no good to her anymore, so she wants to take off with half his pension. He had an all-male jury. They ate it up. Convicted him on the lowest count and gave him a suspended sentence in the penalty phase. What a crock! That was one mean old man," said Thaddeus Call. "Autopsy showed she had about five fractures—probably a battered woman, but the judge wouldn't admit that into evidence."

"No domestic violence records?" Elena asked.

"Not a one, and the family and neighbors wouldn't admit that he'd been beating her. Hell, the poor woman had had a

radical mastectomy. He probably hit her in the breast and
caused that too."

"Would you know if she went to the Socorro Heights Senior
Citizens Center?" Elena asked.

"Not that I remember. But I don't see that it would have had
any bearing on the case. She was home when he shot her. Oh,
and he got his. Someone shot him in the same house." The
A.D.A. sounded pleased about that.

Elena had been taking notes as he talked. After the call, she
bowed her head, fingers forced back through the thick black
hair that fed into her French braid. Another battered wife—
murdered, in this case; another daylight robbery-murder; medals
stolen, jewelry off the body. She'd have to start interviewing
survivors and people at the center. Survivors first. If the
murderer was at the center, she didn't want to tip him off. There
weren't a lot of men over there. She'd have to ask her mother
about the two taking the weaving class. And she particularly
needed to find out more about T. Bob Tyler. But what was the
killer's motive? Did he think he was some sort of knight—
rescuing elderly princesses from their abusive princes?

"How'd my instructions work?"

Elena looked up to see Maggie Daguerre swinging down the
aisle on her crutches. "Pretty well. Mostly because I ignored
the complicated stuff."

Maggie laughed. "You want to do lunch, as they say in the
business world?"

"Do lunch? You mean like go somewhere where they serve
cocktails and appetizers and—"

"No, I mean like pig out on Mexican food—any place they
don't have stairs."

"You're on." Elena collected her notes, slung her purse over
her shoulder, and preceded Maggie out of I.D. & R. "Are you
and Manny an item?" she asked.

"I don't know. His kids like me now, but that doesn't make
him any taller. Maybe if he'd grow—four or five inches; that
would do it."

Elena laughed. "I don't think there's much chance of that.
You'll have to shrink."

"No way. Not for about forty years. Not at all if I drink this stuff your neighbor in Chimayo gave me—Joaquina. Some herbal tea that'll keep me young and gorgeous forever and stop my leg from aching."

"Or give you terminal diarrhea," muttered Elena, remembering Sarah's experience with Joaquina's potions.

"All I can say is I hope it works on the young and beautiful part, because it didn't do shit for my leg."

29

Wednesday, October 6, 2:00 P.M.

Bayard Sims and Lance Potemkin met in the reception room at Crimes Against Persons. "Sorry, Bayard," said Lance, glancing at the woman behind Sims. "But since she already knows, I couldn't see letting them continue to think I killed my father."

Elena, who was with Lance, watched Sims turn brick-red.

"Professor Sims, if you'll come this way," said Leo.

The woman behind Sims said, "Where he goes, I go. I'm his lawyer, not to mention his wife."

Carmen, the receptionist, was staring at Mrs. Sims with horror. Carmen looked like a shampoo ad, with a glowing, luxuriously curled head of hair; Mrs. Sims looked like she had a rusty wire brush on her head.

"His lawyer?" asked Leo. "He's not a suspect."

"I suppose you're the boyfriend," said Mrs. Sims, eyeing Lance. "Well, we'd better head for that room with the tacky early American couch and thrash this out."

Lieutenant Beltran, who had been briefed on the progress of the case just an hour before, strode into the reception area and said, "The suspects will be questioned separately."

"Suspects?" snapped Opal Sims. "Neither one of these men did anything—except break the sodomy law."

Carmen's mouth dropped open.

"Opal," muttered Professor Sims, looking pained. He was a

stocky man, handsome in a distinguished, graying way, but shorter than his wife.

"I believe in calling a spade a spade," said Opal Sims.

Lloyd Booker, a black detective in Sex Crimes, who was entering the reception area at that minute, said, "Some of us spades take that amiss, ma'am."

"I'm not surprised," snapped Opal Sims. "Nothing pisses me off more than this politically correct racial and ethnic sensitivity crap. Now, can we get on with this interview?"

Elena had now placed Opal Sims as a tough criminal defense counsel, easily pissed off in court, as well as elsewhere. "Is Professor Sims going to back up Lance's alibi?" asked Elena.

"Whatever he has to say, we're interrogating them separately," said Beltran.

"I'll tell you what," said Opal. She fished in her purse and came up with a notepad, ripped off a sheet for Lance and one for her husband. "Just write down the span of time you were together out at Bayard's tedious country place, then note any time that you weren't in each other's presence while you were at the house. You don't have to say what you were doing because that would be self-incrimination."

"Look, lady," roared Beltran.

"Don't 'look-lady' me," Opal Sims snarled back. "I'm appointing myself counsel for Potemkin too. Now, write!" She glared from her husband to Lance. "You cops can compare what they have to say."

Lance looked taken aback to find himself, willy-nilly, represented by the wife of his lover, the woman who had insisted that they part company. Elena, who was enjoying the scene immensely, managed to keep from laughing out loud because she could see that the lieutenant was furious. Sims sat down, took a cookbook from his expensive soft leather briefcase and, using it as a writing surface, began to jot things down. Lance turned and used the reception counter to make his notations.

"Great hair," said Carmen. "Are you really gay?" Lance nodded and added some more notes to his written testimony. "Too bad," said the receptionist. "Is that a perm or natural curl?"

"Natural," said Lance.

"Shit," said the receptionist. "Who cuts it for you?"

"Mrs. Pargetter, the secretary in Electrical Engineering."

"You're kidding? An amateur?"

"No," said Lance. "She's faster on a computer keyboard than I am, and that's saying something."

"Great," said Mrs. Sims. "Then you can type Bayard's new cookbook. I sure as hell don't want to."

Lance gave her a look, added one last item, and handed his paper to Elena, who read it over. Sims handed his to Leo.

"I don't care what those papers say," muttered Beltran.

"Oh, don't be such a grouch, Lieutenant. I got my husband in here; I told him he had to tell the truth except where he needed to take the Fifth. Now read the damn accounts of their time. I've got a deposition at four. You screw that up, I'll file suit against the department. Wouldn't be the first time."

Beltran gave her a fulminating look and compared the two schedules. Before he could comment, Opal Sims strode off toward the large interrogation room, leaving the others little choice but to follow her.

"You're both swearing to these?" Beltran asked angrily.

Opal plunked herself down on the blue polka-dot couch. "You sit here, Bayard," she said, patting the cushion beside her. "You can sit over there, Potemkin," she said to Lance, pointing to a chair beside the table. "We don't want any hand-holding here. You may not have killed anyone, but you two could get yourselves arrested for—"

"Opal!" grated Bayard Sims.

"Oh, all right, but it was your idea to turn bisexual, not mine," she snapped. "And don't think you're ever getting back in my bed. I'm not risking AIDS."

"I don't have AIDS," muttered Lance.

"Who said I wanted back in your bed?" snapped Sims.

"Right, you want *him*. Well, O.K. It's not as if I ever enjoyed fucking with you, Bayard. It's just too bad you didn't find out you were gay *before* we got married."

"Shut up," shouted Beltran. "We're not interested in your—"

"This is called negotiation," Opal interrupted. "You cops ought to try it. You'd save the taxpayers money. I'd be one of the savees if my husband didn't insist on living out in the boondocks growing a bunch of goddamned grapes and vegetables. I'd a hell of a lot rather eat frozen stuff than something that just came out of a garden with bugs and dirt all over it."

"Always the philistine," muttered the chairman of Gourmet Cookery.

"Philistine, schmilistine. I'm pulling down three hundred thou a year. That buys a lot of Eggs McMuffin."

"I can't believe you said that, Opal. Have you been eating Eggs McMuffin when you could be home having Eggs Benedict?"

"Ah—Professor Sims, counselor." Elena tried to sound tactful but firm.

"O.K.," said Opal Sims. "Here's my offer. No divorce. We stay together for the kids. If I feel like sex, I'll find my own partners. As for you and Potemkin, since it turns out he's not a murderer—"

"That has not been established," said Beltran.

"For God's sake, check the statements. They were with each other. Anyway, as long as you're discreet, you two can get back together."

"I accept," said Bayard Sims, all smiles.

"I don't think so," said Lance quietly.

"It does *look* as if Potemkin is in the clear," muttered Beltran. "On the other hand, Sims lied once. He could be lying again to save his—his—" Beltran obviously had a hard time using the word *lover* in reference to two men.

"His sweetie?" suggested Opal Sims maliciously.

"Lance, I know you're angry because I lied, but you have to understand—the children, the scandal. Our relationship is too precious to let—"

"Could you talk about this somewhere else?" Beltran looked as if he might throw up. Elena, however, thought it was one of the best shows she'd seen in C.A.P.

"Of course," murmured Bayard Sims. "Lance, perhaps we could—"

"There's nothing to talk about."

"*Lance!*" Sims had gone pale. "The way is clear. Our future, within the bounds of discretion—"

"No."

"I beg you—"

"Oh, lighten up, Bayard," said Opal Sims. "It's only sex."

Elena had been comparing the statements of the two men. "I'd have to agree that you're off the hook, Lance," she said kindly. She didn't blame him for dumping Sims. Who, male or female, would want to have a lover with a wife like Opal?

Beltran frowned. "I'm not completely—"

"So they'll both take lie-detector tests," said Opal impatiently.

"They're not reliable," said Lance.

"Christ, what a worry wart! Even if you fail, it's not admissible in court."

"I'm the one they think murdered someone," said Lance stubbornly.

"You can count on my testimony," said Sims.

"What? At a trial?" Lance looked horrified.

"Well, I'm out of here," announced Opal. "Come on, Bayard. You have to pick the kids up at school. If we didn't live in goddamned New Mexico, they could take the bus."

"Am I free to go?" asked Lance as the Sims left.

"Go on," muttered Beltran.

"I've got a new lead, Lieutenant," said Elena when Lance had closed the door politely behind him. "It's kind of weird. Looks like maybe the Potemkin murder was done by a serial killer."

"Nonsense," said Beltran. "Sometimes I think *you're* weird, Jarvis."

"Well, I'm my mother's daughter," she replied cheerfully. She could see that he was about to protest, so she added quickly, "But I promise I won't start any demonstrations in front of headquarters."

Beltran stamped out.

"You want to hear what I've dug up, Leo?"

"Sure." Leo began to practice a tap routine, fortunately without the tap shoes.

"You're going to dance while I'm talking?"

"Yeah. And let's start the cameras going in the other room.

I can take the tape home and check out my routine for the talent show. You could make a few notes. Tell me what you think."

Elena groaned.

"I can listen and dance at the same time." He rushed into the next room, started the camera, returned, and bowed to the one-way window.

"Well, I've got five cases that fit the pattern."

Leo did a slick buck and wing, then tapped gracefully around an imaginary cane. "How's that?" he asked with a flourish.

"Great. The really interesting one was five years ago. This guy killed his wife and got off. The other four wives were at the center when their husbands died. What do you make of that?"

Leo, tapping away madly, didn't answer.

30

∷

Wednesday, October 6, 4:42 P.M.

Elena got home from her shift to find Harmony weaving in the living room and Jose Ituribe repairing the love seat. At the large window that looked out on the front yard, Juanita Ituribe was perched on a kitchen step-stool, measuring. Her position looked so precarious that Elena dashed across the room and grabbed Juanita around the waist.

"You shouldn't be climbing ladders," she cried. "What about your knees?"

"I'm fine," said Juanita. "I've had four Ibuprofen since breakfast."

"The Ituribes are here to help me with your living room," Harmony explained as she started a new row.

Juanita jotted a number down on a pad of paper, retracted the long, flexible arm of the metal tape measure she had been using, and said, "If you'll let go of me, dear, I can climb down. I'm doing your draperies," she added, taking a seat on the step-stool.

"And I'm doing the upholstery," said Jose. "*Que lastima,* what a mess you've got here, but your mother's made almost enough fabric for me to do this love seat—shouldn't take me more than two days."

"Are you and Juanita up to this?"

"Of course we are," said Juanita. "I worked in the pants

172

factories for years. A few draperies won't be nuthin' for me. They'll be a—how do you say it? A wind for me."

"A breeze," said Jose.

"Anyway, lots more interesting than putting in them studs on jeans. I've done some bartacking in my day. And if your mama weaves you up some more of the material, I can make you matching pants."

Elena smiled weakly. She couldn't see herself going to work in a pair of pants that matched the colors of her upholstery and draperies. Coral, Hopi green? No way. "Thanks, Juanita," she said tactfully, "but I can't afford the cleaning bills."

Jose said, "You're going to have the finest living room on the block, *muchacha*."

"I've had the most wonderful idea," said Harmony after dinner. "You're going to love it."

Elena groaned.

"I've signed us up for the police talent show."

"Mom, you're not a member of the department."

"I called Chief Gaitan this afternoon, and he liked the idea. We'll bill ourselves as the new Judds, a new mother and daughter sensation."

"Mom, this is a small talent show in Los Santos, not Nashville, Tennessee, and the Grand Ole Opry."

"Umm. Now, we have to decide on our numbers and start practicing. Where's your guitar?"

"I don't have it anymore."

"You sold it?" Harmony looked shocked.

"No, it disappeared. I figure Frank took it with him for spite."

"Did he?" Harmony looked rather grim.

"So you see, Mom," said Elena, feeling a lot less angry with Frank than she usually was, "you'll have to withdraw our names."

"Ummm," said Harmony and resumed her weaving.

Elena went to answer the telephone in the kitchen, taking her time, hoping she wasn't being called out, since she'd been planning an early night.

"This is Colin Stuart," said the pleasant, formal voice at the other end. "I'm checking to be sure that we're on for Saturday night."

"Oh." Elena had forgotten about that.

"I thought we'd go out for dinner and then some music."

"Fine," said Elena, hoping he wasn't thinking of anything classical, like the Los Santos Symphony. She'd sat politely through classical music at Sarah's apartment when Sarah was trying to inject a little cultural sophistication into Elena's life, but she could usually divert Sarah with conversation so the CD never got changed. Elena had a feeling there was no way she could manage to drag Colin Stuart out of a symphony at intermission, short of telling him she'd just developed acute appendicitis.

"I wonder whether you'd mind if we take Lance along?" Colin was saying. "He's offered to show us a few jazz places in Los Santos that *aren't* after-hours clubs."

"Oh."

"I guess that seems strange, inviting someone else along on our first date."

"Not at all," mumbled Elena, glad Lance was no longer a suspect.

"Poor Lance is feeling rather blue over this business about his father and—ah—other problems."

"Well, he's off the hook as far as the murder's concerned."

"I'm glad to hear that. Why don't you invite your mother? We'll make it a foursome. Shall I pick you up at seven o'clock Saturday?"

"Fine." Now she understood. Colin Stuart was actually taken with her mother, just asking Elena out to please Sarah. "Well, I'll see you Saturday." Elena shook her head as she replaced the receiver on the wall bracket. Amazing. Gaitan knew her mother was married. Colin Stuart, having met the sheriff, definitely knew it, but he still wanted to spend the evening with Harmony, in return for which Elena would get to spend the evening with a homosexual. Lance was nice enough, but if anyone from the department saw her, they'd say, "Poor Jarvis. She's reduced to dating gays. Can't get a straight date."

"Mom," she called. "That was Colin Stuart. He and Lance have invited us out to dinner and an evening of jazz."

"How thoughtful. Lance and I can talk poetry."

"Uh-huh." Elena figured that her mother's attention would be monopolized by Colin, and what the hell was Elena going to talk to Lance about? "Mom, if you don't mind, I'm really tired."

"Then I think you should go straight to bed," said Harmony.

"You do?" Elena looked at her suspiciously.

31
··

Wednesday, October 6, 8:45 P.M.

Harmony delayed forty-five minutes before digging out Elena's address book. Then she leafed through to "J" and called her daughter's ex-husband.

When a gruff, blurred voice answered, Harmony said, "Is this Frank Jarvis?"

"Who wants to know?"

"Harmony Portillo," she replied sharply. "Your ex-wife's mother."

"Mrs. Portillo? I didn't mean to sound like a shit—I mean—well, I was asleep."

"I'd like you to return my daughter's guitar," said Harmony. "If possible, please bring it to the house tomorrow afternoon. I'll be here by two o'clock."

"What? What?"

"The guitar you took when you moved out. I want it returned."

"Hey, I don't have—"

"Of course you do. Unless you've sold it. Have you?"

"No."

"Good. Then return it, please."

"Look, Mrs. Portillo, Elena's always saying crazy things about me."

"You mean like your coming into her house without her permission and playing tricks on her."

"Hey, I don't—"

"You're the person with a key."

"Not anymore," he muttered.

"There, you see. You could and did get in before she changed the locks. I saw you do it. Now Frank, I gave that guitar to Elena, and I don't see any sense in your having it. You don't even play."

"Maybe we could make a deal," said Frank. "If I could find the guitar. You know—look around the pawnshops. Probably someone stole it the night her place was broken into and trashed. She probably didn't tell you, but I took care of the guy who did it."

"That's commendable, Frank. So you're saying you *can* locate the guitar?"

"I might be able to, but I'd like you to do me a favor."

"What favor?"

"Well, Elena's got this restraining order. I can't even talk to her anymore, and I was hoping to get back together. Maybe you could put in a good word for me. Like tell her we ought to start dating again. I wouldn't mind dating. And then we could—"

"I'm not sure anything I say will help, Frank. It's your aura."

"My what?"

"Your aura. It's very bad. I noticed the day you let me into the house. My goodness, you project bad vibrations even over the telephone."

"What's an aura?"

"I suggest, Frank, that you go to a *curandera*. She might be able to help you with herbal medicines."

There was a silence. Then Frank said, "You mean one of those crazy old women who grind up weeds and—"

"The one I have in mind is a woman of great power. Whether or not you consult her, I'd advise you not to say anything unpleasant about her. She might put a curse on you."

"Yeah, right," said Frank and laughed.

"Well, that's my suggestion. You certainly don't have to follow it."

"Hey, I'll go. What's her name?"

Harmony gave him the name.

"Address? Phone number?"

Harmony provided those. She had visited the woman herself
just in case Joaquina, back in Chimayo, decided to take amiss
the scolding she'd received for giving Sarah Tolland that
purgative at the barbecue.

"O.K., listen, I've got it," said Frank. "You think this will
help me with Elena, right?"

"I really can't promise anything, Frank," said Harmony,
"and I don't think even the *curandera* can help you unless you
return that guitar."

"The guitar. Right. I'll look into it tomorrow. And the
curandera."

"You do that. A man with an aura like yours needs all the
help he can get."

"But you'll tell Elena I'm having my aura fixed? What is it?"

"The colors projected by your soul. Good night, Frank." She
hung up before he could say anything else. Harmony didn't
truly think the *curandera* could help Frank where Elena was
concerned. She wasn't even sure she'd want that, although
Elena had been evasive about why they'd broken up. Harmony
did believe in lifetime commitments, having contracted for one
herself and been very happy with it. However she hadn't
always been such a strong advocate of marriage, not when she
was a young woman who believed in free love, free speech,
and the freedom to smoke a little pot when she felt like it.

The important thing was that they'd get the guitar back and
win first place in the police talent show. Harmony was very
proud of Elena's voice. The girl could have been a second Joan
Baez. Humming "House of the Rising Sun," Harmony resumed
weaving.

32
··

As soon as she got to her desk, Elena called Socorro Heights to find out how long T. Bob Tyler had been on their rolls. Six years, they said. That put him within her time frame. Now if she could just take to heart the idea of an old cowboy as serial killer. Glancing across the aisle, she caught sight of Leo rising to leave.

"Where are you going?" she asked.

"Taking some personal time."

"What about interviewing the widows?"

"It's not as if talking to old ladies is a dangerous assignment. You can go on your own. I've got something important to do."

"Like what?"

"Like I'll tell you if I get it off the ground," said Leo mysteriously. "You're going to love it."

"That's what my mother said last night," Elena muttered, "and it turns out she entered us in the talent show. Fortunately, Frank stole my guitar."

"Too bad. I know you can't beat me, but I'd like to see you try." He ambled off, lanky and cheerful. Elena consulted her next-of-kin list. The telephone directory showed no number for Mercedes Castro, but the late Jose had had a son, and the directory listed seventeen Jose Castros.

On Elena's fourth try a surprised voice said, "I'm Mercedes Castro."

179

Elena introduced herself, explained that she was looking into the unsolved murder of Mercedes' husband, and asked for an interview.

"He's been dead a year now, and we told the police everything we knew when he was killed," said Mrs. Castro.

"Still, ma'am, there might be something we missed."

"Come over, then. I've just finished making *empanadas*. Maybe you'd like one with a cup of coffee."

"Thank you. That sounds wonderful." Elena loved the small fruit tarts so popular among Mexican-American families. Aunt Josefina had made them every Tuesday of Elena's childhood, and every Tuesday Elena had stopped by after school. "I'll be there in about half an hour."

She couldn't find a number for Marcia Cox, whose husband, Porfirio, had been murdered four years ago. However, Chantal Brolie, a widow of three years, was in the book. Elena called and left a message on an answering machine. Then she drove to the Upper Valley.

Surrounded by trees, flowers, and bushes, the Castro house had evidently received its water allotment from the canal, because the yard was flooded. To get to the front door Elena had to hop from stepping stone to stepping stone. The lush shrubbery concealed peeling paint on the window frames and front door. Rusted tricycles, wagons, and toy cars littered the porch.

Mercedes Castro answered the doorbell and ushered Elena into a cluttered living room, explaining that her son and daughter-in-law were at work, her grandchildren at school, and she hadn't yet found time to pick up. Elena had to work hard to keep the shock off her face. Mrs. Castro was dark-skinned with heavy, dark hair shot through with white and a good figure, but a terrible scar ran from the corner of her mouth across her cheek—deep, jagged, and disfiguring. Elena doubted that it had been stitched at the time of injury, but surely the poor woman could have gotten plastic surgery. Her husband would have had insurance from the school district.

If not for the scar, Mercedes Castro, who was probably in her sixties, would have been a beautiful woman. And how had she gotten that scar? Elena wondered. From the late Jose? If so, the evidence in this strange case was accumulating, the parallels doubling and redoubling. Mrs. Castro excused herself and went out to the kitchen. Elena moved a teddy bear and three coloring books off a wildly flowered chair and sat down. Mrs. Castro returned almost immediately with a tray containing *empanadas* on a blue-rimmed plate and coffee in matching stoneware cups. Elena recognized the pattern. Her supermarket had sold it last year at five dollars a setting with a twenty-five-dollar grocery purchase.

Taking a sip of her coffee, Elena said, "I understand you were at the Socorro Heights Senior Citizens Center when your husband was killed."

"That's right." Mrs. Castro put two *empanadas* on a plate and passed it to Elena.

"Do you remember what you were doing that afternoon?"

"How could I ever forget? That was the afternoon I lost my dear Jose."

Forking up a piece of *empanada*, Elena nodded sympathetically. Pineapple filling. Not her favorite, but the crust was delicious. Mrs. Castro plucked a Kleenex from a fake marble box on the coffee table, which was strewn with small plastic spacemen and brown flower petals from a bouquet of dying roses. The widow dabbed her eyes. "You were saying—" Elena prompted.

"Surely, you don't think I lied about being at the center?"

"No, I don't."

"Then why do you want to know what I was doing?"

Elena sighed. "I've discovered by going back through the files that at least four older men have been killed in their homes during daylight hours while their wives were at Socorro Heights."

Mercedes Castro looked astonished. "Jose was killed by a robber."

"Maybe, but nothing of great value was taken."

"The things were precious to Jose," the widow protested. Her hand was shaking, and the cup rattled against the saucer as she put it down. "They took the watch the school system gave him. The ring that had been in his family for many years. The Empress Carlotta gave that ring to an ancestor of Jose's, and his father brought it with him from Mexico when they emigrated. He was very proud of it."

Elena didn't know many Mexican-Americans who wanted to claim the patronage of the French colonialist government. "Did you ever talk about the ring at the center?"

"I—I'm not sure," Mrs. Castro stammered. Her fingers went to her cheek, touching the scar. Then she dropped her hand quickly. "You think someone at the center—because of something I said, someone—" Tears gathered in the woman's eyes.

"We don't know, but with four deaths, possibly five, we're trying to make connections, so if you could tell me who you were with and what you were doing that afternoon—"

Mercedes inspected her bright, shapely fingernails. Elena looked at the nails too, wondering if they were plastic, the kind stuck on at nail shops with trendy names. A friend had told Elena it cost forty dollars to get that done, and then your real nails developed fungus infections underneath. Yuck. She finished off her first *empanada*.

"I was playing bridge," said Mercedes Castro.

Two wives playing bridge when their husbands died! "Do you remember who your partners were?"

She shrugged. "Some Anglo women."

"You didn't know them very well?"

"I knew Portia Lemay because she was a realtor; she found this house for my son. The others, I don't remember. I didn't play much bridge."

"How did you happen to be playing that day?"

"I think—" She paused. "One of them had an appointment, and so—maybe, Portia suggested I sit in, and I agreed because she was a nice woman, and she got my son such a good price on this house." Mercedes nodded. "But I felt sort of uncomfortable. Anglo strangers—and me with—" She touched the scar again. "I guess it's silly to be embarrassed, but afterwards I was sorry that I'd agreed to play. If I'd been home, maybe Jose, my husband, wouldn't have been killed."

Two widows who had sat in! "You don't remember the names of the other women?" Elena decided against mentioning the names of Dimitra's bridge partners. If there was a connection to the bridge group, and she couldn't imagine what it would be—Portia Lemay, Margaret Forrest, Emily Marks, and Lydia Beeman, co-conspirators with a serial killer? A bizarre idea. Still, if there *was* some sort of connection, she didn't want to screw up her case by suggesting testimony to a witness. Thinking of Dimitra, she asked, "Did you ride with any of the women—there or back?"

"No. I drove Jose's car. If I hadn't, he might have gone out himself, and then—" Mrs. Castro blinked back more tears.

"Do you remember anyone else who was there that afternoon? T. Bob Tyler, for instance. Do you know him?"

"The *ranchero*?" Mercedes smiled through her tears. "That one is such a flirt. Always calling me pretty." She flushed. "Before. When I *was* pretty."

"Was he there that afternoon?"

Mercedes didn't remember.

"I have another question, and I hope you'll answer me truthfully. Mrs. Castro, before the death of your husband"— Elena heard the front door open and hurried on—"were you a battered woman?"

"What?" Mrs. Castro looked confused, even frightened.

"Did your husband ever abuse you, hurt you?"

"What kind of a question is that to ask my mother?"

A slender man, late thirties or early forties, stood in the doorway. He looked tired and grumpy; his chinos and sport shirt were wrinkled. Shift-worker, Elena guessed. "We're investigating the death of Mrs. Castro's husband," she said to the newcomer.

"My *father* was the victim," said the man angrily.

"My son, Jose, Jr.," said Mrs. Castro, her fingers twisting in her lap.

"A whole year you haven't solved my father's murder, and now you come around upsetting my mother."

Very defensive, thought Elena. "We're following new leads."

"What do new leads have to do with the question you asked my mother?"

Elena said quietly, "Other men have died under much the same circumstances as your father. There's reason to believe that their wives might have been abused."

"Mother wasn't," said the son.

Elena reached out to take Mercedes' hand. "Is that true, ma'am?"

Mrs. Castro snatched her fingers away. "It is as my son said."

"Again, I hate to ask rude questions, but that scar on your face—how did you—"

Again Mercedes' hand rose compulsively to the scar, the slender fingers and beautiful fingernails covering it. "Just an accident," she said, brown cheeks flushing.

"What kind of an accident?"

"A kitchen accident," snapped Jose.

"Please let your mother speak for herself."

"It's as my son says."

"My mother was always clumsy with knives. Now, why don't you leave? Can't you see you're upsetting her? She still hasn't recovered from my father's death."

"That's true," said Mercedes. Tears slipped down her cheeks as the son stood glowering.

Elena sighed. If there were secrets here, she wasn't going to get them from the mother or son. She'd have to try the neighborhood where Mercedes and Jose had lived before his death. "Thank you for your time," said Elena, rising.

The son looked smug. Why? Because he'd gotten rid of Elena without giving anything away? She left, checked for the address of the old family home, which was in East Central, not that far from her own neighborhood. It would take twenty minutes to get there. She drove out of the water-soaked Upper Valley onto Doniphan and from there to the freeway, which took her around the mountain to the other side of town. As she drove, she thought about Mercedes Castro's face and couldn't imagine any scenario involving a housewife and a kitchen knife that would produce a scar like that.

33
..

The Castros had lived in a square, two-story brick house with a columned veranda set high off Copper Street. A fancier neighborhood than Elena's, but probably just as old. It had been only a year since the murder. There should be neighbors who remembered things about the family.

Elena tried the house next door but found no one at home. On the far side, a short, slender woman in her middle forties answered the door. She was wearing a navy blue suit and matching pumps.

"Yes?" she said impatiently.

Elena identified herself and explained that she was investigating the murder of Jose Castro.

"*Him*." The woman made the word into a curse.

An interesting reaction. This lady didn't seem to think the death any great loss. "I'd like to talk to you about the family for a few minutes, ma'am."

"I wasn't even at home when he was killed."

"I wanted to ask about his wife."

"Well, if you think Mercedes killed him, you're wrong. If he'd killed her, I wouldn't have been surprised, but she'd never have killed Joe."

Elena's attention sharpened. "Maybe you could tell me about that."

"Oh, all right, come in. I'm Harriet Upchurch." They walked

185

across a polished wood floor highlighted with a figured runner whose primary color was dark red, then through double doors into a living room furnished with Duncan Phyfe pieces. Elena recognized the style, because she'd been required to take a fine arts course in college. Since she registered late that semester, Rock Music, 1954–1974, was full. Art appreciation courses were closed except for—yuck!—Interior Decoration Through the Ages. Elena had learned more about furniture she didn't like than any sensible person should be expected to know. Mrs. Upchurch's living room did have handsome French doors that led out onto a side patio sheltered by ivy-covered trellises.

"That's lovely," said Elena, admiring the setting and the white outdoor furniture with ivy-printed cushions.

"Yes," Harriet Upchurch agreed, "but I've had to replace the furniture several times, and those doors are another target for thieves. They've been broken open twice in the last four years, but I don't suppose you deal with burglaries. Your card said 'Crimes Against Persons.' Not that I don't feel pretty personal about having my house burglarized. What was it you wanted to know?"

"You said Mr. Castro might have killed his wife. What did you mean?"

"Men like that—they hurt their wives for a while, years even; then they kill them."

"And you think Mercedes Castro was a battered woman?"

"I know she was. Good lord, I think the man beat her up every Saturday night. He was a drinker. One night a week he'd get drunk and go after her. And she adored him. Can you imagine? I told her she ought to leave him, go stay with her son, but she wouldn't. Probably the son thought it was O.K.—what his father was doing. Then I said she should go to a shelter. She said, 'How would that look? For a high-school principal's wife to go to a shelter?' I said, 'How does it look for a high-school principal to be beating up his wife?' Have you seen her?"

"Yes."

"Then you saw that scar. You know how she got that? He backhanded her. He was wearing this huge, ugly ring. Some ancestral thing. It made a terrible gash in her cheek. She didn't even go to a doctor or a hospital. He probably told her not to."

"You know for sure it was his ring that scarred her?"

"Oh yes. After he did it, he stormed out of the house, knocked down my trash cans driving away. I went straight over and found her in the kitchen bleeding into the sink. She tried to tell me she'd cut herself with a knife. I should have called the police then and there, but as it turned out, I didn't have to."

"What do you mean?" asked Elena.

"He's dead. The bastard wouldn't even consider plastic surgery for her face. Mercedes was a real beauty and a sweet woman. Of course, I never see her anymore. Does she look as bad as ever?"

"Pretty bad," said Elena.

"That means the son wouldn't let her have surgery either. Anyway, about a month or six weeks after the ring incident, someone went into their house and shot him. I thought, when I heard, 'There is a God after all.' " Mrs. Upchurch nodded her head vigorously. "Not only did He see that Mercedes was out of the house so no one could blame her for Joe's death, but He sent some lowlife good Samaritan to kill the man. Couldn't have happened to a more deserving victim."

Mrs. Upchurch wriggled uncomfortably on the sofa, her spine upright but not touching the sofa back. "I don't know why I'm telling you all this. I kept my mouth shut at the time. I knew that Mercedes would be embarrassed if anyone knew what she'd been through with him. I hope you're not planning on making trouble for her at this late date?"

"No, ma'am." Elena thought of the widow with that dreadful scar, evidently keeping house for her son and his wife. "Poor woman," she murmured.

" 'Poor woman' is right. Mercedes was so proud of her looks. She didn't have much else. Her rotten husband was always telling her what a dummy she was, and she believed it. Then he destroyed her face and had the nerve to go around the neighborhood telling people it served her right for being so clumsy, and he wasn't springing for plastic surgery. I'd say he got just what he deserved."

"Sounds like it," said Elena.

"Well, a sensible policeman! I suppose it's because you're a woman. If I'd told any of this to those detectives who came around last year, they'd have dragged poor Mercedes off to jail, even though she had an alibi."

"Was there ever any talk of Mercedes having an—admirer?" Elena was thinking of T. Bob Tyler.

"You can't be serious. Joe would have killed her."

"Is there anyone else on the block who knew what was going on with the Castros?"

"Hmm. Maybe not anyone who'd talk about it. You just caught me in a moment of indignation or I'd have kept my mouth shut. It won't help her to tell the police now. He's dead."

"We might catch his murderer."

"Who cares?" Then Mrs. Upchurch reconsidered. "Oh well, you might try Arthur Fallon, across the street and two houses down. The place with the green shutters. I always thought Arthur was sweet on Mercedes, at least since Clara died. Not that he did anything about it," she added hastily. "And don't get the idea that Arthur killed Joe. Arthur left town right after Joe slashed her. Probably couldn't stand to see the wound. Went up to Connecticut to visit his son. He felt terrible when he got back. Mercedes had already sold the house and moved out. He didn't even get to say goodbye to her."

"Thanks, Mrs. Upchurch," said Elena, standing. She was anxious to get to Mr. Fallon.

"Oh, good lord." Harriet Upchurch looked at her watch and said, "I'm going to be late for my lunch date." Elena and Mrs. Upchurch left the house at the same time, Mrs. Upchurch dashing to her car on spindly legs. Elena took a leisurely walk down the street to the house of Arthur Fallon, where she showed her badge and explained her errand.

"What do you want me to say?" murmured Arthur Fallon, ushering her into a living room that had probably once been very handsome but was now covered with newspapers, magazines, and *TV Guide*s. He had a soap opera playing but flipped it off as if he were embarrassed to be caught watching. "I wasn't here when Castro died."

"I want to ask you about the relationship between the victim and his wife. Your neighbor, Mrs. Upchurch, said you knew them."

The tall, stoop-shouldered man with thin, graying hair narrowed his eyes anxiously. "Mercedes was at Socorro Heights when it happened. That's what everyone told me when I got back."

"I know," said Elena.

"So why do you want to know about them?"

"I'm trying to find out how she got that scar."

Arthur Fallon winced. "What did Harriet tell you?"

"That Castro cut her with his ring."

Fallon nodded. "That's what everyone in the neighborhood believed. I didn't see it happen, and she didn't tell me, but I—I'll swear I saw dried blood on that ring the next day at church. He made her go to church. Looking like that. She had the edges of the cut taped together with Band-Aids, and he was talking about how clumsy she was, cutting herself on the cheek."

"You saw blood on the ring?"

"He was waving his hands around, and that ring had—it looked like rust in the carving around the stone. But the setting was silver; silver doesn't rust. The stone was red too, maybe a ruby. He said it was. If so, it was poor quality. A muddy color."

Elena made notes. If Castro left the ring uncleaned, he must have been pretty sure his wife wasn't going to accuse him—neither she nor anyone else in the neighborhood.

"I never understood how he could treat her that way," said Arthur Fallon sadly. "Such a beautiful woman. My wife told me—this was years ago, before Clara died—that he'd come home from school and shout at Mercedes, accuse her of having affairs. The man was crazy. Mercedes was a virtuous woman. A good Catholic. She deserved better."

"Do you yourself know of any abuse, Mr. Fallon? Not gossip but—"

"Bruises. She always wore long sleeves, but we were having a block party one night, and Mercedes was lifting a pot of beans. Her sleeves slid back, and I saw the bruises. And she knew I'd seen. She turned red and left the party early. The poor woman was ashamed. And for something that wasn't her fault."

"Anything else?" Elena asked. She hated to quiz him, to remind him about the unhappiness of a woman he'd obviously cared for.

"Black eyes. She claimed she couldn't get used to her bifocals and ran into things, but the truth was she never wore them except for reading and driving, and no one saw her run into anything. There was a broken arm once. Harriet said that Mercedes claimed the dog had tripped her. I hope she's doing well at her son's. Have you seen her?"

"Yes," said Elena. "She fed me some wonderful *empanadas*, but she said her husband never abused her."

Arthur Fallon sighed. "She would say that. Even now she's defending him."

"Why don't you visit her, Mr. Fallon? I'm sure she'd appreciate a call. She's home by herself out there in the Upper Valley with everyone at work or school. She must be lonely. Away from her old neighborhood and friends."

"Do you think I should?" He looked eager and hopeful.

"I really do," said Elena, hoping that her suggestion would generate happiness, not trouble.

34
##

Elena headed for her cubicle with the intention of typing in reports on the interviews with Mercedes Castro, Harriet Upchurch, and Arthur Fallon before she went out to lunch. She had discovered things, significant things. She just wasn't sure yet what they meant. A few feet from her desk, she stopped short. "What are you *doing* here, Mom?"

Harmony swung Elena's chair around from the lighted computer screen. "Amusing myself until you got back. I thought maybe you'd like to go out for lunch. I'm buying."

"Wonderful," said Elena, "but you shouldn't be using the police computer."

Harmony laughed, tossing her hair back over the shoulder of her deep rose blouse. "Well, you don't have a typewriter or a computer at home. No wonder you don't write very often."

"Frank took the typewriter with him."

Harmony frowned. "Something needs to be done about him."

"That's why I got the restraining order."

"Anyway, I was typing in some recipes for you." Harmony handed Elena a small pile of printouts.

"When did you learn to use a computer?"

"Just now. It doesn't seem too difficult."

Elena groaned. Everything about computers seemed difficult

to her, but her mother had evidently mastered the art in fifteen minutes.

"By the way, I've sent for an herb garden. It will fit in your kitchen window and provide you with all the medicinal and culinary herbs you need."

"Come on, Mom! I don't have—"

"And it won't take any time. Just water it while you're fixing your own dinner, then clip the herbs and follow these recipes. They're mostly herb teas—for insomnia, headaches—"

"O.K., O.K." Elena accepted another handful of printouts, folded them and stuffed them into her large handbag. "Where do you want to go to lunch?"

"I have one more to type."

Because she had reports of her own, Elena agreed and used Leo's computer while her mother labored across the aisle. Then, since Harmony was still staring at the screen, Elena went through her messages. Ah! Chantal Brolie had returned her call. She dialed the number and reached a lady with a delightful accent. The widow had taught high-school French, a language Chimayo schools hadn't even offered. "What time would be convenient for you?" Elena asked after identifying herself and her reason for calling.

"Two-thirty," said Mrs. Brolie pleasantly. "This is a secure enclave, so I'll tell the guard to expect you." Elena hung up and turned back to her mother.

"Done," said Harmony and zipped the recipe from the printer. "Sergeant Escobedo was telling me about a place where they have *salpicon*. You know we don't make that at home. I'd like to try it."

"That would be on the Westside near the university or way up northeast off the interstate on the access road. Either one's a long way."

"Now Elena, I'm sure Manny won't mind if you take an extra few minutes."

Elena threw up her hands and said, "Which did he recommend, Julio's or Casa Jurado?"

"Both," said Harmony, "so you can pick whichever one's closer since you're in a hurry."

"O.K., we'll take Brown over the mountain to the Westside.

The interstate's bound to be pretty crowded. And I'll drive," she added. Before her mother could object, Elena had to take another call.

"Detective Jarvis?"

"Yes."

"This is Michael Futrell. We met at the bicycle race."

"Oh sure." The good-looking criminology professor.

"I'm sorry to call you at work, but your home phone isn't listed."

"Most cops' aren't."

"Of course. Look, I wondered if you'd like to go out Saturday night."

"On a date you mean?" she asked, surprised. She'd decided he wanted to interview her, not date her.

"Well, yes. On a date. Is that against the rules?"

"No, but—well, Saturday?" Shoot! She was tied up with Colin Stuart, Sarah's ex-beau. "I'm afraid I already have plans."

"O.K." There was a pause. "Well, goodbye." He disconnected before she could say that she'd like to have gone out with him. Now he'd probably never call again. Elena hung up and went to the car with her mother.

"Who was that?" asked Harmony. "It sounded as if you were turning down a date."

"It was Michael Futrell, the—"

"—criminology professor. He seemed like a nice young man. Why would you—"

"Because I'm going out with you and Lance and Colin Stuart, Sarah's hand-me-down."

"Well, you could have asked for a rain check. I hope your experience with Frank hasn't soured you on marriage, Elena. No matter how Grandmother Portillo feels about divorce—"

"Mom!"

"I won't say another word," Harmony promised. "Let's see. What shall we talk about that won't set you off. Ah! Today I suggested to my weaving class that we have a sixties fashion show. I thought it was a wonderful idea, but it seems that they aren't interested in the sixties."

"They probably remember those years with horror."

"Oh, surely not. Anyway, they voted for a regular fashion show. And then that Lydia Beeman—do you know what she said? She said she didn't object to a fashion show because, in her opinion, older women should pay attention to their appearance as well as their health, but she refused to wear heels. She said high heels are the American equivalent of Chinese foot-binding, and whatever outfit she wore in the show, she'd wear sensible walking shoes with it. Isn't that something?"

"Well, Mom, you're always wearing sandals—or boots. I don't know what you're complaining about."

"Sandals can be dressy. So can boots," said Harmony loftily. "Lace-up walking shoes don't go with anything but slacks, and not even dressy slacks."

Elena grinned and accelerated from the Murchison light.

Harmony exclaimed over the houses in Kern Place on the other side of the mountain. At Casa Jurado on Cincinnati she said, "Just order me the *salpicon*," and went off to examine the paintings for sale, not to mention the neon cactus at the cash register and the thick stained-glass windows inset in the front wall.

"Delightful," she said to the owner and introduced herself. Elena had to lure her back to the table for lunch.

"I think Leo's idea is absolutely charming, don't you?" said Harmony once they were seated.

"What idea?"

"He hasn't told you? You didn't notice the article in the paper this morning?"

"I didn't see the paper. You had it."

"Well, I'd have shared. Leo is organizing a Tap Night for Los Santos. It's something your friend Sarah Tolland told him about. The idea is that all the Los Santos tap dancers will gather at the Main Library downtown and tap their way to San Jacinto Plaza."

"Wonderful," said Elena.

"Isn't it? I happen to know quite a bit about the plans because Leo's wife called him, and I took the call."

"Mom, you're not supposed to answer Leo's phone."

"Well, I did. Unfortunately, Concepcion's very upset. The

article listed his home telephone number, and seventy people have called there to sign up."

"Oh lord," said Elena. "Does she still have the flu?"

"She does, poor thing. Imagine taking all those calls when you're feeling terrible, aching in every joint, throwing up. I'm going to take her a nice herbal tea as soon as I get back to the house."

"You do that, Mom." Here she was pursuing a serial killer, getting all sorts of crazy information that had to mean something, and Leo was organizing Los Santos' first Tap Night. Wait till she got her hands on him.

"It's to be Saturday," said Harmony. "Naturally, we'll want to go."

"What time?"

"Eight in the evening."

"He wants to go tap dancing downtown after dark? When the library closes, that area's a hangout for prostitutes."

"Well, Leo's a policeman. I'm sure he can take care of it. We'll have to call Colin and Lance. We'll need to eat dinner before or after the event."

"Ummm." Elena wondered how Colin Stuart would feel about attending Tap Night.

"Concepcion said Leo left this morning talking about television coverage."

"He might just get it. They'll put anything on the weekend news programs."

"Yes, doesn't it sound exciting?"

"I can hardly wait," said Elena dryly, trying to picture gangly Leo and seventy other Los Santoans tapping their way from the Main Library to San Jacinto Plaza, possibly trailed by flamboyant transvestite prostitutes. Too bad the city no longer had alligators in the plaza pool. With all that tapping, the creatures would probably leap out of the pond and attack the dancers, getting Leo and Tap Night on the national news as well.

35
..

Thursday, October 7, 2:30 P.M.

Mrs. Brolie lived in Casitas Coronado, well up the mountain on the Westside. When Elena entered the apartment, it *looked* expensive. The living room ceiling soared two stories, with track lights and lovely pictures hung at odd but pleasing intervals up and down the high north wall, and they sat on an immense white sofa that curved around a large marble coffee table. Chantal Brolie was not beautiful, not young, but she was beautifully dressed.

"Lovely place," said Elena.

"Yes." Mrs. Brolie looked around with pleasure. "My husband, being an insurance salesman, was heavily insured. When someone killed him, I got it all."

Elena considered the notion that Hank Brolie had been killed for his insurance. "I'm looking into your husband's death and several others, Mrs. Brolie. I found in the reports that you were at the Socorro Heights Senior Citizens Center when it happened."

"Yes, I taught a French class there once a week. I was a French war bride many years ago, you see."

"So when Mr. Brolie died, you were teaching a class?"

"No, playing bridge."

Bingo! "Did you do that regularly?"

"As seldom as possible," said Mrs. Brolie dryly. "I was sitting in for someone that afternoon."

Widow number three—sitting in. "Who?"

She looked thoughtful. "Some friend of Margaret Forrest's. Margaret was our accountant for ten years or so before she retired. Hank's taxes were fairly complicated because he had a lot of business deductions."

"And Mrs. Forrest asked you to play?"

"Whether she asked me or I offered, I couldn't say."

"And the other members of the foursome?"

"There was a funny little woman named Emily. I'm afraid I don't remember her last name. But she was a terrible player, worse than me, and my husband always said I was hopeless."

Emily Marks, thought Elena. "And the fourth woman?"

"I remember her very well. Portia Lemay. After Hank was killed and the insurance companies paid off, Portia found me this condo." Chantal glanced at her home contentedly. "The previous owner had died, and the family wanted to get the will through probate in a hurry, so she got me a very good price. Can I offer you a glass of wine?"

"No, thanks. I'm on duty."

Mrs. Brolie picked up a crystal decanter and poured white wine for herself. "I've always been very grateful to Portia for finding me this place. And she helped me sell the old house, which I didn't want to stay in."

"Why was that?" asked Elena.

"Bad memories," said Chantal Brolie.

"Of spousal abuse? The computer turned up several domestic-violence calls involving you and your husband."

"But none the year before he died," said Mrs. Brolie bitterly. "After the police came the third time, Hank found a new source of amusement that didn't make any noise to alert the neighbors or leave any bruises to alert my friends."

"You were a battered woman?"

"Yes. Whoever killed Hank did me a favor."

"What happened that last year before he died?"

Mrs. Brolie stared bleakly through the sheer draperies beyond which the rugged, looming presence of the mountain was like a mist-shrouded dream. "We played Russian roulette. He'd put a bullet in the gun. He'd spin the chamber. Then he'd put the gun against my head and pull the trigger."

Elena shivered.

"Or he'd hold my hair and point the gun at my eye. He told me people shot through the eye had been known to live, but they wished they hadn't." She was trembling and had to set her goblet down on the green-veined marble table. "That happened about once a month. I don't know why I'm not dead." She picked up the wine again. "There must have been some higher power looking out for me."

Elena nodded encouragingly.

"Then he decided I wasn't terrified enough, so he put two bullets in the gun, spun the chamber, and pulled the trigger twice. He said next time it would be three bullets and three shots. I went to pieces that month, waiting for him to kill me. And he was building up to it, accusing me of being unfaithful."

Her mouth twisted wryly. "While I was working, he thought I was having affairs with the principal and various teachers in the school. When I retired, he was sure every time I went grocery shopping I was on my way to an assignation. Of course, I never had any affairs. I'd have been afraid to. But Hank—Hank thought because I was French, I must be prowling for *l'amour*. That's what he called it. And his French was execrable."

"What happened?" asked Elena, thankful once again that she'd divorced Frank after the first attack.

"He died," said Chantal Brolie. "Someone shot him. Can you believe it? I couldn't. For a month I thought he'd show up and say it had been one of his tricks, that now he was going to finish me off. It wasn't until I moved that I finally began to believe I could live my life out in peace." She took another sip of her wine. "Now I even go out with gentlemen friends."

"Is T. Bob Tyler one of them?" Elena asked quickly.

"The cowboy?" Chantal laughed. "He's like a character in one of your Western films. But I wouldn't *date* him. I prefer—oh—more sophistication. Hank is probably watching me from the grave, seething every time I accept a social engagement. But he needn't worry. I won't remarry. Because, you see, I thought Hank was the sweetest man I'd ever met, the kind American soldier who gave me food and silk stockings, after the war when we French were starving. And he wasn't

rying to seduce me. Hank wanted to marry me." She shook her
head. "Women are so easily fooled. Or maybe it's that men are
so cunning."

Elena mulled over this story. "Did you ever tell anyone what
was happening to you? A friend? Maybe someone from the
center?"

"About the Russian roulette?" Her eyes became distant as
she thought back to that time. "Margaret and I had lunch
together about once a month, and the last time, the time he put
the two cartridges in and pulled the trigger twice, I called her
the next morning and told her that I couldn't keep our luncheon
date. Margaret didn't argue, but she came over. Hank had left
to play golf, and Margaret found me crying. She fixed me *café
au lait*, she defrosted croissants—I hadn't had any breakfast—
and she got the whole story out of me.

"Isn't that strange? I'd forgotten. I guess she's the only one
I ever talked to. She offered to call the police or take me to a
shelter, but I knew if she did, there'd be one last game of
Russian roulette. I remember she said it was a wonder I'd
survived, that mathematically, I should have been dead already.
At three bullets and three shots, she didn't think I had a chance.
I told her I'd try to decide what to do.

"But of course, I didn't do anything. After years of my
husband getting drunk and violent, hurting me, telling me that
I could never get away from him, that he'd kill me if I left, I'd
stopped believing I could escape. I went to a psychiatrist for
several months after his death because I couldn't sleep. I still
thought he'd be coming after me." Chantal Brolie spread her
hands and smiled lightly. "Well, it's over now, isn't it? Does
that help you?"

Elena nodded.

"You think his death had something to do with the way he
treated me? Margaret was the only one who knew, except for
the police, and they didn't do anything. Neither did Margaret;
she was with me at the center when he died."

"Would she have told anyone?"

"I hope not."

But Elena wondered. Women gossiped. Rumors might have
reached T. Bob. Mrs. Brolie thought of him as a character in a

Western. Maybe he saw himself that way—the gallant sheriff, protecting womanhood from the bad guys. "You don't by any chance know a woman named Marcia Cox, do you?" asked Elena. It was a long shot, but she hadn't been able to find Porfirio Cox's widow.

"Of course I do. Or I should say, I did. I met her when I moved in here. It's strange, you know. Someone shot her husband too. Porfirio Cox. He was a builder. Very wealthy."

"She lived *here*?"

"We were neighbors."

"You keep saying *were*."

"Marcia died last year. She had a stroke." Mrs. Brolie sighed. "I still miss her. Marcia moved in from a big place up on Rim Road. Her husband was killed while she was at the center too. We often commented on how strange that was. Such a coincidence."

"Was she a battered woman?"

Chantal Brolie looked surprised. "If she was, she didn't mention it, but then he was dead by the time we became friends."

"Did she seem to—well—mourn his death?" Elena knew that didn't necessarily mean anything. Mercedes Castro mourned her husband.

"No, I can't say that Marcia seemed to miss him. In fact, was a very happy woman. She relished every day as if it were a new source of delight. I thought the world of her. It's such a tragedy when someone like that dies, someone so happy."

"Do you know how she happened to move into Casitas Coronado? If she was wealthy and had a place on Rim Road, one would have thought she'd want to stay."

"Yes, but a big house is a lot of work, even if you have maids, which I'm sure she did. Portia found a condo for Marcia too and sold the house on Rim Road. If I remember correctly, Marcia said she got close to a million for it. Imagine that! I got a hundred and ten thousand for mine, and I considered myself lucky. Portia is a wonderful realtor. Everyone comes out of her deals feeling that they've had the best of it."

Elena nodded. More and more connections. "What was Mrs. Cox doing at the center the afternoon her husband was killed?"

"I've no idea."

And the real estate connection. Were husbands being killed off so Portia Lemay could get the fees for selling their houses and finding their wives new places? The commission on a million dollars would be a hell of a lot. Were Portia and T. Bob in league?

Elena thanked Mrs. Brolie and, having said goodbye, took one last look at the beautiful condominium purchased with the insurance money of a man who liked to play Russian roulette. Then she looked at the happy, tranquil widow. Maybe Harmony was right. Maybe God did have a hand in setting these women free, giving them a decent end to lives that had been painful and frightening.

36
..

Friday, October 8, 8:00 A.M.

Elena reread photocopies of the Porfirio Cox and Herbert Stoltz files. In the robbery/murder of Herbert Stoltz five years ago, one of the items stolen had been a Tokarev, a Russian sidearm, which had never been recovered. Stoltz had been killed with a Beretta Modello. All those World War II weapons, she thought. Porfirio Cox, according to Ballistics, had been killed with a Tokarev. The one stolen from Stoltz?

Elena shook her head and glanced across the aisle. Because Leo wasn't in, she went to Manny Escobedo's office to ask if her usual partner was out on another case. "He's taking a day of vacation," Manny told her.

"Tap Night?" she asked, laughing.

"What do you mean?"

"Leo's organizing a big meeting of tap dancers at the Main Library downtown. They're going to tap their way to San Jacinto Plaza, waving flashlights." There'd been another story in the paper this morning, mentioning the flashlights and banners that various dancing clubs and schools planned to carry as part of the festivities. Local restaurants would be selling their specialties at the plaza. The food sounded great; Elena wasn't so sure about the event itself. Maybe Colin and Lance would want to snack at the various booths. Elena had loved doing that at the yearly Los Santos Festival before they stopped serving beer and then canceled the whole thing.

"You think Maggie would be interested in going?" asked Elena's sergeant.

"Beats me." Elena sat down across from Manny and gave him the information she'd accumulated: the possible connection between the weapon stolen from Herbert Stoltz and that used to kill Porfirio Cox, all of the men killed with World War II handguns; the fact that Chantal Brolie, Mercedes Castro, and Dimitra Potemkin had all been substituting in bridge games at the senior citizens' center when their husbands were killed; that the late Marcia Cox had been a member there; that three of the women had been battered.

"Dimitra broke her hip a month or so before the murder. Rumor has it that her husband pushed her downstairs. Mercedes Castro has a terrible scar on her face where her husband backhanded her wearing a big ring, then refused to pay for plastic surgery. A year before Hank Brolie's murder, he started playing Russian roulette, with his wife as an unwilling participant. Not only that, but she told one of the bridge players at the center about it. Frances Stoltz's autopsy showed enough fractures to indicate battering, and her husband killed her. Two of the women's houses were sold and condos found for them by Portia Lemay, another of the players. That's too many coincidences, don't you think? And all the women knew T. Bob Tyler, the guy with the history of assault."

Manny Escobedo mulled over the information. "Too many coincidences," he agreed, "but a senior citizen serial killer? That's crazy."

Elena nodded. "And there are a lot fewer men at that center than women. I took their male membership list and ran it through the computer. T. Bob's the only one I could find with a record of violence."

"Are you saying you've ruled out a female as your killer?"

"How many female serial killers have you read about?" she asked. "Do you know of any in our files?"

"Not many to the first question, none to the second. Well, keep after it."

"I will. I'm going to check Porfirio and Marcia Cox today. With both of them dead, I'll have to locate relatives or neighbors. The Castro woman and her son denied that she'd been abused. Two neighbors told me about that scar."

"Good work," said Manny. "Think I'll call Daguerre, see if she wants to go to the tap dancing thing. She's got a heel on her cast now, so she's off crutches."

"Maggie'll love the food, all sorts of booths with ethnic stuff. You gonna take your kids?"

"What time does it start?"

"Eight o'clock."

"Sure, why not? Can't last more than an hour. I can get 'em home in time for bed. And they like Maggie now, don't you think?"

"In spades. She let them paint all over her cast. They may get her fired, but they like her."

"Her captain's not gonna fire her. We'd have the O.E.O all over us."

"I guess I'll go out on my own today. I really don't need a partner on this."

She went back to her desk, jotted down names and addresses, and headed for the parking lot. She had a lot of people to see, but this case was more interesting than the drive-by shootings or spouses nailing each other with whatever weapon came to hand.

She thought as she pulled out on Montana that it would look great on her record if she solved this one and closed four or five homicides at once. Maybe she'd take the sergeant's exam next time around. Being a sergeant meant more responsibility and more money. Wouldn't Frank hate that? She grinned, thinking she didn't owe him any favors—except for the guitar. Its disappearance meant she wouldn't have to perform with her mother in the talent show.

Not that she didn't miss the guitar sometimes, she admitted as she took Cotton to Murchison, passing the hospital. It was nice, when you'd had a hard day, to sit out on the back patio and play a little, sing a little. Her neighbors liked it too. They'd come out to listen. Elena smiled. It was a neat neighborhood, especially now that Boris was gone. She hoped Dimitra wouldn't sell the house to scumbags.

Had Portia Lemay come around and suggested that Dimitra

move into a condo? Elena didn't see Dimitra in a condo. Of course, with the hip, trying to take care of a house and yard would be difficult, but Lance would pitch in now that he was welcome at home again. He seemed like too nice a guy to let his mother struggle on her own.

A lot of kids, once they had their own places and lives, tended to forget their parents existed. Elena admonished herself to do better about writing and calling home. Not that her parents lacked for company. Maria was the only other Portillo to leave Chimayo, and she was just down in Albuquerque at med school. Elena wondered if Maria would return to practice medicine in the Sangre de Cristos. Johnny, Josie, and Two still lived in Chimayo, along with the grandchildren, but they probably got more help from Elena's mother and father than they gave.

She put the Taurus into the steep uphill climb toward Rim Road. Of course, even her seemingly-ageless parents would get old someday. The prospect made Elena feel blue. Not that she'd mind having her mother live with her. It had been great having her in the house this last week, even if she was a little weird. But Harmony, when she got old, wouldn't want to move to Los Santos. She'd want to stay where she was, with family and neighbors.

Elena chuckled. Grandma and Grandpa Waite couldn't understand it—their bright daughter dropping out of school, marrying a small-town lawman, a minority person (that's how they referred to Ruben), living with a bunch of Hispanics in a tiny village. Grandpa Waite had complained about it with his dying breath, and Harmony just laughed, tears in her eyes, and kissed him. Elena remembered that day.

Grandma Waite didn't come to Chimayo, saying it was too hard to get to for an old lady. Instead she paid Harmony's way to Marin County with any children and grandchildren she might care to bring along. Grandma Waite was kind of a pill, but it had been fun to visit. The bookshelves had been full of sexy novels, which Elena could never have bought or read at home, but she read them under the covers with a flashlight when she was a kid at her grandmother's house.

She didn't understand how her grandparents could complain

about Chimayo. Marin County—yuck—yuppie heaven even before anyone knew what a yuppie was, and they were always having disasters: water shortages, fires, floods, earthquakes. Elena wouldn't live in California if they paid her.

She swung left onto Rim Road and parked in front of the house where the Coxes had lived four years ago. Man, they must have been *rich*! The house looked like it had about twenty rooms. She turned to look out over the city. What a view! Imagine seeing that every day. She savored it for a moment, then turned back to a neighbor's house.

37
··

Friday, October 8, 10:05 A.M.

A maid answered the door, looking like an Aztec maiden incongruously clad in a black uniform with a white apron. Elena introduced herself, showed her badge, and asked to see the lady of the house. She spoke first in English, then in Spanish to be sure she got her message across, making clear that she was not *la migra*, the Border Patrol.

"*La mujer policia?*" asked the maid, dubious. "*La señora* eez having breakfast an' don' like to be eenterrupted."

Elena insisted. Looking resigned, the maid left Elena at the door and disappeared down a hall paved in gray-green flagstones. Elena wondered how much they cost. Her living-room floor would look great with this kind of flagstone, and maybe some Navaho rugs. Not that she could afford a Navaho rug. She wondered if Harmony could make one. The maid appeared at the end of the hall and beckoned to Elena. She was taken to a sunny breakfast room with windows on three sides, looking out on a beautifully landscaped yard. Good grief! These people must pay hundreds a month in water bills to keep enough moisture on that kind of shrubbery.

The owner, angularly thin, deeply tanned, wearing a peach kimono with exotic, hand-painted Japanese designs, nodded Elena to a chair. Her hair was blond, a nice color but probably not natural, waved back from the face. The hairdresser who cut and set it undoubtedly charged more than Elena's monthly water bill. She sat down on a bamboo chair with peach- and green-flowered cushions, across a bamboo and glass table from the lady of the house.

"Would you care for a cup of coffee?" the woman asked.

Because the coffee smelled so exotic, Elena nodded and introduced herself.

"Conchita, *café au lait* for *la mujer policia, por favor.*" Conchita went off to get a cup and saucer while the woman introduced herself as Lucia Barbieri.

The name Barbieri rang a bell with Elena. She thought he'd been the mayor of Los Santos ten years ago. There had been some big fuss about his having thrown city contracts to a friend in construction. Could the late Porfirio Cox have been the beneficiary? The scandal was before Elena's time, but Frank had pointed out Barbieri was an example of local skulduggery among the well-to-do.

"Mrs. Barbieri, nice to meet you," said Elena.

Conchita returned with a china cup and saucer so translucent, Elena could see the maid's fingers through it. The coffee was poured from a matching pot, and Elena took an appreciative sip. "I'm investigating the murder of your neighbor, Porfirio Cox."

"That's years ago, and I assure you my husband had nothing to do with it, no matter what problems Porfirio may have caused us in the past." Mrs. Barbieri cut a small piece from her serving of French toast, chewed it, and said, "I'm surprised to find the police following up on a case that old." She sipped from her own cup. "I myself wasn't home the day Cox died. Neither was Anthony, my husband. He wasn't even in Los Santos. But I can assure you, it caused a lot of anxiety here on Rim Road. Our first murder, at least since I've lived here.

"Let's see. What else? Porfirio was a dreadful man. I never understood why Anthony liked him. Of course, we were all pleased for Marcia."

"Pleased?"

"That he was dead," said Mrs. Barbieri.

"Mrs. Cox didn't care for her husband?"

"Who knows?" said Lucia Barbieri with a delicate shrug.

"She stayed with him. I guess she must have felt something for him. Or maybe she was just afraid to leave."

"I see. Could you explain that?"

"Well, I don't like to tell tales, but Marcia spent her life covered with bruises. She never said anything, never complained about him. Lovely woman. Dead now, unfortunately."

"You're saying she was a battered wife?"

"She had the classic signs. Sunglasses at night. Long sleeves when the weather was hellishly hot, dark hose in summer. Sometimes she wouldn't answer her door when you knew she was at home. Goodness, woman, didn't you see *The Burning Bed* or any of those specials?"

"I know a fair amount about it without watching TV."

"I suppose you do. Crimes Against Persons, you said? I myself saw a burn on her hand once. Ugly. I asked how she got it. I suppose that wasn't very tactful. She said it was a grease burn; she'd got it frying chicken. Well, I ask you! Marcia never fried chicken. She had a cook to do that. I doubt if they even *ate* fried chicken. He was part Hispanic—his·mother. Hispanic women don't fry chicken. And Marcia was a Yankee. From Providence, Rhode Island. Yankees don't eat fried chicken."

Mrs. Barbieri dabbed her mouth with a linen napkin that matched the upholstery on the bamboo chairs. "That was a cigarette burn, perfectly round, just the right size. And Marcia didn't smoke, but Porfirio *did*. Not to mention the fact that he was a mean person. I'm a bit of a detective myself, don't you think?"

"Yes, ma'am," said Elena, finishing her coffee.

"So there you are. Battered woman. Of course, in a neighborhood like this you don't hear screams or people slamming against walls, so there's no excuse to call the police. And the neighbors wouldn't like it if you did. Nobody wants police cars and flashing lights right on the street."

Mrs. Barbieri poured herself another cup of coffee. "Porfirio had a terrible temper. If someone set him off at the country club, he'd shout and curse, act like he was going to get physical. He *was* accused of assault by two of his workers. He bought them off, of course. I will say he never hit anyone at a party, but I'll bet he hit Marcia as soon as they got home."

Elena had taken out a pen and notebook to jot down Lucia Barbieri's remarks.

"The two of them met in architecture school at Rice University in Houston," she continued. "I'll bet she wished she'd never gone *there* to study. They both got degrees, and he became an architect and contractor here in Los Santos—this was his home town—but he never let her practice. Always bragging about how talented she was, but he didn't want any wife of his working. Wives were supposed to stay home. Dreadful man. Well, I *am* going on. And I don't suppose that's even what you wanted to know."

"Actually, that *is* what I wanted to know, Mrs. Barbieri. Were you questioned by the police at the time of the murder?"

"Of course."

"Did you mention anything like this to them?"

"*They* didn't ask. You asked, so I told you." She eyed Elena narrowly. "The police don't really care about domestic violence. Well, I can tell you I wouldn't let my husband treat *me* that way. I'd leave. I'd have him in jail before he could say boo."

Elena nodded but wondered if Mrs. Barbieri really had any idea what it was like to live with a violent man. Putting him in jail, leaving him—either could be a surer way of getting killed than staying.

"Marcia was a fool to put up with it," said Mrs. Barbieri.

Lady, you ought to talk to Chantal Brolie before you go around passing judgment, thought Elena. "We know that Marcia Cox didn't kill her husband, that she was at the Socorro Heights Senior Citizens Center on the day he died."

"Oh yes, the center. I never could understand why Marcia kept going there. They weren't really quite her class of people."

"Did she say what she was doing there that afternoon?"

"Playing bridge. Can you imagine? If she wanted to play bridge, there are plenty of us here on Rim Road who'd have been delighted to accommodate her."

"Did she belong to a regular bridge group at the center?"

"No, I think she was sitting in for someone. It was the first time I ever heard her mention playing bridge there. She *knew* the game but didn't play much. Probably too embarrassed to show up wearing sunglasses, afraid her bruises might show. Do you know, one time I saw her with missing teeth. The two front ones on top — gone. She got a bridge, of course, but she looked terrible for a few weeks. She said she'd fallen and knocked them out. I didn't believe *that*! He probably hit her in the mouth. Dreadful man. He was always talking about some medal the Pope gave him. As if we cared about the Pope."

"Did she say who she was playing with that afternoon?"

"I wouldn't remember names of people I'm never likely to meet socially."

"Was there ever any talk that she was seeing a man at the center?"

"A lover, you mean? Surely not."

Elena heard a distant ringing. The maid came in, plugged a green telephone into a wall jack, and handed the receiver to Lucia Barbieri. "Hello . . . Melanie? . . . How lovely to hear from you. Hold on." She put her hand over the receiver. "Was there anything else?"

"I guess not. Thank you."

"You're welcome. Conchita." Mrs. Barbieri waved a graceful hand, indicating that the maid should show Elena out. "Melanie, I hope you're calling to tell me that you did well on your first round of tests . . . You haven't had any tests? My goodness, you've been there over a month . . . Oh yes, sorority rush. I'd forgotten. . . ."

That was the last Elena heard as she followed Conchita over the gray-green flagstones. "*Gracias*," she said as the maid opened the door.

"*De nada*," replied the young woman politely, and then Elena was outside, looking once more across the urban vista. She went to other houses along the street but gained only one more interview, this with Philburn Cross, a retired lawyer, a prissy-looking man of seventy-five or eighty. He said, "People of our class don't abuse their wives."

Elena doubted that he actually believed that. Still, she'd got good information from the Barbieri woman. Marcia Cox *had* been abused, and now Elena knew that four out of four widows had been playing bridge at Socorro Heights when their husbands were killed—as substitutes, not regulars. Good lord, she thought, and went over in her mind the women of the bridge group with whom two of the incipient widows had played: Margaret Forrest, Portia Lemay, Emily Marks, and Lydia Beeman. A conspiracy of senior citizens to eliminate abusive husbands? To protect battered wives? She couldn't imagine any of those women killing anyone. Or hiring a hit man. But they might have passed information on to Tyler. With or without realizing what he did with it. Was he also using the bridge players to provide alibis for the soon-to-be widows?

38
##

Friday, October 8, 12:35 P.M.

After lunch downtown at a sandwich shop, Elena went to the Los Santos *Times* to read obituaries and clippings in their library. Marcia Cox had no relatives in Los Santos at the time of her death, but Porfirio had two brothers and a sister, whose names Elena took down. If they were still alive, she'd interview them about the relationship between their brother and his wife. Then she looked up the obituaries of Frances and Herbert Stoltz. The couple had had a son and daughter, neither of whom lived in Los Santos. Herbert Stoltz was a military man, graduate of West Point, officer in the Second World War, the Korean War, winner of medals for valor.

Elena nodded. Those had been stolen at the time of his death. She thought back over her list of victims. Porfirio Cox's papal medal had been taken; so had Hank Brolie's N.R.A. medals, Jose Castro's Empress Carlotta ring and school district watch, and Boris Potemkin's czar's medal. It was as if the murderer had been stealing their claims to recognition, their accomplishments or the accomplishments of their ancestors. But so far the missing medals were the only things she had to connect Herbert Stoltz to the others, except for the time, setting, and nature of his death, and the type of weapon with which he'd been killed. Not that the weapons were all the same, but they were all thought to be World War II side arms, none recovered.

Possibly war souvenirs. Had T. Bob Tyler fought in World War II?

She read more of the obituary. Herbert Stoltz had been active in the V.F.W. after his retirement. So had Boris. Elena wondered if they had known one another and if Tyler had belonged to their post. Stoltz was a volunteer in the United Fund drive, member of the Los Santos Historical Society, seemingly a good citizen—except for the killing of his wife.

She began reading about the death of Frances Stoltz. Not a whole lot here that she hadn't found in the police report. The husband's lawyer claimed that Herbert Stoltz had killed Frances in a moment of anguish because she was planning to leave him. Nowhere did it say why she wanted to separate. The lawyer said Colonel Stoltz planned to kill himself after he killed her but had had a "cerebral incident"—did that mean a stroke?—out of which he emerged unsure of what had happened. He'd called the police himself to report his wife's death. There was a trial, and he got probation.

In the obit of Frances Marshall Stoltz, Elena struck gold. Frances had been a graduate of the Arland School in Los Santos, a private girls' school. Elena remembered her mother saying that all the women in the bridge group had gone to a private girls' school in Los Santos. Probably the same one from which Frances graduated. They must have known one another, Elena thought, excited. She didn't know exactly how old the other women were, but Frances, had she lived, would have been in her mid-seventies now, which was what Beeman, Lemay, and Forrest looked to be.

Frances had been active in children's causes, the Red Cross—and there it was! She had been a member of the Socorro Heights Senior Citizens Center. The adrenaline surged through Elena's veins. Next of kin—Herbert Stoltz; a son and daughter, Paul and Tabitha Stoltz, and a sister—bingo! Emily Marshall Marks. Emily, the youngest member of the bridge group, had been Frances' sister. Emily, who had told Elena that Lydia Beeman took her into the group after the death of her sister, with whom Lydia had been lifelong friends.

Could those two, Lydia and Emily, have got together to exact justice from Herbert, then gone on to see that other men were stopped before they could murder their wives as Herbert had killed Frances? Had Margaret and Portia, longtime friends of Lydia and Frances, looked on Emily, the bereaved sister, as a sister of their own? Had they been in on it too? A conspiracy of old ladies? But had they done the shootings themselves— one going off with a gun while the others protected the abused wife by engaging her in a bridge game? A sort of neighborhood watch program for widows? Good lord, it was as strange as anything Elena had ever run into.

Or had they used T. Bob Tyler? At the protest, Tyler had attacked a cop because he thought the patrolman was trying to hurt Emily. Maybe he had been in love with Emily— unrequited because she was so crazy about her husband. Only in the last two years had Tyler transferred his affections to Dimitra, his dancing partner, whose company he lost when Boris pushed her down the stairs. Another motive for murder in a man obsessed with women. But that didn't explain the other murders.

Elena returned the clipping files to the newspaper librarian and had material pulled on the brothers and sister of Porfirio Cox, then went to her car. Her next step was to interview the Cox family, of which Porfirio had been the eldest sibling. The next oldest was Arnoldo Cox, who owned a printing company on Texas Street.

"I'm looking into the relationship between your late brother and his wife," she said, once she'd talked her way past his secretary and introduced herself.

"I don't see that that's any of your business," said Arnoldo, scowling.

Elena scowled back. "Did he abuse her?"

"Of course he didn't. Marcia hasn't got any complaints coming. Did she say something to the police?"

"She's dead," said Elena.

"I mean before she died. The woman got every cent he had and then, stupidly, moved off Rim Road. If she'd held that house another ten years, it would have been worth a million and a half."

"I take it you didn't like Marcia."

"She was all right. Snobbish. Came from back East. Anglo.

Porfirio would have done better to marry like I did. Someone like our mama."

"Uh-huh."

"While you're looking into his murder, maybe you'll find that medal from the Pope. As the eldest surviving brother, it should go to me. Give me a call if you find it."

For the next brother, Carlos Cox, she had to leave her car and gun with customs at the border because Carlos was an executive in a *maquiladora* that made electronic parts. She took a cab into Mexico.

"I don't know," said Carlos. "He may have hit her a few times. So what?"

"Often, would you say?"

"It's a little late to arrest him for abuse. The man's dead. Never speak ill of the dead; that's what our mother always said."

"I'm trying to find out why he was killed," said Elena.

"Well, it wouldn't have had anything to do with Marcia," said Carlos. "She was playing bridge when he got shot. Can you beat that? Porfirio made more money than all of us put together, and some petty thief breaks into his house and shoots him. And you people didn't have a clue. Four years and we still don't know who killed him. Well, I'd say the trail was pretty cold. I hope you're looking for that papal medal. The family would like to have it."

"If we find it, we'll certainly return it," said Elena dryly and had his secretary call her another cab. She reclaimed her car and gun, then went looking for Porfirio Cox's sister, Anna Maria Maitland, who owned a small advertising agency housed in one of the fine old houses on Montana, houses now filled with lawyers' and doctors' offices and places of business.

Anna Maria Maitland was up to her elbows in layouts and insisted that she didn't have time to answer questions about a brother four years dead. The office reeked of cigarette smoke, with two cigarettes burning in the ashtray, although only one person occupied the room. Mrs. Maitland looked as if she'd been tanned by her own smoke, with lustrous black hair pinned up in an elaborate chignon that covered the back of her head.

"We've got deadlines here," she said. "Why are you asking me about Porfirio at this late date?"

"What I'm really asking about is his relationship with his wife, Marcia."

"She's dead too. Died of a stroke a year ago."

"I know that, Mrs. Maitland. Do you think your brother abused his wife?"

Anna Maria Maitland picked up one of the cigarettes, inhaled deeply, and squinted through the smoke at Elena. "What's your idea here? You think maybe he beat her up because she had a lover and the lover killed him? I suppose it's possible. Porfirio had women, plenty. He was a very attractive man. And rich. But he wouldn't have liked it if Marcia got a little on the side, though I'm surprised to hear she did."

"There's no evidence of that. Did you hear rumors?"

"No. So what's this about?"

"My question is fairly simple. To your knowledge, was your brother abusive to his wife?" said Elena slowly.

"To my knowledge," mimicked Anna Maria Maitland, "I don't know anything about it. Marcia and I didn't get on. I never saw her except for holiday dinners at Mama's. And I didn't say word one to Marcia when I did see her. Why should I? Women who sit around doing nothing, letting their husbands support them—that doesn't do anything for me. I divorced young and started my own business." She had been studying a layout as she talked and suddenly drew a big X through it.

"You ought to be able to identify with that, Detective. Having a career of your own, I mean. Of course, my mother's never considered me divorced, but that's neither here nor there, so if Porfirio was beating up Marcia every night of the week, I wouldn't know it. It's not something he's likely to have told me over lunch." She pulled another layout on top of the first.

"How come you're investigating his death now? I always heard if the murder isn't solved within forty-eight hours, you can forget it." She stubbed out one cigarette and picked up the second.

Elena shrugged.

"Well, listen, since you're looking into the case again, maybe you'll find that papal medal. If you do, I'd like to have it. Porfirio always told me he'd leave it to me in his will. So just give me a call if you find it."

"Mmm," muttered Elena and went on her way. She glanced at her watch as she walked toward the car. It was four-thirty, and she should have been off duty a half hour ago. Tomorrow she'd try to find some of the Stoltzes' neighbors. She'd done a lot better with Cox neighbors than with the Cox family. As she started the car, she wondered if Leo would be at headquarters. She'd like to talk over her latest discoveries with him. Of course, he might have gone home, or he might be out organizing his tap-dancing extravaganza.

As Elena entered the department, she stopped to say hello to Carmen, the receptionist, and describe to her Anna Maria Maitland's hair style, a subject that always engaged Carmen's interest.

"I wish I had a photo," said Carmen, whose ambition was to own her own beauty parlor. She'd been a hairdresser before she went to work for the police department.

Manny Escobedo caught Elena there and said, "Good, I've got someone to send out."

"I'm off duty. I just came in to type up my notes."

"Beto," he shouted. "You and Jarvis. Take that corpse they found off Lee Trevino Drive."

"But Manny, I'm still—"

"—working the Potemkin case. Now you've got a new one. That woman who was reported missing two weeks ago, blood all over her kitchen. Well, someone just found a body in the trunk of a car in a garage on Jack Fleck. The I.D. in the purse says it's her."

Elena sighed and agreed, going out with Beto Sanchez. "Two weeks in the trunk of a car?" she complained. "This is going to be fun."

"It's O.K.," said Beto. "I picked up a couple of masks. But I sure do hate to catch this kinda case right at dinner time."

Elena nodded, thinking wistfully of the dinner her mother had probably prepared, which Elena would have to eat cold with the stench of the long-dead in her nostrils.

39

Saturday, October 9, 9:00 A.M.

"You're not on duty today, are you?" Harmony asked. They
were having a leisurely breakfast on Elena's covered patio,
enjoying one of those perfect autumn days in Los Santos—
blue skies, sunshine, the temperature in the low 70's, the
baking heat of summer temporarily gone and the inversion
layers and low-lying smog of winter not yet upon them.

Elena smiled at her mother. "I'll be back before noon. I just
want to ask some questions around the Stoltz neighborhood.
I've found another old man who was killed in his house during
a daylight robbery. This one about five years ago." She spread
some of her mother's peach preserves on a biscuit. "It's really
peculiar, because his wife was dead. She *had* been connected
with the center, but he killed her. And she has ties to people
who may have ties to the other four murders. Including Boris
Potemkin's."

"Really? In that case, I'm sure I could get some information
for you. I'm at the center every day. Who do you want
investigated?"

"Mom, I don't want you saying a thing to anyone about this.
If there's a serial killer, I don't want him or her zeroing in on
you."

"A serial killer? At Socorro Heights? It's mostly women,
dear, and women are *not* serial killers."

"I hope not," said Elena, trying to imagine herself arresting

the Forrest-Marks-Lemay-Beeman bridge group and hauling
them off to jail. The department would be attacked not only
by the Socorro Heights people, but A.A.R.P., the Gray Panthers,
and whatever other groups supported the rights of senior
citizens. "Just stay out of it. O.K., Mom? I don't want Pop
roaring down here because you got hurt messing in one of my
cases."

"Well, I don't want him roaring down here because you got
hurt either, Elena. Maybe I'll check auras at the center."

Elena was sufficiently confused about her case to be tempted
by the offer of an aura check. But she wasn't going to get any
search warrants on aura information. She could just see her
submission to the judge. Informant: Officer's mother, Harmony
Waite Portillo, whose information suggests that Portia Lemay
has a suspicious aura and T. Bob Tyler's is dark red.

"What are you giggling about, Elena? This is a serious
matter."

"You don't have to tell me, Mom. Five people are dead!"

"Not to mention that poor woman in the trunk of the car. You
could hardly eat your dinner last night, and that was an
excellent recipe. I got it from Juanita. *Tlapeno* soup. What a
lovely idea. Pouring the soup over avocado slices."

Elena agreed, her mind wandering off to the interviews she
hoped to conduct that morning. Forty-five minutes later she
was in Kern Place, an older neighborhood near the university,
large trees, delicious houses whose interior walls curved up
into their ceilings, with graceful arches and French doors
leading from room to room. The Stoltzes had owned a house on
a quiet back street, occupied now mostly by young families
with children. Elena had trouble finding people who had
known the Stoltzes. Her first success was an old man who had
been a friend of Herbert's.

"Why shouldn't he get off?" said Mr. Evans, who was short,
stout, bald, and wearing eyeglasses as thick as the bottom of a
highball tumbler. "He supported the woman for forty or fifty
years; then she up and decides to leave him. Marriage is about
loyalty. I'd say she got what she deserved. That jury shouldn't
have found him guilty at all. The suspended sentence was an
insult to a man who served his country honorably in two wars."

"Do you know whether he abused her?" asked Elena.

"What's that supposed to mean?"

"Did her physical injury."

"Of course he didn't! He was an officer and a gentleman. His kind doesn't go around hitting women. I don't know what the police are thinking of. Hiring women officers. A male wouldn't be asking me these stupid questions. Good day to you, young woman." The elderly gentleman slammed the door in Elena's face.

She found one other person on the street willing to talk about the Stoltzes and knowledgeable enough to do so, Mrs. Viola Ramsey, an older lady digging up bulbs and geranium plants in her front yard. "I let the geraniums rest in the garage over the winter months," she said, "and replant them the next year. Do you like spring flowers? Daffodils? Tulips? Iris?"

"I certainly do," said Elena.

"So do I," said Mrs. Ramsey. "When I see the first daffodils, I feel as if life is starting anew. I've been digging up bulbs and separating them. Here. You must take some home with you."

"That's very kind of you, but I can't. It would be con-sidered—I don't know—unethical, I guess, for a law officer to accept—"

"My dear, it's not as if I'm offering you a bribe. I'm just giving you bulbs I'd have thrown away. These irises are the most beautiful red-brown shade, and I have yellow ones too. Some beautiful tulips. Daffodils."

Elena looked longingly at the basket.

"Is your car unlocked?" asked the lady.

"In Los Santos? Of course not."

"Well, give me the keys. You go sit on my front porch in the glider and turn your head. Look at those sweet children playing next door, and I'll just slip these into your trunk. You'll be the victim of reverse thievery."

Mrs. Ramsey deftly snatched the car keys from Elena's hand and pattered off with her woven basket of bulbs to that rotten Ford Escort, whose fuel pump had turned off, leaving Elena stranded on Murchison. Unable to resist the temptation, imag-ining the scene Lieutenant Beltran would make if he knew she had accepted gifts from a witness, Elena sat down on the glider and watched two little girls playing hopscotch on the sidewalk in front of the old Stoltz house.

It was nice to know that little girls still played hopscotch. Elena used to play in front of Grandma Waite's but never in Chimayo because there were no sidewalks on which to chalk the squares. She supposed she should arrest those children for defacing a public sidewalk. Hopscotch graffiti. By the time that bizarre thought had occurred to her, Mrs. Ramsey had plopped herself down beside Elena on the glider, setting it into gentle motion. It had a soft squeak, not abrasive, rather soothing in fact.

"Now what was it you wanted to ask me, Detective? Goodness, I've never been interviewed by a policeman— police person. Is that the thing to say? I do try to be politically correct, but it's hard at my age."

"I wanted to ask you about the relationship between Herbert and Frances Stoltz."

"Well, dear me. That was a tragedy all around, wasn't it? Frances was the loveliest woman. And he killed her. I couldn't believe it. And then someone killed *him*. Almost as if God stepped in when the courts wouldn't."

A familiar theme in this case, thought Elena. "Before he killed her, did he abuse her?"

"You mean did he beat her up?"

"Yes, ma'am. That's pretty much what I mean."

"Well, I wouldn't say so. Of course, she broke some bones, but then that's old age for you. Our bones get brittle. I think I'd have noticed anything else because I saw her most every day. She did spend a lot of time at the center, which Herbert didn't like at all."

"Why not?"

"He thought she should be home working in the house and yard. He fired their maid when he retired. Herbert was an Army officer. He had a good pension, so he had no call to fire the maid. It's not as if maids are all that expensive around here, and with Frances getting older, it was downright unkind.

"The thing is, Herbert must have been forty-some odd years in the Army if you count his cadetship at West Point. By the time he retired, he was used to running things. Commanding, you know? So he commanded Frances. Poor woman. Herbert trailed her every step, telling her what to do and how to do it. That's probably why he fired the maid. He didn't speak Spanish well enough to boss her around.

"So there was Frances, who'd been running her own house all those years, often as not without him because he was fighting in some war or on maneuvers. Then Herbert retired and took over. Not in the sense that he helped. He would have thought that beneath him.

"Even in the yard. Frances was so proud of her yard. She may have wanted a maid for indoors, but she did all the outside work herself. And Herbert trailed right after her, telling her how to do it. Deciding she should dig up something in one place and plant it somewhere else. Even telling her how to water. I can remember him standing behind her, saying, 'Stop putting that water in the ground, Frances. Get some on the leaves there. They look thirsty.' Insisting that she stand around holding the hose, watering every plant and tree separately. Well, that's not the way to do it, not here in Los Santos. Because of Herbert, she lost a lot of shrubbery. You just don't put water on the leaves, but then you probably know that. You seem to be interested in gardening."

Elena nodded. The man had evidently abused Frances Stoltz physically (the A.D.A. hadn't thought those breaks were the result of osteoporosis) *and* psychologically. And it seemed that Frances Stoltz put up with it, at least for a time. "Was that why she wanted to leave him?"

"I think it was the yard that did it. She had a beautiful rose garden out back, and it developed the worst case of black spot you ever saw. She lost six bushes that last summer. And all because Herbert had her out there in the evening watering the leaves. No matter how often she told him, he insisted that was the way to do it. Losing those rose bushes was the final straw for Frances. She told him she was leaving."

"And that's why he killed her?"

"I imagine so. Frances was a quiet woman, not given to arguing. But they had a couple of humdingers once she announced that she was leaving. Herbert had a *fit*! He simply told her he wouldn't *allow* it, and Frances went right on packing her things. She was going to live with her daughter in Ohio. And she would have if he hadn't shot her.

"My goodness, I *cried*. I can't tell you how many tears I shed over Frances. If I'd known what he was going to do, I'd have gone right over there and taken her home with me, called the police. Maybe I should have guessed. The man had a house full of guns. Military, you know. They're all in love with guns.

"And then he hired some smart lawyer who got him off. Must have cost him a fortune. That's another thing. Herbert was so stingy. Frances had to have a radical mastectomy ten years ago. She must have been about sixty-five then. The cancer didn't come back, but she wanted reconstructive surgery.

"Now if a woman wants reconstructive surgery, she ought to be able to have it, don't you think? I certainly do. Frances said those special brassieres hurt her scars. Poor thing. She went through all that therapy to redevelop the muscles, and Herbert, who was as tight as a tick—I guess I told you that—he said a woman her age didn't need that kind of surgery. It was just vanity. If he didn't mind the way she looked, she shouldn't. She could have had it done for nothing out at the Army hospital, but Herbert wouldn't let her. I call that mean and stingy, him talking so self-righteously about the taxpayers having to pay for cosmetic surgery and he was a better citizen than to ask it of them. It wasn't his chest that hurt, was it? Anyway, that's the story."

They were still rocking gently in the glider, but tears slipped down Mrs. Ramsey's wrinkled cheeks. "Dear Frances. I still miss her. I visit her grave every year, and do you know, someone puts flowers on it, on both his and hers. I can understand on hers, but why his? He doesn't deserve flowers. It's not as if the children are in town.

"You know what I did? I hope you won't arrest me for this. I took those flowers off his grave and threw them away. I didn't even transfer them to Frances' stone. I didn't think she'd want his flowers, not after he killed her."

Elena stared across the street at a house where a young man was scraping paint off his windowsills. The whole story was pretty depressing. "Do you know if Herbert Stoltz had any enemies?"

"No, not really," said Mrs. Ramsey. "He didn't see that many people, and at our age, even your enemies begin to die off. I'm sure it was a burglar, caught robbing the house. Must have killed Herbert and run out the back way. That's why I didn't see anything. I did hear the shot. I was having a nap, and I heard that gunshot. Knew just what it was. When I was a girl, out on the farm, we used to hunt or just shoot guns for the fun of it, my brothers and I, so I recognized the sound."

"But you didn't see anyone."

"No, there wasn't a thing you wouldn't ordinarily see in this neighborhood. A few children playing. Ann Malone pedaling her bicycle up the street. She rode every day up to the week she died. Imagine having the nerve to shoot someone in the middle of the day with people around the neighborhood. It's become a violent world since I was a girl."

A bicycle? There had been one behind the Potemkins'. "You're sure the bicycle rider was your neighbor?" Mrs. Ramsey nodded. "Did she have any reason to dislike Herbert Stoltz?" Mrs. Ramsey thought Ann Malone had considered him husband material, even considering that he'd killed Frances. "Did Mrs. Malone belong to the Socorro Heights Center?" No she hadn't. Elena gave up on Ann Malone.

"Did you know any of Francis Stoltz's friends at the center?" she asked.

"Can't say as I did. I guess our lives were sort of compartmentalized. I knew her from chatting when we were working in our yards. Saw her at the grocery store. You know the one down on North Mesa and Kerbey? Occasionally, we'd have a block party but not very often. Frances had two sets of friends, same as I do. The neighbors and the outside friends. Hers were at the center. Mine are at the church. I go to St. Clement's. Work a couple of days a week at the Bargain Box. You know the Bargain Box? You can get the most wonderful clothes there for practically nothing. If you have children, it's a great saving. I'll swear, some of the things have never been worn."

"I don't have any children," said Elena. "I'm divorced."

"Oh, I'm sorry, dear. So many young people are. I think it's sad."

"Well, thank you for your time, Mrs. Ramsey." Elena rose from the glider.

Mrs. Ramsey rose with her, picking up her trowel. "Back to the geraniums," she said cheerfully. "Now, you plant those bulbs in November, and next year you'll have wonderful spring flowers."

"It's really kind of you."

"Not at all. It does my heart good to see young people taking an interest in growing things, when you're all so busy. Jobs and homes and children. I don't know how you do it." Mrs. Ramsey preceded Elena down the steps toward the geranium bed. Elena climbed into the Escort, hoping it wouldn't quit on her before she got back to headquarters and switched to her own truck, carrying all those bulbs. Red-brown iris. They were going to be a real joy next spring.

Frances and Herbert Stoltz—he drove her crazy for years and then shot her when she wanted to leave. A wonderful woman, according to Mrs. Ramsey. Probably well-loved by her friends at the center. But would they murder for her? It was hard to believe. They didn't seem like crazies, those women she'd interviewed between hands of a bridge game. Had T. Bob been a friend of Frances Stoltz?

40
..

Saturday, October 9, 7:30 P.M.

"I planned something a little more upscale in the way of dinner," said Colin Stuart as he popped a blob of sticky rice covered with raw fish into his mouth. "However, this sushi is excellent. Won't you try one?"

"No thanks," said Elena, having read in the newspaper that sushi caused horrible diseases. Of course, she'd once read that broccoli could kill you, so it was hard to know what to believe. Still, the idea of raw fish didn't appeal to her. She didn't eat *ceviche* in Mexico, although the lime juice was supposed to "cook" it, and she had turned down the opportunity to try beef tartare, which was raw meat with raw eggs. Sarah Tolland had tried to introduce her to beef tartare on one of their weekly dinners out. Elena had a paper plate that contained Tandoori chicken, which was quite nice and unquestionably cooked. It came with a small mound of bright yellow rice.

She and Colin were sitting on a bench in San Jacinto Plaza, waiting for the tap dancers to appear, and sampling the wide array of ethnic cuisines. On the other side of Colin, Elena's mother and Lance Potemkin sat discussing modern poetry and eating spicy Mongolian beef. Colin devoured the last piece of raw fish and rice, then said he'd go for more food and was taking orders. Elena asked for *nachos* from the G & R booth. Her mother said she'd try the Tandoori chicken this time, plus any vegetarian dish they offered at the Delhi Palace booth.

Lance wanted sushi, having sampled Colin's. "Beer all around?" asked Colin and off he went.

Lance turned to Elena and said, "I hope now that I'm off the hook in my father's murder—I am, aren't I—?"

Elena nodded and forked up the last piece of chicken.

"I hope that you haven't gone back to thinking my mother killed him. The way he treated her while he was alive was bad enough without her getting blamed for his murder."

Elena's mouth was full of chicken so she couldn't answer, but Harmony said, "I'm sure no one thinks your mother did it, Lance. She was at Socorro Heights."

Elena swallowed. "Do *you* think she killed him?"

"Of course I don't!" Lance exclaimed.

Elena wondered if that was why Lance had wanted to come along. So that he could argue his mother's case with her, not to mention give his poetry a boost with Harmony.

"Here we are," said Colin Stuart, distributing food from a shallow cardboard box.

"Oh, good," said Elena. "You brought me some of their hot sauce. It's the best in town."

"Really? What makes it the best?"

"A lot of cilantro, for one thing," said Elena, "maybe garlic, besides the usual tomatoes and jalapeños. You want a bite?" She was applying salsa to a *nacho* with a white plastic spoon. Once she finished, she held the *nacho* out to Colin. Looking somewhat surprised, he opened his mouth. The salsa dribbled onto his chin and from there onto the lapel of his sport coat.

"Elena, look what you've done," cried Harmony. She poured beer onto a paper napkin and rubbed the stain off the lapel, leaving the dignified Colin smelling like a brewery.

"The sauce is excellent," he said politely. Having ordered a tortilla and a small helping of *fajitas* from Wings, the restaurant at the Ysleta Pueblo, he offered Elena a bite, and she accepted. She'd only eaten once at Wings, when she and Leo were on an agg assault out east. She had thought the *fajitas* were great.

"I wonder when the tap dancers will arrive," said Colin.

Elena peered into the street. "I don't hear any tapping. Maybe they had trouble at the library. It gets kind of sleazy over there after dark."

"At a library?" Colin looked surprised.

"Prostitutes of both sexes hang around there, particularly the transvestites from Mexico."

Harmony quirked her eyebrows. "Elena, I really don't think that's a proper—"

"Good grief, Mom, I'm sure Colin's heard of prostitutes."

"I meant that it sounds racist to say the cross-dressers come from Mexico. The universities are into political correctness these days, you know."

"My mother once belonged to a church group that was trying to find new occupations for prostitutes," said Lance. "You can tell from that that she's a good woman and would never—"

"I'm really sure, Lance, that nobody thinks Dimitra a murderer." Harmony patted his arm. "I told Elena the first time I met Dimitra that your mother didn't have the right aura for murder."

"You see auras?" asked Lance.

"How do they look?" asked Colin. Immediately he, Lance, and Harmony became involved in an aura discussion while Elena finished off her *nachos* and filched *fajita* meat off Colin's plate, along with a tasty fried green onion. She'd like to have taken his tortilla and added onions, salsa, beans, and guacamole. Earlier Colin had been taking separate samplings of each item with a plastic fork. He should have been mixing everything into the tortilla and rolling it. Maybe he was worried about getting more food on his sport coat. Suddenly Elena heard a sound that cut through the crowd noise on the plaza.

"I think they're coming," she said. The aura discussion ended abruptly as the tap dancers erupted onto one of the streets edging the square. There were silken banners attached to poles carried by the dancers: NORTHEAST TAPPERS ASSOCIATION; TIPTAP CLUB. They weren't dancing in unison, so the sound was chaotic, like many snare drums, each going its own way. Elena watched as various dancers leapt out in front and did fancy steps while their cohorts cheered. A sort of contest, she thought.

"Look, there's the Socorro Heights group," cried Harmony, standing up because other people had crowded in front of them.

Lance helped Harmony onto the bench. In seconds they were all teetering on the wooden slats. Elena spotted five or six dancers who appeared to be over sixty-five.

"I didn't know they had a tap-dancing class at the center," said Elena.

"Oh, yes," said Harmony. "When you go on the twelve-to-eight shift next week, you can come with me mornings."

"Good idea," Elena agreed. She'd ask questions about the five murders, the bridge group, and T. Bob Tyler—but discreetly, under cover of spending time with her mother. Undercover at a senior citizens center—she bet that didn't happen too often.

"As soon as Concepcion told me about Leo's event, I told Mrs. Galindo. She's had her own tap-dancing school for the last ten years," said Harmony. "She calls it Elder Terpsichore-ans, but she donates her time to the center. She's sixty-nine."

Elena watched Mrs. Galindo, attired in a red, white, and blue satin jogging suit with U.S.A. embroidered on the front. Twirling small American flags, she broke ahead of the proces-sion, danced alone for about thirty seconds, then clicked her heels in the air on the left while crisscrossing the flags with her upper body leaning to the right.

The crowd roared appreciatively, and a young man standing in front of Elena shouted, "Viva, Abuelita!" As she picked out another strip of Colin's *fajitas*, Elena wondered whether Mrs. Galindo was really the young man's grandmother.

"Have you spotted your partner?" Colin asked.

Elena studied the oncoming phalanx of tap dancers. A young woman in a tutu was now at the point doing her solo. As the dancers turned to pass her vantage point on the bench, Elena said, "There he is."

Leo was tapping along the edge of the group, keeping the dancers in order, doing some step in which his feet were twinkling while he flung his arms out periodically. He wore, of all things, a tuxedo, and carried a cane in one hand and his flashlight in the other. He did a sort of tap-dancing bow to various lady performers, top hat held over his heart, the cane now tucked under his arm.

Elena grinned. Gallant Leo! If Concepcion was somewhere

in the crowd, watching, she just might give him a kick in the shins for his mobile flirting techniques. "That's him in the tuxedo," Elena murmured to Colin.

"And who's that woman in the garish outfit that just grabbed him?" asked Colin.

Elena had seen it too. The woman had shiny black hair, blunt-cut at her shoulders, long bangs, heavy eye makeup, a short black leather skirt, and red knee-high boots with black mesh stockings. The stockings were dotted here and there with red rosebuds, and she wore a black satin blouse with a red rose at the low V-neck. Very exotic. She looked as if she should be holding a rose between her teeth as she gave Leo an unsubtle, come-hither look from under long, patently false eyelashes.

To the astonishment of both Elena and the watching crowd, Leo grabbed her arm and twisted it up behind her back. She shrieked. They were now close enough that Elena could hear Leo roaring angrily, "You're under arrest for offering to commit an unnatural sex act with a police officer."

"You're a cop?" yelled the woman. "Is this a sting?"

Leo whipped his handcuffs out from under his cummerbund and cuffed her, bringing the whole tap-dancing procession to a halt. Camera units from three TV stations were whirring. A reporter from the Los Santos *Times* jogged over to Leo and shouted, "What's up?"

"Goddamn transvestite prostitutes," Leo muttered.

"Can I quote you on that, sir? What's your name?" asked the reporter.

"Bug off!" said Leo and gave the transvestite's arm a yank. "Hey, Officer," he yelled to a cop standing by his patrol car blocking off traffic from one of the streets that fed into the plaza.

The patrolman sauntered over. "What's up, mister? You making a citizen's arrest here?" He grinned.

Leo produced his detective's badge. "Take this prisoner over to Central and book her, or him, or whatever the hell it is. You better check the sex before you put it in a cell."

"I'm not an *it*," snapped the prostitute. "I've probably got a bigger dick than you, you asshole," and he burst into a stream of vituperative Spanish.

Harmony jumped off her bench and said to Leo's prisoner, "I consider myself a fairly broad-minded woman, and I do consider prostitution a victimless crime, but there are children in this crowd, and I think you should watch your language."

"Some victimless crime," said Elena. "You can bet he/she's got AIDS."

"I do not. I'll sue you for slandering me and causing irreparable damage to my source of income," said the prisoner.

"O.K., dancers," shouted Leo. "Once around the plaza." The tap dancers, now looking confused, tapped away, the patrolman hustled Leo's prisoner across the street, and the newspapers interviewed Harmony. Elena didn't want to hear it. She shuddered to think of what inappropriate thing her mother might say, like introducing her daughter as the partner of the officer who had stopped the parade by making an arrest.

"My husband is the sheriff in Rio Arriba County, New Mexico," Harmony was saying, "where people, happily, seem to have less trouble with their sexual identities. I think the Los Santos police need to take a much more tolerant view of sexuality. This young man, for instance, was a murder suspect"—Lance looked horribly embarrassed as she pointed to him—"although he's a noted bicycle racer and poet. One has to suspect that he was harassed because he's gay."

"Mom, we didn't harass him," Elena muttered, tugging at her mother's elbow. "For God's sake, we escorted him up to Chimayo to the damn race."

"Would you care to make a statement, ma'am?" a reporter from the *Herald Post* asked Elena. "What's your connection with this incident?"

Elena cast a look of frustrated appeal at Colin Stuart, who promptly and gallantly said, "I think we've enjoyed most of the entertainment available here. Let's go to the Border Folk Festival. Lance tells me there'll be jazz groups there that we wouldn't otherwise get a chance to hear." He gathered his party together, cold-shouldering the reporter, and herded them off before Harmony could make any more inflammatory remarks about the Los Santos Police Department and Lance's gay-ness.

41
..

"For Pete's sake, Mom," Elena muttered once they'd climbed into Colin's Oldsmobile. "Do you have to keep criticizing the department?"

"Public scrutiny is what keeps public servants on their toes," Harmony replied. "That was certainly a memorable finale to Tap Night, don't you think?"

"Stunning," said Elena, giggling. Leo's picture would be in the paper, along with the transvestite he'd arrested. A memorable finale indeed. The whole city ought to turn up next year if Leo could get permission to hold Tap Night again. As Captain Beltran always said, an officer was never off duty. She wondered how he'd like the television coverage of Leo's particular off-duty police action.

They drove to the Chamizal National Memorial's Folk Festival, where tents and stages perched all over the grassy, almost treeless hills that surrounded the building. Lance and Colin accepted programs from a ranger and located the area where a jazz performance was to take place.

"This is a Boston group," said Colin knowledgeably. "Very *avant garde*."

Lance agreed. Elena groaned, but silently. She wasn't into *avant garde* music, things you couldn't sing along with.

"Oh, we must stop and hear these folk singers," cried

233

Harmony. "And just look. At nine-thirty there's a storyteller. Indian myths. I don't want to miss that."

Lance and Colin looked unhappy. They had come for the jazz, and Harmony's choices overlapped theirs. "If you wouldn't mind," said Colin, "perhaps we could all separate, hear our choices, and meet back at—how about the Lone Star stand at ten o'clock?"

Some date, thought Elena and trailed off with her mother. Evidently Colin Stuart found Lance a more interesting companion than her. Or maybe he was just a music fanatic. Not that she cared; Colin was nice, but she didn't feel any overwhelming attraction to him.

"You really ought to talk to your date more, Elena," said Harmony.

"It was your idea to listen to stuff he didn't want to hear."

"Well, I didn't mean for you to come along with me."

"I think he did." They took folding chairs in a tent where a Bluegrass singer was plunking on a banjo while another strummed a guitar and a third played a fiddle, elbows flying. They all sang in nasal tones, but Elena agreed with her mother; she did like folk music—all those maidens pining for dead lovers. An hour and a half later, having crossed paths on the grass several times, the foursome met at the beer stand and walked to Colin's car, a long hike away in the Bowie High School parking lot.

Colin dropped Lance off first, then drove to Elena's house where he asked if she'd like to go out for a drink. Elena was surprised. At first, when he suggested that she bring her mother along, she thought he had the hots for Harmony. Then she thought, during the evening, that he was basically indifferent to both Portillo women. Now it occurred to her that he intended to ask her out again. Did she want to go? All she had to do was say no to the drink, and that would take care of it. Still, they hadn't had that much time to talk, and Sarah was hoping that they'd be friends. "Sure," she said.

"Goodnight, children. Have a good time," said Harmony when Colin had unlocked the door for her.

Children? Harmony was closer in age to Colin Stuart than

Elena was. They drove off toward the Camino Real bar downtown.

"I wanted to talk to you privately," said Colin once they were sitting in comfy leather chairs under the Tiffany dome and drinking Bailey's Irish Creme.

"Uh-huh." Elena took a handful of tidbits from the dish on the table.

"My guess is that you're not particularly interested in me," said Colin.

Now what was she supposed to say to that?

"The truth is, I was married for a long time to a woman who, unfortunately, decided to divorce me several years ago."

Oh lord, thought Elena, another unhappy divorced man about to tell her his problems.

"Looking back, I have to admit," said Colin, "that the marriage was never very successful. There just wasn't any—I don't know—*spark* between us. We had a lot in common professionally—my wife was an engineer too—but personally—"

He shrugged.

"That's too bad," said Elena, *but none of my business*, she added silently.

"And strangely enough, it was pretty much the same with Sarah and me. You know we dated for several months."

Elena nodded. Sarah had noticed the same thing. No chemistry. *Now what's he going to say: "I've finally developed a great lust, and you're its object? Let's hop into bed together."*

"And I think I've finally figured out why my relationships with women have been so unsatisfying."

"Oh?" She crunched another tidbit.

"Yes, I think all these years I've been repressing a homosexual proclivity."

Elena blinked. Now, that had to be a new topic of conversation on a date. A first for her, at any rate.

"I find myself—well—amazingly attracted to Lance. And the feeling seems to be mutual."

"I see." Elena had to suppress a giggle. Laughter would not be politically correct under these circumstances. "Well, I—ah—wish you both the best."

"That's very kind of you," said Colin. "I'm sure many women would be highly offended to hear my explanation of why I wasn't going to ask them out again. And it's certainly not that I didn't enjoy your company this evening."

What company? thought Elena. He'd spent his time with Lance. "Well, that's great. You have a lot in common—bicycle racing, jazz."

"Yes, we do." Colin beamed at her.

"Good luck." Elena didn't know what else to say.

"Thank you. Would you like another drink?" Colin now looked quite cheerful.

Elena wondered whether he was a virgin—homosexually speaking. Not that it was any of her business. "No thanks," she said. If he took her home right now, he'd have time to go over and visit Lance. They left the bar, and she bade him goodnight twenty minutes later.

She wondered whether he expected her to pass the big news on to Sarah. What a time to change your sexual orientation, Elena thought wryly. Right in the middle of the AIDS epidemic. Although she remembered Lance telling Bayard Sims's wife that he didn't have AIDS. Of course, probably you couldn't tell that from one year to the next unless you were into chastity.

Her mother had already gone to bed, so Elena went into the kitchen and fixed herself a cup of herb tea, sitting down to think about the visit she was going to make Monday to the Socorro Heights Senior Citizens Center. She had to do it without spooking the serial killer or killers. What a strange case! What a strange *evening*! She washed out her cup and went to bed. She'd spend Sunday digging irrigation ditches. You always knew where you were with a shovel in your hand.

42
..

Sunday, October 10, 8:30 A.M.

"Finally you have a day off," said Harmony. "We can get some practice in."

Elena had been enjoying the Sunday *Times*, her *huevos rancheros*, and the anticipation of a pleasant morning digging trenches and installing the new irrigation system. "What practice?" she asked with a sinking feeling.

"For our act. I've settled on 'House of the Rising Sun.'"

"I told you, Mom. The guitar's gone."

"Frank returned it," said Harmony smugly.

"How? Did he meet you on neutral ground or ignore the restraining order?"

"He honked, and I went out to his truck."

Elena cut another bite after spreading the yolk of her egg into the melted cheese and salsa. Ambrosia! What was Frank up to? Had he given up bugging her? Or had her mother— "What did you do to Frank, Mom?"

"Nothing, dear. I asked him to return the guitar and gave him some advice on his aura."

"Frank doesn't know he *has* an aura."

"He does now." Harmony smiled radiantly. "Don't you think 'House of the Rising Sun' is a good choice?"

"The guys from Vice will love it," said Elena dryly.

"Of course they will. You sing beautifully."

Elena groaned and went back to her newspaper. On B-2 in

237

the local section, she found an article that might explain Frank's having returned the guitar. He'd completely flipped.

MUSHROOMS FELL NARC

Detective Frank Jarvis of the LSPD Narcotics Squad was hospitalized Saturday afternoon at Thomason General after erratic behavior at Police Headquarters. Dr. Rama Bahadna, the attending physician, speculated that Jarvis might have ingested an hallucinogen such as peyote. Test results are not yet in. When contacted, Jarvis' superior, Lieutenant Paul Costas, had no comment on the incident.

"Look at this," said Elena, passing the paper to her mother. Poor Frank. He wouldn't be the first narc to fall victim to the product. But peyote? She'd have taken him for the cocaine type. Thank God, she'd divorced him. She glanced across at her mother and noticed that Harmony had gone pale.

"I think we should visit him," said Harmony.

"No way," said Elena. "I'd rather pay a conjugal visit to Charles Manson."

Harmony's eyebrows went up. "Frank can't have been that bad! And I'm sure hospitals frown on conjugal visits."

"I'm sure," Elena agreed.

"I really think—"

"Where's the guitar?" Anything to distract her mother from the crazy idea of visiting Frank. He was bad enough when he wasn't taking drugs. She couldn't imagine what he'd be like hallucinating, and she didn't want to find out.

43
..

"You hear about Frank?" Leo asked.

Elena had answered on the cordless phone because she and Harmony were eating on the patio. "Yeah, I read the article yesterday." She tucked the phone between her head and shoulder so that she could pour herself more freshly squeezed orange juice. Harmony didn't hold with juice in cartons. She claimed the little vitamin C's escaped once they'd been separated from the rind more than an hour. But then that was her mother: full of crackbrained ideas. Not that Elena didn't appreciate drinking extra-fresh orange juice.

"The newspaper didn't tell the half of it," Leo was saying. "Frank came in for his shift, and they had this scumbag drug dealer in interrogation. Everyone agrees that Frank was acting peculiar before he spotted the dealer: calling people by the wrong names, complaining about dangerous alien rays coming off the main departmental computer. Then he sees the dealer. 'What are you bastards doing to my wife?' he yells at the narcs, and he grabs the dealer and kisses him. Course the guy, being the macho type, gets all upset. He doesn't want to be kissed by a male narc.

"The lieutenant, who's in on the interrogation, tries to drag Frank away from his true love, the drug dealer, while Frank's yelling, 'Were you trying to come back to me, sweetheart?'

239

Then Frank turns and punches Costas and yells, 'Why are you bustin' my wife, asshole?'

"And the drug dealer, he's screaming, 'I ain't his wife. Bad enough you accuse me of sellin' smack. You think you're gonna break me down by callin' me queer and gettin' some scruffy Anglo to kiss me?' He's scrubbing his mouth like he's trying to get Frank's kiss off. I got all this from Harry Rainbow Trout—you know, the guy they say can sniff out narcotics better than their drug dogs?

"Anyway, Rainbow grabs Frank's arms. Says it's like trying to hold a madman or someone on LSD, 'cause Frank, he wants to hit the lieutenant again, only he doesn't get a chance because the lieutenant slugs him in the gut. Whoomp! Frank folds. So the upshot is they haul Frank off to the hospital, babbling like an idiot. The drug dealer's threatening to file suit for sexual assault."

Elena groaned.

"They're trying to keep it hushed up. The reporters got a little, but not the whole story."

"I can see that," said Elena.

"But you haven't heard the best of it. When Frank came off his high at the hospital, he claimed some *curandera* down in Segundo Barrio told him she was giving him an herbal tea that would improve—get this—his aura! So they tested Frank's blood, right? And he shows positive for some frog venom hallucinogen.

"Then they head straight down and arrest the *curandera*, who's claiming the only way to improve an aura is with a religious ceremony, which she put ole Frank through. So the *curandera's* in the slammer, and all her customers are trying to raise her bail, and she's screaming racial, ethnic, religious, and practitioner discrimination. She thinks it was a sting set up by the County Medical Association.

"Man, it is a *mess*! They tell me Chief Gaitan wants to fire the whole narc squad; the *curandera* wants to sue the department, Frank, and every M.D. in town; and Frank wants to sue her for endangering his job and his—get this!—his aura. You ought to ask your mother what's going on. She's the big aura expert."

"I'll do that," said Elena grimly. "Thanks for the info, Leo. Any news on the baby front?"

"Nah. Concepcion's talking about fertility drugs now. She says if she puts out more eggs, my two sperm per orgasm will have lots of eggs to take a shot at, and we won't have to worry about having five babies, because I don't have that many sperm. That made me feel great."

"Listen to your wife," Elena advised. "She's probably read every book on baby-making ever published." Elena pressed the Off button and stared ominously across the breakfast table at her mother. "So Frank returned the guitar out of the goodness of his heart, right?"

"How should I know?" Harmony replied. "I can't divine the motives of a man with an aura like Frank's."

As far as Elena was concerned, that was the wrong thing to say. "How did Frank happen to be going to a *curandera*?"

Harmony rounded her eyes innocently.

"Mom, come on. Frank wouldn't go to a *curandera* on his own. Frank wouldn't know an aura from an anteater. What did you tell him?"

Harmony gave a delicate shrug and poured herself a second cup of coffee. "I told him a *curandera* might—might, mind you—be able to help his aura."

"And then what? He wouldn't care about his aura."

"Well, Frank was interested in establishing friendly relations with you, Elena, and believe me, I didn't promise him a thing."

"Oh, Mom." Elena groaned. "God, I hope he keeps his mouth shut about our involvement in this. You and I will probably end up getting sued too."

"By whom?" asked Harmony, astonished.

"By the *curandera* because you sent her a narc; by Frank because you recommended the woman who fed him a hallucinogen; by the scumbag drug dealer who's suing Frank because Frank took him for me and kissed him."

"Frank kissed a drug dealer?" Harmony started to laugh.

"Mom, it's not funny. It's a disaster." Then Elena broke into laughter too, because it made such a ridiculous picture. "The chief is beside himself," she gasped.

"Oh, well, I'll fix that," said Harmony.

"Leave it *alone*, Mom," Elena begged and went to her bedroom to dress. She wasn't on duty till noon, so she was going with her mother to the senior citizens center to see what she could find out about T. Bob Tyler. First she wanted to know whether *anyone* had seen T. Bob at the center on the afternoon of Boris Potemkin's murder.

As soon as her daughter left the patio, Harmony called Police Headquarters and asked for Chief Gaitan, identifying herself and getting him immediately. "My dear Armando," she said, "this is Harmony."

Dear Armando was delighted to hear from her and told her how much he was looking forward to the performance of her and her daughter at the talent show. He offered to take them out for celebratory champagne afterward. Harmony told him how sweet she thought his offer but admitted that he might not want to have anything to do with her after he heard the story she had to tell. Then she proceeded to admit responsibility for his narcotics officer, Frank Jarvis, going to a *curandera*. "I was hoping she could help him get over having lost the love of my daughter," Harmony confided.

"That would be a hard thing for any man to get over," said Gaitan.

"Yes, it would. Unfortunately, Frank must have offended the *curandera*, and you know that can be disastrous with a woman of power. I'm sure your own mother explained to you about *curanderas*."

Gaitan agreed that one had to deal carefully with a *curandera* who was also a *bruja*, which this woman was. Sylvia Balderrama was well known and respected in Los Santos, he added.

"Well-known throughout the Southwest and Chihuahua as well," said Harmony. "She makes Los Santos a place of awe in the eyes of all Hispanics who know their own culture, as you obviously do. I always think a man who knows his culture and holds in respect the power of the holy women is a man to be trusted and honored."

Gaitan told Harmony how much he appreciated her kind words and her understanding of the spiritual and magical aspects of Hispanic life. They traded several more compliments, and Gaitan assured her that he did not hold the debacle in Narcotics against her or her daughter. He was even prepared to forgive Frank when Harmony told him that one could hardly expect an Anglo to understand what he was getting into. Harmony now felt that she should have better prepared poor Frank for his meeting with the *curandera*.

"I'm sure you did your best," said Gaitan.

"I thought I had, but things don't always work out as one expects. I can't understand how my daughter came to marry an Anglo. I'm certainly glad I didn't make that mistake."

"The sheriff is a lucky man."

Harmony told the chief how much she was looking forward to seeing him at the talent show, and mentioned that she and Elena would be singing "House of the Rising Sun," which she thought had a folk quality that would appeal to both Anglo and Hispanic. She told him how beautifully her daughter played Spanish guitar, as well as other types of guitar music, and hung up.

Elena was standing in the doorway when Harmony went back to her cereal. "I can't believe you called the chief," Elena groaned.

"It's all straightened out, dear. He doesn't blame you, me, or even Frank, and he's very excited about our performance at the talent show."

Elena threw up her hands. She'd been hoping to get out of that. Now with the chief involved, she didn't dare back off.

44
..

Monday, October 11, 9:30 A.M.

While Harmony went on to her classroom, Elena stopped at
the business office to ask for a list of people who had signed
into the center on the day of Boris Potemkin's death, Monday,
September 27.

Hallie Markham, the director, ran her hands through hair that
was already disarranged and said, "I'm sure we have it." She
looked hopelessly around her cluttered office.

"Maybe if you'd tell me where to look, I can do the
rummaging."

"Oh, would you? I have to referee the shuffleboard tournament. You wouldn't believe the things they say to one another
if I'm not there to keep the peace." She shook her head at the
recalcitrance of senior citizens, then looked around once more.
"Try that Seagram's box." She pointed to a whiskey carton
stuffed with papers. "Or the boxes to either side." She started
to leave, then stopped. "I don't want you to get the idea that we
allow alcohol at the center. It's just that when we have to store
things, we need sturdy boxes, which we can't afford to buy.
And now I really have to go." Hallie trotted out, hair flying in
every direction.

It took Elena three-quarters of an hour to find the sign-in
sheet for September 27. Then she looked at every name,
puzzling over signatures, especially the spidery ones and those
that wandered above and below the line. T. Bob Tyler's name

was there. He'd signed in at 10:30 in the morning, but that didn't mean he'd stayed through the afternoon. There was no sign-*out* sheet.

She doubted that she'd find all these people at the center today, and it was going to be touchy checking T. Bob's alibi if he was here. A small table at the door held a sign-in sheet for that day, so she checked it. No T. Bob Tyler. She'd have to ask questions as fast as she could, then get a list of telephone numbers from Hallie so that she could call others who had been here on the day of the murder.

Photocopying both sign-in lists on a machine that made ominous sounds when she punched the print button, she produced copies that looked as if they had been caught in a fire. Then she went out to the main room and started at the top of the list, cross-referencing as she went. In less than two hours she'd located fifteen of the thirty-five people on the September 27 list. None of them remembered seeing T. Bob Tyler on the fatal afternoon. "If he'd been here," said Rolf Hankins, whom Elena caught as he came out of Harmony's weaving class, "you can bet he'd have been hanging around the bridge group. Dimitra played that day, and T. Bob always did like her, mostly because she was a bang-up country dancer. Don't reckon anyone here at the center could do the Cotton-Eyed Joe with more pizazz than Dimitra. 'Fore she broke her hip, anyways."

All the more reason for T. Bob to hate Boris, thought Elena; Boris had crippled T. Bob's dancing partner. If Dimitra got the post hip-replacement therapy, she and T. Bob could do the Cotton-Eyed Joe on Boris' grave. "Hey, Mom," she called to her mother, who was leaving the classroom. "You going to eat here?"

"Absolutely not," said Harmony.

"What's the matter?" Elena hustled after her mother, who was leaving the center at a fast clip.

"I don't want to have to look at that Lydia Beeman for one more minute."

"What did Lydia do this time?" asked Elena, suppressing a grin. They had reached Harmony's pickup.

"Lydia had the nerve to say she's quitting my weaving class because weaving is too sedentary a pastime. She told me that if I had any interest in my health, I'd take up something more active." Harmony climbed in and slammed the door, leaving Elena on the parking lot pavement. "Where does she get off saying that to me? I don't weigh an ounce more than I did when I was twenty. I'm certainly as slim as she is."

"Not to mention prettier," said Elena. "She's probably jealous."

"No, she isn't. She's arrogant and supercilious. A woman like me, who's raised five children in the Sangre de Cristos and walked the loom besides, is not sedentary."

"O.K.," said Elena. "How about a quick lunch at Señor Fish? They have great *sopa pescado*. You'll love it."

"Oh." Harmony looked mollified. "Well, that sounds good to me."

"It's on Montana too, so I think I can just about wolf down the soup and get to work in time for my twelve o'clock shift."

Once Elena had signed in and checked her messages, she realized that she'd forgotten to get a membership list. Accordingly, she drove back to Socorro Heights and asked Hallie for a printout of the names, addresses, and telephone numbers.

"You're not going to make trouble for any of these people, are you?" Hallie asked.

"You don't think any of them committed murder, do you?"

"Of course not," said Hallie. Blushing as if she'd slandered her clients, she printed out the list.

Elena stuffed it in her purse and checked the main room to see if anyone else had arrived while she was at lunch.

"How nice to see you back, my dear," said Lydia Beeman, who seemed to be between lunch and the daily bridge game. "Won't you have a cup of coffee?"

"Thank you." Elena accepted the plastic foam cup Lydia handed her, and the two sat down at an empty table.

"I suppose your mother's been telling tales on me," said Lydia.

"What tales?" asked Elena innocently.

"Well, we had a set-to about exercise this morning, but I assure you, I was thinking of her health. When she gets to be my age, she'll wish she'd followed a more varied program.

Walking a loom may seem strenuous to your mother, but it doesn't involve enough of the important muscle groups. I myself try to follow a well-balanced program of physical activities."

"Well, you certainly seem in excellent health, Mrs. Beeman," said Elena politely.

"Lydia."

"Lydia," Elena agreed. "You're very sprightly."

"*Sprightly*?" Lydia cocked an eyebrow at Elena. "That's an old woman's word. I may be an old woman chronologically, but my body, my doctor would be happy to tell you, is that of a woman forty-five or fifty. Your mother should take that to heart. I imagine my physical age corresponds to her chronological age."

"Ummm," said Elena.

"Now, *you* seem to be in very good shape, my dear. What exercise do you participate in?"

Elena grinned. "House repair, gardening, and chasing criminals."

"Gardening is good," said Lydia approvingly. "As for house repair, can't you afford to hire it done?"

"I'm not that well paid," said Elena, "and I'm divorced. I don't intend to let the house fall apart, since it's all I have to show for the marriage."

"Very wise. A good citizen takes care of her property. As for chasing criminals, I don't suppose you meant that literally."

"Sure I did," said Elena. "I have quite literally run down drug dealers, murderers, drive-by shooters who abandoned their cars. You name 'em, I've run 'em down."

"Good for you," said Lydia. "I'm an ardent walker and bicycle rider, but I can't say I do much running."

Bicycle rider? Did she mean a real bicycle or one of those stationary things? Elena wondered, remembering the bicycle in the Potemkins' alley.

"Aren't you worried that you'll suffer joint injury?" Lydia asked. "I've heard runners do."

"They're probably the kind who run ten miles a day." That Ann Malone, whom Mrs. Ramsey mentioned, had ridden a bicycle outdoors at an advanced age. Maybe Lydia did. "I just

run when somebody who shouldn't be at large needs catching,"
said Elena.

"Yes." Lydia nodded. "There are, unfortunately, many people
whom society is better off without. I admire your career choice
and your devotion to it. Had I had a daughter, I'd want her to
be a good deal like you."

"Why, thank you, Lydia." Elena was touched. That was a
real compliment coming from a woman who didn't seem much
given to sentimentality. Because Lydia was part of the bridge
group and had been absent on the day of Boris' death, Elena
would have to check out the bicycle angle, but she didn't really
believe that a woman as hung up on law and order as Lydia
Beeman would take the law into her own hands. *If I'd had a
daughter, I'd want her to be like you*—what a nice thing to say.

"It's surprising that you turned out as well as you did with a
mother like yours."

Elena's warm feeling vanished, and she said sharply, "I
couldn't have asked for a better mother."

"I'm sure she was very loving, but she does have peculiar
ideas. Auras, for instance. Do you know anyone, besides your
mother, who claims to have seen an aura?"

Elena grinned, her momentary anger dissipating. "We all
have our idiosyncrasies. Mom's are harmless." She murmured
that she had to get back to the police station and excused
herself.

At headquarters she began to call more people who had been
at Socorro Heights the Monday of the murder. None of them
had seen T. Bob Tyler that afternoon and claimed that if he'd
been there, they'd have noticed him hovering around the bridge
group. Elena remembered him from the day she'd interviewed
the four ladies. He'd been very protective. Had he been afraid
they'd reveal something incriminating about him?

One woman laughed and said T. Bob Tyler had a crush on
anything in skirts. That information didn't add any evidence to
Elena's case against the old cowboy, but it did hone her
suspicions. And he had no alibi. No matter what he'd said, no
one had seen him at the center that afternoon.

She called to remind Harmony that dinner would have to be

served at eight-thirty since Elena was now on the twelve-to-eight shift.

"We'll eat fashionably late," Harmony agreed. "How about something French and sumptuous? I'll go shopping."

"If you're willing to cook it, I'll eat it," said Elena. She had a suspicion of French cuisine as admired by her friend Sarah Tolland: snails, brains, and goose liver. But Harmony would never serve her anything like that.

"And I forgot to tell you about something I discovered," said Harmony. "I've been asking questions—"

"About the murder?" interrupted Elena, alarmed. "I told you not to do that."

"Well, it's not as if I learned anything about anyone dangerous, Elena. Just a curious little item. Did you realize that each time a wife substituted in that bridge group and her husband was killed, Lydia Beeman was the person whose place the wife took? Not that I think Lydia killed anyone; she's too strait-laced. But it is odd."

Damned odd. Especially added to the bicycle-riding. Elena decided to talk to the members of the bridge group again. At their houses if possible. She glanced at her watch: 3:45. Some of them should be home from the center. By 4:15 she had appointments with Portia Lemay, Margaret Forrest, and Emily Marks. She hadn't been able to reach Lydia, but she could pick up that appointment tomorrow.

45
..

Margaret Forrest lived in an older ranch house in the Mission Hills district on the Westside. Elena wondered enviously how she kept her grass so green. It looked like emerald velvet, although the huge, fruitless mulberries must keep the yard in shade all day. There were beds of asters and crysanthemums and impeccably trimmed bushes. Well, this was the woman who, because she wanted to pinch her crysanthemums back, had left Dimitra to find the body alone. Elena had to admit that the pinching results were spectacular. Huge globes of luscious yellow.

Elena knocked at the door, was admitted after a short wait, and offered a cup of tea. In Margaret's living room were antiques that had been lovingly tended, probably with beeswax, by generations of women.

"I don't know what I can tell you," said Margaret as she poured from a silver teapot. "I haven't remembered any more about the day Potemkin died. That is what you wanted to talk to me about?"

"That and other cases."

"Really?" Looking surprised, Margaret offered Elena almond macaroons on a hand-painted china plate.

"Surely you've noticed that three other men beside Boris Potemkin were killed while their wives were playing in your bridge group."

"Yes," said Margaret.

It had been a fishing trip, an attempt to confirm that Mercedes Castro and Marcia Cox had actually been playing with the same three women.

"If I believed in such things," said Margaret, "I'd say we're jinxed. However, my husband died a natural death—cancer."

"I'm sorry," said Elena politely. She was finding it hard to ask questions while juggling her teacup, napkin, and cookie.

"I was at his bedside at the hospital, not at the center playing bridge. So a jinx theory wouldn't quite work. And let's see. Emily's husband is still alive, Portia never married, and Lydia—her husband had a heart attack but then seemed to be getting better. He and Lydia took walks, rode bicycles."

Bicycles? Elena's cup rattled in the saucer.

"Stationary, of course."

Damn!

"Couldn't have him falling down in the street or attempting hills. Unfortunately, he had a stroke six months later, but Lydia wasn't at the center. They were both at home. Ambrose died after becoming terribly angry that evening about something on TV. Another macaroon?" Margaret passed the plate. "Of course, if you are a choleric person with high blood pressure, anger is a killer."

"Can you see any other connections between these four deaths beyond the fact that the wives were substituting in your bridge group?"

Margaret looked thoughtful. "No, not really. The men were all killed in the course of robberies, but I'm sure you know that. Do you think the robbers somehow found out that the husbands would be alone?"

Elena had had that thought and dismissed it.

"Frankly, if I were a robber, I think I'd choose a day when the wife was alone, not the husband."

"Umm," Elena murmured. "There is one more case. The death of a Mr. Herbert Stoltz."

"Well, yes," said Margaret. Her face darkened. "But his wife wasn't playing bridge with us," she said grimly. "Frances was dead."

"I understand she was friendly with all of you."

"We went to school together. Same class. Except for Emily, who was several years younger." Margaret sighed. "Lydia was heartbroken. She's not a woman to show emotion, but she wept inconsolably at the funeral, and it took her quite some time to recover."

"Mrs. Forrest, do you think Frances Stoltz was a battered woman?"

"Of course."

Ah, thought Elena. *Now we're getting somewhere.*

"He killed her, didn't he? That's the ultimate battering."

"Before that?"

"I wouldn't think so. But you know situations like that are best not talked about. At least, in my opinion."

"Where they're not talked about, the wife often ends up dead," said Elena.

"Perhaps, but there was no indication that Frances was abused before Herbert shot her, and we all know why that happened. She wanted to leave him, and he objected. He was the sort of man who had to have his way in everything."

"So perhaps on earlier occasions when she disagreed with him, he hit her," Elena suggested.

"Lydia would have known. She and Frances were closer than sisters."

"Were any of the women whose husbands died"—how should she put it?—"the object of attentions from T. Bob Tyler. You know, the—"

"Of course, I know T. Bob. He's been going to the center as long as any of us. Every woman is the object of T. Bob Tyler's attention. The man adores women. He brings flowers, though I've often wondered how he can afford them. My guess is that he's on a tight budget. Not that he ever says anything. Too proud. If you're thinking T. Bob could have killed those husbands, in some sort of love triangle, that's ridiculous. The man's harmless."

Much you know, thought Elena, remembering all the assaults. "Perhaps out of a chivalric instinct to defend a battered woman."

"Goodness, we don't know that any of those women were battered."

"Even Dimitra? There's her broken hip."

"I wouldn't want to accuse Boris Potemkin without evidence, and Dimitra never *said* that he was responsible."

"Her country-dancing fling with T. Bob Tyler was certainly ended by the broken hip."

"My dear young lady, you're clutching at straws. I hope you can find better evidence than wild guesses and gossip if you plan to arrest anyone."

That was the end of the interview. Elena climbed into her car and wound her way up the mountain to King's Hill, where Portia Lemay had a small condo furnished in Early American.

"I understand you've found condos and sold houses for some of the women whose husbands died," said Elena midway into the interview.

"Yes, I did," Portia agreed, "although I was semiretired at the time and acting out of friendship and sympathy. We all have to do what we can for others. Margaret, for instance, cuts flowers from her garden and puts them on the graves or gives the flowers to the widows to do so. Flowers can be very expensive if you have to buy them."

Margaret hadn't mentioned that, thought Elena.

"I don't know why women marry," Portia was saying. "A woman can save herself a lot of heartache by remaining single."

"Do you think the women whose husbands died had difficult marriages?"

"I don't discuss people's marital problems with them. I was thinking of the shock of having a husband murdered. Are the police doing anything to catch those robbers?"

"We're trying," said Elena.

"I don't see what good it does to interview me. I don't know any robbers." Portia Lemay did not take T. Bob Tyler any more seriously than Margaret Forrest had. "What a funny man," she commented. "I know he'd love to get married. He's even proposed to me, but the chances of anyone accepting T. Bob are slim. After all, who wants to marry a Western stereotype? And I'll wager he doesn't have a penny, not even social security. Goodness knows where he lives. I once offered to find him an apartment, and he said no thank you, that he was quite happy with his present lodgings. But he doesn't strike me as a man who's living comfortably. I can look at a person and tell whether they're well housed."

Uh-huh, thought Elena. *The way Mom can look at a person and tell whether they're happy.*

Elena's last appointment of the day was with Emily Marks, who lived with her husband in Chaparral Park on the Westside, white brick and green shutters with a steep, shingled roof. Not very Southwestern—inside or out. The living room was a riot of flowered chintzes and fussy furniture, Emily herself fluttering about as if she were entertaining a celebrity.

"I'd invite you to dinner," she apologized, "but George isn't here, so I've already had a TV dinner. Isn't that terrible? If my sister Frances were alive, she'd say, 'Emily, if you don't eat well, you'll never live to a ripe old age like Mama.' Our mother lived to be ninety-two. She outlived Frances." Emily blinked back tears. "I don't suppose I'll live as long as Mama. I like sweets too much, *petit fours* particularly. I can eat a whole box at one sitting, and then I have to diet for a month. I like to keep my figure. For George's sake. Of course, George says he'd still love me if I weighed three hundred pounds, but I always ask him if he'd still want to take me to the dinner dances at the country club."

Elena decided that she had to overcome her familial strictures and interrupt Emily. "You mentioned your sister, Frances. Her husband was killed in a daylight robbery, I believe."

"And he deserved it too," said Emily. "He *killed* Frances." Emily began to cry. "How could anyone kill a woman as sweet as Frances? She was always so good to me. And Lydia was devastated. I don't think she's ever got over Frances' death. They were best friends from girlhood. Both married military men and kept in touch all those years when their husbands were at different posts. Then they moved back here when their husbands retired, so happy to be together again. They saw each other every day." Emily smiled through her tears.

"And then Herbert killed my sister, and they didn't even send him to jail. Lydia was just furious," Emily confided. "She attended every day of the trial. I couldn't. I kept crying, and the judge made me leave. But Lydia went. If looks could kill,

Herbert would have been dead long before that robber shot him. Poor Frances. It wasn't fair." Emily sighed and blew her nose into a dainty handkerchief which she had extracted from the pocket of her blue-flowered dress. "We try to comfort each other—Lydia and I. We both lost a sister in Frances."

Elena had begun taking notes as soon as Emily talked of her sister's death. If Herbert was the first victim of a serial killer, she wanted to know as much as she could about him. "Do you think her husband ever hurt your sister before he killed her?"

"You mean like Boris Potemkin did Dimitra?" asked Emily. "I'm sure Frances would have told us—Lydia or me—but she never said anything."

"You're saying Boris Potemkin hurt Dimitra?" That wasn't what Emily had said at the center. Everyone Elena interviewed had waffled on that point.

"Of course he did. No one wants to talk about things like that, but he pushed her downstairs and broke her hip."

"You're sure of that?"

"Well, we weren't there, of course, but that doesn't mean he didn't do it. When Lydia heard, she went as white as a sheet. Who wouldn't? Broken hips are dangerous. Life's dangerous," said Emily, looking very upset. "People getting hurt and killed. I try not to think about it. George tells me not to fret over what I can't change."

"Actually, Mrs. Marks, I'm looking into the deaths not only of Boris Potemkin but of several other men who were killed while their wives were at the center."

"Exactly." Emily shivered. "It makes me so nervous, I bought George a gun for his birthday. I told him to keep it right beside him when I wasn't home. In case that robber tried to kill my George. Of course, George just laughed. He doesn't know anything about guns, and I'd forgotten to get bullets. George said, 'Am I supposed to carry it to the grocery store?'— George does the grocery shopping since he retired—and he said a gun would ruin his golf game." Emily giggled. "George is so funny. I never think of any jokes, but he said even if he had a holster for the gun, it would make him slice or—what's the other word for hitting the ball the wrong way?"

"Hook," said Elena. They were all aware that men were

getting killed while they played bridge. Well, why wouldn't
they be aware? Murder wasn't exactly an everyday event in the
lives of older middle-class women. But they all believed
robbers to be at fault. Elena didn't.

"Did T. Bob Tyler ever show any interest in the widows of
the men who were killed?"

"What a strange question!" Emily squirmed on the flowered
upholstery of her sofa. Elena gripped her pen, thinking some
important revelation might be coming. "I just can't stand it,"
said Emily.

She knows something, thought Elena, elated. *Finally, a real
breakthrough*.

"Would you like a chocolate-covered cherry?" Emily jumped
up and rushed to an ornate cabinet, opened a door inset with
leaded glass, and pulled out a box of candy. "I promised myself
I wouldn't eat any more until tomorrow, but when I have them
in the house, I just can't resist." She whipped off the lid and
offered the box to Elena.

Disappointed when it turned out that Emily was fighting a
desire for chocolate rather than a desire to reveal some secret
about T. Bob Tyler, Elena selected a cherry, which was terrific,
bathed in some kind of tasty liqueur, covered with rich, dark
chocolate, stem sticking out the top so you didn't get your
fingers sticky when you picked one up.

"Have another," said Emily. "Aren't they scrumptious? Let's
see. You asked about T. Bob. Well, of *course* he was interested
in the widows. Poor T. Bob wants to get married in the worst
way. He keeps asking women out, not just the women whose
husbands were murdered."

"Did he date Marcia Cox?" asked Elena, wondering if a man
would kill a husband in order to free the wife for courtship.

"Well, he asked." Emily giggled and pulled another cherry
off the stem with small white teeth. "Marcia told him that it
was much too early for her to consider dating. So he asked her
about six months later. You know, she stopped coming so often
to the center after that. I expect she didn't want to go out with
him. He's a sweet man, but I'm sure he hasn't a dime. Women
have to be careful they're not married for their money, you
know. Especially widows."

"What about Chantal Brolie? Did he ask her out?"

"Oh, yes. He even took her French class before her husband was killed. Can you imagine a cowboy talking French? Everyone knew it was because he was sweet on her. And he asked her out when Hank died. Chantal does date, so she couldn't very well use that excuse, so you know what she said?" Emily's delighted laugh tinkled into the air, which smelled of potpourri. A small basket of it sat on the coffee table, making Elena's nose itch. "She said she really couldn't understand him well enough to consider dating him. His accent was beyond her. T. Bob was terribly disappointed, but he *does* have a country accent. Our teachers at the Arland School wouldn't let us have accents. I don't sound like a Texan, do you think?"

"Not at all," Elena assured her.

"There, you see. And I've lived in Texas all my life."

"How about Mercedes Castro?"

"Poor T. Bob. He waited quite a while to ask Mercedes, and she told him she didn't date Anglos. Actually, I don't think she dates anyone. That son of hers has turned her into a housemaid-baby-sitter. I tell my children that I love the grandbabies, but I don't want to spend all my time baby-sitting. They're quite well enough off to hire someone. Anyway, Mercedes has that terrible scar. Poor thing. I'm surprised T. Bob asked her out. But Dimitra's had several dates with him, and Boris is hardly cold in his grave."

It was seven-thirty before Elena got out of Emily Marks's house, but she felt she'd made progress. She went back to headquarters to type up a report, wondering all the while what her mother was fixing for dinner.

46
..

Elena was cruising toward her house when she spotted an agitated threesome at the gate to Dimitra's courtyard. Dimitra, wearing a red and white polyester dress, was leaning on her walker, expostulating; T. Bob Tyler waved a fistful of lilies and shouted at Omar Ashkenazi, who was rocking back and forth on his heels and talking earnestly. Elena slammed on her brakes and dashed toward the fray in time to hear Omar say, "I just want to switch nights. If you understood my sleeping habits—"

"I don't care none about yer sleepin' habits," said T. Bob, shaking his bouquet in Omar's face.

Omar sneezed. The cloying scent of the lilies tickled Elena's nose too, although she was five feet away. No one seemed to notice her.

"I don't see why you won't switch, T. Bob," said Dimitra. "If we go at five tomorrow night, the paper says drinks at Big Andy's Saloon and Dance Hall will be two for one."

"You're breakin' our date?" demanded T. Bob, outraged.

"No, I'm just saying, since Omar happens to be awake tonight, I should go with you tomorrow instead."

"I believe in natural sleep," explained Omar. "If you're tired, lie down and sleep; that's my motto. You should try it. Natural sleep might improve your disposition, Mr. Tyler."

258

"You're standin' me up after all Ah done for you?" T. Bob demanded of Dimitra.

All he'd done for her? Did that include killing Boris? Elena felt a surge of excitement. Maybe her case was finally about to break. She had reached the warring threesome, but not in time to stop T. Bob from shouting, "Ah'll teach you to steal mah gal," and hitting Omar with a left hook, followed by a fistful of lilies to the ear.

Dimitra shrieked and pushed her walker into T. Bob, surprising him, but doing no damage. Omar staggered backward, then regained his balance. "*Hai!*" he shouted, hands whipping into a position Elena had seen in those stupid kung fu movies her ex-husband, Frank, loved. Then Omar kicked T. Bob Tyler in the balls.

"My lord!" cried Dimitra.

T. Bob doubled over, groaning.

Omar, the first to notice Elena's presence, said, "That man assaulted me." Omar's nose was bleeding, and a lily dangled raffishly over his protruding right ear.

"I have to tell you both," said Dimitra angrily, "I don't like violence." She began to maneuver her walker through the gate.

"You going to press charges, Omar?" Elena asked. Having seen the whole thing, she realized that Omar could, even though T. Bob seemed the worse for the encounter.

"Absolutely," said Omar and chased Dimitra into the courtyard, explaining anxiously that his only fighting skills were self-defense tactics, which he'd learned in his pursuit of Oriental disciplines.

"I give her them flowers, an' she stood me up fer that there lil furriner," groaned T. Bob. "He kicked me in mah privates. A man don't do no dirty fightin' in front of a lady. Ever'one knows that."

"I'm afraid I'm going to have to take you downtown and book you, T. Bob," said Elena, cuffing his hands in front rather than trying to uncup them from his genitals. At least he'd be off the street until she could find out if he was the serial killer. Otherwise, Omar might have been his next victim.

Dimitra and Omar were still arguing in the courtyard, so Elena stuck her head in and reminded the kung fu-yoga-vegetarian-carpet expert that he'd have to come downtown to press charges.

"We could catch a late movie at one of the malls," said Omar to Dimitra.

"That would be past my bedtime," Dimitra retorted.

"Don't step on them flowers," said T. Bob, still bent over and sweating as Elena started him toward her truck. "I went to a heap of trouble to bring her them flowers, an' look what it got me."

47
∴

Because they'd been called out on another case the night before, Elena and Leo didn't get to T. Bob Tyler until the next morning. "The interesting thing," Elena told Leo, "is what T. Bob said to Dimitra. 'You're standing me up after all I've done for you?' What's he done for her? Taken her out a few times. Gone to the funeral and protest with her."

"You think he killed Boris for her?" asked Leo. "Would he have said that in front of you?"

"I'm not sure he noticed I was there. He'd be crazy to hit Omar if he had. T. Bob's got one bar assault here in Los Santos. He came within a whisker of getting charged with assaulting an officer at the demonstration; Lydia Beeman got him out of that. Then there's a long record in Otero County even if charges were never filed."

They parked across the street at Central Division, walked down the ramp to the basement of the jail to check their weapons into lockers, and had T. Bob called down for an interrogation. He was in loose jail clothes and complaining about the breakfast he'd been served, the bed he'd had to sleep in, and the manners of the men in his cell block.

"Have you tried to bail out?" Elena asked.

"With what? Ah cain't afford it," said T. Bob.

"You want your lawyer present while we question you?" asked Leo.

261

"That little pipsqueak ain't gonna do me no good. If he could, Ah wouldna spent the night in jail."

"Should we take that as a no?" asked Elena. "You're willing to talk to us without counsel present?"

"Damn right," said T. Bob indignantly. "'Scuse the profanity, miss. Ah don't usually swear in front of ladies, but then Ah don't usually spend no sober time in jails neither."

"You said to Dimitra, just before you hit Mr. Ashkenazi, 'You're standing me up after all I've done for you?' What did you mean by that?"

"Ah don't 'member sayin' that. How come Ah'm in jail an' he ain't? What he done to me, he oughta be hung. Kickin' me in mah privates. Ah may never be able to pleasure a woman agin."

Elena sighed. "I was there, Mr. Tyler. You assaulted Mr. Ashkenazi. He simply defended himself."

"He was tryin' to steal mah gal."

"I'm afraid you don't have exclusive rights to Dimitra," Elena replied.

"Ah been courtin' her, ain't Ah? Brought her flowers, din' Ah?"

"What else did you do for her?" asked Leo. "You haven't explained yet what you meant by the remark Detective Jarvis overheard."

"Ah meant Ah took her out to them fancy clubs an' spent big money on her—three-dollar cover charges an' drinks. Once we went when they didn't even have one of them dollar wine an' well-drink specials. *Nachos*. Ah bought the woman *nachos*. Don't that mean we're at least goin' steady? Ah ain't no millionaire. Ah had to stand around at the hirin' depot an' git mahself hired on to move someone's furniture outa one a them big semis into a house. An' Ah'm always the last one took. Them drivers don' wanna hire a man mah age. They think Ah'm gonna throw mah back out an' sue 'em. Like after bustin' broncs an' punchin' cows all them years, movin' a few sticks a furniture's gonna do me in."

"What else did you do for her?" asked Leo.

"Ah brung her flowers. She saw 'em." He pointed to Elena. "Ah shore hope Miz Dimitra put 'em in water."

"Were you and Dimitra dating before Boris died?" asked Elena.

"'Course not," said T. Bob. "We was dancin' partners in the country-dancin' class, but that wasn't no date 'cause it didn't cost me nothin'."

"But you killed Boris for her, didn't you?"

"Me?" T. Bob looked astounded. "Ah ain't never killed nobody. That what you think Ah done? Murder? Ah ain't sayin' one more word. Ah want mah lawyer. Even if he is a dumb pipsqueak."

As they left, Elena said, "Let's get a warrant to search his apartment and his truck. Maybe the judge will go for the idea that T. Bob killed the husband, since he just attacked a suitor."

While Leo went to court, Elena kept the ten o'clock appointment she'd made to interview Lydia Beeman, who received her with warm hospitality and served excellent coffee and bran muffins with an ambrosial plum jam. "When I was a girl on the ranch, we used to pick wild plums and make preserves," said Lydia when Elena complimented her.

Leo would be at least two hours getting the warrant, and there was no great hurry now, with T. Bob in jail, so Elena settled back. She could afford to let Lydia talk, direct the conversation now and then, and see what came out.

"I believe you're a gardener," said Lydia, passing the cream and sugar.

"Why yes, I am. How did you know?"

"You told me, my dear, but I could have deduced as much from your hands. If I may offer some advice, you should always wear gloves, not just gardening but whenever you're outside. Look at *my* hands." Lydia displayed them, palms down, fingers spread.

They were surprisingly youthful, Elena had to admit.

"I'm seventy-six years old, but I have the hands of a much younger woman, no age spots, few wrinkles. That's because I never leave the house without gloves on. Also sunscreen and a sun hat."

Elena's first thought was a cop's reaction. Lydia Beeman wouldn't leave fingerprints anywhere but in her own house and

at the Socorro Heights Center. "You do have lovely hands an
skin," Elena agreed.

Lydia nodded. "If I'd had a daughter, I'd have given her th
advice I'm giving you. If you follow it, you'll be very gla
when you're my age. Vitamins, exercise, and a sensible diet ar
important as well. I attribute my good health and vigor to those
And sensible shoes." Lydia looked at Elena's low-heele
pumps. "You'd do much better to wear a sturdy lace-up shoe t
work, my dear. That way you won't find yourself with bunions
calluses, and arch problems when you turn forty."

Elena thanked her for the advice and took a bite of muffin a
she sought an opening in which to introduce the Potemkin case
Lydia gave her one by asking about her progress. "Not much,
said Elena. "We thought Lance might have done it, but he ha
a good alibi. Now, since T. Bob Tyler's in jail, we're lookin;
at him as a suspect."

"What's *he* in jail for?" asked Lydia.

"Assaulting another of Dimitra's gentlemen callers. There'
the possibility that Dimitra talked him into killing Boris."

"Nonsense," said Lydia. "T. Bob Tyler is a silly old man wh
thinks he's some kind of Western hero in the old-fashione
mold. Which he isn't. I have twenty ancestors who were rea
heroes, so I know one when I see one. T. Bob wouldn't have th
nerve to plan and execute a murder."

"Even for love?" asked Elena, smiling.

"Love for whom?"

"Dimitra. She certainly had reason to wish Boris dead. Th
man pushed her down the stairs and broke her hip."

Lydia shrugged. "*If* that were true, and *I* certainly don'
know it to be, I doubt that Dimitra would have the gumption t
solicit his murder. Even to protect herself. I have no doubt tha
Boris was murdered by a robber."

If that were true, Lydia had said and, *I don't know it to b*
She was lying. Emily Marks claimed they all knew ho
Dimitra's hip got broken, that Lydia had become very upse
about it. Had Lydia lied because she, like so many women he
age, didn't think such subjects should be discussed? "Nothin
of much value was taken," said Elena. "If a robber killed Bori

it's lucky you happened to ask Dimitra to take your place at bridge that day."

"Actually, I think she offered."

"Either way you may have saved *her* from being killed too."

"I suppose it *was* fortunate. I don't miss many games, but of course, that was a special day."

"Oh?"

"The anniversary of my husband's death. I always visit his grave. Bring him up to date." Lydia smiled.

Elena wasn't really surprised that Lydia had an alibi for the twenty-seventh, probably verifiable too, since her husband would be buried at Fort Bliss.

"I suppose talking to a dead man sounds daft to you, especially after I criticized your mother for thinking she sees auras, but of course, my husband doesn't reply to anything I tell him. Those yearly conversations just make me feel closer to him."

"I'm investigating the deaths of other men whose wives were at the center," said Elena, feeling her way cautiously.

"Umm. Yes," said Lydia thoughtfully. "There have been other robbery-murders. Old people are targets. There's no question."

"Do you remember anything particular about those days?" They weren't all on the anniversary of Colonel Beeman's death, yet Lydia had been gone each time.

"Goodness, my dear. I can't even be sure what years they occurred, much less what was happening on a particular day. I believe your mother was asking about those days too. Is she assisting in your investigation?"

"Mom? No, not at all. She's just indignant about older people getting killed."

Lydia nodded. "Of course she is. Well, it's been delightful to have you visit, Elena. I hope you'll come back another time."

Elena wasn't nearly finished with her questions.

"I'm afraid I have to be at the center at eleven today, and I need to change my clothes." Lydia rose.

Elena, looking for an excuse to stay longer and ask about bicycling, spotted the beautiful mahogany gun cabinet. "What a wonderful collection you have!" she exclaimed. "I think I remember Mom saying that you liked to keep the guns in pristine condition because they belonged to your husband."

"Your mother has an excellent memory," Lydia muttered, her tone reminding Elena that the two women always struck sparks off one another. "They were his pride and joy," Lydia added.

"Being a law officer, I'm very interested in guns," said Elena, planting herself firmly in front of the cabinet. The side arms were labeled and carefully mounted. Elena read the cards rapidly, trying to commit the types to memory. Lydia had a Nambu and the unsightly, inefficient Type 94 from the Japanese army in World War II, a fine Italian Beretta Modello, stylish Lugers, Walther P38's, PP's and PPK's; there were Colts, Smith and Wessons, Enfields, and Webleys from the British and American armies, Nagants and Tokarevs from the Russian—

"It is a fine collection," said Lydia, taking Elena's arm. "And valuable. I really need to put a lock on that case, especially considering how many people know about the guns." She steered Elena gently toward the front door, saying, "I get requests all the time to show them to collectors and to lend them out for gun shows, local theater, even several movies filmed here in Los Santos."

"Do you?" Elena held back. "I'd love to hear about them."

"Then you must come back when we both have more time," said Lydia. "I'd be delighted to show you the collection and tell you the stories of how my husband came to own them."

A murderer with access to this cabinet wouldn't need to go elsewhere. Elena wasn't sure, but she thought every one of the five men had been killed with a weapon represented here.

"You will excuse me," said Lydia.

"Of course," Elena acquiesced. She wasn't going to get into a tug of war with the woman, but she'd love to have Ballistics run a check on all those guns. Of course, she'd never get a warrant. She didn't have anything against Lydia except absence from the center when the crimes were committed and a lie about Dimitra's hip. The lie could be explained by old-fashioned reluctance to talk about wife-battering. And female serial killers were as rare as low-fat meals in a Mexican restaurant. Not to mention the fact that Lydia didn't have an alarm system; Elena checked on the way out. Anyone could get in and borrow a gun from that unlocked cabinet. Still, she'd tell Leo about the guns. They'd quiz T. Bob about his relationship to Lydia Beeman. Damn! She'd never got a chance to mention bicycling.

48
##

"Did Leo get the warrant?" Elena asked Manny Escobedo.

"Yep. He didn't find anything in the truck, but he's had it towed." Manny swiveled away from the litter of paperwork on his desk. "The address is a fake. The apartment complex exists, but the apartment number's for a floor they don't have, and Tyler never lived there."

"Did Leo check it against the address Tyler gave the center?"

"Same fake. Mail goes to a P.O. box. Turns out he has a room at one of those fleabag hotels downtown. Used to live at the Y, but he had to move when they closed down the living facilities."

"How did Leo find out?"

"By going back to the jail and yelling at the old man. He's getting another warrant now."

"Why would Tyler lie about his address? Unless he's got something to hide in that room."

Manny shrugged. "You'll find out pretty quick, and if there's evidence in his room, he won't have had a chance to get rid of it since his arrest. He never called anyone from the jail."

Were they about to close this case at last? Maybe they'd find the gun that killed Boris. Or if—and she still considered this a long shot—T. Bob had got a weapon from Lydia Beeman and given it back after the murder or left it for Dimitra to get rid of, still, they might find the czar's medal. "I'm working overtime, you know," she said to Manny. "I wasn't supposed to be in until noon, but we wanted to talk to Tyler."

Manny nodded. "You're cleared."

"Got it," said Leo, coming in from Reception, waving the search warrant. "I can't believe that old s.o.b. let me go after a warrant for premises that didn't exist."

"He didn't know we wanted to search his place," said Elena.

"Well, hell, if being lied to and wasting most of the morning doesn't bother you, you can get the warrants next time, and I'll talk to the old ladies."

"No way. I had bran muffins and homemade plum jam while you were hanging around some judge's chambers."

"Stop arguing and go toss his room," said Manny. "Beltran's getting antsy about this case. Since that demonstration, both Stollinger and the chief keep asking him if we've closed it."

They had to climb four floors, up stairways and through corridors that smelled of urine and dust, unwashed clothes and bodies. "I can't believe he lives here," said Elena. "He always looks neat and respectable."

Leo opened the door with the key the manager had given them. The room was clean and bare: narrow bed with a worn quilt over patched sheets; a dresser with a round mirror whose silver backing had long since disintegrated and left blurred patches in the reflection. The closet contained two Western-style suits, two pairs of worn jeans, two pairs of polyester trousers, one with snags, and three shirts, all with yokes and studs down the front. In the dresser they found tattered underwear, one pair of flannel pajamas—"I hope he doesn't have to wear these in the summer too," muttered Elena—and a picture of a blond woman who must have been young in the late thirties if the clothing and hairstyle were any indication. "His wife?" Elena wondered aloud. The picture was in a small oval frame—white enamel and gold.

In the bathroom they found a chipped toilet with a cracked seat, a sink whose porcelain was wearing thin, a shower curtain encrusted with soap scum, two shirts hanging from the shower rod, an ironing board without legs, an old iron with a frayed cord, carefully preserved slivers of soap, straight razor and shaving brush, comb and hair oil sitting on the sink. That was it. No TV, no extra pairs of shoes or boots, no reading material, no weapons, no czar's medal, nothing in the waste basket or lower drawers of the dresser, nothing on the shelf above the closet rod.

Only when they opened the door to the empty medicine cabinet did they hit pay dirt. Scotch-taped to the wood were pictures of women and in some cases obituaries of their husbands. The couples Elena had investigated, except for the Stoltzes, were there, not to mention obituaries of men who had died of natural causes and pictures of their wives. Elena and Leo exchanged glances.

"So we go back and talk to him," said Leo.

"And take the door with us," Elena agreed.

"My God," said Leo. "What a way to live."

49
::

"Look what we found," said Leo, displaying the door they had removed from T. Bob's medicine cabinet.

The old man, who usually looked neat and healthy, was now rumpled and pale. No women, no sunshine, no ironing board explained it, Elena surmised. It was sad really, thinking of him in that awful room, washing his clothes in the sink, drying them on the shower rod, and ironing them on that little board, probably set up across the sink. All so he could look spiffy for the ladies at the center. But it would have seemed a lot sadder if he hadn't killed their husbands.

T. Bob stared at the door with its load of obits and women's pictures. "How'd you git that?" he asked, face reddening. "If Ah'd known you was goin' to tear up mah room, Ah'd never a tole you where Ah lived."

"It's evidence," said Leo.

"Of what?"

"You killed the four guys, didn't you? Saved their obituaries? Got pictures of their wives?"

"Ah tole ya. Ah ain't never killed nobody. Even in the war. Ah was stuck in a supply depot stateside."

"Why the obits, then?"

T. Bob shrugged.

"All these women were abused by their husbands," said

271

Elena, leaning forward. "I think a jury would understand that
you killed the husbands to protect the wives."

"Ah didn't do no such thing. Ah was at the center when
Potemkin died."

"But you did know what he'd done to Dimitra, didn't you?
Broke her hip?"

"Ever'one knew," T. Bob muttered.

"I imagine you felt guilty about it, didn't you?"

"Ah don' know what you mean."

"He didn't like her dancing with you, so he saw to it that she
couldn't dance anymore. How did that make you feel, T. Bob?"
Elena asked sympathetically.

"Bad," T. Bob admitted.

"So you picked a day when she wouldn't be home and killed
him," said Leo.

"No!" the old cowboy exclaimed.

"And started courting the widow before he was even in the
ground."

"She din' mind."

"Don't be so hard on him, Leo," said Elena. "If the woman
you loved were hurt, you might want to kill the man who did
it."

"Ah din'—"

"And Mercedes Castro. Such a pretty woman," said Elena to
T. Bob.

"She sure was. Prettiest Mex Ah ever seen."

"And when her old man cut her like that, you killed him.
Right?" said Leo.

"No. Why would Ah? She wasn't never interested in me."

"You asked her out," said Elena.

"Well, yeah, but she wouldn't go out with no Anglo. Kin you
beat that? You'd think she'd be glad of the chance."

"And the other two, Chantal and Marcia. You asked them out
too."

"After you killed their husbands," Leo added. "What did you
do with the guns?"

"Ah don' have no guns. Sold mine long since. An' Ah din'
kill no one. Ah was at the center."

"I've asked every single person who was there that afternoon," said Elena. "Not a one of them saw you."

The old man turned pale. "Well, don' matter. Ah was there," he said stubbornly.

"Maybe you got the guns from Lydia," suggested Elena, just to see how that would fly. "Are you and Lydia Beeman friends?"

"Beeman?" he echoed. "She wouldn't give me the time of day. Ah asked her out once." T. Bob looked hurt. "She laughed."

"So where did you get the guns?" asked Leo.

"How come you've got the obituaries of all those men who were shot? Why keep them if—"

"'Cause of their wives," said T. Bob desperately. "The obituaries tell where they live, so Ah kin git their telephone numbers. Jus' cause Ah want to git married an' have someone to take care of me in mah old age don' mean Ah'm a murderer. There's other widders on mah board. Din' you see that? Ah need a woman to support me an' take care of me. Ah'm gittin' old. Ah gotta marry before Ah cain't take no more day work to pay for courtin'. Nothin' wrong with that. A man needs a wife." He looked to be on the verge of tears.

"Ah lost mine," he mumbled. "Lost mah ranch. Now Ah gotta git me a *new* wife. It ain't that easy when you're mah age. Wimmen, they ain't so anxious fer a man. Ah been workin' real hard at it. Ever since Ah moved here. Ain't had no luck a-tall. But Ah had me a good chance with Dimitra. Then you went an' arrested me. If you'd jus' let me out, Ah might could go over to her house an' tell her the only reason Ah hit him was 'cause Ah love her, an' Ah din' want her goin' out with some furriner. She's maybe mah last chance. Ah gotta git outa jail."

"Where were you the day Boris Potemkin died?" asked Leo.

T. Bob Tyler brushed a fist across his eyes. "Ah ain't talkin' to you no more. Why should Ah? You ain't listenin'."

Once the guard had taken their suspect away, Elena asked, "What do you think?"

"Hell, I don't know. He wants a wife. I guess one way is to make a widow and then court her."

Elena sighed. "I hate to think about giving this case to the D.A.'s office."

"It's the best one we've got. Unless you think that old lady with the guns did it." Leo laughed. "Try to sell that one to the D.A. War Hero's Wife Kills Off Old Men. He'll love it. Well, I'm off shift. You can type this one up."

"Thanks," said Elena.

At a little after seven Elena had just returned to her desk from the investigation of a freeway assault that occurred after an accident in rush-hour traffic. She found a message from the jail. T. Bob Tyler wanted to see her. Not Leo, just her. Maybe playing good cop-bad cop had paid off, and T. Bob wanted to hear what she had to say about a jury sympathizing with his championship of battered women. She asked Bob Allency, her partner on the freeway assault, to do the report. "I've got a murder suspect ready to confess," she explained.

"Be sure he's been Mirandized," said Allency.

"Thanks, Bob," she retorted dryly as she picked up her handbag. "Do you give that reminder to the guys too?"

"You broads are so touchy," said Allency, grinning.

"You guys are such sexist pigs," replied Elena with good-humored relish, and headed for the jail.

"I hope you've been thinking about what I said, T. Bob. About juries understanding a man who feels called upon to defend women," she began as soon as he was brought in. "You might be able to cut a deal with the D.A."

"Ah tole you," he said reproachfully. "Ah ain't a murderer. So Ah'm gonna tell you where Ah was that afternoon, but you gotta promise you won't tell no one."

Elena frowned. "If you really have an alibi, we can't very well keep it to ourselves."

"Look, Ah wanna git outa jail. Ah gotta go see Miz Dimitra. Ah 'splained all that."

Telling her where he'd been when Boris died wasn't going to absolve him of the assault charge filed by Omar, but Elena didn't mention that. "So where were you?"

"At the cemetery."

"Which one?"

"Fort Bliss. Ah go to different ones, but Ah was at Fort Bliss hat day."

Great. Maybe he saw Lydia there. They could alibi each other. "What do you mean you go to different ones?"

"Fer the flowers. You think Ah can afford flowers fer mah dates? Ah watch the paper fer funerals. Then Ah go later an' pick up some flowers. The dead folks don't care, an' ever'one knows ladies like flowers."

"The ones you hit Omar with—the lilies?"

"Got 'em at Evergreen. Wish folks wouldn't send them lilies, though. They're too much like funerals."

"They're *for* funerals."

"Don't mean folks can't send somethin' else. Hell—'scuse me—heck. Five years ago it was a lot easier. Now folks give the money to some charity. If the death notice says to do that, Ah don't bother to go. Just save mah gas."

"Anyone see you at the cemetery that Monday?"

"Guard prob'ly did. Ah don't call attention to mahself. Gotta sneak out with the flowers. Say, you're not gonna arrest me fer—"

"For stealing flowers? Not until I've checked it out, anyway," said Elena.

"You don't believe me?" he asked incredulously. "Would Ah admit to a thang like that if it warn't true? Now jus' you remember, you ain't tellin' nobody about this."

"I never promised."

"Ah mean any a mah lady friends at the center. Like Dimitra. You ain't gonna tell her them lilies come from the grave of some lady named Pearl Abbott, are you? Ah said a prayer for Pearl before Ah took the flowers. Prayers, they're worth more to the dead than flowers, Ah reckon."

"Probably," Elena agreed. She'd check the cemetery tomorrow. For right now, it was almost eight, and she was going home before she accumulated any more crazy information.

50
..

Elena came in the back door to find her mother watching a program on TV. "I wish I had more time to spend with you, Mom," she said. "Here I just worked a twelve-hour shift and left you by your—"

"Oh, my dear, no one needs to tell me about policemen's hours. Come into the living room. I have a surprise for you." Harmony grabbed Elena's hand and tugged her out of the kitchen.

Elena gasped. Her love seat was finished. She'd seen the material growing on the loom but never clearly envisioned how it would look. A stylized desert-and-mountain scene in navy, Hopi green, coral, and beige repeated itself across the cushions of the love seat. It was beautiful! And it was hers! "Oh, Mom. It's—it's—"

Harmony smiled. "There'll be solid-color pillows in different sizes matching the colors in the design. I plan to hand sew the fourth sides on those tomorrow. And I should think we'll have the sofa and the drapes done in a week to ten days."

"It's fantastic." Elena hugged her mother. She was used to life on the Spartan side. Now she was going to have one room that anyone could envy. She wondered how her friend Sarah would like the design. A bit unconventional for Sarah's taste, but still Sarah'd have to see how beautiful it was. Elena would

276

invite her over to dinner, preferably before Harmony left so the food would be up to Sarah's standards.

"Now for the bad news," said Harmony. "Do you want to eat first?"

"Oh, what the heck," said Elena, getting a beer from the refrigerator as her mother put leftover *caldillo* on the stove. "I might as well hear the bad news. Then I won't have to wonder what it is while I'm eating."

"Your guitar's gone again."

Elena's first, elated thought was that she wouldn't have to sing in the talent show. She manufactured a look of indignation. Then she realized that Frank must have taken it. "How did he get another key?"

Harmony sighed. "The truth is, I was playing it on the patio before I left for the center this morning. Then I got a call from Juanita Ituribe about the drapes. I did put your guitar in the case before I answered, but then I forgot it. Someone must have taken it while I was away teaching my class. It might not have been Frank, although I suppose he's irritated about the *curandera*, especially since I got her an ACLU lawyer who's going to say the police have interfered with the practice of her religion after Frank specifically asked for the ceremony."

Elena started to laugh. "Irritated" was too mild a word for the emotions her ex-husband must be feeling. "Mom, you're the best. The very best," she said, hugging Harmony.

"I am? I thought you'd be upset about the guitar. I'll get you another, of course, but—"

"No, you won't. You weren't the woman who was dumb enough to marry Frank after your father told you not to."

"Well, Elena, *my* father told me not to marry Ruben, and our marriage has been a success. Just because your father—"

"Father knew best in this case. I'll buy my own guitar, and be more careful if I marry again."

"So you should. Now sit down and eat your *caldillo*. I have a favor to ask."

"Anything," said Elena. "The ACLU, huh? Frank must be livid." She picked up the spoon.

"I've been thinking about heredity," said Harmony. "If I can see auras, there's a good chance you can if you'll just try."

"Mom!" cried Elena.

"You did say *anything*." Although she had already eaten, Harmony sat down across the table and broke a piece off Elena's roll. "The first thing we'll try is the easiest—a mirror. The pale walls in your room are the right color; we can get soft lighting by using only lamps, no overheads."

"My room doesn't have an overhead."

Harmony nodded abstractedly. "What you have to do is look into the mirror, focusing two feet behind your image and—oh—six or eight inches above your head. Then relax and wait. Before you know it, you'll see your own aura. If you're very calm, it will be blue. If you're being stubborn, gold. And just remember, Elena, you promised, so I don't want to see any angry red."

"Mom, how can I see something I don't believe in?"

"As Coleridge said, I expect a 'willing suspension of disbelief.'"

"He was talking about fiction."

"Just wait till you see that aura! It's very exciting, dear."

"Then how come we haven't tried this before?"

"The *curandera* told me what to do when we were chatting after her conference with the lawyer. Your aura, or any human aura, is strongest at seven Greenwich mean time."

"The *curandera* told you *that*?"

"No, Elena, I got that information from the library. Unfortunately, I don't know how Greenwich time corresponds to mountain time. I didn't think to ask. But if we fail tonight, I'll call the library reference department tomorrow. Did you know you can ask them questions and they'll look up the answers for you? What a delightful service."

Elena sighed. If she actually saw an aura, she'd probably jump out of her skin. But if she didn't, Harmony would be disappointed.

51
..

Wednesday, October 13, 12:30 P.M.

Elena slept in, exhausted after the aura lessons. Staring into a mirror when you'd just put in a twelve-hour day and knew you were disappointing your mother was tiring business. She signed in for her shift at noon and typed up her solo interview with T. Bob Tyler at the jail, detailing the alibi of a man who claimed he had been stealing flowers in a cemetery at the time a murder was being committed.

Leo was out on another case, domestic assault; there sure was a lot of that, in the Potemkin-maybe-serial-killer case as well as elsewhere. Elena decided to visit the Fort Bliss National Cemetery by herself. It wasn't as if she'd need backup while she checked out cemetery visitors.

She discovered very quickly from obsessive military record-keeping that T. Bob Tyler had signed in at 1:45 P.M. on the day of Boris Potemkin's death. "Old boy comes by regular," said the soldier on duty. "Visitin' comrades from World War II, don't you reckon? Kinda touchin'. Hope someone comes to visit me when I'm dead."

Elena nodded. "When did he sign out?"

"We don't sign folks out. Who'd want to stay in a cemetery after it closes?"

Boris had been killed between two and three. "I don't suppose you saw Mr. Tyler leave?"

"Hey, lady, I don't even know if I was on duty that day. I'm just tellin' you what the records say."

So T. Bob could have come straight out, driven over to the Potemkins', and killed Boris. Maybe he'd figured on establishing an alibi by coming to the cemetery. Still, was he clever enough to have thought up the flower-theft alibi? Elena had seen the lilies he claimed to have stolen for Dimitra from the grave of Pearl Abbott. "Could I use your telephone?"

"Sorry, ma'am. Only military personnel—"

"This is official police business." Elena flashed her badge again.

"Well, I guess," said the soldier and allowed her into his guardhouse, from which she called Evergreen Cemetery to see if Pearl Abbott had been buried the morning before T. Bob hit Omar with his fist and a handful of lilies. Pearl had. Shoot! Another suspect down the drain. Unless T. Bob was smarter than she thought. Then Elena remembered Lydia. "Did you have a visitor that day named Lydia Beeman?" she asked.

The guard, looking pained, checked the records again. "No, ma'am."

"No?" She had pretty much believed Lydia when the woman said she was visiting her husband's grave on the anniversary of his death. "Would you know the date a Colonel Beeman died? He's buried here."

"No, ma'am, I wouldn't, but I can point you to his grave. I've got a directory. What was the name?"

"Beeman. B-E-E-M-A-N."

"First name?"

"I don't remember."

"Well, we might have more than one. Got a lotta graves. Lotta dead soldiers. Kinda depressin' when you think about it. Still, you know that name rings a bell. There's this old lady who comes out to visit a grave. Reason I remember her is she rides a bicycle."

"A bicycle?" A shiver ran up Elena's spine. "What color?"

"I don't know. Strange enough, a woman her age ridin' in on a bicycle. One of the gravediggers told me she talks to the stone. Tall woman. Kinda snippy. 'Course it could be she hates blacks. That wouldn't be anything new," said the black soldier cynically. "But she wasn't here that day."

"The guard couldn't have missed her?"

"Not likely. 'Course I don't know who had the duty on the twenty-seventh." The soldier checked the plats, found only one Beeman, and gave Elena directions to the grave.

Elena located it. In the new section. Ambrose Beeman had died on May 17, not September 27. If Ambrose was indeed Lydia's husband, Lydia had lied twice. She *did* know that Boris had broken Dimitra's hip. And she hadn't been visiting her husband's grave when Boris died. On the other hand, T. Bob Tyler didn't really have an alibi either. Sifting through the new information, putting it together with the old, coming up with nothing conclusive, Elena went back to headquarters. She and Leo had a meeting with Lieutenant Beltran to discuss the case.

52

Wednesday, October 13, 2:00 P.M.

The meeting with Beltran started promptly at two. He described the pressure he was getting from upstairs. Leo described the case against T. Bob Tyler: his previous and present assaults, his previous dancing association with the widow, the fact that he began to date her immediately after Boris Potemkin's murder, the discovery of the obituaries of all the murdered husbands and the pictures of the wives.

"Sounds like a serial killer to me," said Beltran. "Keeping a scrapbook of his victims. Even his alibi involves a cemetery. And funeral flowers. A psychiatrist would make something of that. What did you find out about the alibi, Jarvis?"

"Well, he was there. He signed in. The problem is they don't sign people out, so if he left quickly, he could have got over to the Potemkins' and killed Boris within the two-to-three time frame the coroner gave us. On the other hand, no one saw him or his truck near the Potemkin house that day. Admittedly, people in my neighborhood might not notice an old man, but you can't miss that truck. Looks like a pile of rust held together with Silly Putty."

"So he parked it on another street and walked over," Leo suggested.

"It's possible," Elena agreed. "Still, no witnesses put him at the scene, and we've got no fingerprints. I had his from the jail booking compared to those we took at the Potemkin house."

"So he wore gloves," said Beltran.

Elena stared at her lieutenant. Lydia was the one who always wore gloves.

"As for eyewitness reports, they aren't that great," said Beltran. "We've had three cases this month blow up in court because the eyewitnesses didn't know what they were talking about."

"One of them was mine," muttered Leo. "And Tyler's got motive. I guess. He doesn't approve of husbands hurting their wives. The men were all batterers; Elena's pretty well proved that. And Tyler wants to get married. He asked the women out after their husbands were killed, so he obviously had his eye on them as ladies who could support him and take care of him in his old age."

"Lieutenant." Elena hesitated to bring up the second possibility, knowing Beltran would find fault with it. Still— "There's another suspect who's, in one way, more unlikely than T. Bob Tyler. In another way—well, we could make a case against her."

"*Her*?" Beltran stared at Elena. "You're suggesting we've got a female serial killer at work here?"

"I know what you're thinking. Statistics are against us, but still you ought to hear what I've dug up," and she began to detail the case against Lydia Beeman. "Everybody agrees that she was devastated when her friend was killed by the husband, Herbert Stoltz. Even more so when the court gave him probation. And then he was murdered. Now, we can't really tie T. Bob Tyler to that one because there was no wife left for him to court."

"Frances Stoltz wanted to leave her husband. Maybe she was going to move in with T. Bob," said Leo.

"She planned to move in with her daughter in Ohio."

"So she was lying to her husband about that. Then the husband kills her, and T. Bob kills the husband in revenge," Leo speculated. "Anyway, we can't for sure tie the Stoltz murder to the rest."

"Well, I don't know. Frances was close from childhood with everyone in that bridge group. Emily Marks was her sister, Lydia Beeman her best friend."

"You're postulating a conspiracy of old ladies? What was this woman's name you think did the actual killings?"

"Lydia Beeman."

"She wouldn't be Ambrose Beeman's wife, would she?"

"Yes," said Elena, surprised. "Did you know him?"

"The man held the Congressional Medal of Honor," said Beltran. "You want to go to the D.A. and ask him to prosecute the widow of a war hero?"

"At least hear me out, Lieutenant," said Elena.

Beltran sighed, long-suffering. "I'd be a lot happier if we were talking about poisonings. A woman might poison five men. It's been done. But shoot them?"

"She grew up on a ranch, married a military man. She probably knows how to shoot. She certainly knows how to take care of guns. Anyway, all those women whose husbands died were substituting in that bridge group at the time of the murders, and the person they substituted *for* was Lydia Beeman."

"I didn't know that," said Leo.

"That's what my mother says. She's been asking questions at the center, which I wish she hadn't done."

"That doesn't mean Mrs. Beeman wasn't out running legitimate errands at the time the crimes went down," said Beltran.

"Yeah, I know, and for the other four murders, it's going to be hard to check alibis, but it's also hard to believe that her being gone every time one of them died is just a coincidence. And she's talked to me a lot about justice. She's really hung up on the subject."

"That a crime?" demanded Beltran. "If more people were hung up on justice, you wouldn't be carrying a forty-two case load."

"Maybe she thinks if the courts won't do the job, she has to mete out punishment herself," said Elena doggedly.

"What about the Potemkin murder? You can check her alibi for that."

"I did. She lied."

"That's what you found out today?" asked Leo, frowning.

"Uh-huh. In fact, she's lied a couple of times. Yesterday she acted like she didn't know that Boris was responsible for

Dimitra's broken hip, but Emily Marks says Lydia knew it. And then Lydia said that on the day Boris died, she was at the Fort Bliss National Cemetery visiting her husband's grave. Well, that sounded reasonable to me, but when I went over to check whether T. Bob had been there, I checked on her too. She wasn't on the sign-in list."

"Well, hell," said Beltran. "The soldier at the gate could have been talking to a pal or sleeping, and she just drove through. It's not as if they keep the place locked."

"You're right, but she said she went for the anniversary of his death. I looked at the stone. It said he died in May, not September. And there's the matter of the weapon. Or weapons. When I visited her yesterday, I got a quick look at her husband's gun collection. She hustled me out of the house after I showed an interest, but she had a lot of World War II side arms, and that's the vintage used in the murders."

"You're saying she took a gun out of the gun cabinet, loaded it, went off and shot some old guy, came home, cleaned it, and put it back in the cabinet where anyone could see it?"

"I don't know," said Elena, "but she did have access to the right kind of weapons. We didn't find any guns at Tyler's place or in his truck, which is not to say that he couldn't have dumped the weapon after each murder. Or maybe he keeps them somewhere else. Or borrows them from her. Even steals them from her. The cabinet isn't locked, and she has no alarm system. But there's one last thing."

"Which is?"

"Bicycles. She rides a bicycle to the cemetery. The guard remembered that, and the Ituribes saw a bicycle in the alley behind the Potemkins' the afternoon he was killed."

"You're right," said Leo, "and didn't you say they identified two women's bikes in the lineup?"

"Uh-huh. Both with baskets. And Viola Ramsey saw a bicycle near the Stoltz house when Herbert Stoltz was shot, although she thought a neighbor was riding it."

Beltran shook his head. "You've had how many weeks on the Potemkin murder? And this is the case we've got? An old cowboy or an old lady as our serial killer?"

"I guess it's back to the street with more questions," said Leo gloomily. "Let's just hope nobody else abuses a wife from the center before we—"

"Detective Jarvis," said Beltran's secretary, popping into the office, "there's a call for you. I said you were in conference, but she insisted that it's urgent."

Frowning, Beltran waved at his phone, and Elena picked up. "Detective Elena Jarvis, Crimes Against Persons," she said.

"Elena," whispered her mother, "I'm sorry to bother you at work, but I was sitting out on the patio stitching pillows when Lydia Beeman showed up."

Elena stiffened with alarm.

"She opened the back gate and rode right in on her bicycle."

"Her bicycle?"

"Of course, dear. Lydia never goes anywhere except on a bicycle or on foot. She bores anyone who'll listen about how healthful—"

"Where is she, Mom?"

"In the house. I'm outside on the cordless phone. That's why I'm whispering. She complained about the heat out here, so I sent her in for lemonade. I know that's not very polite, but it gave me the opportunity to—"

"What color is the bicycle?"

"Green," said Harmony.

"Oh God!"

"Well, there's nothing wrong with a green bicycle. It's actually rather nice-looking," said Harmony. "I suppose I'm silly for calling you. I know how you feel about auras, but I swear I've never seen one like hers. It's tight and gold with these frightening flashes of red."

"Mom, tell her to leave. Tell her you've got a migraine."

"I've never had a migraine in my life."

"She doesn't know that. Better yet, you leave. Run around the side of the house, get in your pickup, and drive down here."

"I don't have the keys. Why in the world would you want me to leave a strange woman in your house?"

"Because she's the one who murdered all those old men."

"Are you *sure*?"

"I am now. Listen, Mom—"

"Well in that case, dear, I'll keep her here until you can come to arrest her," Harmony whispered.

"Mom, don't do that! Just leave. Go to the Ituribes' or Gloria's."

"Nonsense. The arrest will look marvelous on your record," said Harmony, her voice dropping even lower just before she hung up.

"Mom? *Mom!*" Panic-stricken, Elena turned to Leo and Beltran. "Lydia Beeman's at my house with a dangerous aura."

"A dangerous *what*?" asked Beltran.

"We've got to get over there before she hurts my mother. She's on a green bicycle, looking mean."

"Your mother?"

"Lydia." Elena was halfway to the door. "Get a SWAT team," she called over her shoulder.

"You think she'd hurt Harmony?" asked Beltran, finally taking the situation seriously.

"Why, not? She probably thinks my mother's responsible for us zeroing in on her."

Beltran grabbed the telephone.

"No sirens," Elena shouted at him, and she raced down the hall with Leo at her heels.

53
##

Wednesday, October 13, 2:45 P.M.

Lydia Beeman a murderer! No wonder I never liked her,
thought Harmony as she picked up the pruning shears, which
Elena had left on the patio table. Harmony used them to clip
gaping holes in the tires of Lydia's green bicycle. Then she
went into the house to find her guest, who was sitting on the
newly upholstered love seat, fanning herself with a copy of
Newsweek and drinking lemonade.

"I hope you don't think me rude for sending you in ahead,"
said Harmony, "but I did want to finish that pillow. I told my
daughter I'd have all the throw pillows done when she got
home."

Lydia nodded. "I suppose she'll be here a bit after four."

"Actually, Elena is on the twelve-to-eight shift this week."
Harmony picked up the shuttle and began to weave. "Now I'm
working on material for the sofa," she remarked, pointing to
the ruined piece of furniture. "Would you like some more
lemonade?"

"No, thank you," said Lydia. She glanced at the fabric on
which she was sitting and said, "What a strange pattern."

"My own design," Harmony replied. How amazing to think
the woman sitting across from her in neatly pressed beige
slacks and blouse, face slightly flushed from her bicycle ride,
was a murderer. Had Harmony not been able to see those

warning explosions of red highlighting the gold of determination in Lydia's aura, she'd never have believed it.

Feeling a bit smug, Harmony began a new row. Elena would certainly make sergeant on the basis of this arrest. What a bright daughter she had! Not many police officers would be smart enough to suspect Lydia Beeman; the woman might be opinionated and tactless, but she certainly maintained a respectable façade.

"You don't have much to say for yourself," said Lydia. "Do you spend *all* your time weaving?"

"I've raised five children and have four grandchildren. That's time-consuming, but yes, I do a lot of weaving. I find it a source of great satisfaction."

"A machine could do it just as well," said Lydia. "With a daughter who makes such a positive contribution to society, I think you'd be ashamed to spend your time so self-indulgently."

Harmony raised her eyebrows. "At least you approve of my daughter."

"She's a fine young woman, whereas you have devoted yourself to snooping and troublemaking among women who welcomed you in a spirit of friendship and trust."

"I have no idea what you mean," said Harmony. Lydia was beginning to make her nervous. The room vibrated with hostility.

"Do you think I'm unaware of the questions you've been asking at the center? About where I was when certain old men died? About my husband's gun collection? That's why your daughter came to visit me yesterday. Because you've made her suspicious. It's very unfortunate that you've seen fit to meddle in things that don't concern you."

"You act like I've been playing detective, Lydia," said Harmony, trying to laugh naturally, as if the conversation were a joke. "I was just chatting with—"

"You've put Elena in a difficult situation. She and I are very close. Now, because of your gossiping, her feelings for me will be conflicted."

"I really doubt Elena is *that* fond of you, Lydia," snapped

Harmony and, forgetting caution, added sharply, "Certainly not fond enough to overlook murder."

"Justice," said Lydia. "Not murder. I have simply done what the courts seem unable to do: I protect women who have no other protection."

Harmony watched with sudden horror as Lydia rose from the love seat and drew a pistol from the large fanny pack she wore around her waist. It was like Berkeley all over again—when she had been naively astonished, then helplessly terrified the first time the police beat her to the ground with clubs. Why hadn't Elena arrived? Five Points wasn't *that* far away. "For heaven's sake, Lydia, surely you don't mean to shoot *me*?" Harmony quavered.

"Yes, I do."

"That's not going to improve your relationship with my daughter," said Harmony, trying to swallow her fear. *I can't die*, she thought. *I have to get home to Ruben.*

"Elena will take your death for just another daylight robbery-murder."

"*Just?* I'm her *mother*!"

"But she should have been *my* daughter," said Lydia, her mouth and eyes softening with the look of a woman thinking of a beloved child. "Once you're dead, she will be."

Harmony could see a gentle blue flickering in that killer's aura. The change was doubly disturbing because Lydia's gun hand was steady, and she had moved toward her target. "She'll never be your daughter!" cried Harmony. "You'll be in jail. I've slashed your bicycle tires and called the police. Even if you kill me, you can't get away."

"I am not a gullible woman, Harmony," said Lydia, taking aim, left hand now supporting her right elbow. "And I know you to be much too frivolous and lacking in foresight to—"

Seeing no other way to defend herself, Harmony shoved the heavy loom over on her attacker and dove aside. The gun fired, shattering one of the brass lamps on the chandelier, as Lydia went down and Elena and Leo burst in from the kitchen.

"Are you all right, Mom?" asked Elena, white-faced.

"Yes." Harmony scrambled off the floor, then dropped, trembling, onto the slashed sofa. "You certainly took your time getting here," she said in a wobbly voice. "And look at my loom. And your chandelier. Will the department pay to repair them?"

Elena, with her gun in a two-handed grip pointed at Lydia, edged the stylish German Luger out of reach with her foot.

Lydia was sprawled under the loom, groaning, "She's broken my hip."

"You were going to shoot me," said Harmony defensively. "*I'm* not the violent person here."

Beltran, entering from the front door, rushed to Harmony's side. "Are you all right?" he asked solicitously.

"No," she replied. "A spring just poked me." She moved to the left and scowled at him as if he were responsible for the damage to Elena's sofa. "And you took an interminable length of time getting here."

Beltran flushed and snapped an order at the SWAT leader to call an ambulance and a shooting-review team.

"The suspect's the only one to fire a gun," Elena pointed out, "and no one's been shot."

"Shooting would have been kinder," groaned Lydia.

"Too bad *I* didn't have a gun," Harmony muttered.

"Do you know the statistics on women who die of broken hips?" retorted Lydia, her voice gaining strength from her own indignation.

With her police revolver in one hand, Elena knelt carefully to get the Luger. Lydia reached out and caught Elena's free hand, which Elena jerked away. "Don't pull back," Lydia whispered. "I'd never hurt *you*. I'd have made you a fine mother when she was gone."

Elena stared at the woman in horror. "You *were* going to kill my mother?"

"Some things are necessary. For the greater good. There are still women who need protecting. Watching. She should have realized that. She shouldn't have interfered. I'm sure you understand, Elena. We share—"

"Mrs. Beeman, you've killed five people!" Elena exclaimed.

"But never a *good* person. Only the guilty."

"It doesn't matter. You're not the judge or jury. Your actions constitute capital murder. And you were going to kill my mother, who never hurt anyone. At the very least, you're going to jail."

Lydia smiled weakly, her face gray with pain. "I won't live to stand trial. Statistics are against me." The keening wail of the ambulance siren cut her off. Then she said, when two members of the SWAT had lifted the loom away, "Will you go with me to the hospital, child? I want to explain. I want to make you understand."

Beltran nodded to Elena, and his nod was a command, one she didn't want to obey. It was too macabre. Lydia Beeman seemed to feel no guilt, seemed to be sure that Elena would understand and approve. Elena had no desire to hear what the woman had to say.

The attendants bustled in and moved her to a stretcher, as Lydia, gasping, said, "I killed only those the law can't or won't deal with. Like Frances' husband." Her grip on Elena's hand tightened as the attendants lifted her. "You said yourself that you could make arrests, but the courts set the criminals free. They do."

"Go along," Beltran murmured to Elena. "Have you got a tape recorder?" Elena nodded.

54

Elena knelt by Lydia's head while the ambulance attendants worked on her hip.

"We'll give you a shot for pain in just a minute, ma'am," one of them said.

"You killed them all?" Elena asked. She'd had to holster her gun because Lydia still clung to one hand, and Elena was holding a tape recorder in the other. "Stoltz, Cox, Brolie, Castro, Boris? All five?"

"Six," said Lydia. "I killed Ambrose too."

Elena stared at her. "Emily said your husband died of a stroke." Was Lydia's confession part of some fantasy?

"I let him," said Lydia. "I watched him." She gasped softly when the needle went in, then said, "Ambrose beat me. If I didn't obey orders fast enough, he beat me. So did my father. That's why Mother sent me away to school. To protect me. And then I married a man just like my father. But I was a woman then, so I tried to stop it."

"What did you do?" Elena found herself waiting breathlessly for the next revelation.

"Told his commanding officer." Lydia laughed bitterly. "He said if a hero like Ambrose was beating his wife, it must be because she deserved it. He told me to go home and be a better wife. I had no place to turn. Neither did any of the others. The system ignores us. So I bided my time, and as we got older,

293

Ambrose, with his bad heart and his high blood pressure, had to be careful about getting angry. He couldn't afford to attack me."

"So you're saying he stopped the abuse? When? After you moved back here?"

"Mmm." Lydia looked indescribably weary. "Only he made a mistake. One night he said, 'Lydia, call 911. I think I've had a stroke,' and I said, 'How do you know?' That's when he forgot about staying calm. He shouted, 'Do you want me to die, woman? Call 911.' And he hit me with his cane. On the legs—back of the thighs. I'd almost forgotten how much that hurt. I was sick with pain, stumbling away from him, heading for the telephone to obey.

"And then I remembered his question: 'Do you want me to die, woman?' And the answer was, 'Yes.' That's what I'd been waiting for all those years, through two wars. So I didn't call. I told him I had. And I stayed away from his good arm. He was paralyzed on the right side by then, but he could still talk. He kept cursing E.M.S. Saying it had been ten minutes, twenty minutes, and I should call again. And I said, 'No, Ambrose, it's only been a minute. Two. Three.' In case he lived. Of course he didn't. He was furious and died shouting at me. Then I called 911.

"So Ambrose was the first one I killed. I buried him and froze his Congressional Medal of Honor in a box of okra. Ambrose hated okra. It's in my freezer to this day. Along with the other medals and jewelry. All in vegetable packets. Perfectly preserved while the men are rotting in their graves, shot with the guns I inherited from Ambrose. One day there'll be nothing left of them but the medals they didn't deserve. And Ambrose—I always go to tell him when I kill a new one. So he'll know that *I'm* the hero. I never bring flowers; I bring vengeance."

"You really did kill them all," marveled Elena.

"Of course I did. They deserved to die. Maybe you don't understand what they were doing. You don't understand about Frances. If I'd started earlier, she'd be alive."

"Did you know he was abusing her?"

"We never told each other. That was the only secret between

s, and it killed Frances," Lydia sighed, moved restlessly on
e pallet, moaned. "But her death led me to save the others.
Marcia, always bruised and burned. Porfirio Cox couldn't
elieve it when I shot him. A woman. And an Anglo." Lydia
miled weakly.

"And Chantal?"

"Margaret told me about her."

"Russian roulette?"

"You knew about that?"

"Mrs. Brolie told me just a few days ago."

"If she'd told *me* earlier, I could have saved her all that
error. And poor Mercedes. So beautiful, and he took it away
rom her. And then laughed."

"Did she tell you what happened? About the ring?"

"She told—who was it?—Portia, I think. The ring's in a pack-
ge of New England boiled vegetables—Marcia's favorite—
along with Porfirio Cox's papal medal. Those men would have
ated New England boiled vegetables."

"They were all in on it? The bridge group?" Dear God, this
was going to be awful. They'd have to charge all four women
or murder and conspiracy.

"The Goren vigilantes," Lydia mumbled.

Elena had to lean close to hear over the wail of the sirens.
She didn't think the cassette recorder was getting it all,
although maybe the experts could separate Lydia's voice from
he rise and fall of sound that threatened to drown her out.

"My ancestors were vigilantes. Did I tell you that? When
here was no law, they saw justice done. I did the same."

"And the others—Emily, Margaret, Portia?"

"All vigilantes. Goren vigilantes. Still play Goren rules.
Old-fashioned, but we like the old ways." Her voice slowed as
he medication took hold; her eyes closed, then flicked open
again as she strove to stay conscious. "They told me about the
battered women . . . I arranged for the wives to take my
place at the bridge table . . . while I killed the husbands."

"So you thought of yourselves as the Goren vigilantes?"
Elena prompted, moving the recorder microphone closer to
Lydia's mouth.

"*I* did. The others didn't know. Never realized what I was

doing. Poor Emily. She'll be shocked . . . and she depend
on me . . . since Frances died." Tears welled under Lydia
flickering eyelids. "If only I'd started earlier. I wouldn't hav
lost Frances."

Elena thought Lydia had fainted, but as the ambulanc
turned toward Thomason General, Lydia whispered, "The
were very happy . . . those women I saved. Women give an
give . . . all their lives. They have a right to be happy . .
in old age. But you understand. I only had sons, but you'll b
the daughter I wanted. Take over my work."

"Never," Elena whispered. "Killing, except in self-defens
makes us as bad as the criminals."

"I don't want you to kill, child. Just see justice done."

"Maybe you should rest now," said Elena, shivering at th
woman's vision.

"Yes. Beside Ambrose. Whispering in his ear through a
eternity . . . that he was the villain . . . and I the hero."

Elena sighed and squeezed Lydia's hand. The woman ha
been wrong, very wrong, but she'd acted out of love for he
friend and a sense of what was right. Elena could see that.

As if she understood Elena's unspoken relenting, Lydi
smiled. "They were all . . . vigilantes . . . and didn't . .
even . . . know it. . . ."

Lydia's eyes closed as the full flow of the sirens washed ove
Elena before they ebbed and fell silent.

"What'd she do?" asked one of the attendants.

"Vigilante justice," said Elena.